Also by Judith Ingram:

A Devotional Walk with Forgiveness

MOONSEED TRILOGY
Bridge to the Past
Borrowed Promises

To Janet:

The past isn't always behind you —

Enjoy!

Judith Ingram
August 2015

Katherine's Family History

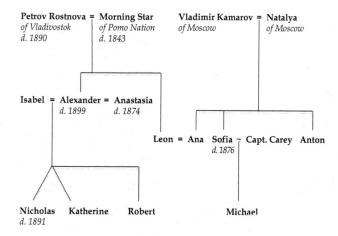

The *Moonseed* Trilogy
Books 1 & 2

Book One: BRIDGE TO THE PAST

Victoria Reeves-Ashton longs to escape her meaningless life. Trapped in a loveless marriage, haunted by dreams she can't remember, she craves the love and safety that have always eluded her despite her breathtaking beauty and privileged life among the San Francisco elite. Then her careless wish on a mysterious coin causes a near-tragedy that snatches her back over a century in time, into the life of the coin's previous owner. Victoria awakens in the body of Katherine Kamarov, a rancher's daughter living in rural California in the late 1800s — a selfish, friendless young woman who is accused of murdering her husband.

Ryan Ashton hates to admit that his marriage to Victoria is failing. Still stinging from a disastrous first marriage, he had hoped for a second chance at happiness with the quiet and beautiful Victoria. But after ten months of fruitless attempts at intimacy, he is ready to concede defeat. Then a tragic accident nearly takes Victoria's life, and his wife regains consciousness no longer shy and repressed but sexually brazen and defiant. Baffled by the change, Ryan is repelled by her ruthlessness yet also excited by her new sensuality, and he dares to hope that here at last is a woman who can satisfy the longings of his lonely heart.

Book Two: BORROWED PROMISES

After three months of pretending to be Katherine and laboring to repair relationships damaged by Katherine's brash and selfish personality, quiet and gentle Victoria finds that her heart is putting down roots in Katherine's world, in her family relationships, and especially in a deepening friendship with Katherine's winsome cousin Michael.

Hidden letters reveal the story of other "moonseed" — time-travelers like herself — and Victoria realizes that she and Katherine will likely be returned to their own times the following spring. Tension mounts when a rich and handsome suitor applies to marry her, and Victoria must choose whether to accept him for Katherine's sake or to follow her own heart.

This second book of the *Moonseed* trilogy follows Victoria and Katherine through a summer season where love ripens, family ties deepen, and each woman must decide how deeply she can invest in a borrowed life that may be snatched away unless she can find some way to keep it.

Into the Mist
Book Three in the Moonseed Trilogy

Judith Ingram

Vinspire Publishing
www.vinspirepublishing.com

ISBN: 978-0-9964423-1-2
PUBLISHED BY VINSPIRE PUBLISHING, LLC

This book is for my grandmother
Ekaterina Vasilievna

Judith Ingram

Part Four

FALL

Judith Ingram

Katherine

Chapter One

Ryan Ashton pulled the Jaguar into his reserved parking space and shut off the engine. In the sudden silence he slumped forward and laid his head on the steering wheel. Just for a moment he allowed his mind to drift in an unfocused haze, temporarily cushioning him from the unpleasant task awaiting him.

He faced it every night—that rush of heat and ice in his veins as he rode the elevator to his apartment and unlocked the door, anticipating his first glimpse of her. He longed to see her graceful body sway toward him with that light in her eyes that set his heart hammering. Because he loved her. But he always met her gaze with hard eyes and kept his hands fisted at his sides so he couldn't pull her into his arms and savor the sweetness of coming home to her. Because he hated her.

Day after day, the memory of her betrayal made him taste the bitterness of his shame. His only defense was to steel his heart against her. He couldn't help loving her, but she would never make a fool of him again.

Silence met him as he stepped into their foyer, but Ryan knew his wife was home. Intriguing aromas wafted from the kitchen, and the table was set for two. He'd called to let her know he'd be home for dinner, mostly because he couldn't think of a good enough reason to stay away. He wanted to see her even though he knew he would suffer.

It drove him crazy, this desire to feed his love for her while fanning the flames of his resentment. He watched her when she wasn't looking, inhaled her scent like oxygen to keep himself alive, but he wouldn't let himself touch her. He knew if he crossed that line, he'd be helpless to resist her. So he nursed his resentment to keep that boundary firm.

He located Vicki in their bedroom. She lay curled on the bed, asleep in the soft light of the bedside lamp. Ryan stood over her and allowed himself to feel the slow ache of loving her. She looked young and soft, like an angel child, her hand fisted close to her mouth, her blond hair tousled against the pillow.

She stirred and opened her eyes, blinking in the light. Seeing him beside the bed, she looked up quickly into his face before he could tuck away his tenderness. A corresponding warmth flickered in her eyes. Then wariness dropped a veil, and she looked away.

"I must have fallen asleep." She yawned and stretched herself in a way that was unintentionally sensual. "I just lay down for a minute. I think the pregnancy is making me tired."

"How did it go at the doctor's?" Ryan heard husky tenderness in his voice and winced. *Careful, Ashton.* He turned quickly away and shrugged off his jacket.

"Healthy baby, healthy mama." The guard was back in her voice. *Good.*

"When's dinner ready?" He crossed the room to get away from her, away from the soft glow of lamplight on her hair and the pronounced curve of her breasts under the silk robe she was wearing. A stunning wave of heat and need slammed through him and left his ears ringing.

"It should be ready now." She slid off the bed and padded into the bathroom.

Ryan blew out a tremulous sigh and flexed his hands. *Don't fall for it, Ashton*, he reminded himself. *She's not what she seems.*

He'd be a fool to go down that same road twice.

* * *

Ryan had to admit she knew how to cook. If he weren't so keyed up, the subtle flavors and tenderness of the lamb stew would have left him wholly satisfied. As it was, the meal lodged in his stomach in an uncomfortable lump.

They ate mostly in silence, their wineglasses unused, the candles unlit. Ryan couldn't risk a romantic atmosphere breaking down his resolve. He needed his barriers intact.

"Are you and Chris playing tennis tomorrow?" she asked. The husky edge in her voice reminded him that she wasn't Victoria and stirred up a curious mix of emotions.

"Yes. Court's reserved for one o'clock. Oh, and by the way." He reached into his pocket and passed her a folded envelope. "Alice Andrews sent this to the office. It's addressed to you."

His wife tore open the envelope, and as she drew out a sheet of paper, a copper coin clattered onto the table.

With a shriek she seized the coin and immediately circled its rim with her thumb, just as Ryan had seen the old Vicki do a hundred times. She picked up the note and read it aloud.

> Dear Vicki:
> We've started work on renovating the attic at Summerwood Cottage. A workman found this coin when they pulled up the floorboards. I remembered you'd said you lost a coin in the attic, so I'm betting this is yours. Please tell Ryan thanks again for his ideas—you're both invited to come up and see the results when the work is finished. Be sure to send us an announcement when your baby is born. Hoping all is well with you.
> Regards,
> Alice Andrews

"My coin, Ryan! My good luck coin." She gave a delighted little laugh and cradled her treasure in the palm of her hand.

Ryan frowned. "I don't understand. That's Vicki's coin. She carried it everywhere with her." His frown deepened at his wife's look. "She must have dropped it the last time...when Vicki and I were up there in March."

"What are you talking about?" His wife clutched the coin inside her fist. "This is *my* coin. I paid a nickel for it at the state fair."

"That's *Vicki's* coin," Ryan insisted. "It has a nick in the rim. Take a look for yourself."

She opened her hand and stared at the coin. She

touched a finger to its rim. "A wheel ran over it," she said quietly. "I was afraid it was ruined. The woman who sold me the coin promised it would bring me good luck."

She fingered the coin, so uncannily like Vicki that Ryan caught his breath.

"Well," he said. "The logical explanation is that Vicki bought a coin that used to belong to you." He shrugged. "It's a coincidence—far-fetched, I'll grant you, but not impossible."

She shook her head. "No, Ryan, not a coincidence." Her expression turned dreamy. "It's part of the circle. Don't you see?"

"What circle?"

"Dora—my Indian nurse—used to say that life is a circle. Everything comes back around in some way. Birth and death, night and day, a year of seasons, love and hate—everything comes back to its start. This coin"—she held it up reverently—"in some way I don't understand, linked Vicki and me in a circle of time. And here it is, back in my hand." She met his gaze across the table. "I'll wager it's in Vicki's hand, too. Maybe right at this very moment in that other time."

Ryan watched her and said nothing.

She continued slowly. "It must be by design. It must mean that God intended this all along for us, that it isn't our doing." She shuddered. "What a relief it is to know that our lives are in wiser hands than our own." Her gaze turned thoughtful. "I wonder if Vicki knows that."

Ryan couldn't speak. He felt as if he were floating above a surreal landscape, his feet dangling, his hands clutching at dissolving wisps of cloud.

When his wife rose to clear the table, he followed her into the kitchen, deciding he'd have that glass of wine, after all.

* * *

In his dream, the night was dark and moonless because his mission required stealth. His face and hands in blackout camouflage, Ryan slipped through the trees above Two Trees Creek, ears straining for sounds of the enemy, eyes scanning ahead for the bridge. His architectural firm had been commissioned to reconstruct the bridge. His secret job was to blow it up.

He saw the bridge—a great dark monster looming against the lighter blackness of the night sky. He lowered his backpack to the ground and pulled out six bundles of dynamite.

A squirrel the size of a small dog leaped into the tree behind him and began to screech. He had to act quickly now before others came to stop him. He had to destroy the bridge before…he couldn't remember exactly why. But everything depended on it.

Ryan waded into the water, preparing to swim to the wooden underpinnings where he would secure the explosives. His next step, however, plunged him into a deep hole. Inky water instantly closed over his head. He kicked his way back to the surface but had lost the dynamite. Shaking water from his eyes, he saw a woman emerge from a knot of trees on the bank and start toward the bridge. Another woman appeared on the opposite bank. Ryan shouted at them to go back, but the wind whipped his words away.

The current suddenly grabbed him and hurled him

downstream, away from the women and the bridge. Strands of creek-bottom weed coiled around his feet like dead fingers and dragged him under. He tried to scream, but water filled his lungs, and the coils tugged him deeper into the silent dark…

Ryan jerked awake, flailing his arms and gasping for air. He opened his eyes and blinked stupidly at the only light source in the room—a late-night comedy show on TV. He still felt the coil of something deadly around his ankles, but he couldn't remember what it was or why his body was trembling and slick with sweat.

He ran his hands over his face and through his hair, trying to clear away his fear. Pushing aside his empty tumbler, he reached for the remote control and clicked off the TV. The pounding in his head told him he should have stuck with wine.

Ten minutes later he heaved himself into bed and stretched out beside his wife. Despite their mutual distance, they continued to share the same bed, keeping to their own sides by unspoken agreement. Ryan refused to sleep in his den again. If Vicki didn't like sharing her bed with him, she could sleep on the floor, pregnancy or no.

He fell instantly asleep.

In his dream, Ryan stood on the cracked sidewalk looking at his old house on Beacon Hill Avenue. His dreamer's body glided through the weedy front yard, up the porch steps, and passed invisibly through the patched screen door.

The living room still smelled of rotten food and human waste. The hallway was dark. He passed by his bedroom but did not look inside, not wanting to disturb the memories sleeping there. He passed Mark's room and shut out the pain of his brother's leaving. He couldn't think about that now. He had to go into his parents' room and discover the body.

He turned into a doorway and was shocked as always by the relentless pink of the walls and bedspread. Her slippers lay at odd angles close to the bed, one on its side, where her feet had shaken them off. The room smelled of his mother—the rose talc she liked after her bath and the stale sweat stained a dirty yellow into her clothes. She wore her faded pink bathrobe, the one he had snuggled his face against for comfort ever since he could remember. He couldn't look at her face yet, only at her feet hanging over the edge of the bed. Carefully, he fitted each with a slipper, dressing her like a doll. He adjusted the robe to cover her thin legs. Then he picked up her cold hand and held it against his cheek. Still unable to look at her face, he wrapped his arms around her waist and buried his head against the soft flannel covering her breast. And he wept.

Her arms came around him and held him gently. "Ryan." Her voice was tender. "Darling, don't cry."

"Ma?" He couldn't lift his head, afraid of what he would see, afraid she would still be dead. He imagined the beat of her heart under his ear, and he clung tighter.

"Ma, don't go away! Please don't leave me." He was weeping again, and his tears dissolved the dream. Still the warm arms held him, and the voice crooned in his ear, repeating his name, lovingly, over and over…

Ryan came fully awake and realized who was

holding him.

He pushed himself away from her, angry and embarrassed. She let him go without a word. Discovering he was in her half of the bed, he shoved himself to his own side and wiped his pajama sleeve impatiently across his eyes. Then he punched up his pillow and turned his back to her. Laying his head down, he stared for a long time at the dim shapes of his orderly bedroom and wondered how many more times he must walk that dark, silent hallway into the blinding pink before his dreams would finally release him and let him forget.

Chapter Two

Francine Shepherd's patient spoke. "Last night I dreamed about the lioness again. She was on the mountain ledge, like always, pacing. I was walking up the trail, and suddenly I saw her!"

The beautiful green eyes sparked with fear. Francine knew it was Elizabeth speaking and was probably Elizabeth she had encountered in the early days of their therapy together—Elizabeth who guarded Katherine's secrets with her muteness, whose blindness had shielded Katherine from further hurts. Elizabeth, the Protector.

"What happened next, Elizabeth?"

Her patient began to gnaw at her thumbnail. "The lioness had left her cub alone in the forest. I wanted to go back for it, and it was as if she heard my thoughts. She snarled at me, like she wanted to rip me to pieces!"

Her patient tore at her thumbnail more savagely.

"Katherine tried to kill her baby," she went on, "but she failed. I know it's alive. I helped give birth to it."

Francine struggled to follow her patient's train of thought. "You mean, when you and Katherine went back in time briefly last week?" Her patient nodded. "You say Katherine tried to kill her baby?" Another nod. "How?"

"Poison." The thumbnail gave out, and her patient started on another nail. "She made a tea of mistletoe. It was supposed to make her miscarry, but she used too much. She nearly killed herself. She should have asked Dora."

Francine studied her. "Elizabeth, why would Katherine want to kill her child?"

The green eyes darted away. "Katherine was...indiscreet. She always was reckless, but she finally landed herself in a trap that she couldn't escape."

"And coming here, to this time?" Francine spread her hands. "Was that an escape?"

The young woman shrugged. "I guess so."

"Yet the lioness is still trapped on the ledge."

Her patient shrugged again.

"Maybe we should ask the lioness to explain herself.

"What?"

"We could do another guided imagery. We'll recreate your dream and see if the lioness will talk to us."

"No!"

Francine eyed her patient. "Why not?"

"She hates me!" Another nail gave out. "I'm afraid of her!"

"And yet," Francine reflected, "it's your presence that keeps the lioness trapped. Know what I think, Elizabeth? I think the lioness is afraid of *you*."

The nail-tearing slowed. The young woman regarded her, half-skeptical, half-curious.

"Remember how I said that people who have been badly hurt or frightened sometimes get so confused about their feelings, they feel like two different people?" A wary nod. "They're afraid to feel powerful emotions together, like love and anger, afraid they'll never survive it. They end up closing off parts of themselves so they can feel the other parts. Do you see?"

The young woman frowned and said nothing.

Francine gentled her voice. "I know you're scared. And I promise we won't attempt the imagery exercise until you tell me you're ready." She leaned forward and touched her patient's arm. "But sooner or later, you *will* confront her, either alone in your dreams or with me here in the office. Until you do, neither of you can be truly happy or truly free."

* * *

Lisa Knight chewed her sourdough bread thoughtfully and observed her friend sitting across the table. Vicki's chin rested in her hand as she stared out the restaurant window at the boats bobbing on the water. She seemed thin and tired, with a new sadness in her eyes that she refused to talk about.

"So, what did the doctor say?" Lisa took a sip of Coke, keeping her eyes on her friend. Vicki pulled her gaze away from the wharf and looked at her. The sudden warmth in her eyes made her sadness even more pronounced.

"She said I'm in good health, and there's no reason to expect any complications with the pregnancy." Vicki laid a light hand on her stomach. "She said to limit my alcohol intake, which isn't a problem because I never touch the stuff. Not since I was fifteen and got violently sick on peach brandy." She grimaced.

"Do you hope it's a girl or a boy?"

"A girl, I think. I don't know why." She shrugged. "Ryan says he doesn't care."

Lisa nodded. "How is Ryan these days?"

Vicki didn't answer right away. Her gaze wandered out to the boats. "Working hard. He stays late at the office every night. When he does come home, he works in the study until I go to bed. We haven't..." She trailed off.

Lisa frowned. "Are you worried about Jessica?"

Her friend turned careful eyes on her. "Jessica?"

"Yeah, that lady architect who's been after Ryan for months." At her friend's look, she faltered. "Chris said you knew—" She swallowed. "Look, Vicki, I don't know anything. Honest." She shifted uncomfortably.

"I guess it's no secret that things are...uneasy between Ryan and me." Vicki pushed a fork listlessly through the greens on her plate. "He's unhappy and it's our...it's *my* fault. If I could just help him with this Golden Springs Ridge project. It may be the one thing I can do for him, something that will really make a difference, before I have to...before next March comes."

"You're helping him design the resort?"

Her friend nodded slowly. "I know the area. It's a very special place, sacred to the Indians for time out of mind." She dropped her voice. "No one has ever been able to settle that area. The Russians, the Spanish, the European settlers all failed because Indian shamans drew a magic boundary around the area to keep it sacred. This new resort will succeed only if it honors the sacred nature of the place. Although he doesn't know it, that's what Ryan has been searching for. And that's where I must help him."

Lisa swallowed and glanced away. Vicki Ashton had

to be the most glamorous, intelligent, inquisitive, and exciting friend Lisa had ever known. She was also the strangest. Lisa was drawn to her for a number of reasons and some she couldn't explain. While she enjoyed Vicki's wit and avid interest in practically everything, her occasional hints of otherworldliness also fascinated Lisa despite the unexpected jolts of unease they gave her. Sometimes Vicki talked as if she were two different people, neither of whom had knowledge basic to anyone living in modern times. And she seemed to believe that the world would somehow come to an end next March, when her baby was due.

Lisa shrugged off her thoughts and refocused on what Vicki was saying.

"—respect for the spirits residing in the rocks and the mountain. If I could just capture that essence in the design, I think the resort could succeed. Harmony with the earth is the key thing."

Lisa nodded politely and wondered if Vicki were only eccentric, that last outpost before crossing the line of sanity. Without meaning to, she gave blunt voice to her thoughts. "Any progress with your psychiatrist?"

She flushed as her friend drew back. Darkness moved like a cloud over Vicki's features. It lingered only a moment and then cleared, leaving her green eyes distant.

"You've reminded me that I have an appointment with Francine in less than thirty minutes. I'd better go."

Before Lisa could speak, her friend rose, extracted a bill from her wallet, and dropped it on the table. Lisa put a hand on her arm.

"Vicki, I didn't mean—"

"I know." Her friend paused and gave her a weak smile. "Sorry to run out on you. I really do have to go." She turned away.

Lisa frowned as she watched her go. With a sigh, she picked up her unfinished Coke and signaled the waiter for the check.

* * *

Francine assessed her patient: limbs relaxed, breathing slow and deep, jaw loose, eyes closed, expression serene. She settled the writing tablet on her lap and proceeded with the guided imagery.

"You are walking through a pleasant meadow. The sun is warm on your face. The air smells sweet. You feel rested and strong." Her patient smiled faintly. "Now you see a path leading away from the meadow. You follow it, and it begins to rise. You climb higher and higher, but you're not tired. You are strong and healthy, and the climb is easy."

She paused, giving her patient time to adjust to the imagery and feel her strength.

"Now, when you're ready, look up the path. You'll see a ledge." Frown lines appeared between her patient's brows. "Do you see the ledge?"

"Yes." A small voice. Then, "She's there already."

"The lioness is there?"

"Yes."

"What's she doing?"

"Pacing. Grumbling because she's trapped."

"How did she get trapped?"

"There's a monster in the forest. She left her cub and

ran away to save herself, up the mountain, and then she couldn't get off—" Her body gave a sudden start. "She sees me! She's glaring at me!" Her voice rose. *"She hates me!"*

"Why does she hate you?"

"I don't know. *I don't know.*" Her limbs twitched; she threw her head from side to side.

"You'll feel safer if you take a step back." Her patient quieted. "What is she doing now?"

"Nothing. Just staring at me."

"What would you like to say to her?"

Silence.

Francine waited. She watched the young woman's facial features slowly contort, as if in pain. "What's happening?" she asked quietly.

"She's telling me it's my fault that she's trapped on the ledge. If it weren't for me, for my conscience, she would be free."

Francine's pen paused above the tablet. "She says *your conscience* keeps her trapped on the ledge?"

"Yes. She says I'm brave and good and people love me." Her voice dropped to a whisper. "No one loves her. She's very angry about that."

"Whose love does she want?"

"Mama's. Papa's." Tears glistened beneath her thick sweep of lashes. "Ryan's."

She began to nod her head, and tears leaked out the corners of her eyes, rolling into her hair.

"What does she say now?"

"Nothing. She's sitting with her back to me. But I know what she's feeling. I feel it, too. She's so terribly alone!"

Fascinated, Francine watched her patient's hands lift as if on puppet strings and slide through the air.

"What are you doing?"

"Stroking her." Francine drew in a sharp breath and blinked. Her patient murmured, "Don't be afraid. I can help you. I'm not your enemy."

Francine pressed a hand over her heart and fought to keep her voice steady. "It's almost time to leave. Is there anything you'd like to say to her before we go?"

The young woman nodded. "I'll come back," she whispered.

"Now I'm going to count backward from ten. When I reach one, you will be fully alert and present in the room. Ten, nine, eight…"

The young woman opened her eyes and sat up slowly. She took several tissues from the box Francine held out and pressed them to her face. Francine heard her muffled sob.

"What is it?" she asked gently.

"Such an awful, dark emptiness inside her. I don't know how she stands it!"

Wordlessly, Francine joined her patient on the sofa and wrapped her arms around her. The young woman leaned against her and sobbed while Francine cuddled her. Eventually her sobbing quieted, and Francine felt her stir.

"You were right, Francine. She *is* frightened. She only acts fierce to hide her fear. And her loneliness." The young woman sighed. "All this time I've been afraid of her, and I never knew how afraid she is of herself."

Francine raised an eyebrow. "Afraid of herself?"

Her patient looked up and frowned. "No, she's afraid of *me*. She hates *me*."

"You said she's afraid of *herself*."

"I did?"

"Yes."

They were silent for another long moment. "If what you say is true," her patient began, "if Katherine and I are really parts of the same person"—her voice caught—"then what happens to me when it's just Katherine again?" She pushed herself away so she could search Francine's face. "Will I just disappear?"

Francine met her gaze steadily. "You won't disappear, Elizabeth, because you are as much Katherine as she is. The lioness told you today that you are Katherine's conscience. You are also her courage, her goodness, her sweetness. You hold her capacity to love others. You showed her your love today when you felt her suffering and tried to comfort her." Tears brimmed the young woman's eyes again. "And she seems to hold most of the pain and anger over the terrible things that were done to you as a child. She holds them inside herself so you won't have to feel them. Because she loves you."

Francine patted her hand gently. "What neither of you realizes is that you can be stronger together than either of you is alone. You are not that helpless little girl anymore. You're a strong, caring, courageous young woman who can take care of herself. You can feel your love and your anger together, and nothing bad will happen. You no longer have to be afraid of monsters who come in the night."

"Or monsters in the forest," her patient added. Then, slowly, "The lion cub we left behind. She isn't the baby at all, is she?" Green eyes searched Francine's face for confirmation. "She's Katherine, the little girl Katherine, alone and afraid. Still alone and afraid." She crossed her arms over her stomach and hunched over. "I feel an awful ache, Francine," she groaned, "such an awful ache inside me."

Francine pulled her close again. "It's your heartstrings tugging. That little girl is bound to you with strong ties no one can break. Now that we know where she is, it will be our task to help you find a way back to her."

Chapter Three

Chris Knight threw back his head and chugged a third of the water in his plastic bottle. "You're off your game, Ashton. What's up?" He wiped sweat from his face with the towel draped around his neck and gave his tennis partner a measuring look.

Ryan looked haggard, his handsome face lined and shadowed. He seemed to sag in his chair. Even on the court, his body was sluggish, slow to respond, as if his feet were too heavy. He appeared to be losing weight.

His mind was somewhere else; that was obvious. Chris took another swig of water and shifted his gaze discreetly to the green lawns of the club.

"Bad night, I guess," Ryan said finally. He gave a sour laugh. "Bad week."

"Work?"

Again he was slow to answer, and Chris nodded to himself. Lisa had told him Ryan and Vicki were having problems. What was up with those two, anyway? They were either faced off in battle or barely able to keep their hands off each other. Vicki was a little odd, but it was hard not to like her. And with the baby coming, everything had seemed to settle into a happy groove. Until the last couple of weeks.

"Vicki still seeing that psychiatrist?"

Ryan's glance was sharp. "Yeah."

"Is it helping?"

Ryan shrugged. "Her, maybe. It's not doing a thing for our marriage." He rubbed an open hand over his face. "I feel like crap."

"You look like crap."

Ryan flashed him an annoyed glance, but Chris's grin was benign. After a moment Ryan shrugged again and took a swig from his water bottle. He shifted in his chair. "They're breaking ground in November on the Golden Springs Ridge project," he said. "The plans are good. Solid." He frowned and met Chris's gaze, colleague to colleague. "I wish I knew what the problem was. I'm just not satisfied. Something in my gut tells me it's all wrong." He studied the younger man. "You ever feel like that?"

Chris colored a little, flattered that Ryan would seek his opinion as an equal. He tried to think of a worthy response.

"You mean, like when you want a building to blend into the landscape and sort of echo the land around it? Like a Frank Lloyd Wright thing?"

Ryan nodded slowly. "Maybe. Yeah, that's part of it. I guess the plans are okay, as far as that goes. But there's something else. Something I'm missing." He sighed. "I don't know." He tipped his bottle again and was silent.

Chris glanced at his watch and stood. He reached under his chair for his racket.

"Time to shove off. Lisa and I have plans for tonight."

Ryan squinted up at him. "Vicki mentioned you've

got a big night planned."

Chris swiped the air with his racket. "It's more Lisa's thing than mine. She wants to dress up and go to a fancy restaurant. You know, the whole nine yards. She wants romance." He rolled his eyes. "I guess it won't be so bad. Especially when we get to the end of the evening." He grinned.

Ryan's mouth tipped in response. He cut his gaze to the tennis courts, but Chris didn't miss the empty look in his eyes.

* * *

The sun was already slanting low across the balcony when Ryan unlocked the front door and stepped into the apartment. *The days are getting shorter*, he thought, and the realization somehow depressed him. Summer was gone; fall had arrived. Soon it would be winter.

Ryan dropped his tennis bag behind the sofa and strode to the kitchen for a glass of water, trying to shrug off his sense of foreboding. He leaned against the counter, holding his glass and surveying the kitchen. It was neat and clean, countertops clear, food put away. No sign of dinner started.

He suddenly realized that the apartment was deathly quiet.

She's gone.

The thought shocked through his body and lodged under his diaphragm, twisting a knot so tight it hunched him forward.

Don't be stupid, Ashton. She wouldn't do that.

Yes, she would. She said she would. She'll take the baby and go where I can't find them.

He forced himself out of the kitchen and into the hallway. He could see the walls of his bedroom at the other end, the last rays of September sunlight washing them in soft colors of cream and gold. Not blinding, puking pink. He had a sudden, fearful image of what he might find lying across the gold satin bedspread in the room at the end of the hall. His feet faltered, and he braced his hand on the wall to steady himself. His head began to buzz.

The door opened next to his hand so suddenly that he jumped and dropped the glass of water he'd forgotten he was holding. His wife stood in the doorway, her smile of greeting vanishing with alarm when she saw his face.

"Ryan! Lord in heaven, what's the matter?" She gripped his arm while he stared dumbly at her. "You're white as a sheet!" Instinctively, he pulled away from her and backed up against the wall. It felt hard and cold through his suddenly damp shirt.

"I'm fine." His voice tremored, annoying him. "You startled me, that's all." Then, peevishly, "You made me drop my glass."

His wife glanced down at the glass leaking a wet circle into the carpet. She looked back at him, searching his face. "What's wrong, Ryan?"

"Nothing. I was on my way to the bedroom, and you startled me." He couldn't keep the stiffness from his voice as he added, "I didn't think you were home."

"I've been working hard on something all afternoon. I'm sorry. I didn't hear you come in." She added, touching his arm briefly, "I didn't mean to give you a fright."

She stooped to retrieve the glass, feeling the stain with her fingers. "Water?" she asked, looking up.

He nodded, his body still pressed against the wall. It anchored him, kept him from foolishly grabbing her into his arms and crying into her hair how much he loved her, how the thought of losing her terrified him.

He was still pressed against the wall when she returned from the bathroom with a towel. She eyed him with surprise before stooping to soak up the water stain. "I made some iced tea. It's in the icebox." She smiled shyly. "I want to show you what I've been working on, Ryan. Maybe we could sit at the dining room table for a little while?" Excitement in her eyes penetrated his paralysis and sparked his curiosity.

"Sure." He felt relieved that his trembling had stopped and his voice sounded normal. Relieved that she wasn't pressing him for an explanation. "I'll just be a minute." He stepped away from the wall and added, "Thanks for cleaning that up."

He proceeded down the hallway. Entering the bedroom, he risked a foolish, fearful glance at the bed and was reassured to see its pillows fluffed and neatly arranged above a smooth, empty expanse of gold satin.

* * *

Ryan emerged from the hallway to find his wife bending over papers she'd spread across the dining room table. A dewy pitcher of iced tea lured him to the breakfast bar, and he poured himself a glass. He had to admit she made the best iced tea—the secret seemed to be in the assortment of fruits she added in the steeping process.

He took a long, satisfying gulp and moseyed to the table. "What's all this?" He looked curiously from the gleam in her eyes to the drawings spread for his perusal. His mind snapped to attention when he realized they were drawings of buildings.

"Well, Ryan." She looked nervous. "These are my drawings for the Golden Springs Ridge Resort. My lucky coin gave me the idea."

He leaned over the table with her and recognized at once the ridge overlooking Golden Springs Valley. In her five different perspectives, she had included hills, trees, rocks, and views with dead-on accuracy. The woman had a keen eye and an excellent memory. And he wasn't even addressing her buildings yet, which were already exciting him.

She was watching him anxiously, and he turned to her. "Tell me," he said simply.

Her cheeks flushed a pretty pink, deepening the emerald of her eyes. "Have you ever looked closely at my...at Vicki's coin?" She pulled it from her pocket and held it out to him. "See? On this side it says 'Sonoma County State Fair 1887,' with an American flag. And on the other side"—she leaned closer, and Ryan couldn't help inhaling the warm scent of her hair—"is the theme of the fair: 'All Brothers of the Land.' The word 'brothers' is written out in the languages of the different inhabitants of Sonoma County—native Indians, Russians, Spanish, Chinese. I got the idea that your complex should represent all the different people, an integration of cultures." She gave a wry grin. "I guess that's Francine Shepherd's contribution. She's forever going on about integration."

She pushed her hair back and pointed to the center drawing, an aerial view of the main lodge. "I propose starting with a medicine wheel in the central courtyard because the wheel creates a sacred space. This will honor the spirits of the land and the spiritual significance the ridge has for native Indians. Then we construct the buildings around the wheel, radiating out like this." She traced a finger over the primary buildings circling the courtyard, and the paths leading out to other small buildings and recreational areas. "Everything about the place should reflect the mixed cultures of Sonoma County—architecture, landscaping, decor, cuisine. The restaurant can offer specialty dishes from Russia and China and Spain and, of course, from the Indians indigenous to the area.

"Right here," she said, pointing, "we could build a cultural center to educate people about the history of Sonoma County and make sure all the cultures are fairly represented." She looked up at Ryan, her eyes shining. "I think it would succeed, Ryan, because it honors the land instead of dominating it. Harmony with the earth is the key here, not control. I don't know if there's really a magic circle protecting the area. But I believe this is the right way to go. It *feels* right."

She blew out a breath, punctuating the end of her speech. Ryan moved his gaze from one rendering to the next, seeing it all come together. Her drawings were hastily done and crude to his professional eye. But they were stunningly effective, and he knew she was right. This was the answer to the dilemma that had plagued him for months. Her solution was so simple, so intuitive, he wondered how no one had stumbled across it before.

He recognized genius in her work, cleverness and sensitivity, and he felt a swell of admiration alongside a twinge of envy. He knew she had given him a design that his boss, Larry Morgan, was bound to jump at. Her plan would raise their project from mediocre to a level of brilliance worthy of their best efforts, certain of achieving success.

Surely this was proof that she loved him.

But even as the enormity of her gift to him slammed home, Ryan steeled his heart against it. *Don't be a fool, Ashton. You know that kind of thinking can only get you into trouble.*

He took a small moment to still his emotions before he looked at her. "Your work is excellent." The coolness of his tone pleased him. "Your idea is sound and intuitive. This design is so unique, people will come just to experience a walk through it. And the circle is what does it, everything arranged to come full circle." He scanned the drawings again, visualizing how it would nest into the clearing, spreading out like rings in a pond from the central wheel, anchored in place. Words like *sacred*, *natural*, and *balanced* came to mind, confirming what he already knew was a perfect plan. "I congratulate you. I will, of course, present it to Larry and the others on Monday. I'm sure they'll all go for it. You have my sincerest thanks and admiration."

She flinched as if he'd struck her. The shine in her eyes darkened with hurt and then flared into anger. She tightened her jaw and thrust out her chin.

"Jealous, Ashton?" Her voice was soft, taunting. "Jealous because you didn't think of it yourself?"

Ryan's anger erupted like a volcano but just as quickly cooled to a prickling shame. "Yeah, maybe." He regarded her soberly. "You've found the solution to a problem that has stumped me for months. I confess I never would have thought of this on my own. It's all you—your insight, your talent, your knowledge of the area. I am grateful, truly, and I apologize if I sounded harsh or mean. You don't deserve that. I think your design is magnificent."

The honesty of his words quenched the fire in her eyes, leaving a soft glow that quickly misted over. She lowered her head and began to gather her drawings together. "I didn't realize it's so late." He noticed her hands were shaking. "It's high time I started supper."

Ryan hesitated. Then he reached out and took the drawings from her, careful not to touch her hands. "Let me take you out. You've worked hard, and you deserve the night off." At her look, he added lightly, "It's the least I can do for a colleague."

She searched his face. "All right, Ryan. That would be lovely. I'll just go and change."

She walked away, and he forced himself not to watch her. He was fighting the urge to follow her, to sweep her up from behind and carry her into the bedroom and forget about dinner entirely. To distract himself, he raised the glass of tea to his mouth and discovered all the ice had melted. Annoyed, he walked into the kitchen and dumped the tea into the sink.

He leafed through the drawings in his hand, letting

the clever simplicity of her design strike him afresh. Then he noticed the name she had signed to each picture, in a sloping hand that decidedly wasn't Vicki's: *Tori Ashton*.

* * *

The restaurant hummed with crowds of Saturday-night couples, many of them dressed for the opera or the theater. Phoning ahead for reservations had helped, for it wasn't long before the hostess called their name and led them to a tiny table squeezed up against a window. Ryan allowed himself the guilty pleasure of watching his wife settle into her seat and glance around the room. It seemed her guard was down, for he saw fatigue and pain etched plainly on her face. There were smudges under her eyes and a pinch of lines between her brows and around her mouth. She was pale and, despite the pregnancy, didn't seem to have gained weight. If anything, she looked thinner.

Ryan felt a twinge of guilt but mastered it quickly, letting the memory of the words she'd written in her journal harden his heart: *One day he'll come home and I'll be gone. I just hope I can get so far away that I never have to go back...*

In his weaker moments, he recited lines like that to remind himself why he couldn't trust her. His heart pleaded with him to go to her and try to rekindle the love they had shared and lost. But following his heart had opened him up to a pain he hadn't known since childhood. He'd been right to close off access to those feelings and rely on his reason to get him through life. And reason told him now that she was the enemy. Beautiful, intelligent, alluring, but still the enemy.

So, when her gaze returned to the table and found his eyes on her, he knew they revealed nothing. He saw her disappointment before she looked away, and he allowed himself to feel only grim satisfaction.

When their salads came, she picked at hers without interest, and she didn't touch the specialty bread sitting warm in a basket between them. She mostly sat, chin cupped in her hand, and stared out the window into the city street still busy with people and glowing amber under the streetlamps. Ryan swallowed down an ache in his throat and resisted the urge to reach out and take her hand.

Instead, he spoke up in a conversational tone. "Have you heard from Stephanie lately?"

She turned her sad eyes away from the window and rested her gaze on him, bringing the ache back into his throat.

"Yes. I got an e-mail yesterday." She wrapped her fingers around her glass of mineral water and began turning it in small, precise increments. "She sounds unhappy."

"Anything specific?"

"Not really. She just says how much she misses us, how she's looking forward to spending her Christmas vacation out here, how she wears her locket every day." She wrinkled her forehead. "She doesn't mention her mother or her new stepfather. She talks about her skating but doesn't mention her friends. She sounds lonely. I know she's lonely for us." Her eyes glistened. "And I'm lonely for her."

Ryan steeled himself. "You behaved very nicely to

her over the summer."

The mist in her eyes suddenly glittered. "*Behaved?* It wasn't an act, Ryan." Her voice was hard. "You know it wasn't an act."

He shrugged. "Okay. I admit, you two seemed to develop a real relationship. I know she loved you, and you seemed to love her. But then"—he honed the edge in his voice—"I'm not the best one to judge your motives about love, am I, darling?"

He saw something flash in her eyes as she leaned forward.

"You know the facts, Ashton. It's all been explained to you. You think you're protecting yourself, but don't you know that every day you let slip by you can *never* get back? You don't have so much time that you can squander these days and weeks nursing your pride and turning away love. Love isn't that easy to come by. Are you so rich in it that you can afford to just throw it away because you got your feelings hurt?" He saw another flash of emerald fire. "When are you going to grow up and stop whining? You'd better learn to take love where you find it because there are no guarantees—"

"You think I don't know that?" Ryan shouted, startling diners at the next table. He lowered his voice, but it was still seething. "What could you possibly know about love being snatched away, leaving a hole so big you're afraid you'll drown in it?"

Her reply was grim. "I know plenty."

"Oh, yeah?" Ryan glared at her. "What do you know about coming home from school one day and finding your mother lying on her bed, dead from an overdose of

41

sleeping pills? What do you know about your older brother, the one who was supposed to take care of you, suddenly taking off and never coming back? About a father so self-absorbed that he was always off on some trip, throwing our money into get-rich-quick schemes, leaving his family alone to cope with no food, no money. Until his wife couldn't stand it anymore, until she...until—"

Rage and pain choked off his breath, momentarily blinding him. He fought against a tide of old memory— the horror, the helpless fury, the despair and longing that made him feel sick with shame.

He couldn't stop the humiliating sob that tore from his throat and brought his wife around the table to sit beside him, shielding him from curious stares. He felt her grip on his arm and heard her voice easing him back into the present.

"Ryan, darling." Her voice was tender, the voice from his dream. "Ryan—"

It took every ounce of strength he had not to turn and bury his face against her. Instead, he rubbed his free hand over his eyes and tried to wrest his arm away from her.

"Leave me alone."

"Not a chance."

"Don't touch me!"

"I *will* touch you." She tightened her grip. "I won't let go of you, Ryan. Do you hear me? *I won't let go!*"

Something in her voice made him turn and look at her. Love shone in her eyes, warm and deep as it had ever been. He saw sweetness and patience there, too, achingly familiar, waiting to welcome him home.

But flames burned in the emerald depths, shooting hot bursts of fire above the steady warmth. Her mouth was set in a stubborn line; her fingers gripped his arm in an iron clasp. There was a lift to her head, a fierceness in her expression he suddenly recognized.

The warrior goddess.

Baffled, he stared at her, feeling stupid and light-headed. Her eyes narrowed as she studied him.

"We're going home, Ryan." She leaned closer and locked gazes with him to make sure he was hearing her. "Stay here while I take care of things. Then we'll go. All right? We'll go home together."

She touched his cheek before she left him. He shut his eyes and tried to steady himself, aware that his body was trembling, terrified he was going to burst into tears. Then he felt her hand on his shoulder. She helped him stand and led him from the table, through the restaurant into the night air. He drew car keys from his pocket, but she took them away.

"I'll drive, Ryan. I have a driver's license, remember?"

He caught the wryness in her voice, but he was too weak to argue. He slid into the passenger seat without comment and leaned his head back. And he let his wife take him home.

* * *

In his dream, the soft spring grasses rose knee-high. Ryan ran bare-legged, knowing he'd catch trouble if his mother found out. But he loved the squish of damp earth between his toes and the slap of tender grass blades

43

against his legs. He could run like this for hours without tiring.

Ryan ran in wide circles but skidded to a halt when he remembered the land mines. They were planted everywhere. He looked behind him, trying to remember exactly where he had stepped, wondering if he should go back or go forward. Across the street a woman emerged from a house and stood on the porch, shading her eyes. Ryan knew he had to get to her. Perhaps, if he stepped very carefully, he would be safe.

His next step set off a mighty explosion. The air burst into a cloud that lifted him high into the air. The cloud carried him, miraculously unhurt, and set him down in a garden of flowers. He knew he had been here before. This was where he was going to build his house.

On the ground beside him lay a woman frozen in marble casing. Ryan knew he had the power to release her. He touched her lips with his finger, surprised to find them soft and warm. He leaned over her and covered her mouth with his.

The woman came alive, as he'd known she would. He deepened his kiss, and her breath swirled down into his body, filling his lungs and then his blood, heating it until it ran strong through his limbs and spilled into his abdomen, hot and red…

Ryan understood that he was no longer dreaming. Still, he couldn't pull away from her. Languor from the dream weakened his defenses and muffled the warnings in his brain. For the moment he was content to hold in his arms a woman who was warm and soft and exquisitely responsive.

The warnings, however, clamored louder, reminding him of danger until, with a savage groan, he wrenched his mouth away. Rolling on top of her, he raised himself on his arms and glared down into her eyes, which were wide open and fixed on him.

"I hate you!" A lump of tears in his throat threatened to break. He bounced the bed under her head. "Do you hear me? *I hate you!*"

"I know, Ryan. And I love you." She slid her hands under his T-shirt and raked her nails down his back. "So go ahead and hate me, Ashton. Hate me all you want. I dare you."

He saw the challenge in her eyes, wild and taunting, and was tempted. But stinging words from her journal burst across his mind: *He reminds me of a puppy with his eyes still closed…so easily brought to heel…his wet tongue, his clumsy paws…*

With a grunt of disgust, he shoved himself off her. "No way," he said through gritted teeth, "are you getting your claws into me again." He glared at her before he turned away and punched up his pillow.

"Oh, no, you don't, Ashton." He felt her teeth on his earlobe, her leg sliding over his. "You're going to finish what you started, or I'm going to finish it for you."

She wrenched his pillow away, forced him onto his back, and swooped down to capture his mouth with hers. When she finally released him, he tasted blood on the tender interior of his bottom lip.

"You—"

She cut off his speech with another crushing kiss.

Anger, lust, hate—Ryan couldn't tell what drove

him, but he suddenly seized his wife's head between his hands and took control of the kiss. Clamping his body along the length of hers, he rolled her onto her back and continued to kiss her until she gratified him with little moans and soft whimpers.

"I *do* like to finish what I start," he said, his lips brushing her ear. By the time he did finish, her heart was thudding under his and her breath erupting in quick, shallow gasps. Satisfied, he tried to roll away from her but miscalculated the width of the bed. Still locked together, they tumbled off the edge and landed on the carpet with simultaneous grunts.

His wife's expression of surprise instantly gave way to merriment. "I like your style, Ashton," she said with a chuckle. In a burst of energy she reasserted her position, pinning him on his back, and Ryan braced himself for another assault on his mouth.

This kiss, however, was gentle, soft and searching. She draped her body over his, settling herself into the hollows and crevices between them. With her lips she grazed his chin, his temple, his closed eyelids, and murmured his name over and over. Just that—light kisses and his name like a song on her lips—melted through the last of his defenses.

He quietly wrapped his arms around her and shifted her weight until they were lying side by side, their kisses slow and lingering now that passion had been satisfied.

It's like coming to center, Ryan thought with wonder. As if all the push and urgency and sex were just to get to this deep place, to the heart. To the love.

He thought of his wife's design for the resort, those

rings like ripples in a pond, emanating from the center circle, anchored by the sacred core. Love.

He felt her lift away. Reluctantly, he opened his eyes. She was staring down at him, her eyes wide and dark and so deep with love that he felt his eyelids prick. She was smiling her feline smile but without malice, only contentment. She reached back to the bed for a pillow and slipped it tenderly under his head, then pulled down the blanket and covered them both. She nestled her head into his neck and sighed.

Ryan held her gently and stared into the dim shadows of their bedroom, slowly realizing what she had done for him. She'd baited him and made herself a sexual target so he could heave up his anger and his pain and release them. And then, in the stillness that followed, she'd guided him to the love buried beneath. He cast his thoughts back, remembering the words they had spoken. He had no doubt she was Katherine, the warrior goddess, the enchantress who disappeared with the dawn. But when he'd told her he hated her — and believed he did — she'd told him that she loved him.

And now, the woman he held in his arms so quietly had the tenderness of Elizabeth. He caught his breath and tightened his arms around her. "Are you asleep?" he whispered.

"No."

"May I ask you a question?"

She stirred and raised her head. "What is it?"

"Right now, are you Elizabeth, or are you Katherine?" Her eyes widened, and he rubbed her chin with his thumb. "It seems...I've fallen in love with you both."

She stared at him for a long moment, her mouth a soft *O* of surprise. Then she pressed her face into his neck. "I love you, Ryan," she said. "That's who I am." He felt the hot breath of her muffled words. "Please, darling, let that be enough for now."

Chapter Four

"And this one I picked up in Vienna." Eleanor Prescott held up the doll for her granddaughter to admire. "See this fine stitching on her petticoat and panties? You won't find that on dolls made in America."

Victoria murmured appreciatively and fingered the doll's petticoat. Christine sighed and tried to concentrate on her newspaper. Eleanor was showing off her doll collection. They'd already been through sixteen dolls. That left seven more to go.

"And this one belonged to my grandmother. She brought it with her when she married my grandfather and came over to this country. It was the only doll she ever had."

Here it comes, Christine thought. *The selfish-American-children speech.*

"In those days children learned to be content with very little. Not like children nowadays who grow up so spoiled. In Germany they didn't have all the luxuries you and your mother have enjoyed, Victoria."

Christine rattled her newspaper and held it up higher. She heard Victoria's soft answer. "You're right, Grandmother. We've been very fortunate."

Grandmother. Christine shook her head, unable to focus on the news story about an impending teachers' strike. The old lady didn't even wince at the name anymore. Amazing.

"And this is an original Shirley Temple doll. I've kept the box because it makes the doll more valuable to collectors."

She's my doll, a small voice shouted in Christine's head. *She was my Christmas present, but you said I couldn't play with her because she was too valuable. Somehow she ended up in your display case, and you forgot that she was mine.* Christine blew out an impatient breath. *Let it go, Christine. It doesn't matter.*

It does matter.

The Scottish Highlander was next. Then the Eskimo doll, dressed in real leather and mink with a tiny silver dagger in her belt. Then the Queen Elizabeth doll.

Christine kept her newspaper high, shielding her from the offensive sight of her mother caressing her dolls, handling them carefully because they were valuable. *Women like Eleanor should never have children*, she thought, *only dolls because they have no feelings to hurt.*

With a snort, Christine flung her newspaper aside and stood up.

"The coffee's cold," she announced. "I'm getting a fresh pot."

Her daughter looked over, but Eleanor continued a seamless flow of speech without glancing up.

Christine stormed out of the room.

This is about Dan, and you well know it, she chided herself. *You've been a prickly hedgehog for weeks, ever since you sent him away.*

She'd hardly seen Dan since the night of Stephanie's

birthday party. He arranged to be at the office on days when she wasn't, and he rarely spoke to her at business meetings. He'd said he would give her space, and Daniel Winslow was a man who kept his word.

Just this once, she wished he'd break it. She hadn't known how much she loved him until the night she had ordered him out of her life.

You did the right thing, Christine. He could never be happy with you. And a man like Dan deserves happiness.

When she returned with fresh coffee, Eleanor and Victoria were sitting together on one of the twin sofas.

"Mother!" Her daughter jumped up and held out the Shirley Temple doll. "Look what Grandmother gave me. Isn't she lovely?"

Christine's gaze slid from her daughter's radiant face to the staring glass eyes of the doll. Jealousy and rage licked through her with astonishing force. She set the pot clumsily on the coffee table and looked at her mother.

The old lady was sitting quite still, her shrewd eyes fixed on Christine. *Why, the old witch,* Christine thought. *She remembers perfectly well.*

Her body clenched with rage.

"I always liked that doll," Christine said briefly. She sat on the sofa, but her hand, she noticed, shook as she reached for her cup.

Her daughter was suddenly beside her, pouring her coffee for her, sitting companionably close. Across the coffee table, the Shirley Temple doll leaned against Eleanor, her glassy brown eyes staring at a corner of the ceiling.

"It's not a doll for children to play with," Eleanor

said crisply. She smiled at her granddaughter. "I'll give you the box, Victoria. You keep the doll for your own daughter when she grows up."

Victoria poured herself a cup and leaned back beside Christine. She splayed a hand over her stomach. "This could be a boy, Grandmother," she said with a smile.

Eleanor held out her cup, but as no one offered to pour for her, she sniffed and reached for the pot herself. Christine tensed, knowing the pattern, knowing there was a barb coming.

"Victoria, why aren't you modeling our maternity clothes?" Eleanor pursed her lips as she stirred her coffee. "Even though you've ruined your beautiful hair, I'm sure they could get some decent shots."

Christine rolled her eyes. "Give it a rest, Mother," she said. "Victoria's not going back to modeling. She's told you enough times."

Eleanor brushed her comment aside like an unpleasant odor. "Talk to Ray, Victoria. He'll set you up. Or I'll talk to him for you."

Victoria shook her head. "Mother's right—I have no intention of going to work right now, as a model or anything else."

Eleanor sniffed. "Well, I frankly don't understand why someone with your looks and your education insists upon wasting her life doing absolutely nothing." Her green eyes narrowed over her raised cup.

"An active businesswoman like you might see my life as nothing, but I don't see it that way." Christine marveled at the calm assurance in her daughter's voice. "Ryan and I are having a baby, and I'm happier than I've ever been. I'm in love with my life exactly the way it is. I don't want to change a minute of it."

Eleanor hunched a shoulder as if deflecting her granddaughter's reply. She pushed the Shirley Temple doll away from her, letting it slump over on the cushion. "You're too thin, girl," she said. "You won't have a baby at all if you don't start feeding yourself properly."

"My doctor says I'm a healthy weight. Anyway, I expect I'll balloon out fairly soon now, fat enough even to please you, Grandmother." Victoria chuckled.

"Tart as the skin off a May plum, aren't you, missy?" Eleanor scowled, but her eyes twinkled with amusement. Victoria was grinning.

How does she do it? Christine wondered. *Eleanor coils and strikes, and the words slide right off Victoria, as if she's immune to Eleanor's venom. If it were me, I'd either be striking back or crawling off to lick my wounds and nurse my resentment.*

Christine had noticed a new peace in her daughter, and she envied it. Over the summer she'd watched her daughter grow into her womanhood, watched her begin to live outside her fear and open herself to love. Like those beautiful roses on her balcony, she'd found the courage to push beyond that tight little bud and blossom.

And look at the results. A close relationship with Stephanie, a fast friendship with that nice girl Lisa, and a solid marriage with her husband. Ryan was so in love with her—you could tell just by looking at him, by the way his eyes lit up at the mere sight of her. And now they had a child on the way. It was like a fairy tale come true.

I can't tell her, Christine thought. *Francine Shepherd is wrong. Victoria might not be as strong as she seems, and what I have to say could destroy the life she's trying to build for herself. What kind of mother would I be to risk ruining her chance for happiness?*

You're a coward, Christine. It's your own happiness you're worried about. You're afraid she'll blame you and hate you when she knows the truth. And when you lose her, there will be no one left to love you.

* * *

Christine closed her eyes and listened to strains of Mozart lifting on the air, realizing as never before how well her daughter could play the piano. She allowed herself to be carried up on the swell of the crescendos and set down in the valleys beyond. When the piece ended, Christine kept her eyes closed and hoped Victoria would continue, relishing the peace of this time they had alone together.

The library fire gave warmth to the room, welcome now that Indian summer was over and fall weather had officially arrived. The smell of fallen leaves, the subtle nip in the air, the deeper blue of the sky made Christine think of buying plaid uniforms and school supplies, and of Victoria's small, soft hand in hers as her daughter glanced fearfully around the new classroom and edged closer to her mother. Every year it was the same — Victoria's pleading eyes, her tearful entreaties not to leave her, and Christine sitting in the car afterward, alone, with tears streaming down her face.

Victoria, baby, I'm so sorry.

Her daughter was playing a folk song Christine

didn't know, German or maybe Russian. It was sweet and sentimental, and Christine sighed when it slowed to a finish. In the tender silence that followed, she heard her daughter rise from the piano bench and cross the room. She opened her eyes as Victoria sat down beside her.

She was carrying a framed photograph, one from the group sitting on top of the piano. Wordlessly, she handed it to her mother.

Christine stiffened at the old black-and-white photograph of herself and Luke taken at age four. Wisps of old pain curled in her stomach.

"Tell me about Luke." Her daughter's green eyes were curious. "Grandmother tells me how much I look like him, that I have his hair and his eyes. She says he was a saint." She rolled her eyes. "It's horrible to have your brother canonized by your mother and held up as a standard you can never hope to match." Christine gave her a sharp look. "Is that how it was for you, Mother?" She laid a hand on her mother's arm. "Please tell me. I really want to know."

"You've already heard the story," Christine said in a flat voice.

"You may have told me before, but I won't hear it the same way today." Her daughter's hand on her arm tightened. "I want to hear it again, not Grandmother's version but yours. Because you were his twin."

Surprised by her daughter's urgency, Christine studied her. Then she risked a look inward. That memory had been locked away for years behind a door that was old and rusty. It wouldn't be easy to open it now.

She looked at the two childish faces in the photo, and

as always, she saw them in contrast—Luke's light curls to her straight dark hair, Luke's laughing expression to her solemn one, Luke's eyes that he got from his mother to her eyes that she got from the gypsies. *The gypsies left you on my back porch, and if you don't behave, I'll put you out there again so they can take you back.* Christine had believed it for years.

She made herself look away from the photo, into her daughter's waiting face. She saw Luke again in the Rhineholdt features—the sensitive mouth, the delicately arched brows, the creamy skin with the translucence of alabaster. And Eleanor's green eyes.

Yet not Eleanor's eyes. Her daughter's gaze was soft and earnest, without that emerald bite that could draw blood with a single glance. And there was something else that Christine had never seen in her own mother's eyes— a desperate longing for connection.

Christine set the photograph carefully on the coffee table and smoothed her hands over her knees. She cleared her throat.

"I don't remember much about Luke."

Her daughter helped her. "Did you always live in this house?"

Christine shook her head. "We lived in a small house. Luke and I were five when we came here to live." Her voice grew soft as memory tiptoed back. "I remember playing dominoes on a navy-blue rug. I used to win at our games, but Luke never seemed to mind. He was my best friend. In those days I didn't care about anybody but Luke. And maybe my father."

Christine stared at her knees. "I don't remember

much about my father, either. Only that he was very tall and had big hands that were always gentle. He smelled like pipe tobacco and chewing gum. He used to take Luke and me for walks and an ice cream in the park every Saturday." She smiled suddenly at her daughter. "I had forgotten about our Saturday trips to the park. Father would sit on a green bench by the lake and watch us feed the ducks." Her smile faded. "Mother was hardly ever at home. She was always working. When she was home, she was either thinking about work or yelling at the servants. Father always liked our house, but Mother wasn't satisfied until she bought this place. She always had her mind set on something bigger, something better, lovelier." Christine shrugged. "That's why I always disappointed her. I've never been lovely. Not like Luke."

She took the photo into her lap and stared at her twin. "Luke was a beautiful child. It wasn't just his looks. It was *him*. He was gentle and sweet and loving. I remember taunting him to see if I could make him angry, but all I did was make him cry. And then I felt guilty. He had a way of charming Mother. Not just flattery—he really loved her, and she knew it. Just like she knew I didn't."

Christine's voice dropped. "I used to wonder if my jealousy killed him as much as the illness. It wasn't that I was glad when he died; truly, I was heartbroken. But a tiny little voice inside me whispered, 'Well, now that he's gone, maybe Mother will love you instead.' But she didn't. In fact, things got worse. She blamed me. And then Father died, and she blamed me for that, too. She said he died pining for his son that I'd killed."

Christine's eyes were so dry they began to burn. "After years of trying to be good, I guess I decided to be bad. I started smoking when I was fifteen. I practiced cursing and started stealing from stores. Nobody ever caught me, and maybe that's too bad. I think I really wanted them to. I wanted my mother to know. I hated her, but I hated myself more.

"Then I met Jack. Your father." She glanced at her daughter's solemn face. "Mother had a fit because he was a nobody and didn't have a steady job. But he was strong and handsome, and he was good to me. I got pregnant, and you were born." Christine's jaw tightened. "You were beautiful, just like Luke. Everyone loved you, even Mother. Jack adored you."

Her words stumbled as they came faster. "I was so jealous. I went...sort of crazy. I started picking fights with Jack, accusing him of things I knew weren't true. I went back to work and flirted and went home with men. I...it was like I was suddenly on a mission to prove how bad I really was—not to myself, because I already knew it. But to Jack. To my mother. Maybe even to you.

"You were such a good baby, Victoria. So sweet and good-natured. And so beautiful. Next to you I felt ugly, just like I did with Luke. But it wasn't your fault; it was mine. And Jack loved you. I think he stayed in the marriage longer than he wanted to because he loved you so much."

Tears were threatening. Christine pressed her hands over her heart, trying to slow it down.

"The night he left me, we had a terrible fight. He accused me of being a rotten mother, and I hated him for it because I knew he was right. When he stormed out of the house, I assumed he was going for a drive to cool off. He'd done it before, and he always came back. But that night he stayed away. And the night after. Four days later the police came to the door and told me Jack was dead. They'd found his car turned over in a ravine just north of Sacramento. It had been there for two days before a jogger discovered it."

Her voice shrank to a whisper. "It was my fault that he died, you see. Just like Luke. Just like my father. I loved them all, and they all died because of me." She paused, fighting down the sobs gathering in her chest. She couldn't look at her daughter, who sat still and silent, watching her. "You and I moved in with Mother, and I lost all interest in living. I started to drink. I took up with men again. My life became a blur of parties and waking up with strange men in smelly beds. I let the servants look after you because I told myself they would be better at mothering than I was. Nearly anybody would be."

She caught her breath, realizing she was on the brink of confessing what she'd never wanted Victoria to know. She risked a look at her daughter's face and saw green eyes soft with compassion. *Maybe it will be all right. Maybe she'll understand and forgive me.*

Christine wet her lips and swallowed.

"I was a terrible mother to you, Victoria." She shook her head as her daughter opened her mouth. "No, let me finish. I neglected you because I couldn't stand myself when I was around you. I was jealous and resentful of the attention you got. When my mother spoke of you, there was pride in her voice that I never heard when she talked about me. People turned their heads and smiled at you when we walked by—I imagined they looked at me and wondered how someone like me could have such a magnificent daughter."

Christine dropped her gaze. "The men—they liked you, too. When I brought them home, they wanted to hold you and touch you. I knew you didn't like it. I knew it wasn't right." Tears brimmed her eyes. "That time when you were eight. I knew what happened. God help me, I knew that he went to your room while I was lying in a drunken stupor on my bed. I should have protected you, Victoria. You deserved better. And then you kept having those awful nightmares, but I wouldn't let you talk about it. As long as we didn't talk about it, I could pretend it never happened. I know that was selfish. I'm so ashamed. Victoria, darling, I'm so, so sorry."

Raw sobs tore from her throat, spilling a horrible sound into the silent room. Christine smeared away tears with the back of her hand and looked fearfully at her daughter.

Victoria had pulled back and was staring at her mother with round, stricken eyes. She rose without a word and crossed the short distance to the fireplace. Resting both hands on the mantel, she stared into the fire.

Neither woman spoke. The bright flames crackled; a log dropped and hissed. The mantel clock struck the half hour.

And still they were silent. Christine bit her lip and stared at her daughter's stiff back. She felt as though she had leaped off a cliff and was suspended midair, not sure whether she would make it to the other side.

At last her daughter turned. Christine searched her face, trying to read her expression.

Victoria moved to the sofa and sat down, just out of reach. She folded her hands on her knees and stared at them. When she spoke, her voice was soft.

"I think what you really want is to hear your daughter say that you are forgiven." She looked up then, and her green eyes were solemn. "I'm not trying to be cruel, but I can't give you what you want today. Perhaps sometime in the future, you will hear those words of forgiveness. I can't say for certain."

Christine nodded, hardly daring to breathe.

Her daughter continued. "Francine told me once that people always do things for a reason. We may not understand what the reason is, but that doesn't mean there isn't one. The things you did—hurting yourself, hurting your husband and…your daughter. I don't condone them. But I do think I understand the reasons why you did them."

She was on her feet again, crossing to the fire, staring once again into the flames. Her body sagged a little against the mantel.

"When we're filled with hate, it leaches into the life around us, spreading like a spilled bottle of ink. We're capable of acting in ways that are shockingly evil. And we hurt the ones we love most. Choosing to live in hate is choosing to live in perpetual darkness. But Francine has taught me that we all have a choice. As long as I choose to hate—myself or anybody else—I'll go right on hurting and distancing myself from the one thing that can heal my hurt and make the darkness disappear—love."

She returned to the sofa and, this time, sat close enough to take her mother's hand.

"The forgiveness you seek may come to you on another day. But I can tell you this from my heart. You are the mother I've always wanted. We are more alike than you will ever realize. And for the present, the past doesn't matter to me. I don't want it to spoil our opportunity to be close. I want you to love me and give me the chance to love you back. Let love drive away the darkness that's made you suffer for so long."

Christine searched her daughter's face, hardly daring to believe the gift she was being offered. Fiercely she pulled her daughter into her arms.

"I think love's work has already begun," she said.

* * *

Francine watched her patient closely.

"It was the same dream, Francine. The lioness was on the ledge like always, pacing, trying to find a way off. Then she saw me and stopped."

Rather than fearful, Francine noted, her patient seemed excited.

"She told me, 'The only way I'm going to get off this ledge is through you.' I looked into those golden eyes and thought, *She's going to kill me!* But I wasn't afraid, Francine. I just nodded and opened my arms, ready for her. And the most amazing thing happened!" The green eyes shone. "She leaped off the ledge, straight at me. But instead of landing in my arms, she leaped *into* me, right into my chest. And then, as one body, we leaped off the mountain and landed, easy as anything, on the soft grass at the forest edge. But we weren't a lioness anymore,

Francine. We were a *deer*."

She flattened a hand over her chest.

"Inside, though, I still felt strong, like the lioness. It's funny; when you talked about integration, I always feared the lioness would swallow me up, and there would be only Katherine left. But it feels as though *Elizabeth* took Katherine inside, and *Elizabeth* is in charge of my life, not Katherine." She searched Francine's face. "Does that make sense to you?"

Francine leaned forward, crossing her arms over her knees. "Well, we've talked about how you split yourself into two halves. The part you decided was "bad" you called Katherine, and all your anger and pain got frozen in that childlike personality. Meanwhile, the rest of you grew up, maturing into the woman you call Elizabeth. It seems natural that the adult—Elizabeth—would embrace the younger self and lead her into the present. I think that's why you feel you're now living Elizabeth's life."

Her patient smiled shyly. "Ryan told me he'd fallen in love with both of us, both Katherine and Elizabeth. I think his words, more than anything, convinced me that Katherine and I need each other. I wanted Ryan to admire in me what he admires in Katherine. I wanted to take it all back inside me, to be everything that I could be." She wrinkled her forehead. "This sounds confusing, but even the name Elizabeth doesn't fit anymore. And neither does Katherine. I just realized that for some time I've been thinking of myself as *Tori*." She grinned at Francine's bewildered look. "Stephanie gave me the nickname last summer. It's how she addresses her e-mails to me. I sign all my paintings 'Tori Ashton.'" She paused. "It's like that time when I cut my hair to stake a claim on my new life. Remember?"

Francine nodded. "You want a new name that fits the new way you feel about yourself."

"Yes, that's it. That's it exactly."

Chapter Five

Dan Winslow picked up his empty dinner plate and his glass and carried them into the kitchen. As he turned on the tap and waited for hot water, he couldn't help feeling disappointed. It wasn't that he minded eating alone. He'd done it for years, enjoying the quiet time to play his music and reflect on his day. But Erin was supposed to come over tonight and bring his little grandson, Sean. She'd called at the last minute to tell him Sean was coming down with a cold, and they'd come over when he was feeling better. Dan had understood; of course, he'd understood. But he was still disappointed.

It didn't take him long to wash his few dishes and hang up the towel. Cooking for one, he didn't bother with the dishwasher. Besides, he enjoyed tidying the kitchen—wiping the counters, polishing the chrome faucet, putting things back in their proper places. Even when Deborah was alive, Dan had enjoyed domestic chores more than she did. Putting his environment in order helped him relax.

Deborah. His eyes automatically sought her picture sitting on the top of the old upright piano she'd brought from home when they were first married. He had loved Deborah; they'd shared a happy life raising two daughters and making a home together. Seven years after losing her to cancer, he still missed their talks. He missed her quiet voice and her practical nature. He missed the constancy of having her to come home to.

But it wasn't Deborah who filled his thoughts these days. His gaze moved from the piano to the table under the window, where the soft light of the lamp illuminated a bright bowl of chrysanthemums, the first of the season. He picked up the picture sitting beside it and stared hard at the smiling faces of himself and Christine on their first dinner date at the Fairmont Hotel. He recalled the corsage he'd brought to surprise her, the dance when he'd held her in his arms for the first time, and the way his palms sweat, making him feel like a lovesick teenager. That was the night he'd fallen in love with her. And fallen hard.

Interesting how he didn't feel he was betraying Deborah. When she'd died, Dan had resigned himself to living alone and looking to his daughters' families to fill the empty space left by her passing. When he met Christine Reeves, he wasn't looking for romance. The last thing he'd expected was to fall in love.

This love was different from the one he'd had with Deborah, born of a different age in life, seeking a different kind of fulfillment. The love he'd shared with his wife had started young and simple and had later taken on the layers of family love. When Dan looked at his daughters now, he couldn't help feeling his love for Deborah intertwined with his love for them—seeing traces of her features and her personality in them, watching their lives reflect the values he and Deborah had shared. Deborah would always be part of their family, a welcome presence who wasn't threatened by other loves.

Oddly, his love for Christine had initially made him miss Deborah more. For seven years he'd told himself that he wasn't really lonely, that he didn't need anyone special in his life, that lust and physical need were no longer a concern. After all, he was fifty-two years old. His days of sowing oats were over.

He'd met Christine a few times at Prescott's, passing through the office, smiling politely over casual remarks. Then he'd sat beside her at a business meeting for one of the longest hours of his life. He couldn't remember anything about that meeting except Christine. His senses were flooded with her spicy fragrance, with the swell of her breast catching his eye when she moved her arm, with the dark intensity of her eyes when she turned to speak to him. He listened to her quiet, cultured voice and couldn't understand why anyone in the room would question anything she said, except perhaps for the pleasure of hearing her speak again. He remembered flushing with annoyance and pulling himself closer to the table to hide his sudden, unbelievable hardness.

When the meeting was over, he'd loitered by the door, murmuring to others as they filed out, waiting for her. And he'd asked her out, shocked by his uncharacteristic spontaneity and grateful that he wasn't stammering over his words. But she'd turned him down. Cold. He'd backed off for a while, taking little opportunities to speak with her, cultivating a casual relationship. Then he'd asked her out again. And she'd said no. Finally, after two more tries and a bouquet of roses, she had agreed. He'd worn his best suit, taken her to the Fairmont, and lost his heart to her.

That painful night in August when she sent him away—he should have seen it coming. But even if he had foreseen it, he couldn't have prevented it. Christine was a complex woman with secrets to protect. He'd done his best to honor his promise and give her enough space to work through whatever was tormenting her. But he couldn't help showing up some days at the office when she wasn't expecting him. Loving her as he did, he couldn't resist the physical urgency just to see her, to touch her lightly on the arm and hear her voice speaking his name.

Dan sighed as he propped the photograph on the table and switched off the lamp. He left the gay chrysanthemums and the smiling faces in darkness and headed for his bedroom, knowing exactly what he would dream about that night.

* * *

"Mother, we've been over this a dozen times at least. I will *not* talk to Victoria about going back to work for you. It's the last thing in the world I want for her right now. She's happier than I've ever seen her. Why would you want to spoil that?"

Sitting behind the wide mahogany desk in her personal study, Eleanor waved a dismissive hand at her daughter. "That girl doesn't know what she wants. Her job at Prescott's gave her something important to do. What does she do now? Just sits around that apartment all day."

"What's wrong with just sitting around?"

"It's wasteful. It's a waste of her looks and her talent. If you'd raised her with a decent work ethic, I wouldn't have to explain it to you now, Christine."

Her daughter bristled. "So you're telling me I've been a bad mother?"

"I'm telling you if it weren't for my positive influence, Victoria would have grown up completely undisciplined. As it is, she's spoiled and lazy. I admit she has a sweet temperament and some degree of the Rhineholdt charm. But you've done your best to ruin that girl. I suspect she married the first man who asked her, a *divorced* man much too old for her, just to escape you."

Eleanor snapped off her computer and leaned back in her chair. She gave her daughter a pained look. "I am grieved to say what a disappointment you are to me, Christine. Frankly, I can't understand where I went wrong with you."

Her daughter looked stunned. Pleased with the effect of her words, Eleanor continued.

"I've spent my best years building up this retail empire so I could pass it on to my children and my children's children." She sighed and shook her head. "I admit you do an adequate job of handling the buying end, Christine. You've made the most of your abilities, I suppose. If my son had lived—" She sighed again and watched her daughter's expression darken. "I'm sure Victoria could still learn to take over for me when I'm gone. She's got a lot of me in her, except for that streak of stubborn laziness. But I credit you with that. Or maybe she inherited her propensity to waste time from her...unfortunate father?"

Christine's dark eyes smoldered. "Leave it alone, Mother."

Eleanor saw the fire in her daughter's eyes and sneered. "Don't threaten me, girl. You haven't got the stomach for a real fight. You never did." She leaned forward over her desk. "You think I don't know what you're up to? You're keeping Victoria from coming back to work for me because you're jealous of her. Always have been, from the moment she was born. Couldn't stand the attention she got, couldn't stand the fact that she was beautiful like you never were. Spoiled little rich girl, you didn't want to move over and let someone else be the center of attention for once."

"Look who's talking!" her daughter shrieked, and Eleanor flinched. "*You're* the one who can't stand giving up center stage! Even now, you're not concerned with what's best for Victoria. You only care about what's best for you. Always what's best for Eleanor Prescott!"

"What's best for me is also what's best for my granddaughter. Not being a true Rhineholdt yourself, you can't understand the bond she and I share."

Christine leaped to her feet. "Don't give me that gypsy crap! Like it or not, I'm your flesh and blood even more than Victoria is. I'm your child. *I'm your child!* Just as much as Luke was." Her voice dropped to a hiss. "But don't think that fact gives me any more pleasure than it gives you!"

"You spoiled, ungrateful girl!" Eleanor was shocked to find herself trembling. "How dare you speak to me in that fashion?"

"I dare because I am sick and tired of being blamed

and hated for something that wasn't my fault. I didn't do anything wrong! I was a child, and I got sick, and it was nobody's fault." Tears choked her words. "I loved my brother. I was heartbroken when he died. But no one was there to comfort *me* in *my* pain. You were so wrapped up in your own narcissistic grief—"

"Don't you speak to me about my grief!" Eleanor rose also and shook a fist at her daughter. "I forbid you!" Her voice thundered. "Do you hear me, girl? *I forbid you!*"

"Did you forbid Father, too?" Christine's voice was loud and angry, sending daggers of pain through Eleanor's head. "Is that why he died? Because you didn't allow anyone in the house except you to feel the loss of Luke, and Father didn't have enough hate to help him survive?" Eleanor heard the words muffled as if through cotton; she tried to see her daughter's face through a sudden, shimmering fog. "Did you know that hate was the only thing that kept me alive all those years? Hating you, hating myself…Mother? What is it? *Mother!*"

Pain the color of blood burst behind Eleanor's eyes. She tried to raise a hand to slap her daughter's insolent face. But the red turned inky black and seeped into her body, and she couldn't move her arm.

The last thing she saw was a look of alarm on her daughter's face before the inky black crept into the room blotted out the world.

* * *

Christine sat by the hospital bed and watched her mother's face, alert to the faintest change. She recalled sitting by Victoria's hospital bed not so long ago, and she wondered if her suffering was God's way of punishing her.

Please, God. Don't let one more person die because of me.

She shuddered, recalling the quarrel and her accusations hanging in the air like gun smoke in the moments after her mother collapsed. Her angry words rang in her ears and paralyzed her as blood trickled a bright red stain into Eleanor's white hair, showing where the corner of the desk had clipped her as she fell. Christine's body didn't belong to her anymore. She willed it to bend and see if her mother was still alive. But it wouldn't budge. All it would do was stand still and scream.

She was still standing there when the paramedics arrived. Agnes must have called them. One of the team—a woman—took Christine by the arm and gave her face a quick appraisal.

"Is there someone I can call to be with you?"

"My daughter." Christine whimpered. "I want Victoria." And then, "Oh, God!" as the horror hit her. She covered her face with her hands.

Ryan was out of town, so Victoria had come alone to the hospital. She sat with her arms around Christine for the interminable wait, and then stood with her, supporting her, when the doctor came to tell them about the stroke.

"It's too soon to tell the extent of the damage." He took Christine's elbow and helped her to sit down again. "Right now she's in a coma. She has a history of high blood pressure, but this is her first stroke. I can't make any promises; we'll just have to wait and see."

She felt Victoria's arm slip around her shoulders and tighten, triggering a wave of emotion through her body. It should have brought tears, but her eyes wouldn't cry.

When Christine walked into the intensive care unit and saw her mother, her first reaction was surprise. She hadn't realized that her mother was so small. Always wearing heels, with her hair coifed and fire in her eyes, Eleanor had seemed larger than life. Now she looked like an old woman in a child's body, the mound of her feet under the blanket nowhere close to reaching the foot of the bed. As Christine stepped closer, she saw that her arms lying over the blanket were thin and spotted, and the eyelids covering her emerald eyes were wrinkled.

She looks so old, Christine thought. *She almost looks dead already.* And she pressed a hand against her trembling lips. But still the tears wouldn't come.

She stood by the bed and touched her mother's arm. "I'm so sorry, Mother," she whispered. "Can you hear me? You must get well so I can tell you how sorry I am. I didn't think. I never imagined—"

Her legs wobbled, and she sat down abruptly.

Fifteen minutes later, the nurse found her rigid in the chair, straining toward her mother. The nurse touched her on the shoulder.

"Time to leave her now, Christine." She spoke kindly. "You can come back later."

"But if she wakes up—"

"We'll let you know." She took Christine's arm and led her to the door. "Here's your daughter."

Christine felt Victoria's hand slip under her elbow. "Come sit down, Mother. You look worn out."

Christine allowed herself to be led to the waiting area. She sat down beside her daughter and wrung her hands.

"Oh, Victoria. We had a fight. I said the most awful things to her, just before she..." The memory of her words horrified her into silence.

"The stroke wasn't your fault, Mother. Grandmother is old. These things just happen. It doesn't have to be anyone's fault."

Christine shook her head. "No, I baited her. I wanted us to fight. I wanted everything out in the open. I wanted to make her angry—" She squeezed her hands together. "But I never wanted this. Dear Lord, I never meant for this to happen!"

"Of course you didn't." Her daughter hugged her tightly. "You love her."

"I told her I hated her."

"But that doesn't mean you don't love her." Her daughter gave her shoulders a gentle shake. "You didn't do anything wrong, Mother. Even if the worst happens, it isn't your fault."

Christine nodded without conviction. Not only wasn't she crying, she realized, but her eyes felt abnormally dry. In fact, her whole body felt dry and brittle, like an old leaf tossed on the breeze and dropped uselessly into a corner of the yard. She couldn't seem to feel anything but guilt.

She recognized his sweater first. It was blue, one of her favorites because it brought out the blue of his eyes. A little cry caught in her throat as she rose from her chair and stood on shaky legs. Her eyes met Dan's, and she saw hesitation in his as he slowed his pace, unsure of his welcome.

Something broke loose in Christine's chest, dislodging the cry in her throat.

"Dan!"

And then she was running. His arms caught her and folded her close, and his warm, familiar voice murmured into her hair, "Christine, my love, my love."

* * *

The clock on the waiting room wall inched past eleven. Victoria had gone home a little after nine, but Dan stayed with Christine. The ache in her back and the grit beneath her eyelids reminded her that she'd been at the hospital for over seven hours.

"You can't do anything more here." Dan squeezed her hand. "Let me take you home, so you can get some rest."

Christine nodded dully. With his arm firmly around her shoulders, Dan guided her along the polished corridors, down the elevator, and out through the lobby. The shock of cold night air made her gasp and realize that she'd come away without a coat.

"Here." Dan pulled off his jacket and helped her into it. The lining was still warm with the heat of his body and smelled faintly of him. She cocooned herself in his essence as he helped her into the car. The San Francisco night was thick with fog, insulating them from the rest of the world as Dan got in beside her and started the engine. With comforting detachment, she watched him drive out of the hospital parking lot and turn right, heading for the Prescott mansion.

"I don't know what it is, Dan." Her voice sounded dreamlike and far away. "But I don't want to go back to that big, empty house tonight."

She felt his glance.

"Then come home with me, Christine."

She roused herself a little. "Well, no, I couldn't."

"Yes, you could."

"Dan, it's very kind of you. Thank you. But—"

She broke off as Dan suddenly swerved the car to the curb and stopped. He turned to face her, his expression hidden by the misty darkness.

"I'm not being kind, Christine. Don't you know by now that I've imagined you in my home almost every day since the first time I saw you? Sending me away didn't lessen your presence in my life. You're with me in the morning when I'm fixing my coffee and picturing how you'll look at the office that day, wondering if you'll be wearing your green suit or your paisley dress with that funny little pin. When I come home in the evening, your photograph is the first thing I see when I switch on my lamp and the last thing I see when I switch it off again. You're in my bed with me every night because all I ever dream about is you."

His hands were on her shoulders, his eyes gleaming at her through the dark. Then he pulled her roughly to him, and his mouth came down on hers, hard. His kiss crushed against her teeth, but his lips were warm, and the light stubble on his chin grazed hers with little strokes of delicious pain. Overwhelmed by the sheer comfort of his body against hers, Christine clung to him. She felt his hands move up to cradle her head, and his kiss softened. Her hands crept around his neck, and she answered his tenderness by deepening her kiss, knowing she was surrendering to him, believing she would do anything to keep those strong male hands holding her.

At last he pulled away but still held her head gently in his hands.

"Well?" he said quietly. "Are you coming home with me, Christine?"

She nodded without speaking, not wanting to break the magic of the moment. He smiled and kissed her forehead. Keeping an arm around her, he released the brake, eased the car into a U-turn, and headed off in the opposite direction from Eleanor's house.

* * *

"Erin left some of her clothes here." Dan hung up his jacket and offered Christine a seat on the sofa. "I think I can find something to fit. She's tall, like you."

He disappeared into the hall, leaving Christine to wander around his living room on her own.

It was her first time in Dan's house. She had never allowed him to bring her here, afraid it would make things too intimate between them. As she looked around now, she was sorry she'd waited so long. The personality of the man she loved was evident everywhere she looked — in the soft colors of the sofa and armchairs arranged for intimate conversation, in the orderliness one would not expect from a man who lived alone, even in the bowl of yellow chrysanthemums sitting beside the picture of the two of them on their first date. She looked curiously at the photos on the piano, guessing these were his daughters and his wife, Deborah. Christine studied the sweet, pretty face and felt an uncomfortable stirring of jealousy.

"Here we are." Dan emerged with a robe and nightgown over his arm and slippers in his hand. "Bathroom's down the hall." She took the garments without a word, and he rubbed his hands together. "Okay, then. I'll get a fire going."

He knelt before the hearth and fussed a little with the firewood. Christine found her way to the bathroom, closed the door, and stared at herself in the mirror. *I can't do this,* she thought. *What am I doing here?*

The burst of desire and certainty she'd felt in Dan's arms had dissipated, leaving her with the stark reality of her gray face, exhausted from shock and strain, and the realization that she was about to break a barrier of isolation she'd spent years perfecting. She put on Dan's daughter's nightgown and robe and tried not to grimace at the irony of it. The slippers warmed her cold feet somewhat, but still she shivered. She splashed water on her face, ran a comb through her hair, and sighed over the impossibility of looking even remotely attractive. Shutting off the light, she crept back to the living room.

Dan had a cheerful blaze going and two glasses of red wine set out on the coffee table. Violins and the full richness of a tenor voice filled the room.

Dan smiled at her from the sofa and reached out a hand. She went to him and sat close, resting her tired head on his shoulder. Neither of them spoke as they stared into the leaping flames. Dan stroked her hair and planted a kiss on the top of her head. Christine relaxed into him, snuggling her cheek against the soft blue sweater she loved while the tenor sang a love song in Italian. She didn't understand the words, but she understood the song.

The tears that had refused to come earlier suddenly filled her eyes and slipped quietly down her cheeks. Dan tightened his arms around her. When the tears began to pull up painful sobs, he stroked her back and kissed her hair, her forehead, her cheeks. For a time the only sounds in the room were her choking sobs, the snapping fire, and the tenor's pulsing vibrato.

Gradually her sobs withered, and her body succumbed to a pleasant hum that sang along her limbs and filled her head, cushioning her from everything but the comforting feel of Dan's arms around her. She was scarcely aware when he swept her up and carried her into the bedroom, only dimly realized when he slipped off her robe and laid her gently on cool, smooth sheets. She rolled onto her side and curled into a ball, and warm covers settled over her body, tucking under her chin. A kiss whispered over her forehead and lips. Then the hum overtook her completely, and she slept.

* * *

Christine awoke to bright sunshine and the rich smell of fresh coffee. She blinked and squinted until her eyes made out the shape of Dan standing over her, smiling and holding two brown mugs. Reluctant to emerge from her warm nest of bedcovers, she nevertheless pulled herself to sitting, rubbed her eyes, and accepted a mug while Dan adjusted the pillows behind her back.

"Good morning." His greeting held such warmth

that Christine glanced quickly into his face. She saw the warmth there, too, in his caressing gaze, in the tenderness of his smile, in the little lines crinkling from the corners of his eyes. Warmth—and love.

Christine took a sip from her mug and said lightly, "A man who can brew a decent cup of coffee. That makes you a catch for any woman, Dan."

"I was hoping you'd think so." He grinned as he sat on the bed and rested his hand on the blanket, or rather, on the long stretch of her legs beneath it. Christine shifted uncomfortably and glanced at the other side of the bed. The pillow was hollowed with the imprint of his head, the covers rumpled.

Dan followed her glance.

"It was too cold last night to sleep on the sofa." He removed his hand from her leg and leaned it behind him on the bed. "I hope you don't mind."

"It's your bed, Dan."

He couldn't miss the stiffness in her voice. He took a sip of coffee and eyed her thoughtfully. "Feeling rested?"

Christine bit her lip and nodded. "I must have gone out like a light. I don't think I moved all night."

Dan nodded. "You were exhausted. You needed the sleep." He added softly, "I'm glad you let me bring you here, Christine. Last night wasn't a time for you to be alone."

He studied her frankly over the rim of his mug, and Christine felt her cheeks flush. She raised a self-conscious hand to her hair.

"I must look an absolute fright this morning."

"On the contrary," he murmured. He didn't reach

for her but held her with his eyes, and Christine felt his gaze caress her, stroking her face, triggering little sparks along the length of her body.

What does he expect of me? I'm not good at this. I shouldn't even be here.

She took a nervous sip of coffee, and then another, pulling her gaze away from his with an effort. She stared at the little hairs along his arm, glistening blond in a shaft of morning sunlight. Her stomach turned a slow somersault as her gaze traveled up his arm, and she remembered how it felt to be held inside the circle of his embrace, pressed against his chest, her heart beating against his.

If you touch me now, Dan, I will shatter like old glass. And I'll never find all the pieces to put myself back together.

"Christine." His voice was soft but compelling. She looked up and met unexpected compassion in his quiet blue eyes. "I love you," he said simply. "And I want something from you. But I'm not going to take it until you're ready to come to me and offer it freely."

He leaned toward her, and she flinched. He saw it, but still he reached out and laid a gentle hand on her cheek.

"Don't be afraid of me, Christine. As strong and as deep as my love is, it will never hurt you."

Christine brought her hand up and clasped his wrist. "It's not your love I'm afraid of Dan," she whispered. "It's mine."

He caught her hand and brought it to his lips, smiling.

"I'm stronger than you think, my love. And so are

you. In fact"—he tilted his head and studied her—"you are without a doubt the strongest, the smartest, and the most efficient woman I've ever known. And," he added, kissing her fingers again, "probably the most stubborn."

His grin was infectious. Christine couldn't help grinning back.

"As if all that weren't enough," he continued, "you are so incredibly beautiful that I can't concentrate at work, but then I go crazy if I don't see you or hear that intoxicating voice of yours."

Her grin softened at his words, and he leaned over and kissed her. His mouth was warm and giving, asking nothing of her, only wanting to love her. She closed her eyes and gave herself up to the kiss. When he lifted his mouth away, he gathered her in an embrace so tender that she buried her face in his neck and clung to him. Neither spoke for a long, deep moment.

At last Dan stirred. "I'll let you get dressed now." He spoke against her hair, his voice gruff with emotion. "And I'll make us some breakfast. Then we'll go to the hospital to see your mother."

Chapter Six

Ryan stood in the exact center of the medicine wheel, holding in his hands his wife's elaborate drawings. The circle had been staked off, and the ground directly beneath his feet served as the anchoring center for the entire building site. They had broken ground last week, thankful for the California autumn weather that kept these early November days warm and dry. If the forecasters were correct, they would get at least two good months before heavy rains interrupted the building of Golden Springs Ridge Retreat.

"Retreat" had been Larry's idea. He'd loved Vicki's ideas, just as Ryan had known he would. Larry was the successful head of his own architectural firm because, while taking a conservative attitude toward labor and building materials, he was not afraid to risk a new idea if his intuition about it was positive. And in the eight years he had worked with him, Ryan had never known Larry Morgan to be wrong about the feasibility of a new idea.

"This is good, Ryan," Larry had said, after a full fifteen minutes of silently studying the drawings Ryan and Vicki had worked out together for presentation. "Insightful. Clever." He pulled absently on the little goatee he groomed with inordinate pride. "Changes the whole concept. Not so much a fun vacation for the family as a getaway spot where they can escape the busyness of their lives and get reacquainted in peace and quiet. Could bring in conventioneers too, looking for a retreat atmosphere instead of razzle-dazzle. *Retreat*, that's the ticket. Golden Springs Ridge Retreat."

And that was that.

Vicki had wanted to come up for the ground breaking, but Ryan wouldn't have it. "No way am I risking you anywhere close to that area," he'd told her, shuddering. "Besides, there's no need. I understand your concept—finally." He'd grinned at her, and they both remembered her hours of patient coaching.

"Explain to me again about the medicine wheel," he had pleaded, once they'd begun collaborative work on the plans. "I understand about a circle being sacred. That concept isn't unique to Native Americans. But I don't get the rest of it, the four directions and the significance of the animals."

"It's an ancient tradition," she said. "Simply put, the medicine wheel reminds us of our spiritual kinship with the earth and with every living creature. The wheel creates a sacred space, physically symbolic of the wonder and mystery that holds us in natural balance with our spiritual source."

She pointed to her drawing. "The wheel depicts the four directions of nature—north, east, south, and west— and ascribes meanings and symbols to them. Shamans traditionally chose which animals or forces would represent the village in the wheel, but individuals can make their own wheels. This is the wheel I would design for myself, with animals that have meaning for me. The particular animals aren't important—people can assign whatever animal they want as long as it leads them to the center of the wheel."

"Which is?"

"The center of your life. Your spiritual center."

"So it's basically *you* in the center of the wheel."

His wife smiled. "No. And that's the point. The wheel is a reminder that you are *not* the center of your life, that there are forces working in and around you over which you have no control. The power of the wheel is in accepting this truth and surrendering to it."

"Surrendering?"

"Giving up the illusion that you have supreme control over your life. Acknowledging that you are part of a greater design. Part of a greater power."

"You mean, like God?"

"Yes, like God. Dora explained it like this: We become sick, spiritually and physically, when we forget where we come from. The wheel symbolizes the dignity and power of the earth and its creatures but only as they reflect the central spirit."

She saw Ryan's hesitation. "Think of a candle flame in a dark room. You'll see a halo, a circle around the flame. You might think the halo is the heat and the fire, but it's only the radiation of the true flame, a reflection that cannot sustain itself. It would be foolish for the halo to think of itself as the source of light and heat. Without the candle flame, the halo would disappear. But," she smiled, "the halo is beautiful, and it's warm and alive as long as the candle flame burns at its center."

Ryan frowned. "Okay," he said slowly. "I

understand when you explain it. But the people who visit the resort." He gestured at her drawing. "How are they going to understand all this?"

"It should be intuitive, Ryan. The beauty of the wheel is in its simplicity and its universal appeal." She studied her drawing. "I suppose we could put up little signs of explanation for each direction." She pointed to the north-facing path. "Next to the carving of the squirrel, we could post an explanation that north is the direction of grounding, and the squirrel points us in the direction of our deep home as creatures made from dust." With her finger she traced the other three paths. "On the path facing east, the direction of change, the deer reminds us that our spirits release us from the earth to leap and dance on the air. Facing south, the lioness represents the direction of love and passion, symbolized by her loyalty and her boldness in the face of danger. And facing west is the bear, ancient symbol for the unconscious, who rises from the dark depths of our dreams to bring us healing."

Standing now on the leveled ground of Golden Springs Ridge, Ryan looked around him. He imagined a low circle of white stones in place of the stakes, and the four paths leading out from center. Six months ago he would have laughed off the idea as silly superstition, knowing he was in control of his life and could determine his own destiny by the sheer force of his will. But now—well, now he wasn't so sure.

Consequently, he wasn't surprised when a ground squirrel scampered into the clearing and edged its way toward the circle of stakes. When it came to a halt, raised itself on its hind legs, and chattered at him, Ryan didn't need a compass to know that it sat squarely on the path that faced north.

* * *

"Hi. It's me."

"Ryan!" The gladness in her voice sent a little thrill through him. He clutched the phone tighter, as if he could bring his wife closer. "How did it go today?" she asked.

"Good. There's not as much clearing to do as we thought. And here's a bonus. They think they've got an artesian well on the property. The owner is very excited about that."

"The owner." Ryan heard the wary edge in her voice. "Does he still have reservations about the design?"

"Nothing Larry can't handle. Besides, it's mostly little things. We may have to compromise on a few details, but that's true of most jobs." She was silent, and Ryan imagined the little lines that appeared between her brows when she was frowning. "They won't change the basic idea, and the wheel is nonnegotiable. I insisted on that, and Larry agrees."

He heard her husky laugh. "I don't know why I'm so possessive about this project. Goodness, you'd think I was the architect in charge!"

"It's your baby, Vicki." Ryan winced as he said her name, knowing it no longer fit her but not knowing what else to call her. "Speaking of babies, how are you feeling?"

"Wonderful, Ryan!" There was joy in her voice. "I've never felt so well in my life."

"Well, you certainly sound healthy. And beautiful and soft and sexy. And you smell good, too." He heard her chuckle. "In fact, I've half a mind to drive down there tonight, make passionate love to you, and drive back before dawn tomorrow morning." His voice grew serious. "I regret every day I'm not spending with you."

She was silent again, and Ryan knew he'd touched on a subject they never discussed. She believed she would be forced to return to her own time next March. Sometimes he caught her studying him, as though she were memorizing every detail of his face, and his heart would lock in a painful grip. It terrified him to think that she might be right, so he daily told himself that he would never allow it. Somehow, he would prevent her from going back.

He broke their heavy silence. "How's Eleanor?"

She sighed. "There's been no change. She's still in a coma. She doesn't respond to anything or anyone."

"How is your mother doing?"

"Surprisingly well. Did I tell you she's seeing Dan again?"

"No kidding."

"She's like a different person when she's with him. If anyone can break down her barriers, it's Dan. She's seeing him again tonight. I understand he's cooking dinner for her."

"I know you've been seeing a lot of her, too. Ever since the two of you had that mysterious talk you won't tell me about—"

"Ryan, you know I can't break Mother's confidence."

"Yeah, I know. Have you been staying over with her

at night?"

"No." Her voice softened. "I sleep here because this is my home, Ryan. And I want to be here when you come home. I want to be the first thing you see when you walk through that door."

Ryan caught his breath, knowing that she understood what he needed to hear and loving her for it. "I'll be there day after tomorrow." His voice was suddenly husky. "It'll only be for a day. But I couldn't stand to wait a whole week before seeing you again."

"Me, neither." There were tears in her voice. "I'll cook something special for your dinner."

"Forget the dinner." He tightened his grip on the phone. "All I want is you."

* * *

"That was wonderful, Dan." Christine dabbed her mouth with a neatly pressed napkin and sighed. "A man who knows how to poach salmon, toss a superb Caesar salad, and brew a perfect cup of coffee." She smiled at him across the table. "Is there anything you can't do?"

Dan chuckled and leaned back in his chair. "Well, I never could make a decent pie crust. And I always overbeat the whipped cream."

"Minor flaws." Christine waved dismissively and admired his table: Chinese blue china on a tablecloth of snowy Battenberg lace, tapered blue candles, and a bowl of white lilies in the center. "And my favorite flowers. If I didn't know better, I'd think you were trying to romance me."

"My, but you have a suspicious mind." Dan's blue eyes twinkled in the soft light of the candles. "But I'll admit, when it's just me, a frozen dinner microwaved and an hour in front of the TV is as fancy as I get."

"Somehow I doubt that," she murmured, and raised her wineglass for a last sip. It was a superb Chardonnay, so subtle that she'd already had two glasses and hardly noticed.

"So, Christine. Would you prefer to wash the dishes or dry them?" Dan pushed back his chair and piled silverware on his plate. Christine gaped at him, and he chuckled. "Sorry, but this isn't uptown. Around here, we clean up our own dishes."

Christine flushed. "Dan, I didn't mean—"

He chuckled again as he stood up. "I know. I didn't, either. But it's important that you realize I live a different life from the one you're used to." He picked up his plate and reached for hers. "Besides, doing dishes isn't so bad when you have good company."

She rose and followed him into the kitchen with the empty fish platter. Dan tied an apron around his waist and rolled up his sleeves.

"I think I'll wash." He grinned as he took the platter from her. "I don't know if I'm ready to trust a rookie with my best china."

He filled the sink with hot water and liquid detergent, raising a warm, moist scent of lemons into the air while Christine brought more dishes from the dining room. As they worked, Dan suggested that they have Thanksgiving dinner at his house. "I'd like to invite my daughters, and you could ask Victoria and Ryan. It won't be fancy, but I think it would be fun." He glanced up from his soap suds, his eyebrows raised in question.

"I think that would be wonderful," Christine said. "I hadn't thought about Thanksgiving yet, not knowing if Mother…" She trailed off, and Dan continued to work quietly, soaping the dishes and rinsing them under hot water. She took a warm, wet plate from the rack and rubbed a towel over it. "I think Victoria would like it, too. It would be so depressing to have it at home…now."

Dan nodded. "Good. I'll invite Erin and Kelly. Erin had it at her house last year. But with little Sean scooting around, I think she'll be just as glad to have it here." He smiled at her. "So, it's settled."

"Yes." She smiled back. "Settled." And they fell into a comfortable silence.

What a good man he is, Christine thought, watching him drain the soapy water and begin to wipe down the counter with a sponge. *And he's right; he's stronger than I thought he was and, goodness knows, more patient than Job himself. And I love him so much. It doesn't have to be like it was before, the other times with men I didn't love, or with Jack when I was still a headstrong, rebellious girl barely out of her teens. I can handle this — I can love and not destroy. Dan will help me. I want this; I need this, now, before I lose my nerve…*

With fingers suddenly trembling, she stood behind Dan, untied his apron, and slipped it off. When he turned in surprise, she reached her hands behind his head and pulled him toward her, bringing his mouth to hers, a little clumsily but determinedly. She felt his startled response before his mouth recovered and began to give back her kiss, while his hands fumbled behind his back, pulling frantically at the yellow rubber gloves. Then she felt his hands, warm from the hot water, pressing into her back, wrapping her closer, and she heard the pleased little moan in his throat.

Christine kept her eyes closed and focused all her attention on the softness of his mouth and the delicious sensation of her breasts crushing against his chest. Eyes still closed, she unfastened the row of buttons down the front of his shirt. When she reached his belt, Dan groaned and pulled his mouth away. Christine opened her eyes.

His eyes, blue and brilliant, locked on hers with hungry intensity. He pulled her hands from his belt and raised them to his lips. Kissing her fingertips, he slowly shook his head.

On a hot wave of confusion and embarrassment, Christine pulled her hands away and stepped back. "You don't want me?"

She watched him back up to the counter and lean heavily against it.

"Not want you?" His voice shook. "I want you so much, I can hardly stand up. I want you so much that if I loved you any less, I wouldn't even make it to the bedroom but would take you right here on the kitchen linoleum. Of course I want you, Christine. Good Lord, do you think I'm crazy?"

He gave a desperate little laugh, while Christine regarded him in baffled silence, twisting her hands.

"I'm not crazy, Christine, but I may be old fashioned. I can't think of anything that would give me more pleasure right now than taking you to my bed and satisfying the hunger for you that I carry like an ache in my body." He sighed. "But I want more from you. I want more for us. And I won't take it until you allow me the privilege of giving you my name and my vow to love you and protect you and honor you for the rest of my life." He grinned sheepishly. "I realize I drive a hard bargain. But you're worth waiting for. Maybe I'm greedy, but I want the whole package. I won't take less." He added quietly, "I won't let you take less, either."

His smile turned solemn, and his blue eyes studied hers intently. Christine's heart fluttered in her chest like a small bird trying to find a place to perch. She returned Dan's gaze with an equal measure of solemn intensity, and a taut silence stretched between them.

A yellow glove, hastily tossed onto the counter, suddenly slipped over the edge and hit the floor with a soft plop. It had the effect of a bomb exploding, and they both jumped, startled into smiles.

Christine laughed shakily.

"Well, Dan." She stepped up to him and laid her hands lightly on his chest. "I realize it's sudden and sounds suspiciously as if I'm just trying to lure you into my bed." She looked steadily into his eyes. "Daniel Winslow, will you marry me?"

Dan sucked in a breath and caught her up in his arms. "Will I marry you?" he said, twirling her in a full circle before setting her down with a gentle laugh. "I thought you'd never ask!"

Judith Ingram

Chapter Seven

"Well, I think Dad is making a fool of himself." Kelly Winslow fished a plastic bag from the diaper satchel and handed it to her sister. "He's too old to go mooning around over a female." She added emphatically, "It's undignified!"

Erin folded Sean's used diaper into a compact bundle and thrust it into the bag. She glanced at her younger sister before reaching for the baby wipes. "Who says love has to be dignified?" She smiled down at her son as she raised his legs by the ankles and wiped his bottom clean. "And you're never too old to be in love, Kelly."

Kelly snorted and sat on the bed, dangling a colorful ring of plastic keys above her nephew's face. He squealed and made a grab for it with his chubby hands. "I don't know what he sees in her, anyway. I suppose she's attractive. But with enough money you can make anyone look attractive." She glanced at the nightstand beside her father's bed, where her mother's picture used to sit. "Thanksgiving should be reserved for his family. She has no business being here."

"She's here because Dad wants her here." Erin centered Sean's bottom over the new diaper and pulled at the tapes to secure it. "It feels funny to us because

94

Christine isn't our mother. But Dad's happy—you just have to see them together to know how much he loves her." Her sister snorted again. "Dad has a right to his happiness, Kelly."

"It's too soon."

"It's been seven years!"

"It's *still* not right!" Kelly set her chin stubbornly. "And did you see Victoria? What a cow. She isn't half as pretty as her pictures. I'll bet they're all computer enhanced, anyhow. I've got a better figure than she has."

"Kelly, she's pregnant!" Erin threw her sister an exasperated look as she sat beside her on the bed and settled Sean on her lap. "Give them a break. Dad deserves this chance. He's been so lonely." She saw her sister's face set and sighed. "I think Christine's nice. And she adores Dad."

"Yeah, right."

"You need a man, Kelly. You've been in a foul mood ever since you broke up with Brandon." Kelly glowered as Erin stood and eased Sean to the floor. "I think you're just jealous."

* * *

The call came near the end of Thanksgiving dinner. In the excited commotion following Dan's and Victoria's announcements, Christine nearly missed the quiet ringing of her cell phone.

Dan's announcement had come first. Christine had watched him all through dinner as he made special efforts to put everyone at ease, especially his daughter Kelly. Christine had found Erin easy to like; inheriting more than sandy hair and blue eyes from her father, she had accepted Christine from the first, giving her Sean to hold, sharing little stories with her about being a first-time mother. Kelly, on the other hand, had been offensively aloof. Slim and dark, she looked like her mother's picture on the piano, which somehow made Christine more nervous as she tried to make conversation with the young woman. After five painful minutes, Ryan had sat down with them, and Christine watched the girl slowly unbend as he skillfully maneuvered her through topics and eventually hit on a favorite of hers: cross-country skiing. Feeling grateful and a little cowardly, Christine politely excused herself and headed for the kitchen to find a task that needed urgent attention. Alone at the sink, she leaned on trembling arms and fought back tears of anger and frustration.

Now, as they finished dinner, Dan tapped his spoon against his water glass for silence. Knowing what was coming, Christine put a nervous hand to the pearls at her throat and glanced around the table.

"Thanksgiving seems like a good time to recount our blessings," Dan began. "Christine and I are so thankful for you, our beloved children, and we want to share our happiness with you." He raised his eyes to Christine's, and she felt her smile tremble. Kelly's dark head whipped around to face her. "We are...getting married," he finished simply.

Surprised murmurs escalated quickly into hearty congratulations. Dan's son-in-law raised his wineglass and led them in a toast. Victoria slipped from her chair and came around the table to hug her mother. Only Kelly sat still, hands in her lap, stone-faced as she stared at her plate.

Christine saw the nod Ryan gave her daughter, who still stood beside her mother's chair. She felt Victoria's hand settle on her shoulder.

"Since we're all toasting," her daughter said loudly. The boisterous voices quieted. "Ryan and I have some news, too." Christine heard her take a breath. "The sonogram gave us a nice surprise. Guess what? We're having twins!"

Christine gasped and turned in her chair. Her daughter bent and enveloped her in an embrace of pure joy. Ryan was grinning so broadly, he looked about to burst from happiness. Dan beamed and clapped Ryan on the shoulder. Erin rose from her chair and walked over to Victoria, clasped her hands, and then gave her a hug so warm and sisterly that Christine's eyes smarted.

Through the din, Kelly's voice cut a sharp path. "Isn't that someone's phone?"

Voices dropped abruptly, and the phone rang again.

"Oh. It's mine." Christine jumped up, shooting a worried glance at Dan. "I gave the hospital my number."

She rushed into the kitchen and pulled the cell phone from her purse. Minutes later, she returned to the table, still holding her phone.

Dan took one look at her face and was out of his chair, crossing the distance between them.

"It was the hospital," she said weakly. Dan helped her to sit and bent over her.

"And?" he urged gently.

"Mother has regained consciousness. Oh!" Her shoulders shook, and he pulled her against him. "Half her body is paralyzed. She can't speak. The doctor—"

Christine bit her lip to ward off a sob. She glanced around the table and saw tense, sympathetic faces. Even Kelly looked stricken.

"We'll go over right away, of course," Dan said, patting her arm.

"We'll be right behind you, Mother," her daughter echoed.

Dan straightened but kept an arm around Christine's shoulders. "Erin—"

"Don't worry, Dad. Kelly and I will clean up. You go ahead."

Christine didn't pay attention to Kelly's response. All she could think about was how strong Dan's arm felt as he helped her to stand. All she could feel was gratitude for the love that she knew she'd be leaning on heavily in the days ahead.

* * *

Christine stood over her mother's tiny body and choked down rising bile. The old woman was awake and staring, but the stroke had robbed her of dignity. One emerald eye stared vacantly, dull without its usual imperious glint. Her body seemed shrunken, withered like old fruit kept too long on the kitchen sill. The right half of her face sagged, its soft flesh sinking into the bony contours of her skull.

Dan had not been permitted to come in with her, so Christine stood alone, fighting her revulsion and willing herself to touch the dry parchment of her mother's hand.

"Mother?" Her whisper was tentative. Then, louder, "Mother!" The emerald eye didn't flinch, while its mate looked askance under a drooping lid. Eleanor's mouth sagged on the right side, giving the impression of a grotesque leer.

Christine had to look away. She pressed a fist against her mouth and with her other hand groped for the bed rail.

"Mrs. Reeves?" Christine looked around at the freshly scrubbed young man approaching. "I am Dr. Nsouli," he said, in precise English.

Christine gaped at him. *He looks about as old as Victoria,* she thought. *How can he possibly be in charge?*

"Your mother's coming out of her coma is a good sign," Dr. Nsouli said. "We can now better assess the damage to her system and begin therapies to help her."

"Help her?" Christine roused herself with an effort. "Are you saying she can get better?"

The doctor shrugged his slim shoulders. "Difficult to say. Patients with essentially the same damage vary greatly in their abilities to recover. We will know more in a few days. Right now, it is good for you to be here to talk to her. We do not know how much she can hear or understand. She gives no outward responses. But inside, who knows? Touch her, talk to her. Let her know that you care about her."

Christine clamped her mind against a sudden, shocking thought.

"Do you have any questions, Mrs. Reeves?"

Christine stared at him. She shook her head.

Dr. Nsouli stepped up to the bed and gave her mother's face a quick study. He flashed his penlight into her eyes; he tapped her knuckles and listened to her chest with his stethoscope. Finally, he pulled the sheet up over her thin body and smoothed it. He nodded a polite smile at Christine before he disappeared, pulling out the curtain to give them privacy.

Christine stood frozen by horrifying thoughts that refused to be quieted. They grew louder, and she tried to drown them with cheerful chatter.

"You must get well, Mother," she said. "We all miss you at home. Nothing has been the same since you left us."

Die, Mother, die. The house has been so peaceful without you. I've never slept better in my life, never awakened with such joy in the morning.

Christine picked up her mother's hand and squeezed it. "You've always been a fighter, Mother. You can beat this illness if you try."

You've lived your life exactly the way you wanted. Now let me live mine. Don't come back and spoil my chance for happiness.

"Mother, Victoria is going to have twins. Twins! You must be there when they are born. You must be their great-grandmother."

Don't you dare play favorites with them, the way you did with Luke and me. If you can't love them both, it's better if you don't live to see either of them.

Christine gave a cry and clutched her mother's hand tighter.

"I'm sorry, Mother. I'm so sorry for the things I said to you. I love you."

I'm not sorry for a single thing I said to you. It was all true, every word. And I hate you.

"I love you, Mother!"

I hate you, Mother!

Christine sobbed. "No! I love you!"

Through the tumult in her mind, Victoria's voice rose to the surface. Something she'd said the night Eleanor was brought in began to soothe Christine's torment, like sweet oil poured over angry waters. Slowly, Christine lowered herself to her chair.

"I love you, Mother," she said wearily.

I hate you, Mother.

"I love you."

I hate you.

And I love you.

Victoria

Chapter Eight

In the two weeks since her birth, Elise Isabel Kamarov had become the new center of the Rostnova household. The servants doted on her. Robbie assumed with possessive pride his new role of uncle. Dora took to squatting beside her cradle at all hours, rocking her and singing in a low, chanting voice. And I could barely stand to leave her out of my sight.

On the night of Elise's birth, no one had been unduly alarmed at my failure to return home for supper. Apparently, Katherine had slept away from home more than once. Shortly before dawn, however, Isabel had called for Dora and insisted that she take the wagon to Summerwood at first light to look for me. Dora had arrived to find Elise already born and me unconscious. After bundling us up in blankets, she drove us home in the wagon, promptly put us both to bed, and took personal charge of our recoveries.

In the two weeks since her birth, Elise had also become the new center of Springstown gossip. Ana argued that Elise's facial features were due to Russian heritage and that her sister—Michael's mother—had been born with a similar look of slanting, lidless eyes and moon-shaped face. Despite Ana's insistence, neighbors who came to see the newborn left with eyebrows raised and tongues they could barely keep still. Looking at my new daughter every day, I began to suspect, as they did, that Anton Kamarov was not her father.

My hunch was Kim Soo, the Chinese apothecary's eldest son.

I slept for most of that first day after Elise's birth, surfacing only when Dora roused me and laid Elise beside me to nurse. I remember little of those hours except the feel of Elise's tiny mouth sucking with surprising vigor on my nipple and the new tingle of my breast answering her need. It was late evening before I awoke at last on my own. Dora brought Elise and laid her in my arms, and in the tender light of the lamp, I got my first real look at my daughter.

She was exquisite. Her eyes were closed, her long dark lashes fanning cheeks blotched with newborn ruddiness but promising an ivory complexion. Surprisingly thick, dark hair framed a face as round and perfect as a rising moon. Her tiny fists flailed, and her little rosebud mouth worked, anticipating a meal.

I gave her my breast and watched her agitation suddenly quiet as she attached herself and began to suck greedily. With my free hand, I smoothed the dark hair over the soft flesh pulsing at the top of her head, and my eyes filled with tears. I looked up to find Dora smiling down on us, her arms folded across her chest, her dark eyes gleaming. I smiled back at her, unable to speak. Dora nodded, and words weren't necessary.

My milk came in the next morning. I felt awed and

humbled to realize how dependent upon me Elise was for her very life. Silently I made the vows mothers make to their newborns, to care for her and to shield her from harm, believing I would give up my life to protect hers. I can't describe all that passed between us that day because so much of it was understood but not spoken, so much was felt at a depth I had never before navigated. The love I felt for her was at once brand new and ancient as the primal instinct that dates us back to our first mothers.

Ana came to see me, and I learned from her that Isabel had not yet seen her granddaughter. When I suggested that we take Elise to her immediately, Ana shook her head.

"Your mother is very ill, Katya. Elise is too small to risk a visit." She added softly, "Your mother understands this and is content."

I imagined Isabel lying in her bedroom, hearing the cries of her granddaughter but unable to see her. I became indignant.

"Nonsense," I snapped. "We can take precautions." I flipped back my covers and stood, but quickly grabbed the bedpost and sat down again. "I'll need your help, Ana."

Ana pursed her lips, but I glared at her until she finally let her shoulders fall and nodded. She gathered Elise into a tight bundle and followed as Dora helped me walk down the corridor to Isabel's room.

Isabel lay listless against her pillows, the book she had been reading cast aside. When she saw me and the bundle Ana was carrying, she cried out and clamped a hand over her mouth.

"Katrina, you shouldn't be up—" She coughed violently into her pillow, and despite my determination, I hesitated.

Dora found her a clean handkerchief, which Isabel kept over her nose and mouth as Ana held up the baby. The wonder and joy in those blue-violet eyes restored my confidence.

"Mother, I'd like you to meet your granddaughter, Elise Isabel."

Isabel lifted her eyes to me, and I tried not to flinch at the pain and weariness etched in them. "Ana told me the name you've chosen." She arched an eyebrow. "Not 'Anton'?"

I shook my head. I had decided against the Russian tradition of making the child's middle name that of the father. "I want her to have her grandmother's name."

With most of her face covered, it was her eyes that spoke her gratitude as she turned her gaze once more on Elise.

Ana opened the blanket, and I saw the effort Isabel made not to reach out and touch the waving little feet, not to offer her finger for the tiny fist to grasp.

"Katrina, she is beautiful." Isabel's voice was hushed. "She will look like you, like your grandmother." Her eyes crinkled with her hidden smile. "The old man would be pleased." She leaned back against the pillows and shut her eyes. Dora bent over her.

"You should rest now, Isabel," Ana said. She secured the blanket around Elise and glanced at me. "We'll bring Elise back tomorrow for another visit."

Isabel nodded and lowered her handkerchief when Ana left the room. "You should be in bed, Katrina," she scolded mildly.

"I know." I sat in the chair beside her bed and touched her sleeve. "I'd rather be here with you."

Her tired eyes studied my face. "Dora told me about your ordeal. And it's so strange. While you were all alone, giving birth to Elise in that horrid little attic, I had the oddest dream about you."

She stretched and settled herself. "There wasn't much to it, but it seemed to go on for the longest time. I was in a dark tunnel, searching for you. I couldn't see you, but I sensed you were there and that you needed me. I called out to you, 'Don't be afraid. I'll find you.' Then you brushed past me, Katrina, like a breath of wind, and I could swear there were *two* of you. For the briefest moment, I held you both in my arms, and I felt so peaceful. I woke up and told Dora where to find you. And I wasn't afraid. I knew you were all right."

I couldn't speak. I glanced at Dora, who was standing by the window, her arms akimbo, watching us protectively. I took Isabel's hand.

"I wasn't alone, Mother." My voice shook. "In the darkest moments, I *did* hear a voice telling me not to be afraid. And my fear went away." I clasped her hand tighter. "It must have been you with me."

She laid her other hand, pale and wasted with her illness, over mine.

"Always, Katrina *mía*."

* * *

Robbie came to see his new niece as soon as he got

home from school that afternoon. He sat in a chair by my bed and held himself perfectly still as Dora laid Elise gently in his arms. He hardly breathed. When Elise started fussing, his gray eyes shot up, round with alarm.

"It's all right, Robbie," I reassured him. "Just rock her a little and talk to her. Let her get used to you."

Robbie nodded and twisted his entire torso in a stiff rock. He spoke solemnly: "I am Robert Alexander Rostnova. I am your uncle." Immediately Elise quieted, and Robbie flashed me a look of surprised triumph. "When you are bigger, I will teach you how to swim and how to play with kittens carefully. And I'll help you learn how to read." He relaxed a little and studied her, curiosity and wonder playing over his features.

"How was school?" I asked.

His head snapped up. "Katya, did you know it wasn't the Russians who discovered America but Christopher Columbus? I always thought Grandfather Petrov discovered it when he came on the Russian ship to build the fort." His look turned doubtful. "Do you think Miss Forrester could be wrong about that?"

"Well, Robbie, there's a difference between discovering a place and settling it. Fur traders were hunting up and down the coast for otters long before Grandfather came to help settle the land. And the Spanish were already in California, working their way north. I think a lot of people discovered different parts of America, but Christopher Columbus got the credit."

I noticed Dora standing by the window. She was normally so silent that I often forgot her presence. "Dora," I said, "it must be terrible to see the land that once belonged to your people just taken and divided up by foreign settlers. Does it make you angry sometimes?"

Robbie turned to watch her answer. "The settlers kill many of my people," she said. "They still kill us. For that I am angry, yes, and sad." She shrugged her shoulders. "But the land—it never belongs to us. It does not belong to you. Land does not belong to anyone, only borrowed and used for a time. Like our spirits. The land will be here long after our bodies die." She shrugged again. "My people understand this. Settlers, they never understand it."

Elise began to squall. Dora crossed the room to lift her out of Robbie's arms and place her in mine. "Time for supper," I cooed. Holding the blanket high to give us privacy, I offered Elise a breast. Robbie turned beet red and stared determinedly at his shoes.

"Have you decided who to invite to your birthday party?" I made my voice bright, giving us something to focus on besides my breast and Elise's noisy suckling.

"You're still giving me a party?" His face brightened and then clouded. "Katya, do you think you'll be strong enough?"

His consideration touched me. "Of course, silly. It's not for three more weeks. And Theresa said she'd help me."

"I've never had a birthday party," he said wistfully. "Are you sure you know how to do it?"

I rolled my eyes and grinned at him. "Ever play Pin the Tail on the Donkey?" He shook his head. "Well, it's loads of fun and a must for birthday parties. In fact," I tilted my head, regarding him, "I've got an art project for you, Robbie. That is, if you think you'll have the time between studying for school, helping me with Elise, and making so many new friends."

* * *

The day of Robbie's birthday party dawned unseasonably cold and threatening rain. Sadly, the population of Springstown was no more generous to him. Of the twelve children he invited to his party, only three came.

By midmorning a light shower was settling the summer dust and scenting the air with the first rain of the fall season. An hour before his party, rain began to pour in earnest. Robbie was up at dawn and prowling the house, worrying that the inclement weather would keep his party guests home. He watched Carmen decorate his cake and then helped me give Elise her bath and settle her for her morning nap.

Theresa came early to help me set up for the party. Instead of a picnic outside as I had planned, we decided to set up a table by the fire in the kitchen. Against the side of the house protected by a porch overhang, we tacked up Robbie's drawing of a donkey, ready for the tails he'd painted and cut out so carefully. Carmen was making sandwiches and lemonade, so there was nothing else for us to do but wait for the party guests to arrive.

Josh Hartwig, Robbie's new best friend, arrived first, with his younger brother Steven. Within a few minutes, a boy named Lawrence Crawford and his mother, Laura, arrived. Laura was a quiet, plain woman with a sweet smile, who offered to stay and help with the party. Robbie took the boys upstairs to his room, while Theresa,

Laura, and I waited in the parlor for the rest of the guests to arrive. For the next thirty minutes, Robbie kept running up and down the stairs, checking to see if more guests had arrived. It finally became clear that no one else was coming.

"But where is everybody?" His voice was high and perilously close to tears. "They should've been here by now."

"I guess the weather is keeping them home." As I took his hand, I caught the sharp glance Theresa gave Laura. Eyeing her, I gave Robbie a little push. "Go tell Carmen you're ready to eat. Then tell the others to get washed up."

I waited until Robbie was out of earshot before I pinned Theresa with a grim look. "What's going on?" I asked.

She dropped her gaze and twisted a wayward strand of blond hair. "Well, Katherine, some of the mothers...that is, there is a nasty rumor that, well—" She broke off and bit her lip. "There is some sentiment against you because of...Elise." She looked pleadingly at Laura.

The older woman met my gaze squarely. "The fact is, Katherine, some small-minded busybodies took it into their heads to boycott this party on account of not being sure who Elise's daddy was. Betty Somers is at the bottom of it, and those other nitwits will follow anything she says. That's the plain truth of it, I'm sorry to say. It's mean and spiteful, and I told them so!"

She folded her arms for emphasis.

Comprehension trickled cold down my spine.

Katherine! I fumed. She'd left me with another mess to clean up. Only this time if I couldn't fix it, Robbie and Elise would be the ones to suffer for it.

I blinked away furious tears to find Laura watching me with sympathy and Theresa shifting uncomfortably.

"Thank you for telling me," I said, my voice unintentionally cold. "I beg you not to breathe a word of this to Robbie. Let him think the rain has kept the other children home."

"Of course," Laura agreed.

"That's best," Theresa echoed.

We made the birthday meal as gay as we could, wearing the paper hats I had made for the other children and singing loudly when Carmen brought the cake with its nine lit candles. As Robbie opened his presents, my thoughts surged forward, realizing the games we had planned must be abandoned because of the rain or the small number of guests. I watched the pathetic little group gather around Robbie, who was struggling bravely to hide his disappointment, and I choked on repeated spikes of anger and pity.

That's when the idea struck me. I turned to the two women and whispered, "After they eat their cake, will you take them to the back porch and help them with the 'Donkey' game? There's something I need to do."

Theresa looked apprehensive, but Laura nodded readily. "You go ahead, Katherine. We'll manage here."

I touched her gratefully on the shoulder and left the table. In the hall I found Marta.

"Send one of the men to the cottage right away. I want the large red metal box from the attic there. Then I want you to go up into our attic here and get four shirts from *Señor* Kamarov's trunk. Bring them to the nursery."

Marta looked shocked. "But, *señora*—"

"*Do it!*"

Marta ducked her head and scurried away. I climbed the stairs to the nursery, the walls of which I'd just had painted white in preparation for redecorating. I pulled Robbie's art folder from the bookshelf, found the sketches of circus animals he'd drawn in San Francisco, and brushed away the thought that I might be forcing fate. Taking up a black crayon from his art box, I stood before the blank white wall and studied his sketch of the seal balancing a ball on its nose. Then I raised the crayon to the wall and made the first bold stroke.

* * *

"Katherine, this is such a great idea!" Laura met me at the nursery door as I returned from feeding Elise. I held my daughter tightly, protectively, as if daring anyone to utter a slur against her.

The four boys were busy at the nursery wall. Paint spattered Anton's shirts, which they were using for smocks as they filled color into the outlines I had crayoned. Four of Robbie's circus animals were slowly coming to life. I felt satisfaction, and a sense of relief, to observe that the colors each boy chose were exactly as I remembered them from those faded animals I'd seen on my tour of Rosswood House. It seemed I was to have a hand in fate, after all.

"Mrs. Kamarov!" Josh turned from his French poodle and held a dripping brush carelessly over the tarp protecting the floor. "Can we come back and do some more next Saturday?" The other boys turned in unison and set up a clamor for my consent.

"If it's all right with your parents, I don't see why not." I caught Robbie's shining look and gave him a wink. He winked back shyly and turned back to his tiger.

I walked along the wall behind the boys, deciding that large mistakes could be concealed with more white paint, and that some touching up would be required. But, overall, they were doing a pretty good job, and I said so. I noticed the same irregularities that had struck me on my tour, and I experienced again that eerie feeling of living in a world that was neither Katherine's nor mine but existed somewhere in-between.

I sat down between Laura and Theresa to watch the boys' progress.

"You should probably know that Robbie invited everyone to stay the night." Laura's voice held a smile. "He has such a generous little heart. I told him the boys have to go home so they can get ready for church tomorrow morning, and maybe another time would be better."

I turned thoughtfully to her. "What time is the service?" I asked.

She was smiling at Elise, who had fallen asleep in my arms. "Ten o'clock." She looked up at me. "Are you thinking of attending?"

I nodded slowly. "Maybe." Another idea was hatching. "After all, what better place than church to atone for sins and nip evil rumors in the bud?"

* * *

"But we *never* go to church in town! We have our

own chapel, and the priest comes to see us twice a month. Besides, they aren't even *Catholic*."

"Robbie, it won't hurt us to worship God in a different place this time. God doesn't care about the building, only about our hearts. You can pray to him like you always do, and the priest will still come as he always does. We're not changing that."

"Mama won't like it!"

"She will when I explain it to her. Where is that little bow tie you wore to Theresa's wedding?"

Robbie produced the tie but continued to frown as I folded it under his collar. "Are we taking Elise with us?"

"Yes, of course." *She's the main reason we're going.*

Ana expressed concern at our going but declined to attend herself. "I'll stay here and have devotions with your mother." She peered at me over her spectacles. "Mind, you make Alfred wait for you."

As Alfred drove us into town, I shielded Elise's face from the sun and smiled tenderly at her. She looked like a tiny angel in her lace-trimmed bonnet and pink-ruffled dress. The newborn ruddiness had disappeared, leaving a smooth ivory complexion that might have been inherited from Kim Soo or from her grandmother Isabel. I would defy anyone to say it wasn't from Isabel.

The congregation seemed to stir, then hush, as we entered the church. Robbie walked ahead of me and found us a place beside Theresa and Bruce. We sat down, and I twisted around to smile sweetly into the astonished face of Betty Somers, seated directly behind us. After an awkward hesitation, she nodded back, her cheeks coloring. Before turning to face forward again, I caught

Laura's grin from where she sat two rows back.

After the service people gathered in the patio garden. The previous day's rain had spent itself, leaving a warm, rinsed sunshine and a gentle breeze spiced with autumn. I moved directly to Betty Somers's side.

"So nice to see you again, Betty." I shifted Elise in my arms and smiled winningly into Betty's wary face. "We were so sorry your Billy couldn't attend the party yesterday. We missed him."

"Oh." It took her a moment to recover. "Billy's been down with a slight cold, and I didn't want to risk him in the wet weather."

"I have not." This was from Billy, hovering at his mother's elbow. "Lawrence said Robbie's party was really wizard. They got to paint on the *walls*, and Lawrence said they get to go back next Saturday. Can I go, too, Ma?"

His mother looked confused, and Laura came up behind me. "There she is," she cooed. "May I hold her, Katherine?" She took Elise from me, who seemed quite content to lie in Laura's arms and stare up at her adoring face. "Gerte, have you seen Katherine's daughter yet? Little Elise has the sweetest temperament I've ever seen in a baby." The woman standing beside Laura glanced at Betty before she leaned over dutifully to look at Elise.

Gerte's face softened as Elise opened her rosebud mouth in an exquisite little yawn. "She *is* sweet," she said. She glanced hesitantly at Betty, and then at me. "I declare, Katherine"—with a trace of defiance—"she has your eyes. And that might be Anton's chin, don't you think?"

Theresa and Emily had quietly joined the group and stood watching Betty as her son piped up again. "Can I go next Saturday, Ma? All the other kids are going, and I'll be the *only one* left out!"

Betty flushed as at least nine pairs of eyes trained on her, some of them glaring, some of them curious, all of them waiting.

"Maybe it's best if you don't come, Billy," I said suddenly. "Your mother is only thinking of your health. These colds can turn into pneumonia pretty quickly if you don't watch them."

"But she's fibbing! I'm not sick!" Billy ducked out of his mother's reach and scowled.

"Boys." Betty laughed nervously. "They never want to admit when they're sick." She glanced around the group. "Billy seems to be recovering tolerably well. I suppose there's no reason why he shouldn't go along with the others next weekend." She hesitated, then added, "It is kind of you to invite him, Katherine."

Robbie's small hand found mine, and I squeezed it. "We'll be glad to have him, Betty. And you must plan to stay and have tea when you bring him."

She blinked. "Why, thank you, Katherine."

I smiled. "Now, I must get Elise home. This is her first real outing, and mine, too." I turned to Laura, who settled Elise in my arms and gave me a sly wink and a grin. I grinned back and reached for Robbie's hand. There were murmurs of good-bye and some grudging looks of admiration as we turned to go.

On a glow of personal triumph, I was starting for the carriage when my gaze fell on Emily Stillman. She looked pale and considerably thinner than when I had last seen her. She was studying me with such ferocious intensity that I hesitated and stared back at her, puzzled. Reddening, she looked quickly away.

I was further startled by the unexpected sight of Raymond Delacroix. He stood back from the others, one broad shoulder leaning against the stone wall of the garden, and it struck me that I had neither seen nor heard from him in the weeks since Elise's birth. When I nodded a brief acknowledgment to him, his handsome face darkened and the sensual mouth curled unpleasantly. His pale gaze followed me to the street.

Despite the warm sunshine, I shivered as Alfred handed me up into the carriage.

* * *

When the dream begins, I am once again the deer in a forest clearing. A midnight breeze stirs the grass and strokes my sleek coat. My long ears detect only the normal night sounds, but I know the bear will be coming soon.

My fawn sleeps peacefully at my feet. Moonlight picks out the white spots on her back, camouflage that would protect her if we were nestled in the forest shadows. I wonder vaguely how we came to be in the wide-open clearing, exposed and vulnerable. But it's too late to run back into the shadows now, back into hiding, back into fear. The time has come to face my enemy.

My ears and my nose alert me at the same time. I hear the crashing and snorting even as the smell of the beast reaches me on the air. Instantly, my muscles tighten and pull me closer to the ground. Startled, I look down to see my slender legs shortening and thickening, my sleek coat fluffing into tawny fur, my neat hooves branching into toes that hide tough, curving claws, razor sharp.

I crouch on the wet grass and stare with crescent eyes at the line of trees, waiting. The trees suddenly part, and I cry out with a roar that shakes the air in thundering waves. My muscles tense, ready to leap, and my fear dissolves before a bold new confidence that no matter how powerful my enemy, he will be no match for me.

Chapter Nine

The soft haze of summer surrendered to autumn's crisp clarity as September slipped into October. My strength returned, and the appealing blue skies and mild air edged with autumn spice drew me out for afternoon walks with Elise. I fashioned a crude halter, secured around my waist and shoulders, which allowed me to carry her against my chest while leaving my arms free. Together we roamed the forest paths and made several trips to Summerwood. It occurred to me that I was avoiding Two Trees Creek and the bridge that in a curious, complex way was responsible for my presence in Katherine's world. I had no wish to see it again. Come March, however, the choice might no longer be mine.

Isabel's illness seemed to stabilize. Some days she even seemed improved. About half the time, she was able to come downstairs to dinner, and we sometimes sat together in the large sitting room. Those times were bittersweet for me, remembering our quiet, companionable times in the bright days of early summer when I had learned to love Isabel as the mother I'd never had. Now, with October sun slanting in at a different angle, I knew that, whether or not I was returned to Victoria's time, Isabel and I would never again sit together in the summer sunshine. The thought overwhelmed me with indescribable love for her and unspeakable pain.

The nursery was complete with new furnishings, waiting for Elise, but I could not yet give up keeping her cradle in my room. True to their word, the boys had returned the Saturday following Robbie's party. They brought half the neighborhood with them, including Billy Somers, finished painting the circus animals, and even started painting the new furniture and bookshelves. Robbie became something of a celebrity among them, and he strutted with a new confidence that warmed my heart to see. When I brought Elise into the nursery to see the children's progress, Robbie asked to hold her. He then sat in a chair, displaying his niece solemnly, while the children actually lined up to file by and pay her homage.

We attended more church services in town, cementing the goodwill of our first visit. Betty Somers herself invited us to a potluck supper, and I made a point of bringing Elise. No one said a word against her; neither did they hint at anything other than admiration and acceptance. Our new appearances at town functions, along with Robbie's enrollment in school, broke down the years of isolation and suspicion surrounding the Rostnova family. Robbie blossomed with new confidence, and I could swear he grew visibly taller. Or perhaps he was just standing straighter these days.

I made some friends. Laura took it upon herself to include me in her circle of women, and although stiff at first, they gradually relaxed and seemed to accept me. I was disappointed to find Theresa still holding me at arm's length. Oddly, her sister Emily became like a shadow, hovering on the edge of our circle but not participating, her face drawn, her eyes watchful.

Ana returned to San Francisco. I was doing so well, and Isabel seemed so stable that she felt she could leave us for a time. Knowing that Michael no longer wrote to me, she informed me that he was seen everywhere in New York with the Stratfords — at the opera, in the homes of the publishing elite, photographed with them for the newspapers. She didn't mention when he would be coming home.

I tried not to think about Michael at all. I bound his letters with a satin ribbon and placed them together with Joanne Greenly's in the beautiful wood box Grace Stillman had left to me. Then I shoved the box into the farthest corner of my wardrobe. Like the etching of Michael's words in my mind, I kept the box hidden in the dark and felt a perverse sense of comfort in knowing it was there but having the strength not to constantly take it out and look through it. After a while, the pain of parting from Michael softened a little, and I didn't experience the daily jolt of remembering. It became something like a sore tooth — knowing the tooth would hurt if I tampered with it, I devised ways to avoid it, to live around this tender wound in my life and convince myself that it didn't really matter.

* * *

The mid-October morning was crisp and cool. A sudden cold snap had turned the leaves of Nicholas's dogwood a brilliant red, concealing the clusters of scarlet fruit that hungry birds would find before winter came.

Elise slept peacefully in a wooden cradle I'd found in Summerwood's attic. I imagined gentle brown hands rocking the infant Alexander or Leon to sleep in it, and a sweet voice singing the Native American songs that Dora sometimes sang to Elise.

I knelt in my rose garden, engaged in the never-ending battle against weeds. Left unattended during the long weeks of late summer, the last crop of buds had withered and died, still entombed in their tight sheaths. I picked them off with a pang of regret that stabbed amazingly deep. It was too soon to prune, I knew. That must wait until midwinter, perhaps after Isabel…

I swallowed over a hard lump in my throat.

My life had organized itself into distinct measures of time that strangely coincided with the seasons. The happiest summer of my life had been edged with the pain of Michael's leaving and the shattering reality of Isabel's impending death. Fall seemed to be a time of waiting, still close enough to those happy days to feel their warmth but with a chill on its edges, reminding me that winter was coming. Each day I could still visit with Isabel, still hear her voice and see her love for me in those blue-violet eyes. And I could still recite the memorized phrases of Michael's letters, still feel his slender, sensitive fingers curled around mine, still wrap myself in the sea green of his eyes and briefly recover that certainty of being loved.

But I knew the winter was coming. And even if I could somehow learn to live around the terrible emptiness of losing Michael and Isabel, March threatened to rob me of everything else I held dear.

Elise's fussing roused me from my reflections. I pushed myself up and moved stiffly toward her, grateful for the solid reality of my sore muscles, for the cool breeze on my face, for the pungent fragrance of the autumn leaves crunching under my shoes. When I picked up my daughter, I breathed in the sweet smell of soap from her bath and felt her body, warm and alive, in my arms. And I resolved once more not to live too far in the future but to be as present as I could in each day, cherishing each moment as a precious, unrepeatable gift.

* * *

I sliced lemon for my tea with a sharp knife from the drawer and laid out tea things on the rough wooden table. The old woodstove warmed Summerwood's kitchen, and I could see Elise fighting between drowsiness and the demanding pangs of hunger. I settled at the table to nurse her, knowing it would not be long before she nodded off to sleep. I'd left the kitchen door open, welcoming the cool gusts of wind that relieved the stuffy warmth and blew a few scattered leaves up against the screen. I blew on my tea and gazed around the kitchen, trying to imagine old Petrov cooking his meals, and then a younger Petrov sitting at this very table with Morning Star while their infant son Alexander slept in the cradle now resting at my feet.

Elise quickly fell asleep, but I left her at my breast as she took comfort from occasionally sucking and then drifting off again. I felt sleepy myself, and my head was starting to nod when I heard hoofbeats.

Caught in the beginnings of a dream, I raised my head in confusion. Then I heard a horse whinny and boots striding toward the open door. Impossible hope fluttered instantly in my heart.

But the man who climbed the steps and entered the kitchen without announcing himself was not Michael. It was Raymond who stood towering over Elise and me, his hair disheveled from the ride, his cheeks ruddy, his breathing fast and heavy. His pale eyes were dilated, as I had seen them that day at Golden Springs Valley, and he looked very tall as he stood looking down on us. Tall and threatening.

Flustered, I realized how vulnerable I was, alone and holding my sleeping child to my exposed breast. I attempted to hide myself from his unflinching stare as I disengaged Elise's mouth and buttoned up the bodice of my gown. Without looking at Raymond, I laid Elise carefully in the cradle and adjusted the blanket over her. She was still fast asleep.

On a sheer bolt of instinct, I pushed the cradle deep under the table for safety before turning to face my visitor.

"Raymond," I said shakily. "Whatever are you doing here?"

"Isn't it obvious?" His perfect teeth flashed a chill smile as his silver gaze raked over me. "I came to see you."

I licked my lips. "I was just having some tea. May I pour a cup for you?"

As I stepped toward the cupboard for another cup, however, Raymond seized my arm. He wrenched it behind me with a force that made me cry out.

"I didn't come here for tea," he sneered, his face so

close to mine that I could smell the alcohol on his breath. "But there is something you can do for me."

He pinned my other arm behind me and forced me back against the counter. He shook his head and gave a hollow laugh.

"You certainly made a fool of me, didn't you, Katherine?" He laughed again, the sound made hideous by the dark rage twisting his features only inches from my face. "'I need a year to mourn my poor dead husband, Raymond,'" he mimicked. "And all the time you were carrying some Chinaman's bastard."

He moved so suddenly that I didn't see the blow coming. His fist smashed into my temple with a sickening *thud*, making my head bounce on my neck like a wobble toy. Before the white dizziness passed, his hands, like steel bands, were once again pinning my arms behind me.

"You've made me a laughingstock, Katherine. Everyone knows I'm expecting to marry you." He shook me hard. "You and your sham virtue. Making me wait, making me grovel. Well, not anymore." He shook me again, and the paleness of his eyes shrank to thin rims around his dilated pupils. "Not anymore!"

In one swift motion, he whirled me around and shoved me onto the wooden table. With one hand holding both my wrists above my head, he wedged himself between my legs and pushed up my skirts. "No more waiting, you little slut. Filthy, lying whore. I'll show you who is master here."

I heard my undergarments tear as he yanked them down. I screamed at that, but he silenced me with another blow, this one with the flat of his hand hard across my mouth. Stunned, I stopped struggling and stared mutely up at him.

He brought his face close to mine. The handsome features were at once so familiar and so terrifyingly evil that I tried to shrink back. His mouth curled in a satisfied sneer.

"You've had this coming for a long time." His breath, hot and stale with whiskey, was making me dizzy. He brought his mouth down on mine, his lips fleshy and slippery like a slug's body, slithering and drooling into my mouth. I wanted to shut my eyes, but I couldn't make my body respond. Already it was limp and dead, severed from the thin thread of consciousness that was all I had become.

As he pulled his head away and reached his hand down to loosen his belt and trousers, I stared above him at the blue cornflowers on the ceiling, willing myself into their blueness. They made room for me as they always had, helping me to find that small space where only I could fit.

From a long way off, I heard a baby crying, and I recognized Elise's cries. I also heard harsh, rhythmic gasping and little grunts of satisfaction. Smell and feeling slowly returned to me, and then vision. I saw Raymond arched above me, his eyes clamped shut, his expression pained as he used my body.

With slow understanding, I realized he was raping me. But it took another sharp cry from Elise to shake me loose from my lethargy. My mind accelerated: *rape, Elise, fight, weapon, teapot, lemon, knife, knife, teapot, knife...*

My hands, free from Raymond's grasp, felt for the teapot. My fingers closed around the handle, and with a banshee howl, I smashed it against the side of his head, shattering the ceramic pot and showering us both with hot tea. Raymond shrieked and raised his hands to his head. I managed to shove him off with my knee, and I started to squirm off the table. But he recovered before I could slide to the floor. He grabbed my arm and thrust me back.

"I'll kill you!" he yelled, and he clamped his hands around my throat. "You sneaky, whoring slut, I'll kill you!"

Mustering all my strength, I let out a roar and raked my nails across the tender pink patch on his face where the tea had scalded.

Raymond screamed and let me go. Sobbing, I reached the counter, grabbed the knife, and whirled to face him just as he was about to make another grab for me.

"Don't try it!"

Raymond saw the knife and stopped. In the sudden silence, Elise cried with a sound I had never heard in her voice before: terror. The realization pumped me with new strength, hot and seething.

Raymond eyed me with undisguised hatred. His sneer was back.

"Just what do you propose to do with that?" he said. He took a step forward but jumped back as I lashed the knife across the air between us. I said nothing but held the knife up, showing him the blade. I was too shaken to speak.

He took another step forward. "Put that thing down before you hurt yourself." His words were more confident than his voice, and his skin was pale beneath the angry blotches of burned skin. My claw marks flamed red and oozing across his cheek. "Come, Katherine, let's be reasonable."

"Reasonable!" I shrieked. "Keep coming this way, and I'll show you reasonable!"

There was a dead silence in which even Elise stopped crying. Raymond stood quite still, assessing me, while I tensed my muscles for his attack. Time seemed to move in slow motion. I stared at his handsome face contorted with evil, and I did not recognize it.

Elise let out a sudden shriek, and I glanced toward her. It was all Raymond needed. He pounced on me and grabbed my wrist, trying to twist the knife out of my hand. Knowing my strength was no match for his, I did the only thing I could. With all my might, I jammed my knee into his dangling, unprotected genitals. He jerked his head back and howled, his hand loosening my wrist until I broke free. Without hesitation I brought the blade up and slashed it across his exposed throat.

He staggered back a few steps and stared at me, his eyes wide with surprise. His hands clutched at his throat, and bright blood began to leak through his fingers. He pulled them away and stared at them. Then he looked at me.

Color seemed to drain from his face and leak directly out the gash in his neck. The white collar of his shirt turned scarlet, but still the blood kept oozing. Without a sound, Raymond crumpled to the floor and lay still.

I stared in paralyzed horror as blood pooled on the floorboards under his throat. Then Elise's wailing snapped me back to life. I stepped around Raymond's still body and pulled the cradle out from under the table. Her tiny fists were waving, and she was hot and red from crying. Gathering her up and still clutching the knife, I ran out the door and down the kitchen steps without looking back.

* * *

Alfred met us in the woods. I was stumbling along the path for home, clutching Elise and sobbing for breath, when I heard his horse coming. Having no strength to run and hide, I could only stand, frozen, on the path. I cried out with relief when I saw him.

"Alfred!" I sobbed and staggered toward him as he pulled up his horse and leaped down. "Oh, God, I've killed him! He was...he tried—" My body convulsed. "And I killed him!"

"Miss Katherine!" Alfred took my shoulders in his hands and peered into my face. "We have to get you home, you and your little one." He pried the bloody knife from my fingers. Then he took Elise from me and gently laid her on the ground.

"No!"

I lunged for her, but Alfred stopped me. "It's all right, Miss Katherine. I'll put you on the horse first, then lift her up to you. Now, up you go."

His sinewy arms lifted me onto the horse as if I weighed no more than Elise. She was squalling as Alfred handed her up, and he swung into the saddle behind me. Without a word, he turned the horse and headed for home at a gallop.

Dora was waiting for us on the front porch. She took one look at me, crossed herself, and hurried down the steps to take Elise from my arms.

Alfred helped me down, and I turned to him.

"It's Mr. Delacroix. He's at the cottage—"

"I know, Miss Katherine." His voice was grim. "Right well I know it. I'm the one that told him you were there, God forgive me. I knew something wasn't right. That's why I was on my way over."

He climbed back on his horse and gave me a nod, his normally gentle face set like stone. He turned his horse and vanished around the corner of the house.

Dora held Elise on one arm and used her other to guide me up the steps and into the house. Just inside the door, I turned to her.

"Dora, you mustn't say anything to Mother about this." My whisper was frantic, my eyes pleading. "It would only upset her. Promise me."

Dora nodded. "That Delacroix man." She looked at me steadily. "He does something very bad to you?"

I nodded, beginning to shake again. "Very bad, Dora." Strength seeped from my body as I realized I was home and safe. My face crumpled.

Dora pulled me against her and patted my head. We stood there for a long time, Elise and I held in Dora's huge arms while she comforted us.

Chapter Ten

Raymond recovered from his wounds. Despite all the blood, the knife hadn't sliced the carotid artery, although it did damage his larynx. Alfred found him conscious but unable to speak. He was sitting upright on the kitchen floor, in the same spot where he had fainted, and clutching his neck. Alfred bandaged the wound and, when Raymond could keep his balance, helped him onto his horse. Raymond offered him money to keep quiet about what had happened. In response, Alfred snorted and said he hoped Raymond would fall off his horse and break his neck before he got home. Then he slapped the horse's rump and sent them off.

Alfred stayed and cleaned up the blood. He found the broken teapot and the shreds of my underwear, and he guessed what had happened. He washed the knife he had taken from me and put it away in the drawer. Then he left Summerwood, taking care to lock all the doors behind him.

I was amazed at how quickly I recovered from my ordeal. The blows to my face raised purple welts, and the rape itself left me bruised and sore but nothing that time wouldn't heal. The astonishing aspect was in my emotional response to the trauma—instead of feeling depressed and frightened when I recalled it, I felt fierce and powerful. Somehow that terrifying moment had transformed me into the lioness of my dream. I had faced the enemy and triumphed. I felt strong, unstoppable. I could do anything. If Raymond Delacroix showed up at my door, I believed I could kill him with my bare hands.

I told no one about the rape, and good as her word, Dora kept the truth from Isabel. During the following week, stories reached me of robbers traveling the countryside and how the unfortunate Mr. Delacroix had been attacked and barely escaped with his life. I wondered what story he'd invented to explain the claw marks on his face.

Alfred, bless him, overcame his characteristic reticence and came to see me at the house. Twisting his hat nervously in his hands, he apologized for telling Raymond where to find me that day, and he pleaded with me not to go for any more walks by myself. He offered himself or one of the ranch hands as escorts should I need to go Summerwood again. I thanked him warmly and assured him that Elise and I planned to keep very close to the house in the near future. I tried to reassure him that he was not responsible for what Raymond had done; there was no way anyone could have guessed his evil intentions.

It was two weeks after the incident when Marta roused me from my bed.

"*Señora*, wake up. *Señorita* Emily, from the Stillman ranch—she is downstairs." Her eyes were frightened as she clutched her shawl over her nightgown and gestured toward the door.

I jumped out of bed and threw on a robe, glancing at

the clock. It was just after midnight.

Emily stood in the foyer, huddled in her overcoat. She turned when she heard me coming down the stairs, and I gasped when I saw her face. The entire right side was puffed and purpling. Her lip was bleeding; a cut just below her eyebrow had one eye swollen almost shut.

"My God! Emily!" I rushed to her and took her arm. She was trembling violently, her teeth chattering with cold and shock. "Come, sit down." Her legs wobbled, and I half dragged her into the parlor.

Marta lit the lamps and stood staring with wide, curious eyes. I tried to shield Emily from them.

"Go and wake Dora," I told her sharply. "Then go to the kitchen and make some tea." She nodded and scurried off, no doubt eager to tell her news to the other servants.

I turned to Emily. Her good eye was glazed over, and her head lolled to one side. I took off her coat and helped her lay out on the sofa, raising her feet and covering her with a quilt. As I pressed the quilt against her side, she whimpered and curled her body to protect herself.

"Emily?" She didn't respond but lay with her eyes closed. I took her hand and patted it helplessly.

When Dora's bulky frame appeared in the doorway, I cried out in relief.

"Dora! Thank God! You must come and help Emily."

Dora came around the sofa to look and caught her breath. Tossing her long braid behind her, she knelt with surprising agility and touched the young woman's face.

With the competence of a trained physician, she

raised Emily's eyelids and studied her eyes. Then she proceeded with a swift, methodical inspection of her body. She located swelling and bruises on Emily's neck and arms, in her side and across her stomach and thighs. Emily moaned as Dora pressed gently on her abdomen.

Dora looked up at me, anger flashing in her small dark eyes. "Very bad." She shook her head. "Someone beats this girl and the baby she carries."

"Baby?" I echoed weakly. Dora hoisted herself up from her knees. Marta brought in the tea, and Dora turned to me.

"Get her to take some tea," she said. I heard her giving instructions to Marta as she led her from the room, something about "comfrey" and "poultice."

I poured tea into a cup and knelt beside the sofa. "Emily?" I raised her head and held the cup to her lips. "Here, dear. Drink some tea. It will make you feel better."

She didn't respond. Her good eye was open now, staring vacantly. Her body was limp, her bruised, swollen jaw slack, making her mouth gape. When Dora returned, I suggested we send for Dr. Goodhall.

But Dora shook her head. "Her mind is in a faraway place," she said, "because of this cruelty. Her body heals itself. The baby is not harmed. Best not to tell anyone until Emily can say who beats her."

Unconvinced, I stood uneasily and watched Dora treat and dress Emily's wounds. She slipped off Emily's gown and laid hot, wet rags over the cuts and bruises, all the while chanting in her native tongue. When she was finished, she turned to me.

"Sit here," she said, pointing to the sofa cushion at Emily's head. I obeyed. "Take her head in your lap, stroke her, talk gently." I did as I was told. I stroked the parts of her head not covered with the bandage, careful to avoid the lumps. I lightly stroked her arms and her hands. I kept up a steady stream of reassurances that she was safe and warm and that her baby was not harmed. Dora stood and watched us, her arms folded, her face stern, her small eyes dangerous.

It was almost twenty minutes before the staring eye fluttered closed, and Emily's breathing smoothed and deepened. Dora nodded and motioned for me to stand.

We left her on the sofa, sleeping, while Dora and I both kept watch. I found myself dozing often, but Dora seemed to stay awake and alert the whole time. From the way she fingered her cross, I knew she was praying. I prayed, too, unable to keep out of my prayers the demand for a slow, agonizing death for the man who had done this.

At one point, I opened my eyes, and it was morning. Dora was kneeling beside the sofa, helping Emily to take some tea. I jumped out of my chair and stood behind Dora.

Emily saw me and pushed away the cup Dora was holding. Her attempt to smile made her wince and brought tears of pain to her eyes.

"Emily," I said gently. Dora withdrew, and I knelt on the floor beside the sofa. I stroked her arm. "How do you feel?"

She shut her eyes, and I saw tears leak out and trickle down the contours of the bandage. "I'm so ashamed," she whispered.

"You mustn't be." My voice turned savage. "Whoever did this to you is the one who should be ashamed!"

Emily shook her head back and forth. She opened her eyes and fixed me with her one good eye.

"I came to you, Katherine," she said, "because I thought...I thought if anyone could understand, it would be you." She shut her eyes again. "There's no one else I could turn to. Theresa would never understand. My friends—" She broke off on a sob.

"Emily, who did this to you?"

She hesitated and lifted a hand to her face, gingerly touching her swollen eye. "You won't believe me, Katherine."

Raymond, I thought viciously. *I'll see him in jail for this. I'll see him in hell.* "Try me," I said.

In a dead voice, she said, "It was my father."

"John?" I couldn't hide my surprise. Mild-mannered John Stillman? The man who had wept so inconsolably when his mother Grace had died?

Emily's lone blue eye fixed me accusingly. "I said you wouldn't believe me."

"Emily, of course I believe you. I'm just, well, stunned."

She spoke bitterly. "No one would guess it. No one who doesn't live with us. Everyone thinks he's so quiet and mild. They don't know what happens at home, when one of us crosses him. He's lucky he had daughters, all girls he can beat and bully. A son wouldn't stand for this. If I were his son...if I were a *man*—" Emily's face tightened, and she turned away.

I gave her a few minutes. Dora brought me a chair, and I raised myself into it, feeling weary and disgusted.

"Was this about your baby, Emily?"

She nodded, still turned away from me. "I'm almost four months. I couldn't hide it any longer. June guessed and told Mama. And she told Pa." Her voice was muffled. "He hit me. He knocked me to the floor and called me a whore and a disgrace, and he kicked me, like I was dog. He kept kicking me in the stomach. I think he wanted to kill the baby. Lord, I've never seen him so angry." She raised her arm to shield her face from me, her shoulders shaking with sobs.

Dora, who had been standing silent behind me, grunted. I touched Emily's shoulder.

"You were right to come here, Emily. We'll talk later and decide what's best to do. Right now, I'm taking you upstairs where you can sleep, and no one will bother you." She turned to me, her good eye wide and brimming. I saw her fear. "If your father comes for you, we won't let him in. Come on, now." I stood and reached out my hands to help her up. "You can lean on me."

Dora went ahead of us. By the time Emily and I reached my old room, Dora had laid out one of my nightgowns and turned down the bed. When I reached up to unfasten her hair, Emily stopped me.

"I can manage from here." Her smile was shy. "Thank you, Katherine. Thank you for your kindness."

I nodded and touched her arm.

"Rest now," I said gently. "You're safe, you and your child." I added grimly, "You have my solemn word on it."

* * *

Two days later I was in the sitting room when I heard a commotion in the hallway. As I rose from my chair, someone screamed. Without thinking to arm myself, I ran down the hall and came face-to-face with Raymond, looming like a giant over the cowering body of Marta. I ran to her and helped her up.

"I tried not to let him in, *señora*, like you said," she whimpered.

"It's all right, Marta," I said loudly, alarmed at the way my body had started to shake. Then, into her ear, "Go and get Alfred."

She nodded and slipped by me. But Raymond caught her arm.

"You're not going anywhere." His voice rasped queerly, like a stage whisper. I glanced at his throat, but his wound was concealed by a high, starched collar. He shoved Marta into the parlor and then grabbed my arm. "You, too," he said. "No one's going for help."

I struggled against him, but his grip on my arm was like steel. He wrenched my arm behind me, and I cried out as hot pain seared my shoulder.

"I've come for my cousin Emily." The peculiar hiss of his voice somehow made him all the more menacing.

"You can't have her!" I shot back, and he jerked my arm again, sending a fresh bolt of pain through my shoulder. I screamed, and he clamped his free hand over my mouth.

"You whores stick together, don't you?" He barked a horrible mutation of a laugh. "You've no idea how relieved I am to be rid of you. No matter how much you'll inherit from your father, it isn't worth putting up with an ugly, disgusting slut like you!"

I clenched my teeth against the blinding pain and forced my suddenly wobbly legs to keep me upright. My foolish bravado fled before the stark realization that, without a weapon, I was helpless against him. I couldn't protect Emily. I couldn't protect my mother or my daughter. We were a house full of women trying to survive in a man's world, just as Michael had said in that last letter.

"Let her go!"

At the sound, Raymond jerked his head around. I looked over his arm and found myself staring down the twin barrels of a shotgun Emily was leveling at us. Raymond stared at her for a moment.

"Well, well," he said. "Haven't you caused your family enough grief? Put that thing down before somebody gets hurt."

Emily's voice was cold. "The only one who's going to get hurt is you, Raymond, if you don't let Katherine go." She added, "Don't think I don't know how to use this. I'm a better shot than my father."

Raymond's hand slid slowly off my mouth. Suddenly, he grabbed my other arm and twisted it behind me. He whirled me in front of him, using my body as a shield.

"Put it down, I said!"

Emily kept the gun leveled at us. Raymond wrenched my arm, and I shrieked in pain as my shoulder tendons ripped.

I saw her hesitate.

"Don't do it, Emily!" I cried, and then screamed as Raymond yanked on my injured arm again.

Emily lowered the shotgun. I felt Raymond's body relax and heard the chuckle in his throat. Then, out of the corner of my eye, I saw something flash bright blue just before I heard a crash behind me. Raymond yelled and let me go. I ran to Emily, and Alfred suddenly appeared in the doorway, his rifle cocked and aimed at Raymond.

"High time you was leaving," he said quietly.

I put my good arm around Emily and turned to look.

Raymond had staggered against the mantel and was holding his bleeding head, cut from the ceramic vase Marta had broken over it. With a grunt, he pushed away from the mantel and staggered across the room. As he neared us, I had the good sense to push Emily and her shotgun behind me. Raymond's pale eyes burned through me like acid, but I raised my chin and fixed him with a defiant glare. Nevertheless, his coarse whisper broke out waves of gooseflesh along my arms.

"Don't think you've heard the last of me, Katherine. I'm going to get you where it hurts."

Without glancing at Alfred, Raymond brushed past him and into the hallway. Minutes later, we heard him ride away.

* * *

"But I want to press charges, Sheriff. Raymond Delacroix forced his way into my house, knocked down my servant, threatened me, and dislocated my shoulder, for heaven's sake! What do you mean, you can't put him in jail?"

The county sheriff leaned back in his chair, stroking his walrus mustache stained a disgusting yellow from chewing tobacco. His small, flat eyes roamed over me, lingering on my breasts, sliding down my body like I was a heifer at auction. He glanced at Alfred sitting politely beside me.

"Well, now, Mrs. Kamarov." The sheriff's voice was rough and lazy. "Mr. Delacroix was come to fetch back a runaway girl for his uncle. Ain't no harm in that. Fact is, you had no right to give her shelter. Then that illiterate servant girl of yours assaulted him. He's within his rights to have her punished, but he says he'll forget the whole thing if you will."

"That's outrageous!"

The sheriff shrugged. "Mr. Delacroix has a decent reputation, Mrs. Kamarov. Comes from a fine Philadelphia family." He leaned forward over his desk. "Now I know you women get high strung, and one thing leads to another. Mr. Delacroix is a gentleman. He says he doesn't want to see his cousin's name sullied by pressing charges against her for holding a shotgun on him. He's a right understanding man. You should count yourselves lucky, Mrs. Kamarov."

"And what about the rape? He *raped* me, Sheriff!" My voice shook with fury.

"Well, now, by his account, you two had an understanding of marriage. Says you accepted his engagement ring. Says you two were just doing what comes natural when you turned cold on him. There was no cause to hold a knife on him when a simple 'no' would have done the job. Says he's glad he found out in time what a temper you have." He wagged a finger at me and chuckled. "You ought to watch that, Mrs. Kamarov. Next time, you might not find the man so forgiving as Mr. Delacroix."

I looked at Alfred in shock and disbelief. He twisted his hat in his hands and glanced up at the sheriff.

"It was rape, Sheriff." He colored a little, but his quiet voice was firm. "I'll testify to that, right enough."

"Did you witness it?"

Alfred shook his head. "Not exactly."

The sheriff waved his hand impatiently. His voice became brisk.

"You'll do best to drop these foolish charges at once. Or Mr. Delacroix may forget about being generous and sue you both for slander!" He pushed back his chair and stood up. "Now that we understand each other, I have *important* work to do. Good day, all."

Alfred stood, and both he and the sheriff looked down at me. I rose slowly and gave the sheriff the most contemptuous glare I could muster. With head high and my back ramrod straight, I stalked out of his office into the dusty street.

I didn't stop until I reached the wagon.

"I can't believe this, Alfred." My body shook with outrage. "How can Raymond Delacroix get away with these crimes?"

"Happens all the time, Miss Katherine." Alfred slapped his hat onto his head. "Ain't no help in the law for a woman nor for hired help like me, neither." He settled me on the wagon seat and then swung himself up beside me and took the reins. "Only things that'll stop a man like Raymond Delacroix are a threat to his bank account or a bullet."

* * *

I was in my bedroom nursing Elise when Dora suddenly appeared in the doorway.

"Very bad news!" She planted her feet wide apart and fisted her hands on her hips. "Such wickedness!"

I felt instant dread, remembering Raymond's threat.

"What is it, Dora?"

"The cottage, *señora*. Someone sets it on fire. Gardeners going to work there like you say see the smoke. They work hard to put the fire out." She spread her hands. "But half the house is burned. The barn is gone. And the old man's roses — they are all dead."

Chapter Eleven

Alfred drove us to Summerwood in the wagon. Emily stood beside me, holding Elise, while I stared in numb silence at the blackened walls and gaping holes of the cottage. The right side seemed fairly intact. But the left side—the parlor, the kitchen, the garden workroom— were badly damaged. And the rose garden.

Spidery figures of charred rosewood still stood erect, proud even in death. Through a blur of tears, I walked the rows, naming them for the last time: Morning Star, Isabel, Katherine.

I'm going to get you where it hurts.

Brushing away my tears, I looked up at the sad remains of the workroom wall. With no more need for doors, I stepped between blackened posts and stood amid the ash and debris littering the stone floor. The drawers of herbs and powders and seeds, each neatly labeled in Katherine's slanting hand, were utterly reduced to rubble. I mounted the stone stairs into the kitchen, recognizing the stout iron stove but little else. The wood floor, along with the stains of Raymond's blood, had been destroyed.

I edged my way into the hall. Thankfully, the beautiful buffet looked unaffected by the fire. Opening the door to the master bedroom, I was relieved to discover that it, too, had escaped destruction. The parlor was hopelessly ruined, but I found Leon's beautiful stair banisters untouched. It seemed as though a magic shield had risen before the flames, warning them: this far and no farther.

From the sweep of destruction, I guessed that the fire had been started outside the parlor and workroom. And from the utter devastation of the rose garden, I knew the roses had been a deliberate target.

"Such wickedness," Dora had said. I clenched my fists and willed down the rise of bitter acid in my throat. The violation of Summerwood Cottage was so profound, I felt as if I had been raped a second time.

I started up the stairs to see if the attic was intact. But a hand grasped my arm, and Alfred's soft voice spoke behind me.

"You don't want to go up there, Miss Katherine. Come on out, now. It's not safe."

"Oh, Alfred! Why would he do this? What did he have to gain by such useless destruction?"

Alfred led me gently out of the ruin. "There's no accounting for evil, miss. Evil is its own master and to them that serves it." He added, "No one saw him do it, Miss Katherine. No one can prove a thing against him."

I heard the resignation in his voice and saw my own despair mirrored in his eyes. We turned together and stared at the charred wood still sending curls of smoke into the morning air. It was a full minute, maybe more, before I spoke.

"Have you ever heard of the Phoenix bird, Alfred?"

Something in my voice made him turn to me with a

curious look. "No, ma'am."

I narrowed my eyes at the blackened walls. "The Greeks believed in a beautiful, magical bird called the Phoenix. There was only one of its kind, and it lived for hundreds of years. At the end of its allotted time, the Phoenix would die and burn on a funeral pyre. But then an extraordinary thing would happen. Out of the ashes would rise a new Phoenix, fresh and renewed. It's a continuous circle, you see. Out of suffering and death comes strong new life."

I turned to Alfred. "Raymond thinks he's defeated me. He thinks he's won." I found myself smiling. "He doesn't understand that he's helped me move from one life to the next. Out of this defeat will come my ultimate triumph."

Alfred stared at me, rubbing his chin in bewilderment. "I don't think I follow, Miss Katherine."

I laughed. "I know, Alfred. This is what I mean." I turned back to the defiled cottage. "I'm going to rebuild the cottage, and I know exactly how I want it to look—bigger kitchen, wider porch, more windows in the parlor. And I'm going to replant the rose garden. We'll take slips from the formal garden at the house and make it more beautiful than it ever was."

I met Alfred's uneasy look, and I laughed again. "And you know what else, Alfred? You're going to teach me how to shoot a rifle, starting this afternoon. The next time anyone threatens me or mine, I'm going to be ready for him." My voice became grim. "No man will ever again grind me under his heel and think he's gotten the better of me."

* * *

I gave orders for the work to begin immediately on Summerwood Cottage.

Fortunately, the bearing walls had not been destroyed, so the second-floor bedrooms and the attic were saved. I drew plans for the new parlor and an enlarged kitchen expanding out where the workroom had been. My design for the new porch included a comfortable swing and thick, sturdy balustrades as similar as I could make them to the ones I'd seen for the first time with Ryan.

As the workers were putting up new walls and laying new flooring, I took it upon myself to renovate the master bedroom. Emily looked after Elise while I scrubbed the walls and papered them and polished the old bedstead and dresser. I made curtains for the windows and brought lamps and rugs from Rosswood House. Finding a painting of the old rose garden from among Katherine's canvases, I made a crude frame for it and hung it over the dresser.

"Why are you going to all this trouble?" Emily asked me. She was sitting on the bed, Elise on her lap, watching me polish the andirons for the small corner fireplace. "Nobody lives in this old cottage anymore. What's the use of it?"

I shrugged. "Nobody lives here now. But someday the family will start living here again. And they'll continue to live here long after they've stopped living in Alexander's mansion."

Emily's voice was careful. "How do you know that, Katherine?"

Judith Ingram

I held her gaze with a direct look. "I've seen the future, Emily. I know what I'm talking about."

She stared at me with round eyes. "Sometimes you sound just like Granny used to when she'd tell her stories about the future. I didn't like to tell anyone, but I believed her. There was nothing crazy about that old woman. In fact, she was probably saner than most people I knew." She added softly, "You're like her, Katherine. You have your own way of seeing things and people."

She lowered her gaze.

"I want to thank you again for taking me in. I know I've caused you a load of trouble with Raymond—"

"My trouble with Raymond has nothing to do with you, Emily."

She nodded and swallowed. "Well, I...I also want to thank you for not asking me questions. You haven't asked me...who the father is."

I sat on the mattress beside her. "It's none of my business. If you want me to know, you'll tell me." I lifted Elise from her lap and settled her on mine. "I live in a glass house, you know." I smiled softly. "I'm not about to throw rocks."

"That's exactly why I came to you." Emily's blue eyes were solemn. "When Elise was born, there was all that talk in town about you and that Chinese boy whose family got burned out..."

She broke off, flushing a little.

"Then I saw you at church and the way you talked down that awful Betty Somers. You defeated her with nothing but kind words. And you got everyone to accept Elise, no matter who her father was." Her eyes shone. "I

148

want to be like you, Katherine." She gave a quick laugh. "Knowing you all my life, I never thought I'd hear myself say that. But it's true. You're so changed. Still strong-willed, but also gentle, considerate. Just the kind of mother Elise needs." She laid a timid hand on my arm. "And the friend I need. The change in you seems like, well, an act of providence."

I swallowed hard, too moved to speak. Elise lay quietly in my arms, staring up at me with eyes that seemed to add her own affirmation. I smiled down at her.

"I believe providence is just what it is, Emily," I said.

* * *

Thanksgiving Day was not far off. I discovered that the Rostnova household had never celebrated Thanksgiving, an omission I was determined to correct. After consulting with different members of the household, I gave Carmen instructions for the feast: stuffed, roasted turkey for me; Carmen's special spiced yams for Isabel; Indian corn pudding for Dora; apple dumplings for Emily; and blackberry cobbler for Robbie. Trying to be sensitive to Dora, I endeavored to make this a celebration of blessings rather than a remembrance of the settlers' arrival at Plymouth Rock.

I wrote to Ana, inviting her and Leon to join us. She wrote back, declining, but added that my uncle would be arriving soon to discuss a business proposition with Isabel. She was leaving him to explain it when he arrived in a week's time.

As I read further down in her letter, my heart slipped into my throat:

Irene Stratford has written that her daughter and our Michael plan to announce their betrothal at any moment. Julian has agreed to publish a book Michael has written, and already there is much publicity about it. Irene adds that Michael has become so popular with the publishing crowd, he may choose to settle in New York when he and Vivian are married.

My fervent prayer has always been to see Michael successful and happy. This news has surpassed my best hope for our dear boy, although his uncle and I will miss having him near. I've not heard yet when the family plans to return to San Francisco, but I expect it will be in time for the Christmas holiday.

Give my love to your mother. Stay well, Katya dear.

Ana

I put the letter aside and wondered why the news shocked me. Their betrothal had been inevitable.

But Michael loves me, a tiny voice insisted. *Me.*

Numbly, I folded Ana's letter and put it in my pocket.

* * *

Leon arrived during the second week of November. His black mustache tickled my cheek as he swept me into an affectionate hug and demanded to see Elise. Dora brought her down, and I delighted to see his face soften as he held her small body in his strong arms, looking down into eyes as dark as his own.

"Tiny little thing, isn't she?" His booming voice startled his great-niece, and she started to fuss. I stepped forward to take her, but he held her up and bounced her gently. "Now, now, little girl, it's your uncle Leon. No need for fussing. That's it, sweet pea. My, you look just like your mama."

Amused, I watched Elise stare down into her great-uncle's upturned face, her eyes solemn, all thoughts of crying apparently abandoned.

"Uncle Leon!" Robbie tore down the stairs and threw himself against his uncle. "Wait till you see Elise's nursery! You won't believe it! Remember those animals you helped me draw? Well, see, I had this birthday party, only not everybody came, and then—"

"Robbie, give your uncle a chance to catch his breath, for heaven's sake! He just got here." I laughed and ruffled Robbie's hair. "How about if you show him the nursery after he's had some dinner, hmm?"

Leon laughed as he handed Elise back to Dora. "Sounds like the artist has been hard at work." He swung Robbie up almost as easily as he had Elise and gave him a friendly shake. "Am I mistaken, boy, or have you gotten taller?"

Robbie chuckled as his uncle set him down. "I'm going to school now, Uncle," he said proudly. "I'm learning to read. Soon I'll be able to read to Mama."

Leon glanced at me over Robbie's head. I answered the question in his eyes.

"Mother is doing fairly well. She's determined to prove the doctor wrong and live to see the New Year."

"I'll go up to her now." He gave Elise a fake pinch on

her cheek as he passed her, heading for the staircase.

Isabel, however, was already on the stairs. She wore her black silk dress, her hair neatly arranged, the enamel brooch pinned to her bodice. I caught my breath at her thinness, at the paleness that made her eyes stand out like ink spots.

Leon met her at the bottom step. "Leon, how delightful." Her voice was warm as she extended her hand. He bent over it and then kissed her warmly on the cheek.

"Isabel, how well you look."

She threw him a skeptical look and shook her head, making her earrings bob. "You're either blind or a liar, Brother." She gentled her admonition with a smile. "But I thank you for the compliment. It pleases my absurd vanity to hear it."

Without warning, she burst into a series of violent coughs. She turned away from us, pulling a handkerchief from her pocket, while we all looked away in helpless silence. Robbie felt for my hand.

Marta appeared from the dining room. She looked at me, and I surreptitiously nodded at Isabel.

"*Señora*. Carmen asks if you wish the dinner served now."

Isabel raised her head and looked at Leon. "Can you eat now, Leon? Or did you want to discuss your business first?"

"Business can wait until later, Isabel. No hurry." His voice was a shade too hearty. "Let's eat, by all means."

He offered her his arm, and she took it graciously. As we followed them into the dining room, I glanced down at Robbie.

His face was pale, and his mouth was set in a little frown that suddenly reminded me of Michael. On impulse, I leaned down and whispered to him, "I can see you're being very brave, for Mama's sake." I squeezed his hand.

He looked up at me in surprise. "I am the man of the house, Katya. I have to be brave."

Before I could respond, he moved ahead and pulled out my chair for me. Then he stood beside it, his straight, dignified posture a replica of his mother's.

Chapter Twelve

"It's this north valley I'm talking about." Leon tapped the map with his finger. "And the timberland around it. He's offering a good price, Isabel. I suggest you take it."

Leon, Isabel, and I were seated around the coffee table in the parlor. Time was short—Leon was scheduled to leave for home in little more than an hour. Isabel's appearance downstairs and her efforts as hostess on the previous afternoon had so sapped her strength that the business discussion had to be postponed until this morning. I watched her anxiously now as she sat, pale and silent, listening to Leon's advice about selling off some of the Rostnova land.

He presented his proposal without preliminaries and his opinion without reserve. A neighboring rancher had approached him and expressed interest in purchasing a parcel of land adjacent to his own property. Because the land was not being used, Leon saw no reason not to sell.

Looking at the map, I recognized the valley that would someday house Rosswood Winery. The hills around it, now timbered with redwood, would be striped with neat, narrow rows of grape vines. The idea that we should sell the property for ranching was unthinkable.

I glanced at Isabel and saw her hesitate. She looked

tired but determined to uphold her role as head of the family. She studied the map for a long time before looking up at Leon.

"Do we need the money, Leon?"

He shrugged. "We are not in bad shape, if that's what you mean. But, of course, we can use the capital for investing. That will mean security for your family after... for years to come." He cleared his throat.

Again Isabel looked at the map. I saw indecision and weariness etched on her face, tightening the lines of her mouth, puckering her brow.

"May I speak?" I said suddenly.

Both glanced up.

"Of course, Katrina." Isabel looked relieved. "This concerns you. What is your opinion?"

I took a deep breath, knowing there was no turning back once the words were spoken.

"We must not, under any circumstances, sell this property." I ignored the sudden beetling of Leon's black brows. "The valley and the hills around it are perfect for wine growing. Eventually wine will become this family's largest source of income, not cattle ranching."

Leon made an impatient noise in his throat. Marta, who had just set down the tea tray, was frankly staring. Isabel said hesitantly, "Our family knows nothing about wine growing, Katrina."

Before I could answer, Leon exploded.

"I've heard this drivel all my life!" he declared. "It's the old man's nonsense gotten into her head. He was always carrying on about that valley, experimenting with that Luther Burbank fellow, the two of them cooking up new varieties of grape. Burbank had some success, but the old man couldn't get them to grow around the cottage. He always had his sights on that valley." He pointed an accusing finger at me. "If you're going to be making decisions for this family, young woman, then you've got to get your head out of the clouds. The valley is useless to us. Russ Paxton says he'll pay us top dollar for it, and I say again we'd be fools not to take his offer!"

"We'd be fools *to* take it!" I shot back. "Uncle, I know what I'm talking about. You'll have to trust me about this. That valley is going to produce Rosswood wines for future generations—"

"Rosswood?" Isabel asked sharply.

I looked at her. "Yes. Our ranch will be renamed Rosswood, or 'Russian wood.' This house will become a museum, and the family will end up living at Summerwood...that is, grandfather's cottage." Nerves made my voice shrill. "I tell you, I've been there, Uncle! I've walked inside that winery. I've seen the vines and even tasted the wine! It would be sheer folly for us to sell!"

Silence followed my outburst. Leon and Isabel stared at me, their mouths gaping. Out of the corner of my eye, I saw Marta hovering near the doorway, crossing herself.

Leon suddenly bellowed, "Hell's bells, the girl's demented! She's gone completely off her head, Isabel." He rattled the map at me. "We're talking the future of your family here, girl. You don't expect us to take all this nonsense seriously, do you?" His black eyes glared at me under bristling eyebrows.

I pressed my trembling hands together, as if I were

praying, and met his glare. "Yes, Uncle, I do. I am fully competent and rational, and I am telling you the truth. I have seen the future. And I am begging you to listen to me. Believe what I'm telling you."

Leon sputtered an oath and rolled his eyes. But Isabel was studying me, her eyes thoughtful.

"What else do you see, Katrina?" she asked quietly.

Grateful, I turned to her. "In 1906 there will be an earthquake of huge proportions. Half of San Francisco will be lost in the tremor and the fire that will follow." Marta was crossing herself rapidly. She fled from the room, her crucifix pressed to her lips. "The city will need lumber for rebuilding. These hills"—I indicated the map—"are covered with redwoods that can be shipped down the Russian River. Our lands will become the biggest source of lumber in this area, so big, in fact, that the name of the town will be changed from Springstown to Rossport. You see, not only will the earthquake devastate San Francisco, but its effects will reach all the way up here and dry up the hot springs that give the town its name." I leveled a look at Leon. "It *will* happen, Uncle. Whether or not you believe me now, it will all happen just as I've said."

Leon was shaking his head at me when Isabel turned to him.

"We'll keep the land," she said.

His eyes rounded in horror.

"Isabel, are you out of your mind? Surely you don't believe this fantastic concoction! The girl is obviously...confused. She's always been a little odd. Forgive me, Katherine"—he spread his hands at me—

"but with so much at stake, I've got to speak plainly." His voice rose with temper. "You'll regret this, Isabel!"

Isabel leaned forward to pour herself a cup of tea. "I don't think so, Leon. I believe my daughter. I believe she has the Sight. Besides, she just confirmed what Grace Stillman always said, that there's going to be a devastating earthquake." She stirred her tea placidly. "Perhaps you and Ana should consider moving up here. Your house in San Francisco might be in peril come 1906."

"Rubbish!" Leon exclaimed. He slapped his hands across his knees and gave her a hard look. "Is that your final word, Isabel?"

"It is."

"No possibility of changing your mind, I suppose?"

Isabel stirred her tea. "None."

Leon stifled another oath. "And just what am I supposed to tell Paxton?"

"Tell him we have plans for that valley." Both her voice and her gaze on him were steady.

After a withering glare at me, Leon blew out a breath and sagged against the sofa. "Saints preserve us," he muttered. His eyebrows were a solid disapproving line, but there was a twinkle in his eyes as they jumped from Isabel to me. "Never did I see two such stubborn women. Katherine, you're more like your mother every day." He rolled up the map and stood. "Are you certain I can't talk you out of this foolhardy, pigheaded position, Isabel?"

Isabel smiled up at him. "Brother, you are good to want to protect our interests. But no. I believe we are meant to hold onto that land."

Leon shrugged in resignation and bowed. "In that case," he said, "I shall take my leave. Ladies." He turned, and I heard him muttering, "...mule-headed women...need a man around here..." as he crossed the room and disappeared into the hall.

Isabel's hand shook as she set down her cup. She leaned back against the cushion and shut her eyes.

"You were right to speak up, Katrina," she said. "You can't realize what a comfort it is to me, knowing I shall leave my family in your capable hands."

"Mother," I said softly. "Thank you for believing me. Thank you for not selling the land."

"Of course I believe you, *niña mía*." She opened her eyes and looked at me. "God himself sent you to us. How could I not believe the voice of his messenger?"

* * *

Thanksgiving was less than a week away when Marta appeared at my bedroom door. She stared at the floor and refused to meet my eyes. Since overhearing my revelations about the future, she had treated me with a reverence and fear that were beginning to annoy me.

"What is it, Marta?" I laid down my book and glanced at Elise, sleeping in her cradle beside me.

Marta gave a deep curtsey, another new behavior of hers. "*Señora* Stillman and her daughter have come to see *señorita* Emily. I did not know what to do, so I came to you first."

I rose immediately. "Thank you, Marta. You acted wisely. Is Miss Emily in her room?"

Marta nodded and swallowed. "*Sí, señora.*" She curtsied again and left. I gave Elise another look and headed for Emily's room.

"Your mother and sister are here to see you," I told her, without preamble. "What do you want to do?"

Emily stiffened. "Not my father?" I shook my head. "I guess I'll have to see them," she said, after a moment. "Will you come with me?"

"Of course."

We went down together.

Lillian and Theresa sat in armchairs facing the sofa. Theresa stood as we entered the room, and she crossed to take her sister's hand. Lillian remained seated, her back stiff, her eyes cold as she shifted her gaze from her daughter to me.

"I'm sure you'll excuse us, Katherine," she said. "This is a private matter."

My reply was just as curt. "Emily wants me here." With that, I moved to the sofa and sat down. Emily sat beside me, facing her mother across the coffee table. Left standing alone, Theresa hesitated until a look from her mother sent her meekly back to the other armchair.

Lillian cleared her throat. "I won't waste words, Emily. It's high time you stopped all this foolishness and came home. Your father has forgiven you."

"*He* has forgiven *me*?" Emily's voice was shrill. "For what? For allowing him to beat me almost senseless?"

"Heavens, Emily, how you do exaggerate. Your father was upset, and with good reason. Such shame you've brought down on our heads!" She paused. "However, despite the disgrace you force us to bear, your family has decided that your place is with us. Not with strangers." Her gaze swept me with disdain. "Theresa and I have come to fetch you home."

"No."

"Emily, don't be stubborn!"

"I won't go with you."

Her mother's voice rose. "And are you going to hold a shotgun on us as you did on your poor cousin Raymond?"

Emily's voice was hot. "I'm just sorry I never got a clear shot at him!"

"You take that back, you ungrateful snippet!" Lillian's eyes blazed. "I've heard the lies you two girls are spreading, accusing my nephew of terrible things." Lillian turned a withering look on me. "Raymond is too much the gentleman to tell me what happened between the two of you, Katherine. But, if you ask me, I'd say he's well out of it. Imagine, raising a child—" She left her sentence hanging.

I bit back an angry retort and gripped the cushion under my skirt. Emily touched my arm.

"I'm sorry you've wasted your time, Mama. I'm not going home with you."

"Emily." Theresa's soft voice turned our heads toward her. "Think of your child. You can't live on your own, with no husband. And you can't stay here." Her blue eyes flicked over me. "Coming home is the only sensible thing to do."

"How sensible would it be for me to deliberately have my baby in a home where personal safety doesn't matter?" Her mother started to object, but Emily's glare stopped her. "I tolerated it for myself, but I won't allow him to hurt my child. You know what I'm talking about,

Theresa." Emily turned fierce eyes on her sister. "He's terrorized us all for years. You got out by marrying Bruce. I thought I had a chance to get out, too. To get married—" She laid a hand over her stomach. "I won't go back there again. I've escaped, and I'm never going back. Never!"

Theresa glanced at me and flushed. "You exaggerate, Emily," she said uneasily.

I couldn't sit quiet any longer. "Those welts and bruises on your sister's body weren't exaggerations, Theresa. And she didn't put them there herself."

Theresa flushed deeper. "It's not your business, Katherine. You don't know—"

"It *is* my business, and it's yours too," I snapped. "For God's sake, how can you just sit by and watch—"

"Enough!" Lillian glared me into silence. Then she sighed, and her tone turned wheedling. "Be reasonable, Emily. You cannot continue to impose upon the hospitality of this house. Isabel has been a friend of mine for years, and now you've put her in a difficult position—"

"Mrs. Stillman." I interrupted her. "It was *my* decision to give Emily shelter, not my mother's. And I do not find myself in a difficult position at all. In fact, I take great comfort in knowing that in my house Emily and her child will be safe from danger and fear."

Lillian's smile was thin. "Does that certainty come from your new and much celebrated fortune-telling ability, Katherine?"

I blinked at her. "What?"

"Oh, come now." Lillian lowered her voice. "It's all

over town how you have the Sight. Just like old Grace." Her voice was sarcastic, but there was speculation in her eyes. She added, as if in spite of herself, "Is it true? Can you see things in the future?"

I hesitated and realized pretending was futile. "Yes. Some things."

"Like what?"

I shrugged. "I don't feel comfortable talking about it."

"Is this what you and Raymond quarreled about?"

"What?"

"About whether or not he should invest in Golden Springs Valley?" Lillian narrowed her eyes at me. "It is true, isn't it? You told him not to invest in the land, and he's hesitating now because of all this talk about you having the Sight. But you lied to him, didn't you?"

I stared at her and suddenly saw my opportunity.

"Well, Mrs. Stillman," I began, rapidly formulating my thoughts. "Seeing into the future does pose an awful temptation for wickedness." I lowered my gaze and fidgeted with the folds of my skirt. "I was angry with Raymond. When he took me out to the valley, I could see how much it meant to him. It's spiteful, I know, but I did advise him not to invest." Emily turned her head sharply toward me. "The truth is, that valley holds extraordinary opportunity for the right person. Raymond is both experienced and clever. Short of a *natural disaster*, I can see nothing that would keep him from achieving financial success." I swallowed hard and watched Lillian through my lashes.

She was studying me, her head thrust forward on

her thin neck like an inquisitive turkey. I hung my head a little and hoped she would mistake the trembling of my jaw for profound remorse.

She startled me by suddenly retracting her neck and sitting upright in her chair. She bobbed her head in a triumphant nod.

"I thought so!" she said. "I told Raymond as much, but he wouldn't believe me. Said you wouldn't *dare* lie to him." Her eyes glittered. "So you thought you'd make a fool of him, did you, Katherine? Wicked girl!" Her mouth lifted in a contemptuous curl that made her look shockingly like her nephew. "Be assured, I will set him straight on the matter immediately. Oh, yes, you may depend upon it!"

In her zeal, she practically leaped from her chair. Then her gaze caught on Emily, and she frowned.

"Come, Theresa." Lillian jerked her head at her middle daughter and raised her chin. "Our business here is finished. It's high time we went home"—her gaze swept us meaningfully—"to our *husbands*."

With a sniff and a dismissive rustle of silk, Lillian swept herself from the room, leaving Theresa to trail meekly in her wake.

Chapter Thirteen

Thanksgiving came and went, and the weather turned cold. I dressed Elise in layers to keep her warm and found myself keeping to rooms with fireplaces. Isabel remained upstairs. When I visited her, she seemed very tired, and there was blood again on her handkerchief when she coughed. Hating myself for it, I gave orders to keep Elise away from her grandmother.

I was in the kitchen, fixing a pot of tea, when Alfred came to the back door.

"Afternoon, Miss Katherine." He tipped his hat. "Miss Emily." Emily sat at the table behind me, holding Elise. She dimpled and dropped her gaze. "I just came from town and brought up your mail."

I opened the screen, and Alfred handed me three envelopes. "Would you care for some tea, Alfred?"

"Oh, no, ma'am. I got a heap o' work waiting for me." He touched his hat again. With a quick, shy glance at Emily, he flung himself off the step and strode away.

I set the teapot on the table and took Elise from Emily's arms. Settling into a chair, I gave Elise my breast and felt the tingle as my milk let down. Her greedy sucking gradually quieted to a more sedate nursing, and I reached over to pour myself some tea. I gave Emily a shrewd look.

"I think our Alfred is smitten," I said casually.

Emily blushed and drank her tea. I looked down and smiled at Elise, whose lovely, almond-shaped eyes were fixed upon my face. She blinked and waved a fist in the air before settling it against my breast. I felt her body sigh and relax further in my arms.

I glanced up at Emily, who was also watching Elise. "You could do worse than Alfred, you know."

Her blue eyes snapped up, round and incredulous. "Are you joking?"

"Not in the least."

"Katherine, I'm a rancher's daughter. Alfred is a *hired hand.*" She dipped an eyebrow at me. "You know that sort of thing isn't done."

"Who says?" I countered. "Your family? Your *father*?" Emily's mouth tightened. "Alfred is one of the best men we know. A woman could count herself fortunate to have him for a husband."

"A woman of his station in life, yes."

"And the father of your child?" I said it gently, knowing my words would hurt. "Was he of your station in life, Emily?"

Her expression darkened. "You promised you wouldn't ask about him."

"I'm only pointing out that decency and personal worth aren't determined by social class. I mean, can you imagine Alfred ever abandoning the woman he loved? A woman who was having his *child*?"

She shifted her gaze to the back door, looking through the screen as if Alfred himself were still standing there. Her expression softened.

"No," she admitted quietly.

Elise started to fuss, and I realized my breast had gone soft, drained of its milk. I shifted her to my other breast. She patted it happily and settled herself with a contented sigh.

I glanced up to find Emily staring at Elise, her blue eyes clouded.

"I'm going upstairs," she said suddenly. Without looking at me, she rose and left the kitchen.

Elise's eyes were fluttering closed. In the next few moments, her mouth slackened. Smiling, I reached for the envelopes Alfred had given me and scanned the return addresses.

One was from Ana, addressed to me. Carefully, so as not to disturb Elise, I fingered open the flap and drew out the folded sheets. Flattening them on the table, I perused Ana's neat, elegant script.

Leon was disappointed, she said, not to sell the north valley to Russ Paxton. She hoped I was not paying too much attention to "Dora's Indian nonsense," and she reminded me how Dora had filled my childhood days with medicine arts and spiritual heresy. "You've always been so susceptible to suggestion, Katya," she wrote. "Your family needs you to be strong, now, not given to flights of fancy."

Farther down she described how the city shops were getting ready for Christmas, filling with new merchandise and hanging festive decorations. As with us, the weather in San Francisco had chilled abruptly, promising an early winter. The damp cold ached her joints, she said, and she was hoping to get some of

Isabel's medicine to treat them.

My eyes suddenly caught on a single phrase, which leaped off the page and straight into my heart: *Michael is coming home.*

I backed up and read from the start of the paragraph:

> Leon and I plan to come the week before Christmas and stay with you through the New Year, as we always do. Michael is coming home and will join us there. The Stratfords will be in San Francisco through the end of spring, and will then sail for Europe. Michael has, of course, been invited to go with them. It is unclear when he and Vivian plan to be married. I have all my news from Irene, for Michael has not written me a word about it. Imagine, honeymooning in Europe! It all sounds very grand.

My eyes trailed over the rest of her letter with little interest and returned to the only significant paragraph. *It is unclear when he and Vivian plan to be married.* So, it was true. I had told myself that Ana might be mistaken, that Michael couldn't possibly marry someone else if he still loved me.

And yet, I reminded myself, knowing that I loved him, Michael expected me to marry Raymond.

With a sigh I pushed the letter aside and looked down at my daughter.

She was fast asleep. Her body lay motionless in my arms, her pink mouth open in a soft *O* as her baby breath, sweet with fresh milk, slipped in and out quietly. I raised her and brushed my lips over her downy head.

"Your cousin Michael is coming soon," I whispered. My heart thudded painfully as I said his name aloud for the first time in many weeks. I shut my eyes and said it again, savoring the taste of it on my lips. "Michael. Even though it's not to stay, Michael is coming home."

* * *

The night was dark, the air still and heavy with the threat of rain. Elise was now sleeping through the night, so it was no surprise that I was deep in slumber when Dora came into my room and shook me awake.

The sight of her anxious face, her thick braid falling over her shoulder, so frightened me that I couldn't speak. Silently, I slipped from bed and grabbed my robe, shoving my arms into it as I hurried after her. She didn't wait but was already in the hallway, heading back to Isabel's room.

The warm glow of lamplight kindly softened the stark walls and bare furnishings of her room, bringing my attention immediately to the bed. Isabel lay with her eyes closed and her mouth gaping, her breath loud and wheezing as she gasped for air. There was blood on her pillow, red drops that contrasted painfully with the snowy linen. Her hands were clutched on top of her breast, rising and dropping with the erratic pattern of her breathing.

I rushed to the bed and bent over her.

"Mother?" My voice was rough with sleep and quivering with fright. "Mother, can you hear me?"

Her eyes rolled under the thin lids, and she moaned softly. I glanced up at Dora, who stood on the other side of the bed. Her black eyes were small and bright in the soft lamplight. She closed them and began a soft chant.

I pulled up a chair and sat close, smoothing Isabel's damp hair back from her face. Perspiration dewed her forehead, and two bright fever spots colored her cheeks, looking like overdone theater makeup against the pallor of her skin. I stroked her cheek and murmured to her, and eventually her eyelids stopped rolling and her gasping eased a little. Not knowing what else to do, I slipped to the floor on my knees. Taking her hand in mine, I pressed it to my forehead, closed my eyes, and I prayed for her.

My prayers were disjointed, spikes of solitary pleading against the certainty that Isabel could not live much longer and despair over how I would bear my grief when she was gone. Tears squeezed out of my tightly shut eyelids and trickled down my cheeks, some straying into my mouth and stinging me with their salt. I wasn't sure if I prayed aloud or silently. The sound of Dora's chanting swept in and out of my awareness, and yet I felt terribly alone. With pain that was surprisingly physical, I yearned for the comfort of Michael's arms around me and the warmth of his cheek pressing against mine.

Dora touched me on the shoulder. I raised my head from the bed where it had fallen. Isabel's eyes were open and looking at me.

"Mother?" My voice was thick with tears. A fresh swell of them brimmed my eyes as I tightened my grip on her hand.

"Katrina." Her voice was barely audible, but I read my name on her lips. I moved closer to her head and put my hand on her hair.

"Mother. Mother." I could manage nothing but the one word, caressing her with it, giving myself the small comfort of knowing she could still hear me saying it.

The lovely blue-violet eyes left my face and traveled to Dora's. "Roberto." The effort of words brought on a rack of coughs. Dora held a cloth to her mouth, where blood stained bright red into the white cotton. "My son," she gasped.

I took the cloth from Dora so she could go for Robbie.

"Katrina." Isabel's voice was stronger now, and her eyes held me with an intensity I knew was costing her.

I shook my head. "Please, Mother. Don't talk. You must rest, you must reserve—"

Isabel shut her eyes as if to stop my words. She shook her head faintly.

"Listen to me, Katrina," she rasped. "I regret so many years with you when I did not protect you, when I did not know you. Forgive me, *niña mía*."

"Mother, it doesn't matter. None of that matters."

Her eyes, when she opened them, were solemn. "It does matter, daughter. I beg you now to forgive me, to let me go in peace."

"Mother, with all my heart, I forgive you!" My tears splashed onto her neck and trickled down into her hair. "I waited all my life for you. These last months with you have been my happiest. My love for you is so deep, so much a part of me, that I just don't think I can—"

I pressed my hands against my face and sobbed.

I felt Isabel's hand on my head. "Katrina," she

whispered. "You are my strength now. You will live and be strong for Robbie, for your daughter. For yourself."

I opened my eyes and saw the love in her smile as she blessed me. "You have come from God, and you will walk with God, *querida*. Don't be afraid. If you come again to the dark tunnel, listen for my voice. You will not be alone."

Her hand slipped from my head, and she sighed. I heard the door open and turned to see Father Andreas, the priest who came twice a month to give us communion. Behind him stood Dora, her hands firmly holding the frail shoulders of a white-faced Robbie.

Isabel saw them and reached out her hand.

"Roberto," she called softly.

Robbie looked at me and reached for my hand as he came to stand by his mother's bed.

"Roberto, my son. *My son*." She emphasized the words as she gazed at him, her eyes dark and glittering with unshed tears. "I have wronged you in so many ways, Roberto. For this, I ask your forgiveness. You are innocent. Evil blinded me until it was almost too late." Robbie glanced at me, confusion and fear in his eyes. I put my arms around his waist and drew him close.

As she had done with me, Isabel laid a hand on her son's head. "You will grow to be a man of sensitivity and integrity, Roberto." Her voice strengthened. "Learn from your sister, for God has sent her to teach you what I could not. I…I love you, Roberto. My son."

Isabel closed her eyes, and her hand slipped from Robbie's head onto the bed. Alarmed, Robbie clutched at me, and the priest stepped forward.

"She is still breathing, *señora*," he said quietly. I nodded and raised myself into the chair behind me, pulling Robbie onto my lap. Silently, we watched Father Andreas lay a beautiful sash down the length of our mother's body and make a cross of ashes on her forehead.

Minutes ticked by. The only sounds in the room were the priest murmuring prayers, the harsh rasp of Isabel's labored breathing, and the soft patter of rain that had begun to fall against the windows. At last the priest stood back from the bed. Robbie buried his face in my neck, and I held him tightly while I watched Isabel, watched her chest rise and fall with her last breaths, watched her lovely eyes open and look with wonder at something beyond what the rest of us could see. Then her eyelids fluttered shut, and her chest rose and fell for the last time.

* * *

I stood at the window of my room—the room that had belonged to Alexander—and watched the dawn of the new day. Minute by minute the eastern sky grew lighter and pinker, casting its soft glow over the sleeping hills washed clean by the night's brief baptism. I listened to the song of a solitary bird, up before his brothers, calling them out of their night of darkness into a world newly born.

I felt curiously wide awake and peaceful, as if my hours of grieving had used up all my tears, leaving behind only a deep sense of calm. As I stared at the sky streaked with ever brightening light, I found I could hold no more than this quiet moment of dawn, alive in its fresh colors and waking sounds. I felt oddly content and comfortingly at one with that solitary fellow shrilling out his morning song from a fullness of heart we both shared.

Suddenly the new sun crested the hills, dazzling my poor eyes red and swollen half-shut from weeping. I heard a rustle behind me and turned to find Dora standing there, watching the sunrise.

"The new day," she said simply.

I nodded and said nothing, needing no words to explain to Dora how I felt. Dora knew.

She approached me, and the grief in her small dark eyes sent a fresh stab of pain through my already aching chest. She suddenly looked very old—exhausted and wrinkled and stooped. For the first time, I wondered how old Dora really was. In the pain of my own loss, I had forgotten what the loss of Isabel must mean to her—she who had raised Isabel from a baby and had loved her all her life.

"Dora," I said gently. "Have you rested at all?"

She shook her head. "I rest later." She handed me a flat package wrapped in cloth. She stared at it for a moment, nodded heavily, and turned away.

"Dora?" I called after her, puzzled.

She stopped and turned. "Your mother finds this. Your mother says give it back to you." Without meeting my gaze, she turned away again. I watched her lumber off, her head bowed, her shoulders drooping. Then I looked at the package in my hands.

Carefully, I folded back the oilskin, knowing what I would find even before I saw the familiar red satin of

Katherine's journal.

Part Five

WINTER

Katherine

Chapter Fourteen

From the vantage point of Stephanie's airplane window, Mount Diablo resembled a tiny island anchored in a dazzling sea of whipped cream, its bare summit thrusting up through a thick layer of Bay Area clouds into thin December sunshine. As her plane dipped lower, the fluffy white sea abruptly swallowed them, dimming the cabin and splattering her small window with fine sprays of water.

Stephanie cupped her chin in her hand and stared out, waiting for her first glimpse of Oakland Airport. With her free hand, she fingered her gold locket nervously, tracing the engraved S at its center.

I've got to make them understand, she told herself. *I have to say it just right, so they can't say no.*

She glanced down at the magazine article lying open on her lap. Under the title "Retail Princess Turns Rembrandt," a photo showed a wall of paintings with the artist standing beside them, smiling her beautiful smile. *Tori.*

I hope she hasn't changed, Stephanie thought, as she shut the magazine and slipped it into her backpack. She swallowed hard.

Maybe they won't notice how much I have.

Inside the terminal, Stephanie spotted her father at the same moment he saw her.

"Dad!" she yelled, just as he lifted his arm to wave. She broke away from the crowd of passengers and ran to him, hardly seeing him through the sudden mist in her eyes. He gathered her into a hug, and she buried her face in the soft suede of his jacket. "Dad! Dad!"

"Hey, Stephanannie. What's this?" Her father smoothed her hair back and tried to look into her face. But she kept it buried, not wanting him to see her tears finally released, hot and sour from long weeks of captivity.

At last she pulled away and rubbed the sleeve of her sweatshirt across her face. When she opened her eyes, her gaze fell on a round swell of green silk about twelve inches from her face. She looked up into Tori's radiant face.

"Tori," she said, and carefully tucked her arms around the green swell. Ginger spice fragrance brought those tears crowding to the surface again. She felt gentle hands on her shoulders, and she screwed her eyes shut, holding the sweetness of the moment for as long as she possibly could.

* * *

The phone rang as they entered the apartment. Tori answered it and held it out to Stephanie with a knowing smile.

"It's Brett."

Stephanie took a step back and stared at the receiver as if it had teeth. She shook her head. "I can't talk now.

Tell him I'm not here." Surprise flicked over Tori's face. Before she could speak, Stephanie turned away and started dragging her suitcase down the hall. Guilty relief swept through her when she heard Tori say, "Can she call you back, Brett? We just got in."

Stephanie took a long time unpacking and putting her clothes away, remembering how she'd felt at this same task last June—angry and jealous of her father's new wife. She noted with a sheepish grin the absence of flowers in a vase to welcome her this time. The sight of her plump yellow gingham comforter recalled lazy hours of staring at the ceiling, listening to summer songs and thinking about the blueness of Brett's eyes and the way his hands felt on her waist when they skated together.

A cold fist closed around her heart.

Her father brought in her sports bag and lingered too long in the doorway. Stephanie busied herself with stacking her clothes in drawers and avoided his eyes. Finally he said, "Dinner's in about a half hour. Okay, Steph?" She nodded, and after another moment he closed the door. And those hot, sour tears began to leak from her eyes again.

* * *

"Not hungry, Stephanie?"

Stephanie looked up into Tori's worried green eyes. She tried for a smile.

"Not much. I guess it's the long flight." She pushed her fork around her plate and felt guilty because she knew Tori had gone to a lot of trouble to fix her favorite dish—lasagna with spicy Italian sausage. "Can we save the leftovers for tomorrow?"

"Of course." Tori's hand felt cool against Stephanie's forehead. "You look pale. Maybe we should cancel our outing tomorrow. I'll call Lisa and postpone it."

"No!" Stephanie glanced at her father, who was chewing his bread thoughtfully and watching her. She forced herself to sit straighter. "I'm just tired, that's all. I'll go to bed early and be fine tomorrow. Besides"—she gestured toward the living room, where a freshly cut fir tree stood, dark and lonely in its corner—"you can't leave the Christmas tree like that for long. We should at least get some lights on it."

"Well, if you're sure." Tori was still frowning. "We won't stay out long. I've been getting so tired lately. I can't go all day without resting."

The phone rang, and her father rose to answer it. He brought it back a moment later and offered it to Stephanie, his eyes twinkling. "For you, Steph."

Stephanie's stomach clenched. She took the phone and slipped from the room, escaping their curious eyes. "Hello?" Her voice was a gruff whisper.

"Hey, Steph! You don't sound any closer than you did in New York." Brett's familiar voice cut a jagged path through her body, leaving a wide tingle in its wake. "How come you're not answering your cell? I was wondering how soon we could get together and skate."

Stephanie clutched the phone tighter to her ear and shut her eyes. "I...am not feeling well, Brett. I think the plane ride made me sick. Can I call you back tomorrow?"

"Sure, if you make it a promise." He paused, and his voice dropped a fraction. "Steph? Are you okay?"

As if he could see it, Stephanie nodded. "So, I'll call

you tomorrow, okay? 'Bye."

Before he could respond, she pressed a button, and the phone light snapped off.

* * *

"Vicki, I can't believe you haven't been back to see the doctor!" The stern disapproval in Lisa's voice made Stephanie look up. "Are you telling me you haven't seen her since early *October*? That's almost three months! Does Ryan know?"

Tori lifted her chin. "I'm perfectly healthy, Lisa. Where I come from—" She stopped and started again. "Having babies is the most natural thing in the world." She glanced at Stephanie. "I don't like being poked and, well, exposed that way. I don't see a need to put myself through that again until it's time for the babies to be born."

Lisa shook her head wonderingly. "Where have you been, Vicki? Don't you know how many things can go wrong, especially with twins?" She reached a hand across the table. "If you're nervous, I'll go with you. But you've got to take care of yourself." Her frown deepened. "Think what it would do to Ryan if something happened to you or the babies."

Tori's mouth tightened, and Stephanie suddenly felt uncomfortable. She looked away from the two tense women and turned in her chair to watch the ice-skaters. Sitting in the restaurant at the top of a five-story department store, she had a perfect view of the ice-skating rink that annually materialized in the center of Union Square. She imagined skating there with Brett and afterward buying hot chocolate and sitting with him on

Judith Ingram

one of the glossy green benches, joking casually, as if she hadn't a care in the world. As if it were last summer instead of now.

"Stephanie?" Lisa's voice intruded on her thoughts. "Wouldn't it be fun to skate here with Brett?"

Stephanie turned and picked up her Coke. "I guess."

"Did you two have a fight, Steph?" Tori asked gently.

"No." She shoved back her chair. "I'm done with my lunch," she said, and made a beeline for the restroom, escaping their curious stares.

To her relief, neither woman questioned her when she returned. They left the restaurant and wandered the different floors of the department store, exclaiming over the tall Christmas tree that speared up four floors through the rotunda and displayed ornaments the size of soccer balls. They sifted through baskets of painted glass ornaments, choosing some to buy and take home to decorate the tree. Her father had never bothered to have a Christmas tree, so she and Tori had agreed to share the responsibility for putting one up.

Shopping would have been fun if Stephanie hadn't felt so numb, as if her brain were stuffed with wads of cotton. She fondled ornaments without interest and sighed with relief when Tori announced that she was tired and needed to go home. Laden with bulging bags, they trooped back to Lisa's car, and it wasn't long before they were waving good-bye to her from the front steps of the apartment building.

Chapter Fifteen

Stephanie stumbled down the hall to her room, pushed the door shut, and kicked off her shoes. Then she crawled under her comforter and tucked it close under her chin. Gray gloom from the overcast afternoon filled the window and mirrored her mood perfectly. She shut her eyes and pulled the comforter over her head.

When she awoke, her bedside lamp was glowing softly. Tori must have come in and turned it on. Stephanie yawned and lay quietly for a few minutes, struggling against the need to leave her cozy cocoon and seek companionship. Eventually she shoved the comforter aside and shuffled to the door.

The six-foot noble fir still stood dark and naked in the corner, filling the air with its spicy evergreen scent. Tori was sitting on the sofa, sipping tea and staring into space while a soprano sang an aria on the stereo.

"Stephanie." She welcomed Stephanie with a smile and held out her hand. "I was just thinking about you. Want some tea?"

Stephanie shook her head and sat down. She pulled the quilt off the sofa back and wrapped herself in it.

"You were sleeping so soundly, I didn't have the heart to wake you." Stephanie felt Tori's hand on her shoulder as she asked gently, "Do you want to talk about it, Steph?"

Stephanie found she couldn't speak. Words lay trapped inside her, like her feelings, muffled by the cotton in her brain. Tori lifted her hand and traced a finger down Stephanie's cheek. Somehow the distance between them closed. Next thing Stephanie knew, she'd buried her face in Tori's white chenille robe, and a floodgate deep inside her broke.

Tears rose on harsh sobs that burned her chest. The arms around her tightened, and the soft chenille blotted her tears until they slowed. The soprano finished her aria, and the room was silent.

Reluctantly, Stephanie pushed herself up and rubbed her sleeve over her eyes.

"Sorry," she said. Tears brimmed her eyes again. Would they ever *stop*?

Tori didn't say anything. Stephanie pulled up tissues from a box beside the sofa and blew her nose. She considered what to tell Tori and decided to start at the end.

"I want to live here with you and Dad. I don't want to go back to New York." She raised teary, hopeful eyes to Tori's face. "D'you think Dad would let me?"

Tori tilted her head and studied her. "Why the sudden decision, Stephanie?"

"It's not sudden. I've been thinking about it a lot since last summer." Stephanie attempted a smile. "I like it better here than in New York. It's fun being with you and Dad. And Lisa, too." She looked away.

"And?"

Stephanie bit her lip. "And...I could help you take

care of the babies. You'll need my help. And I want them to know me right from the beginning." She risked a glance at Tori's face.

"And?"

"And what?" Stephanie scowled. "Isn't that enough?"

She squeezed the damp tissues into a ball between her palms. Tori slipped an arm around her shoulders, and at first Stephanie resisted but soon gave in and slumped against Tori's body with a sigh. She stared at the dark boughs of the Christmas fir and imagined it alight with colors, the angel they'd purchased sitting at the top.

Stephanie began to speak but in a voice that seemed to come from outside her body.

"I won't live in that apartment anymore," she said. "I've gotten away from him, and I won't go back."

"Away from whom?"

"Clifford Baines."

There was a pause. "What did he do?"

They'd purchased a silver bell with a red satin bow on top. Stephanie scanned the tree for a good spot to hang the bell.

"Stephanie?"

The cotton thickened in her brain. Stephanie shut her eyes. She felt Tori's chin rub lightly against her forehead.

She spoke again in that strange detached voice. "He picked a Saturday when my mother wasn't home. Kristin called and asked me to go to the mall, but I said no. I wish now I'd gone with her." Stephanie began to tremble. For the first time since it happened, she allowed herself to remember that afternoon clearly. "I didn't think he'd go that far. I mean, he'd made jokes before, even in front of my mother. But I didn't think...he seemed so huge, and I couldn't move. I couldn't scream." She swallowed. "Then he laughed. He *laughed* at me." She turned her face into the soft chenille and sobbed. "I should've gone. I should've gone to the mall with Kristin."

"Oh, Stephanie." Tori tightened her arms around her. "It wasn't your fault, darling. You couldn't have stopped him. It was your mother's job to protect you, not yours." Stephanie felt the kiss Tori planted on the top of her head. "Don't worry about going back to New York. I won't let you. I'll talk to your dad as soon as he gets home."

Stephanie pushed suddenly upright. "But you won't *tell* him, will you? I mean"—she licked her lips—"he doesn't have to know the real reason I want to stay with you. Okay?"

Tori frowned. "Of course he has to know, Stephanie. Don't you think he has a right to know?"

Stephanie pulled farther back. "I don't want you to tell him!" Her voice rose. "What will he think of me? How could I ever let him *look* at me again if he *knows* about me?"

Tori reached for her, but Stephanie pushed her away. "No!"

Tori gave an impatient cry and pushed herself up from the sofa. She stood tall, hands on her hips, eyes flaming like an avenging angel. Stephanie gaped at her.

"There is nothing wrong with you, Stephanie! The

ugliness is in that brute who touched you, not in you."
She leaned closer. "You have *nothing* to be ashamed of.
Do you hear me?" She waited, but Stephanie couldn't
speak. *"Do you believe me, Stephanie?"*

Stephanie's eyes filled, and she looked away. After a
moment, Tori sat beside her and took her hands, not
ungently. "Look at me, Stephanie."

"Please don't make me tell Dad," Stephanie
whispered. Tears spilled over the hot patches on her
cheeks. "Please, Tori."

Tori squeezed her hands. "I won't make you do
anything. But, honey, if you want to stay here with us,
your father has to know the truth." She spoke tenderly.
"He loves you, Stephanie. Don't you think he'd want to
know that someone has hurt you so terribly? And,
besides, surely your mother will tell him—" She stopped
at Stephanie's look. "You haven't told your mother."
Stephanie swallowed and dropped her gaze. "You
haven't told anyone except me?" Stephanie shook her
head. "Don't you think your mother ought to know?"

"She won't believe me."

"Maybe she will. Even if she doesn't, that's no reason
not to tell her." Her voice hardened. "Stephanie, you
have no obligation to protect this man."

"I'm not—" Stephanie broke off and bit her lip. She
stared at their hands, at her fingers laced tightly with
Tori's.

At length Tori spoke again. "Tell your dad,
Stephanie. He loves you and only wants what's best for
you. He can protect you." Her voice shook a little. "Don't
let what this man did eat a hole in your soul. Don't give

him that kind of power over you."

Stephanie heard pain and concern in Tori's voice. She took a steadying breath and looked up. "How about if I make you a deal?" she said. "I'll tell Dad what happened to me if you'll ask him to take you back to the doctor." She stuck out her chin as Tori drew back and tried to withdraw her hands.

"Stephanie, that has nothing to do with—"

Stephanie held on firmly. "Deal or not?" she said. "Dad loves us and only wants what's best for us. You said it yourself."

Annoyance flicked across Tori's face. "Of all the sneaky, underhanded—" She blew out a breath. "All right. I'll ask him tomorrow, when he gets back from his trip." She gave Stephanie a long look. "So we have a deal?"

"We have a deal." Stephanie nodded and tried to smile, but her mouth trembled. At least, she noted with relief, the cotton in her brain was gone.

* * *

Ryan stared in horror at his daughter's pinched face. He looked up at his wife, who sat behind Stephanie, holding his daughter tightly. Her face was a stony mask except for the angry fire in her eyes.

"My God, Stephanie." Ryan spread his hands helplessly. "How—What—"

Tears brimmed his daughter's eyes, and she shrank closer to his wife. Ryan realized that shock must be showing on his face, alarming her. He shook himself inwardly.

"Why hasn't your mother kicked him out?" he said.

"Why hasn't she gone to the police?"

Stephanie looked at him with helpless eyes.

"Gina doesn't know, Ryan," his wife said. "No one knows except us. And, of course, Gina's husband."

Ryan leaped off the sofa and paced the room. He turned to face his daughter. "Why didn't you call me, Stephanie?" His voice shook. "I would have gotten you out of there right away. In all these weeks, he could have—"

Ryan broke off as the horror crashed over him again. "I'll kill him," he muttered. He struck out across the room, heading for the phone. "Slimy bastard; I'll *kill* him!"

His wife's cry of "Ryan!" was drowned out by his daughter's shriek: "Dad! *Don't!*" Stephanie leaped off the sofa and ran to catch her father's arm. "Don't call them yet! Please, Dad! *Dad!*"

Ryan stopped and looked down. Through a white haze of fury, he saw his daughter's stricken face, and she suddenly looked so small, so vulnerable. Such an easy target for a man without scruples.

"Oh, baby." He gathered her into his arms and bent his head over her. "I'm sorry, baby. I'm so sorry I wasn't there to protect you. I should have been there, I shouldn't have let them, let your mother—"

In the agony of his guilt, he held her tighter, feeling the shudders of her slender body echoing his own. *I should have asked for custody last summer,* he thought, *when I knew it was the right thing to do. If I had kept her here, she never would have…he never could have…*

A harsh sob racked his chest beneath his daughter's

dark head.

"Ryan." His wife spoke softly beside him and circled his waist with her arm. He opened his eyes to a film of tears and blinked. "Darling, come sit down. Both of you."

Like a child, he let her lead them to the sofa. Stephanie still clung to him, and they sat for some time in silence. Ryan held his daughter tightly while his wife sat on her other side, a little apart from them. When Stephanie stirred against him, he looked down at her.

"I'm sorry I flew off the handle like that, Stephanie. I didn't mean to frighten you." When she started to speak, he shook his head firmly. "I wasn't thinking about anything except how I'd let you down, how I wasn't there to protect you. I love you so much, baby. I can't stand the idea of someone hurting you like this." He smoothed her hair and looked into her eyes so like Gina's that his heart lurched in a painful, angry twist.

"I want you to stay here, Stephanie. I want you to live with us. Permanently." Her face brightened with joy, and his grip on her shoulders involuntarily tightened. "The first thing I'll do is call my lawyer to see what needs to be done. What Baines did to you was not only outrageous but legally criminal." His voice hardened. "That animal should be in jail." He bit back the rest of his thought—*and I'd like to see your so-called mother in there with him.* But he kept his anger at bay, for Stephanie's sake, and tried for a light smile. "Is that okay with you, Steph?"

Her eyes clouded before she hid her face against his chest. In a tiny voice she said, "Will you tell Mom for me?"

Ryan smoothed her sleek head, and he saw his hand was trembling.

"Yes, if that's what you want. You don't have to speak to either of them if you don't want to."

He felt her body shudder before she nodded her head.

"Okay. You can call your lawyer." It was only a whisper, but Ryan heard the relief and the weariness in it. She sighed and snuggled closer and was still for a long time.

Over his daughter's head, Ryan looked at his wife. Tears had spilled over her cheeks, and he saw wistfulness in her smile as she watched them. Love and sympathy swam in her eyes, along with a sadness that made her seem somehow very young.

* * *

"It went right to my heart, Francine, watching the two of them together. And it may sound strange, but as Ryan comforted Stephanie, I felt the young girl in me being comforted as well. Like the wet leaves Dora used to put on my cuts to take the sting out of them. Watching Ryan and Stephanie together took the sting out of what happened to me." She shook her head. "I don't understand why, but suddenly what my father did to me wasn't as important as it used to be. Not that it doesn't matter, but it doesn't seem as big or as powerful as it was."

Francine spoke gently. "You're telling me you've moved beyond the pain, Tori. You're realizing there's a lot more to you than just being the victim of your father's cruelty."

Her patient nodded slowly. "I guess that's it." She was silent for a long moment. "But there's something I don't understand. Why did Stephanie have to be hurt like this? I mean, what are the chances that what happened to me would happen to her, too? Especially after so many years, when society should be moving forward, improving…"

She trailed off, her eyes angry and confused.

Francine sighed. "I wish I could say that we've progressed. But the sad truth is that our children are as vulnerable as you were to the cruelty of adults. The chances are high — one in four — that a girl like Stephanie will be sexually mistreated, and even worse given her age and living with a new stepfather."

Seeing the other woman's horror, Francine leaned forward. "But Stephanie is lucky because she has you and her father to listen to her story and believe her. You never had that advantage. Because of you and Ryan, Stephanie has a good chance of escaping the self-hate and destructive behaviors that kept you a prisoner of the molest for so many years." She added softly, "Having been a victim yourself, you have gifts that can help Stephanie heal."

Her patient's eyes misted. "I thought I'd been sent here to help Ryan build his resort. Perhaps —" She swallowed. "This might be another reason." Her eyes looked bleak. "If only Stephanie didn't have to go through what I went through. I spent years hating myself, being with all those boys —" She lowered her voice. "I've done some terrible things, Francine. Things I've never told you."

"Listen to me, Tori," Francine said firmly. "When a young girl believes the molestation is her fault, and there is no adult to tell her otherwise, like you told Stephanie, then that girl might respond in one of two ways. She can cut herself off from feeling pleasure in her body and try to earn love by being a 'good girl.' Or she can use her body in sexual ways to try to get the love she needs. Her sexuality becomes a weapon, do you see? She uses it to hurt herself, over and over again—"

"Like I did." Her patient interrupted her. "Oh, yes, I see. All those times with different boys just to reinforce my belief that I was bad, that the good half died—" An unexpected sob erupted. "I never told you, Francine, how I killed my brother. Out of jealousy, out of spite. I killed my twin."

She looked away from Francine and fixed her gaze on a small patch of December sunlight slanting in through the window.

"Nicholas was my parents' favorite. My mother doted on him from the moment he was born. She loved him so much there was never enough for me. My father didn't love either one of us. But Nicholas was his heir." Her voice tightened. "I could never make them see that *I* was the strong one. Of the two of us, *I* was the one who took risks, who could make plans and carry them out. *I* was the one who should have inherited. Nicholas didn't even like horses; he was afraid of them."

She looked up, and Francine recognized Katherine's old glint of resentment. "But *I* wasn't afraid of horses. I wasn't afraid of anything." She suddenly laughed. "Once, when I was nine, my cousin Michael and I rode up to the old haunted caves at Golden Springs Ridge, where Ryan is building his resort now. Michael was three years older than I, and he dared me to stay all night in the caves with him. I surprised him and said I would. But the darker it got, the more scared Michael got, and he wanted to go home. I wouldn't budge. He went back to the ranch and got Uncle Leon, and together they forced me to leave. I would have stayed all night, and Michael knew it. He never dared me to do anything again."

She tossed her head. "I deserved Papa's attention more than Nicholas because I had the qualities he respected. I could ride as well as any hand on the ranch, only my father refused to see it. So I planned for Nicholas's horse to throw him, not to hurt him but just to show Papa that he should be proud of me instead of his son." Her eyes darkened with pain. "God forgive me," she whispered. "When they carried my brother's body out of the woods, and I realized what I had done —" She shuddered and crossed herself.

Both Francine and her patient stared in silence at the tiny patch of sunlight. It had inched across the carpet and was nearly touching the younger woman's shoes. "What had you done?" Francine asked.

"Dora once told me you could control an animal's behavior by putting a spell on its food. So I put a spell on Spitfire's food. He was very spirited. I knew Nicholas was already afraid of him, and it wouldn't take much to throw him. I think Papa chose Spitfire for the hunt because he wanted to make a man out of Nicholas. But Papa didn't mean for my brother to die any more than I did."

Francine spoke gently. "If Stephanie came to you and told you she had caused the death of a friend by putting a spell on her tuna sandwich, what would you say to her?"

Her patient looked up, her eyes filled with misery and a hint of confusion.

"I'd probably tell her it wasn't possible."

"Why isn't it possible?"

"Because you can't do things like that—now."

"What's the difference between then and now?" Her patient didn't answer. "Maybe the difference is that 'then' belongs to a young girl—starved for love, jealous of her brother, feeling guilty when he died but she lived—and 'now' belongs to a mature woman who understands that jealous thoughts and anger don't kill people, that accidents happen, and they are nobody's fault." Francine tilted her head. "Maybe that's why you'd have more compassion for Stephanie than you've had for twelve-year-old Katherine. Your brother's death was tragic, but it wasn't your fault. And there's no reason to feel guilty because you were the twin who survived. It's good to survive, Tori. It's good, not bad, to enjoy being alive and healthy and strong."

"But I thought—" It was hardly a whisper, and Francine had to lean closer to hear. "I thought what my father did to me was my punishment for being alive. He was so angry that it was Nicholas who died and not me." Tears welled up and spilled over her pale cheeks.

"Oh, my dear." Francine quickly crossed to the sofa and cradled her trembling patient. "If your father believed that you should have died instead of Nicholas, then that was his own sickness and selfishness, and it wasn't right. Don't blame yourself for his inability to love you. You are a lovely, caring, infinitely precious young woman. Look how Ryan loves you, how important you are to Stephanie and your mother. And I feel great affection for you, Tori. I admire your determination to become the best person you can be. If your father couldn't see those qualities in you, then all I can say is he was blind and incredibly foolish!"

Her patient clung to her and was silent for some minutes.

"Thank you, Francine," she said at last. "Thank you for giving me back myself."

Francine shook her head as she pulled up several tissues and passed them to her patient. "Don't thank me," she said. "It's your doing. I only helped you find what you've had inside you all along."

Chapter Sixteen

"Mr. Ashton?" Ryan looked up at the nurse beckoning him across the waiting room. "Dr. Walker wants to see you in her office. Your wife is already there."

She led him down a narrow hallway into the obstetrician's private office. Dr. Susan Walker rose to shake hands with Ryan across her desk before he took a seat beside his wife. His polite smile died on his lips, however, when he saw his wife's face.

"Tori?" He reached for her hand. She lifted her eyes to his, unable to speak, and Ryan felt his stomach lurch. He shot Dr. Walker a hard look.

The doctor spoke with practiced calm. "We have some good news and some not-so-good news for you, Ryan." His wife's hand was trembling, and he tightened his grip on her. "The good news is Victoria is carrying a strong, healthy baby with no signs of any problem."

Ryan raised his scarred eyebrow. "A strong baby?"

The doctor nodded. "The other twin has been lost. I'm so sorry."

The words hit him like a fist in the stomach. "How — What happened?"

Dr. Walker lifted a shoulder. "We don't know. I suspect the other baby was lost several weeks ago, during the first trimester. That's when most vanishing twins are lost."

"'Vanishing twins'?"

"That's a name we've given the phenomenon of a multiple pregnancy spontaneously becoming a singleton. It's not as uncommon as you might think. With the advent of ultrasound, we can detect a twin pregnancy very early. But studies show that given the early detection of twins, only half of those pregnancies result in live twin births. That means that, in roughly half the cases, one twin just doesn't make it."

"Does it mean that one twin dies so the other can live?" His wife's voice sounded small and lost. Ryan rubbed her fingers, but she hardly seemed aware of him.

"No, it's nothing like that. In a spontaneous abortion like this, it usually means there was something very wrong with the fetus that nature couldn't correct. Even if it survived to term, it couldn't live outside the mother's body. In practical terms, its little life never really got started."

They sat in silence for a moment, absorbing the information. "What happened to the other baby?" Ryan asked quietly.

"Probably just resorbed into the mother's body. There's usually vaginal bleeding at the time but not always. There may have been no physical signs at all that something was wrong."

"If I had come back sooner—" His wife's voice shook so violently that Ryan put his arm around her and pulled her close. "If I hadn't waited so long to see you—" Her words seemed to die in her throat.

Dr. Walker came around her desk and sat on the corner of it. "There is nothing anyone could have done," she said firmly. "This baby would not have survived, no matter what you did. I don't want you blaming yourself." She leaned back and crossed her hands on her lap. "I've ordered blood work, just to make sure you and your baby are perfectly okay. And I want you to come back on a regular schedule from now on, so I can keep an eye on you both. All right?"

Tori's head was bowed, so Ryan met the doctor's gaze. "I'll see to it," he said.

Dr. Walker nodded and stood. "Do either of you have any more questions?" Ryan stared at her, his eyelids suddenly pricking as the realization that one of their babies was gone hit him afresh. He tightened his arm around his wife and shook his head. Tori was silent, her head still bowed. The doctor touched her shoulder in sympathy. "I'm sorry," she said again, her voice gentle. "Even as early as this, it's so very painful to lose a child."

* * *

It was her soft whimpering that woke him. Vague dream images tangled with reality as Ryan tried to open his eyes. He'd almost given up and drifted back into the dream when a high scream shot daggers through his body and jerked him upright in bed.

"Tori! Tori, what is it?" He grasped his wife's shoulders and tried to see her face through the darkness. Her body writhed under his hands, and she whimpered again.

"Darling, wake up. You're dreaming." Her hair was damp as he lifted her head and rested it against him. She jerked once, violently, and then slipped her arms around his neck.

"Oh, Ryan!" Her body shook with sobs. Ryan held her close until the sobs quieted, and she slumped against him. Gently he laid her back down and propped himself on an elbow, stroking her arms, kissing her fingers.

"Darling, what was it? Can you remember?"

She covered her face with her hands. "I was running through a dark forest. I had left my babies alone, and I had to get back to them. At first I couldn't remember where they were, and I was frantic." She drew her hands away from her face, and Ryan caught the gleam of her wet eyes as she stared up into the dark.

"Then I found the place. But there was only one of them left, Ryan. Only one baby shivering with cold, just where I'd left it. Its twin was gone. There was a hollow place in the grass where its little body had lain."

Ryan sucked in a breath but said nothing.

"There was a crashing noise in the forest. I barely had time to turn before it came rushing out of the trees." She clutched Ryan's arm, her fingers digging into his flesh, and her voice became shrill. "It was a bear, Ryan! A great, ugly brute with claws and fangs. It was so big; it all happened so fast—"

She covered her mouth to stifle another scream. Ryan turned her into him and cradled her while she sobbed against his chest. He reached over her and switched on the bedside lamp, squinting against the painful stab of light.

"No monsters now, darling," he whispered, kissing the top of her head and smoothing her hair. She lay back on the pillow and stared up at him with wide, swimming eyes.

"Ryan, I feel so awful," she whispered.

He bent and kissed her forehead, her cheeks. "I know, darling. I know."

"No, I mean I'm sorry for losing the baby. I'm sorry for what it means to you."

He shook his head and laid a finger on her lips. "You don't have to apologize to me. It wasn't your fault. You heard the doctor. There was nothing anyone could have done." He lifted her fingers to his lips. "You mustn't blame yourself."

Her fingers lingered on his mouth and then moved up to brush his cheek. She traced the little scar in his eyebrow. "I never wanted to hurt you, Ryan. I wanted so much to give you these children before we, before I—" She bit her lip, and her eyes filled.

"Don't say it," he ordered. "You're not going anywhere. Do you hear me? I'm not going to lose you, Tori Ashton. Not now, not ever. We're going to have this baby, this healthy, strong baby growing inside you. And we're going to live a long, happy life together, the three of us."

Ryan saw the doubt in her eyes. He framed her face with his hands, and his voice became urgent.

"Don't be afraid of that bear. Next time he shows up, you tell him he can't have you or the baby. Better yet, call me, and we'll fight him off together." He tried for a lighthearted grin, but he couldn't shape his mouth into anything but a fierce frown. "I swear I would do anything—*anything*—to keep you here with me. If the strength of my love can hold you here, then I promise you, my darling, we'll be together. Tell me you believe it, Tori."

She nodded. "I believe it, Ryan. I believe that love is stronger than anything." She suddenly wrapped her arms around his neck and pressed her forehead against his cheek. "Oh, God, I don't want to leave you, Ryan! I don't want to leave you or our child!"

Ryan pulled away and stared at her in the merciless glare of the lamp. With both hands he pushed her back against the pillow and clamped his mouth over hers, crushing her with his pain, his need, his love until they were both shaking.

"Then don't," he said fiercely. "Fight to stay, Tori. Use everything you've got, but fight it!" He kissed her again, this time a slow, aching kiss that brought tears to his eyes and words to whisper against her lips, "I don't want to live in a world without you."

Chapter Seventeen

Christine sat at her mother's bedside, listening to the Christmas carols playing in someone's room down the hall. She lifted the paper cup of cold coffee to her lips, thought better of it, and set the cup aside with a sigh. She glanced at her watch and caught herself wondering, as she often did, what good it was doing to come here every afternoon.

She watched idly as the physical therapist lifted one leg and then the other, stroking and bending Eleanor's joints while she lay impassive and seemingly unaware, or uninterested, in these efforts being made on her behalf.

"Not very cooperative, is she?" Christine raised her eyes to the young man's pleasant, round face.

"Well, now." He flashed her a smile of hopelessly crooked teeth. "Since I don't know what's going on inside that head of hers, I figure maybe she's doing the best she can." He eased one spindly leg down and began to gently bend and rotate the ankle. "Strokes do funny things to people's minds, you know. Folks can get pretty confused and scared. Just imagine waking up and finding you can't control your own body. Been known to change the personality. A person who was sweet and outgoing may turn into a kind of recluse who just wants to be left alone." He shrugged as he wiggled in succession the toes of Eleanor's foot. "My job is to keep her going, so if she does snap out of this, she'll have a good start on regaining some use of her limbs."

Christine nodded, wondering why compassion for her own mother came so hard. She changed the subject. "Do you mind working on Christmas Eve?"

The young man finished with Eleanor's foot and pulled the covers over her small body. "No. I've got tomorrow off and big plans for tonight." He picked up his clipboard and entered some data. "How about you?"

"I'm having dinner with my fiancé tonight and with my daughter's family tomorrow." Christine felt a twinge at the idea of a family Christmas without her mother. "My daughter is pregnant with her first child." She felt another twinge, remembering Victoria's broken voice on the phone telling her about the lost twin.

"Sounds like it'll be a good one." The young man grinned amiably and extended a hand. "Take care, now. Merry Christmas."

"Merry Christmas." Christine echoed the words mechanically as she rose and took his hand. She watched him disappear into the corridor. Then she looked down at Eleanor's sagging face and felt mild distress because the sight no longer aroused her pity.

"Well, Mother," she said cheerfully. "That's over for today. Now you can rest." The old lady's good eye stared past her, her expression giving no indication that she was even aware of her daughter's presence.

Christine sighed. "I have some bad news, Mother. I spoke to Victoria this morning." She watched her mother's face closely. "She lost one of the babies. A miscarriage of some kind." Was that a flicker in the staring green eye? "But the doctor says the other baby is fine, and she anticipates no complications with the birth. Victoria was pretty broken up about it. You can imagine." The eye drifted, seeming to follow the line of ceiling toward the near corner.

"We're having Christmas dinner at her apartment. Ryan's daughter is there. You remember Stephanie, don't you? Dan is coming with me." *You're such a coward, Christine. Why haven't you told her that you and Dan are getting married?* "I gave Agnes the day off. I think this might be her first Christmas off since I've known her." She paused again, watching for a response. "It will seem strange without you, Mother. But I'll come and see you tomorrow morning before we go to Victoria's."

Christine bit her lip. "I've got to go now, Mother. I'm having dinner with Dan tonight, and I need to go home and get ready." She took a breath and added, "Dan's a good man, Mother. I…like him. A lot."

Her mother's eye seemed fixed on the ceiling corner. *Does she even know I'm here?*

Christine bent down and pecked her dry cheek.

"I'll see you tomorrow, Mother." She added a faint "Merry Christmas" before she hurried away.

* * *

Adrian's was always crowded. Tonight, however, the restaurant was a moving sea of glamorously clad guests and white-coated waiters who scurried among the Christmas Eve revelers with long-necked bottles and corkscrews and silver trays balanced deftly above their heads. Dan surrendered Christine's coat to the cloakroom attendant, and they followed the slender, red-lamé-clad figure of their hostess through a labyrinth of white tablecloths, through open French doors onto an outdoor patio. The night was cold, but tall heaters kept the intimate area pleasant, and Dan was pleased to find himself quite comfortable in his sports jacket. He was even more pleased when the hostess led them to a table tucked away in a corner, nestled between a gurgling fountain and a half-barrel tub spilling pink and red impatiens onto the seasoned brick paving.

He chose his entree quickly from the menu and then glanced around the patio, noting the strings of Christmas lights draping the air above them like colorful electric clotheslines. Candle flames flickered softly inside crystal hurricane lamps on each table. Across from him, Christine was studying her menu. Dan's gaze traveled down to the soft curve of her breasts filling out the clinging cashmere of her bodice. The long, tastefully beaded gown was new and decidedly more daring than anything she'd ever worn: a deep, sweeping neckline revealed more bosom than Eleanor would have approved, and the flowing lines followed her long, slender body like a caress.

A waiter materialized at their table, memorized their dinner orders, and promised to bring the wine immediately. As Christine handed up her menu, she caught Dan's gaze on her and smiled.

"You look stunning, Christine." Dan's voice scraped over an unexpected huskiness that brought color to her cheeks. "You quite take my breath away." His gaze strayed again to the creamy swell of bosom heaving softly with her quickened breath. With an effort, he raised his gaze to her face and grinned. "If you're trying to weaken my resolve, you've made an excellent start."

Her laughter bubbled up, light and happy. "I'm glad you approve the dress, Dan."

His grin softened, and he reached for her hand across the table. "It's the woman in the dress who's got my heart pounding."

Christine laid her hand in his, and the clasp of her fingers sent a current of warmth up his arm and neck. They sat with clasped hands, smiling love into each other's eyes until the waiter reappeared and coughed discreetly. Dan looked up, and the waiter held out the wine bottle, label up, for his approval.

Dan nodded and squeezed Christine's hand lightly before he let it go. He sat back and watched the waiter expertly pop the cork, pour out a sample for his approval, and then fill their glasses. When the waiter turned away, Dan lifted his wineglass to propose a toast. His gaze met Christine's, however, and his smile faltered at the sheer intensity of the love in her eyes. Her lips were moist and parted in a trembling smile, the swell of her breasts pumping noticeably on her light, quick breath.

A wave of desire shocked through his body. For a blinding moment, all he could think about was spiriting her into a private corner and grinding his mouth against those trembling lips in a wild, possessive kiss. No, that wouldn't be enough. He longed to make her his own in every way that mattered, in every way *possible*...

"Christine." His voice, hoarse with desire,

embarrassed him. Sweat pricked along his flesh, and it was on the tip of his tongue to sweep aside his chivalrous intentions and to ask her—*beg* her—to come home and share his bed with him tonight. The sheer magnitude of his lust stunned him. His hand shook, slopping wine up the sides of his glass, nearly spilling it. Clumsily, he set the glass down.

"Dan?" Christine leaned toward him, unintentionally exposing more of her cleavage. "Are you all right?"

He stared at her and gave a weak laugh. "Actually, no." He raised her hand to his lips, torturing himself with a quick inhale of her perfume. "I feel quite intoxicated. So much so that I would like to suggest a change of plans for tonight." She waited, and he took a shaky breath. "I had planned to take you back to my house after dinner. But, under the circumstances, I think it's best if we avoid my house entirely tonight." At her look of bewilderment, he drew a small velvet box from his pocket. "I was going to give you this later tonight, in front of a fire, sipping champagne. But I think now is the right time." Turning her hand over, he placed the box carefully on her palm and closed her fingers over it. "Merry Christmas, Christine."

Christine stared at the small cube of black velvet. "Oh, Dan," she whispered. Eyes shining, she felt for the soft seam and pushed back the lid. A brilliant square-cut solitaire winked at her, bringing on a gasp of wonder and delight. She looked up at him, smiling the lovely smile her daughter had inherited, and lifted out the ring. "It's perfect," she said, turning it slowly so that the light caught on its facets. "You have exquisite taste, Dan."

"Well, we certainly agree on that point." He grinned at her, rewarded by her quick flush of pleasure. "And now," he said, reaching for her left hand, "if I may." Solemnly, he slipped the ring on her finger. "Our bargain is sealed, my love. All that's left is to set the date."

Christine touched the diamond reverently. "Let it be soon, Dan," she said. "I've spent my whole life waiting for this, waiting for you." She raised glistening eyes to his. "I don't want to wait any longer."

He recognized the ache of his own longing mirrored in her tender look. His grip on her hand tightened. "My thoughts exactly, Christine," he said.

* * *

"Ryan gave her a beautiful ring, a blue emerald with two small diamonds on either side. Victoria wore it on her left hand in place of her wedding ring. I wondered about that."

Christine glanced over at her mother, and she realized she was thinking out loud. She'd begun doing that more and more, just rambling on in Eleanor's presence, as if she were talking to herself. Like the other day when, out of the blue, she'd started talking about her father. She told her mother all about her recent memory of Matthew taking her and Luke to the park on Saturdays, letting them feed the ducks and treating them to ice creams. She fancied she saw subtle responses in her mother—the flicker of an eyelid, a twitch of lips, a moistness in her eye—but she could never be certain. For the first time in her life, Christine could say anything she liked, anything at all, without fearing her mother's stern look, those biting words, the threat of reprisal when she least expected it. Sometimes Christine left the hospital feeling lighter, as if she'd just spent an hour talking with a therapist.

"They gave Stephanie a new computer for her room. She's living with them now, did I tell you? Some misunderstanding with her mother, I gather. Victoria wouldn't give me the particulars. But she's a sweet girl. Actually, I'm glad. Victoria can use her help when the twins—" She caught herself and furrowed her brow. "I mean, when the baby is born." She sighed heavily. "Victoria looked tired and pale. Ryan was very attentive to her. When I heard the news, I offered to cook Christmas dinner at Dan's house, but Ryan insisted they could manage. He and Stephanie really pitched in. The meal was lovely." She looked out the window. "Victoria gave Ryan a wonderful gift—a painting she'd done of Stephanie."

She threw a defiant glance at the still figure in the bed. "I told you Victoria was unhappy in her modeling job. Now it seems she's finding her niche as an artist, I can't get over how talented she is. This painting she did of Stephanie was in that new style of hers—a center portrait surrounded by little cameo sketches done in charcoal. She said she worked from baby pictures Ryan had of Stephanie. Ryan was quite touched; I believe he's planning to hang it in the living room, in place of that ugly mirror you gave them." *That was nasty, Christine.* "Victoria signs her paintings with the name 'Tori Ashton.' Ryan and Stephanie have taken to calling her Tori. It seems odd to me." She shrugged. "Victoria told me she's sold four paintings at that new gallery on Polk Street. Imagine that." She narrowed her gaze at her mother. "I'm sure you must be as proud and happy for her as I am, Mother."

Eleanor's sagging features showed no response. Christine walked to the window and stared out at the gray afternoon. "I have more news, Mother." Her heart began to pound foolishly. "Victoria wasn't the only one who got a ring for Christmas. Dan and I—" She faltered. Then she lifted her hand and touched the diamond to restore her confidence. "He gave me a ring, Mother. An engagement ring. Dan and I are going to be married on January sixteenth, the anniversary of our first date." She smiled to herself, remembering the happy faces and Victoria's warm hug when she and Dan shared their plans for the wedding. "It will be a simple ceremony, just family and a few close friends. We don't want any fuss. We just want to be together." She stared out at the gloomy day but didn't see it because she was picturing Dan's face. "I love him very much, Mother. He's kind, and he's thoughtful. Gentle, even when he's being strong. There isn't a cruel bone in his body. And he loves me, Mother. He really, truly loves me." She gazed at her diamond. "The ring is beautiful, Mother. Here, I'll show it to you."

She turned from the window and eagerly held out her hand. But her mother's good eye was closed, and her mouth was slack. Christine choked on disappointment edged with anger. Was her mother really asleep, or did she close her eye deliberately just to deny Christine a response to her happy news?

It doesn't matter, Christine told herself. *I don't need her approval.*

No, but you want her to be happy for you. Before she dies, you'd like to believe she cares about you.

I don't need it. I have Dan to care for me, and Victoria. I'm starting a new life.

Yes, but it would be nice to know your mother loves you.

I don't need it.

That's true. But still, it would be nice to know.

* * *

The phone call came two weeks later on a rainy January night. Christine was yawning in the library and thinking about going to bed when Agnes appeared, carrying the phone.

"It's the hospital, Mrs. Reeves."

Christine gave Agnes's face a quick search before taking the phone.

"Christine." It was that young Doctor Nsouli. "Your mother had another stroke about twenty minutes ago. It's best if you come to the hospital. Her condition is not good."

"Yes." Christine felt surprisingly calm. "Yes, I'll be right down. Thank you for calling."

She clicked off the phone and looked up. A nod of her head answered the speculation in Agnes's eyes. "Mother's had another stroke, Agnes. I'm going to the hospital right away."

Agnes bowed her head. "I'm sorry, Mrs. Reeves."

Christine rose and, on impulse, surprised the older woman by giving her a fierce hug. "I've known you for most of my life, Agnes. I think it's about time you started calling me Christine."

She felt Agnes pull away, and she let her go. The housekeeper's faded brown eyes looked directly into hers. "Yes, ma'am." Agnes took the phone and left without another word.

Christine called Dan, and he agreed to meet her at the hospital. As she traveled the now-familiar route and pulled into the hospital parking lot, she wondered at her lack of emotion. *Well, why not? I've been expecting this.*

But shouldn't I be feeling something?

Her mother had been moved back into the intensive care unit. Christine walked into bright lights and a host of machines beeping and flickering around her mother's bed. A nurse was adjusting a blood-pressure cuff on Eleanor's bony arm, and she looked up as Christine walked in.

"Mrs. Reeves?" she asked, and Christine nodded. "Dr. Nsouli said to tell you he'll be in very shortly. He'll answer your questions for you."

Christine nodded, knowing it was useless trying to get information out of her. Hospital rules were such a pain. Ignoring the nurse, she walked up to her mother's side.

"Mother?" Eleanor's skin had a gray tinge to it, and her eyes, even the bad one, were closed. Her mouth was slack, sucking in faint, quick gasps of breath.

"Oh!" The emotion came late but in full force. Christine seized her mother's hand and pressed it against her heart. "Mother, darling, it's Christine. Mother, can you hear me?"

The nurse left. Knowing she was defying hospital

policy, Christine sat on her mother's bed, still clutching her mother's limp hand. She glanced at the heart monitor and, untrained though she was, recognized the irregularity of the beeping trail. She knew she had very little time to say what needed to be said.

"Mother." She sandwiched her mother's hand between her own and spoke close to her face. "I know we've quarreled often, and you've been disappointed in me. I'm sorry for that. I'm sorry we were never close. I'm sorry you lost Luke, and I know you blamed me for that. You punished me for years, Mother, for years. And that wasn't right. I think I've been angry at you my whole life."

She lifted the frail hand to her cheek as she continued. "But I always loved you, Mother. I wanted to please you, but I didn't know how. Please forgive me for the times I was unkind, when I was rude and selfish and hurtful. I was so hurt, you see, because I knew you didn't love me."

She leaned close and spoke in a strong voice.

"I want you to know, Mother, that I forgive you. I know now it wasn't in you to love me, that part of you died when we buried Luke. I want you to know it's all right now. I've made my peace with it. I love you, Mother. And I forgive you." Then, desperately, "Mother! Can you hear me?"

Miraculously, the hand within her own began to move. Christine pulled it away from her face and stared in amazement as the gnarled fingers twitched and flexed. A sound brought Christine's gaze back to her mother's face, and she gasped to see her green eye open and looking directly at her. Her dry lips moved; Eleanor was trying to speak.

"Yes, Mother? What is it?" Christine bent toward her mother's face, trying to catch the words. The green eye still stared at her and was moistening, whether from emotion or the effort of trying to speak, Christine couldn't tell. At last the old woman managed a rasping string of unintelligible sounds. Frantic to understand, Christine held her mother's face between her hands and leaned close.

"Say it again, Mother. I couldn't understand." The wrinkled eyelid closed briefly, wearily. Then the green eye fixed on her again. Christine felt her mother's body strain to push out her words.

"Why not you...dead...not my boy. Hate you...selfish, useless...*hate you* —"

Her open eye, fixed on Christine, flared. Then the shrill warning of the heart monitor brought a team running. Christine backed away from the bed, the cold, dead eye of her mother still seemingly fixed on her. Loving arms wrapped Christine from behind, but she hardly felt them, couldn't pull her gaze away from the grip of her mother's stare. She stood, frozen, and watched the team make efforts to restore her mother's heartbeat, but it was no use. Dr. Nsouli shut the hideous eye and turned to Christine. He spread his hands apologetically.

"I am so sorry," he said, in his perfect English. "I am afraid your mother is gone."

Christine stared at him. Dr. Nsouli glanced behind her, and she suddenly felt the arms holding her tightly.

Turning, she looked straight into Dan's face, seeing his eyes dark with sympathy and his mouth a frown of concern.

Her frozen shock gave way to an unexpected howl. Horrified, Christine clamped her hands over her mouth but couldn't stop the awful sounds. Her legs wobbled, and Dan gripped her to keep her from falling. He half led, half carried her to a quiet corner and eased her gently onto a chair. Then he pulled up another chair for himself and leaned toward her, folding her against him. He didn't speak but stroked her head and her back until she pulled away enough to see his face.

"How long were you—" She gulped and couldn't continue.

"Long enough," he said grimly. He lifted a hand and cradled her cheek. "You didn't deserve that, darling. It was monstrous of her. Cruel."

Christine nodded, and a small sound strangled in her throat. Dan pulled her close and spoke against her hair.

"She's gone now, Christine. You heard the doctor say it. It's finished. She can't hurt you anymore." Christine began to cry, softly. "The pain of all those years—it's over now. I heard you let go of it. You forgave her, Christine. It was the bravest thing I've ever seen. All the ugliness of those years belongs to her now. You're free of it. You're washed clean." He kissed the top of her head. "I'm so proud of you."

* * *

Dan might claim that her mother could no longer hurt her. It seemed to Christine, however, that the old lady was still giving it a good try.

The family sat in the library, wearing their dark funeral clothes and sipping coffee in restrained silence. Ryan's arm was fixed firmly around his wife; Dan and Christine sat on the sofa across from them. Maureen Walters, Eleanor's personal attorney and old friend of the family, perched uneasily on a chair pulled up to the coffee table.

"More coffee, Maureen?" Christine leaned forward and lifted the silver pot politely.

Maureen shook her head and stood rather quickly. "I should be running along," she said. Then, as Christine rose and stepped around the coffee table, she added, "Please don't bother. I'll see myself out."

Dan rose, and Christine felt his hands on her shoulders as she watched Maureen hurry across the room and disappear into the hallway. Not until she heard the front door slam, however, did she allow herself to sag against him and shut her eyes.

"Sit down, sweetheart." Dan pulled her down beside him. Christine sighed and looked across the table at her daughter, who sat deathly still, her green eyes wide with shock.

"Mother, I'm so sorry—" she began.

Christine interrupted her with a waved hand. "It's not your fault, Victoria. This is pure Eleanor." Her gaze brushed the sheaf of papers Maureen had left with them. She gave a bitter laugh. "Mother always said she wanted you to run the business after she was gone."

Her son-in-law glanced at his wife and cleared his throat. "This is insane," he said bluntly. "We have no interest in Prescott's. Eleanor must have been out of her mind to leave all her shares to Victoria. And the house, too." He raised an eyebrow. "Forgive my indelicacy, but with Eleanor gone, the four of us are free to do whatever we think is best. Am I wrong?"

Christine glanced at the crackling fire, its flames unwittingly cheerful in the cold room. "I should have seen it coming," she said. "Anyway, she did leave me an income of fifty thousand a year. And, of course, her doll collection."

Victoria came around the coffee table and sat down beside her mother. The warmth of her daughter's embrace softened Christine's wall of blind rage, leaving her numb and bewildered. *At least,* she thought, *I don't have to worry about placating Mother anymore.*

Her mother was dead.

Victoria pulled away but kept a hand on Christine's shoulder. "We'd all like to believe that Grandmother was kindly and compassionate," she said. "She had remarkable qualities, and in some ways I admired her. But everyone in this room knows she could be mean and vindictive when she wanted to be. She enjoyed her little power games, making people suffer just because she knew she could." Victoria took her mother's hand. "For some perverse reason, she took special pleasure in tormenting you, Mother. She humiliated you and beat you down, and this is just more of the same. *Well.*" She drew her body upright and tossed her head. "Despite all her careful, spiteful plotting, that hateful old woman doesn't get the last word on *this* deal. *I* do."

In the startled pause that followed Victoria's speech,

Christine regarded her daughter, noting the proud, defiant head, the blazing emerald eyes, and thought how remarkably—how alarmingly—she looked like Eleanor.

"So, here's the new deal," Victoria continued. "Dan, in all that legal jargon, I didn't hear Eleanor specify that I couldn't sell my shares to Mother. Am I right?"

Dan fixed his reading glasses on his nose and picked up the packet of legal papers, nodding. "That was my understanding. The shares are yours to do with as you will." He peered at Victoria over his glasses. "I doubt it occurred to Eleanor that you would defy her wishes. Or that Christine would contest the will. I'm surprised, though, that Maureen didn't advise her to stipulate how you could dispose of the shares. Which is, of course, to our good." His eyes gleamed. "It rather seems that in the end Eleanor's arrogance essentially robbed her of her final coup de grâce." He grinned and reached for his coffee cup. "And I'd like to drink to that." He raised his cup. "Here's to the indomitable arrogance of Eleanor Prescott!"

With guilty grins, they all lifted Eleanor's best Meissen china cups in a triumphant toast.

"You know, Christine." Dan smiled as he settled the fragile cup onto its saucer. "Once you add Victoria's shares to those you already own, you'll have controlling interest in the company." His smile widened at her look. "You were voted by the board of directors to act as chair in your mother's absence. I imagine they'll be happy enough to see you in that job permanently." He squeezed her hand and grinned. "Congratulations, Madame Chair."

Christine didn't know where to look. Dan was beaming at her with pride and pure pleasure. Victoria was watching her with Eleanor's eyes but softened with love. Ryan was staring at his wife with the embarrassing frankness of a man who had just been smitten all over again. She set her cup down with shaking hands.

"I don't know what to say." She turned to her daughter. "Victoria, I can't let you—"

"Hey, you don't think I'm selling you *all* my shares, do you?" She nudged her mother playfully. "I know a good investment when I see one. I expect Prescott's will be more profitable than ever with you at the helm. Am I right, Dan?"

Dan nodded gleefully. "She's already proven she's got her mother's prowess for business." He raised his brows significantly. "But without that insatiable lust for power that sometimes blinded Eleanor." He raised his cup of tepid coffee again. "Here's to the proud future of Prescott's." He took a sip, made a face, and sent a pleading look across the table. "What would you say, Ryan, to something a little stronger than coffee?"

Ryan grinned. "I wouldn't say no." As Dan rose, Ryan addressed his mother-in-law. "Congratulations, Christine. This is how it should be, after all."

"Yes," his wife echoed. "This is how it should be." She gave her mother a quick, fierce hug. "And now, about the house—"

But Christine held up a hand. "The house is yours, Victoria. Yours and Ryan's." She cupped her daughter's face. "Your family's growing, dear. Maybe you'll want to consider moving in. You'll certainly have the income for it."

She kissed Victoria's forehead. "Despite Mother's passing, Dan and I are getting married next week, as planned. After that, I'll be living in Dan's house." She let her eyes wander around the familiar room—over the dark paneled walls, the marble fireplace, the antique library furniture, the expensive Persian rug cushioning her shoes. "This is a home for Prescotts and Rhineholdts." She was pleased that her voice held no regrets and no rancor. "And maybe Ashtons."

Dan returned with his brandy and sat down beside her. Christine cupped his knee with a possessive hand.

"I'll be a Winslow soon. And that makes my home wherever you are, Dan."

Chapter Eighteen

"Larry, that's bull, and you know it!" Ryan rammed his fist down on the table, rattling a cup of sharpened pencils and rolling one off the edge to break its tip on the floor of the trailer. "Gleason doesn't give a rat's whisker what the roofs look like. He just wants to use his money to push us around, make him feel like he's in control."

Larry Morgan leaned back in his chair and folded his hands over his stomach.

"You said the magic words, Ryan. *His money.*"

"*His money* doesn't give him the right to turn a sensational concept into an offense against the eyes. I mean, cedar shingles instead of red tile on white adobe? Where did he learn architectural design? From comic books?"

"He thinks it will blend the structures into the environment better than tile."

"In a pig's eye. Tell him it's a fire hazard."

"I told him. He says he's insured."

Ryan exploded with a string of expletives, nothing Larry hadn't heard before. He clamped his hands behind his neck and squeezed his head between his elbows. "Tell him," he said, squeezing harder. "Tell him…" He blew out a breath and let his arms drop to his sides. "Oh, tell him to go jump off a cliff."

"Love to," Larry said amiably, reaching for his coffee mug, "if I wanted to kiss my ass and this project good-bye. Which"—he eyed Ryan over his mug—"I don't."

"Come on, Larry." Ryan flattened his hands on the table and leaned toward his boss. "You know better than anyone what this project means. I saw it in your face the first time I showed you the concept. You were as excited as I was about the potential here. We both know it's got to be just right. It's got to be *perfect*." Larry frowned, and Ryan amended his statement. "Okay, at least in the essentials," he said. "An integration of Spanish, Russian, Chinese, and Native American cultures, Larry. That's what we all agreed; that's the bottom, non-negotiable line. So tell me, Larry, how do cedar shingles fit into that concept?"

Larry rested his coffee mug on his knee and pulled thoughtfully on his fussy little goatee. He nodded slowly.

"Okay." He drained the last of his coffee. "That's a reasonable angle. I'll give it a shot." He tipped forward in his chair and leaned his elbows on the table. "Why don't you go for a walk, son, while I call Gleason? Give yourself a chance to cool off."

His tone was mild, but the steel in his eyes warned Ryan that this was the last pitch. If Gleason didn't buy the argument, then the tile roof was out. Ryan set his jaw and swung around, cursing under his breath. He slammed out the trailer door and pounded down the makeshift steps, landing his boots in muck stirred up from the morning rain. His long strides splashed through water pooled in the deep ruts of dozer tracks and left tracks of his own across concrete foundations already lifting skeletal walls and roof supports, bringing his dream alive.

Cedar shingles. What a joke.

He walked to the edge of the clearing and stopped, staring moodily across the newly washed valley and listening to the patter of raindrops still dripping from the tall redwood boughs onto the forest floor. He took some deep, sharp breaths and tried to shake off his outrage over Gleason's ridiculous demands and Larry's refusal to insist upon doing the project right.

Let it go, he advised himself. He knew it was always like this, compromising to get the job done. This project was no different from any other. Larry wasn't betraying him, just doing his job.

Why was he getting so worked up about it?

The answer was so obvious that Ryan wheeled around and took off in a new direction. Hands plunged deep in his pockets, he circled the site rapidly, his breath puffing out in steamy curls, his face reddening from the slap of cold air. He ended up, as he always did, in the center of the circle, staring at the stakes marking the perimeter of the medicine wheel. And there his thoughts caught up with him.

The project is important because I love her. Because I'm scared to death that she's right, and I'm going to lose her next month. Because, if this project is completed according to plan, I can come here and still feel her presence – her mind, her spirit, her heart – in the design she created. It will be my own personal temple where I can visit her, where I can worship her and mourn –

"Ryan!" Larry hailed him from across the lot,

waving his clipboard over his head. Ryan stood where he was, hands still in his pockets, trying to read an answer in the language of his boss's body as he approached.

When he was close enough to speak, Larry shook his head.

"Couldn't reach him." He squinted his eyes against the noonday glare. "I left a message. I'll call you as soon as I get an answer from him. Okay?"

Ryan nodded in silence. Larry eyed him and slapped the clipboard lightly against Ryan's jacket sleeve.

"Look, Ryan, it'll come out all right. I won't build anything I'm ashamed to put my name to. You know that."

"Yeah, I know that. Sorry for being such a pain in the ass."

Larry chuckled and laid a companionable hand on Ryan's shoulder, leading him toward the parking area.

"Go on home to that pretty wife of yours, son. There's nothing more you can do here." He slipped on his sunglasses. "Take an early weekend like everyone else."

"Yeah. Thanks, Larry." Ryan shook the older man's hand. He pulled out his keys to the Jaguar and fingered them. "I'll do that after I make one more stop."

* * *

"I'm glad you changed your mind, Steph." Brett sketched a circle around Stephanie on the ice. "I knew my charm was bound to wear you down sooner or later."

"Don't be too sure of that, Mr. Ego." Stephanie lifted her arms over her head and raised a leg behind her. "Maybe I just got bored skating alone. Or maybe I felt sorry for you and decided you needed somebody out here to make you look good."

"Yeah, right." Brett grabbed her hands and pulled her toward him, slipping his hands to her waist. Stephanie gasped and instinctively drew back. *Take it easy, Stephanie. This is Brett, remember? He's your skating partner, not some thug.*

Amy would be proud of her. Amy was the counselor she had been seeing every week since December. It was Amy's idea that Stephanie should get back into ice-skating as quickly as possible and not give in to her desire to become a hermit. Once she was on the ice, Stephanie felt her confidence return. She'd had to spend many hours pounding out her anger and frustration before she could begin constructive, artistic work. At first the idea of pair skating—letting male hands touch her and hold her—had seemed impossible. Brett, however, had gradually talked her into it. She would never admit it to him, but he was right. His charm had played a big part in softening her guard and getting her to trust him.

"Well, at least you've been practicing," Brett said. Stephanie preened as she executed a perfect spiral around him, forcing him to turn and watch her as she glided by. "I think you're taller than you were last summer. Is that possible?"

Stephanie pulled herself upright, still gliding on one skate. "I dunno. I guess." Secretly, she knew she had grown nearly a full inch.

Brett took her hand, and they began to skate side by side, matching strokes. "It's so cool that you live out here now. Do you miss your mom?"

"No." Her response snapped like a firecracker.

"Jeez," Brett muttered. He glanced at the observation lounge. "Who's that with your stepmom? I'm sorry, I mean—"

"It's okay, Brett. You can call her my stepmom." Stephanie grinned and waved at Tori, who was watching them through the glass window. Tori and the woman next to her waved back. "That's her mother, Christine Winslow. She just got married last month. Did I tell you Tori is going to have a baby?"

"Yeah, that's awesome. A boy or a girl?"

Stephanie shrugged. "She hasn't told me. I don't think she knows. If it's a girl, she wants to call her Christina. If it's a boy, they're naming him Mark, after my dad's brother. I have an uncle I've never even met. Isn't that weird?"

"Yeah. But families these days are more weird than not."

Stephanie sighed. "You can sure say *that* again."

* * *

"We'd have four whole weeks to practice, Stephanie." Brett's tone was wheedling. "Come on, we can still put something together. It'll be fun."

Stephanie shook her head. "No, Brett. I'm not ready for competition. For Pete's sake, we just started together. Can't we just skate and have some fun?"

"But practicing for a competition makes it *more* fun, don't you think? It makes you work harder—" He broke off with a frown. "Steph, are you *listening*?"

Stephanie was staring over his shoulder toward the observation area. Brett followed her gaze and saw the red light of an emergency vehicle flashing through the glass doors from the parking lot. Two team workers were bending over someone on the floor. As they lifted a woman's body onto the stretcher, Stephanie let out a shriek and pelted for the nearest exit. Brett took off after her.

"Stephanie, what? Wait a sec—"

Stephanie staggered clumsily up the carpeted stairs ahead of him and burst through the doors just as the stretcher was being wheeled toward the outside doors and the waiting ambulance.

"Tori!" She grabbed the arm of one of the medics as he brushed by her. "No, wait—"

"Stephanie." Tori's mother hurried toward them, carrying Stephanie's sports bag. "Here," she said, pulling out a pair of blade guards. "Put these on. You can change into shoes in the car."

Stephanie stared mutely at the rubber guards she had crazily decorated with Magic Markers. Brett saw that her face had gone sickly white, the way people looked when their body temperature had dropped too low.

"Sit down, Steph." Brett took the blade guards and urged Stephanie down on a bench. Within moments he had wiped her blades dry and fixed each with a guard. The older woman was fitting Stephanie's arms into a jacket with the calm efficiency of someone used to being in charge. "What happened?" he asked her.

The woman didn't look up. "My daughter is having her baby early," she said quietly. She helped Stephanie to stand and picked up the sports bag. "Thank you, young man." The woman's dark eyes touched him briefly. Then she put an arm across Stephanie's shoulders and turned her away. "You can call your father from the car," Brett heard her say as they started toward the glass doors. "Do you have your cell phone?"

Brett didn't hear Stephanie's reply. He stared after them, his arm half raised to wave good-bye, but Stephanie never looked back.

Chapter Nineteen

Ryan stood on the bank of Two Trees Creek, staring down at the bridge and trying to figure out exactly why he had come. His intent had been to stop in at Summerwood Cottage and take a look at the finished attic renovation before he headed back to San Francisco. Alice's Christmas card had invited him to "come see the stunning results of your fertile idea." Her card had also mentioned that the county had assumed the cost of rebuilding the bridge over Two Trees Creek, declaring it an historical treasure.

As he'd locked his car in the parking lot near Rosswood House, Ryan told himself that this was an insane idea. He told himself he'd never be able to find the right path. He told himself that they probably hadn't finished rebuilding the bridge, that his visit was not only ill advised but premature.

Ryan now stared at the completed bridge. He recognized its shape from Elise Delacroix's painting, that scene with the two women from Victoria's dream. He vaguely remembered a dream of his own in which he had tried to sabotage the bridge but failed. He looked at the underpinnings and imagined where he'd place the explosives for maximum effect, how to set the charge to blow the cursed thing out of existence.

He knew why he had come. It was a last-ditch effort to find some way to prevent what he feared most, to destroy the bridge before the bridge destroyed his life.

How about a fire? He didn't have any matches. No problem—he could get some. But a fire could get out of control. It would take the bridge, all right, and half the countryside with it.

He shook his head. There had to be some way to get rid of it. He only had three weeks left.

Ashton, you're crazy, he thought. *It's a bridge, a physical structure made of wood and steel. Made by human hands. There's nothing mysterious about it.*

But Ryan knew better. He held the proof every night in his arms, saw it every time he looked into his wife's eyes, felt it in the warmth of her kisses, heard it in the sweetness of his name on her lips. He wasn't going to waste time denying that an exchange in time had occurred. What he needed was to get control of the situation and make sure it didn't happen again.

A loud screech just above him jerked his head up. A large brown squirrel sat bouncing on a branch, just out of reach. Turning its head sideways, it fastened a dark eye on him. Ryan stared at it, and lightening sheeted across the gray sky beyond the trees, so quick that Ryan wondered if he'd imagined it. Moments later, thunder cracked and rumbled. Unexpected terror shot through his body and paralyzed him.

He stared at the glowering sky until the gray seemed to dissolve into a hard whiteness. He smelled smoke nearby and fish frying. He heard children laughing and shrieking, and he wondered if there was a campground on the opposite bank. He wanted to look, but he couldn't manage to pull his eyes away from the hard white sky.

An eagle swept through his line of vision. The blinding white softened into gray, and Ryan blinked. He lowered his gaze and nearly jumped out of his skin to find himself standing in the exact center of the reconstructed bridge. Far below, the restless creek water rushed and gurgled. Ryan lifted his hands and looked at them, rubbing them together to feel if they were solid. He backed away from the rail, afraid to touch it, and looked at the bank where he had been standing. Without success he tried to remember climbing down the slope and walking onto the bridge.

Lightening flashed across the sky, thunder close on its heels. Memories of another storm broke across his mind—charred planks rushing by on furious swells of water; his wife's body lying cold and still on the wet bank; his own voice yelling at her to stay alive, even though his senses told him she was already dead.

And then the miracle had happened, the unexpected gift that had changed his life. The love that might be wrenched away from him so soon now. *So soon.*

Ryan lifted angry fists to the dark sky. Half blinded by his rage and fear, he turned and stumbled off the bridge. By the time he hit the slope that would take him back to Rosswood House, he was running.

* * *

Ryan reached his car just as the rain began. A hostile sky pelted his bare head with fat, stinging drops and drove all thoughts of visiting Summerwood Cottage out of his mind. The only plan he could focus on was to get himself away.

As he settled in behind the wheel and pulled the door shut, a pair of beeps alerted him to a message on his cell phone. He glanced at the phone lying on the seat next to him and grimaced.

"Screw it, Larry," he said aloud. He started the engine and jerked the Jaguar out of its parking space. "I don't need your problems now. What I do need is a good, stiff drink."

He easily remembered the route into Rossport. In the time it took to drive to Loggers End and park across the street, he was feeling calmer and had shaken off most of his fright. Glancing at his watch, he gave himself forty minutes to relax, have a sandwich and a beer before starting for home.

He took his plate and his bottle of Corona and sat at one of the tables casually set outside, protected from the rain by a solid overhang. He watched the occasional car pass by, slick with rain, wipers going, and realized with a start that this was Tori's hometown, that the old mansion, Rosswood House, was where she grew up. That the beautiful woman in the portrait—was her name Isabel?—was Tori's mother. And that the young sour-faced child holding onto her nurse's hand was Tori herself.

Ryan tipped back the bottle and took a long, slow swig of beer. No, he thought, not Tori. That was Katherine, before her father abused her and split her into two people. She had explained it all to him. Tori—*his* Tori—hadn't existed until she'd come to live in his life, until they'd found love together. And she'd become still another person. She'd become his very reason for being.

In a way, he mused, she was like the resort she'd designed—a blending of heritages and personalities, of talents and strengths and memories. Of betrayals overcome and healed, like the land. Her troubled past had been alchemized into a life of strength and beauty, a new creation centered in love.

It wasn't so hard to believe. After all, hadn't something similar happened to him? He thought back a year, two years, ten years, to the Ryan he had been—the Ryan who had married Gina and thought he could change her; the Ryan who had married Victoria because she was beautiful and malleable. The Ryan who had run screaming from the pink bedroom and, in a way, had been running ever since.

But life with Tori had changed him. He realized now that it wasn't just her loving him that made the difference. It was discovering that he himself could love, that he could value another person's happiness above his own. It was no longer fearing that opening his heart to love would destroy him.

It was also in giving up his illusion of control over his life. Ryan had to admit, he was still working on that one. What was it Tori had told him about the medicine wheel? That it's magic was in realizing that you are not the power in the center, after all, but there are forces greater than you working for your good.

If forces are working for my good, he thought, with a flick of temper, *then they won't take her away from me.* His jaw tightened, and his chin jutted defiantly. Just let them try to take her. There was no way he'd give her up without a fight, no *freaking* way.

Ryan tipped back the bottle and swallowed the last of his beer. Well, like he'd already admitted, he was still working on that one.

The rain had stopped. Ryan glanced at his watch and saw that his forty minutes had stretched into sixty. He pushed up from his chair and stretched, reluctant to leave his solitary island and return to the world of Friday afternoon traffic and dealing with idiots like Harvey Gleason.

But, he reminded himself, it was a world that also held the promise of Tori and holding her in his arms tonight.

With a shrug, he dropped a bill on the table, stepped off the porch, and headed across the street. His Jaguar was waiting for him, its bright paint reflecting in a thousand wet drops the grim glare of a sky that guaranteed more rain.

* * *

Twenty minutes north of the Golden Gate Bridge, Ryan decided to listen to his message from Larry. The beer and the respite had relaxed him enough to find pleasure in skimming along the slick highway on the silky purr of power that gave his car its name. He felt ready to face whatever news Larry had to tell him.

He switched on his wireless headset and punched in the code to retrieve his messages. Keeping his eyes on the road, he waited for Larry's booming voice.

"Dad? Dad, they took Tori to the hospital." Ryan's gaze froze on the car in front of him. "She's having her baby. Can you come right away?" He heard some rustling, and Christine's voice came on, crisp and efficient. "Ryan, it's Christine. Victoria's hemorrhaging. They took her to Mount Cross Hospital. Come as quickly as you can, dear. We're following the ambulance there now."

A rude beep signaled the end of the message. Ryan felt his blood turn cold, running a chill through his body like Novocain just before it removes all traces of feeling. His head pulsed with a faint, persistent *no, no, no…* Then he pounded the steering wheel with his fist: "No! No! *No!* You can't do this! We still have three more weeks!" His howl dropped to a choking whisper. "Please, God, don't take her now." He blinked hard, trying to clear his eyes so he could see the traffic ahead, so he could find his way to her. "I'm asking you. *I'm begging you.*" He fought back tears. "Okay, I know I can't fight you. I know I'm not in charge. You don't have to bring me to my knees; I'm already on them." His voice broke. "Please give us this time. If you do, I swear I won't fight you when it comes time to give her up. But it's not time yet. *Please.*" His face crumpled. "Please, God. I need her. I love her —"

He jumped when his phone rang. "What?" he barked into his headset. "What's happening?" His voice was high and frightened, like a little boy's.

"Ryan, thank God." It was Christine. "She's had the baby, Ryan. A little girl. They've got her in an incubator because she's so early. Only five pounds two ounces." She took a breath. "Victoria is out of surgery, and she's stable. I spoke with her, Ryan. She won't rest until she sees you. Where are you now?"

Ryan's hands shook as the nerves in his body reacted

to the news. "I'm almost at the bridge." He choked on a sob. "Christine—" He couldn't continue.

"She's going to be all right, Ryan. Slow down and be careful, for heaven's sake. Dan's here. We'll take Stephanie home with us tonight." With a smile in her voice, Christine added, "Your new daughter is beautiful, Ryan. She looks just like Victoria. Congratulations."

* * *

His wife was asleep when he entered her room. Christine rose from her chair and silently embraced him.

"You poor boy," she whispered. She nodded at the still figure in the bed. "She's doing fine, Ryan. She's not in danger."

Christine patted his arm reassuringly and left them alone. Ryan moved to the bed and stood over his wife. His heart caught, seeing her hand fisted close to her mouth. How often had he seen that familiar gesture when she was sleeping beside him, looking like an angel?

He picked up her other hand gently, trying not to wake her, and sat down in the chair. Her hair was limp on the pillow, and her face was lined and shadowed with fatigue. But her breathing was soft and regular, and she looked so peaceful that Ryan felt his muscles begin to loosen. Swells of relief and love bloomed in his chest. He shut his eyes and held his wife's hand against his face, unable to focus on anything except the warm feel of her skin and the reassuring pulse of life in her wrist. He kissed her palm and moved his hand to rest on the shape of her leg beneath the thin cotton blanket.

Ryan buried his face in the blanket, shuddered, and lay still.

"Hey, Ashton." Her weak, husky voice brought his head up. She was watching him, her green eyes tired but warm with love. Ryan rubbed his sleeve across his face and tried for a smile. "Lord, Ryan. You look worse than I do." Her light chuckle brought out his smile at last, along with a threat of tears.

Swiftly he reached forward and gathered her into his arms. He tried to speak but couldn't, and he tightened his arms instead. She clung to him, her face pressed against his cheek. Her body felt different without the baby, lighter and alarmingly fragile. When he laid her down again, he saw her eyebrows drawn together in pain.

"Darling, I'm sorry. I didn't realize—"

She waved his apology aside. "I've been waiting for that for hours." She sighed. "But I'm afraid we'll have to postpone the rest for just a while longer."

Ryan caught that feline curl of her smile, and he grinned, even as tears threatened again. He took her hand and laced their fingers together, striving to keep his voice steady.

"You'll have to keep reminding me." He lifted her hand to his lips. "Mmm, you don't know how delicious you are." He sat down and leaned his elbows on the bed, still holding her hand. "Don't worry, Lady Ashton. We'll have plenty of time—"

He broke off as the carelessness of his words struck him. She shut her eyes, and he quickly lowered his mouth to hers, wanting to comfort her, needing to comfort himself. He cupped her face with his hands and kissed her eyelids. "I love you, Tori," he whispered brokenly. "I love you."

Such feeble, inadequate words, but he had no others. Ryan straightened and touched her cheek.

"I saw the baby," he said softly. She opened her eyes, and her sudden smile bloomed like a rainbow. "She's beautiful, Tori. Your mother's right; she looks like you."

He hoped his expression didn't betray the anxiety he'd felt when the nurse showed him their tiny daughter, separated from him by the transparent roof of her incubator. With the warming lights keeping her comfortable, she was dressed in only a diaper, and her frail body seemed out of proportion with her large head. Her skin was pink and blotchy, and she was sleeping with her fist curled tightly against her mouth. Just like her mother.

Ryan swallowed and turned suddenly as Stephanie opened the door and peered in cautiously.

"Okay if I come in?"

"Hey, Stephanannie." Ryan opened his arms, and his daughter rushed into them. She clamped her arms around his waist and beamed up at him.

"Did you see her, Dad? Did you see Christina?"

"Yes. She's amazing." He smoothed his daughter's hair back and grinned at her. "So, you've got a new baby sister to spoil. Guess you'll be learning how to change diapers now."

"Oh, Dad." Stephanie rolled her eyes. "I already know how to do baby stuff. I've been babysitting for two years, remember?" She glanced over at Tori. "Hi," she said and grinned shyly.

"Hi, yourself." Tori grinned back. "I heard you're going home with my mother and Dan tonight. Is that okay with you?"

"Oh, sure. They're nice. Did you know they keep Cookies n' Cream ice cream in their freezer, just for me?" She moved to the bed and took Tori's hand.

"No, I didn't know that." Tori chuckled. "Don't get too used to their pampering. I'm going to put you to work when the baby comes home."

Stephanie dimpled. "Yeah, I know." She glanced down at their clasped hands. "Your mom's really happy you named the baby after her. *Christina Isabel Ashton.*" She tilted her head. "Why 'Isabel'? Is she another relative or something?"

Tori hesitated and then nodded. "Someone I even thought I hated." She looked up at Ryan, over Stephanie's head, and he saw her eyes shine. "Right now, though, all I can feel is how much I love my family—the two of you, my mother, Christina." She smiled her beautiful smile. "With so much love in my heart, I don't have room for hate anymore."

Chapter Twenty

The coarse March wind had nearly blown itself out, diminished to an occasional defiant gust as late afternoon softened into evening. Ryan stood at the balcony rail, hands thrust deep in the pockets of his suede jacket, and stared absently at the city streets below him. He missed the exact moment when the ranks of streetlamps came on, didn't take his usual pleasure in the neat green symmetries of the neighborhood park, deserted now as children were called home to dinner and lovers had not yet ventured out for the evening.

His gaze was turned inward, fixed on the image of his wife curled on their bed, asleep. Ryan had come home early, unable to keep his mind on his work, anxious to begin his evening with Tori and stretch it out for as long as possible. He'd found the apartment quiet except for the dull pulsing of Stephanie's stereo behind her closed door. He'd peeked in on Christina, still so tiny, lying asleep in her crib. Then he'd tiptoed down the hall to his bedroom and stood for several minutes by the bed. His pleasure in watching his wife sleep was mixed with pain as he shut his eyes and tested himself, seeing how perfectly he could recall her features. It was always like that now, this pain of dread spoiling his delight in her, assigning him the relentless task of trying to memorize and store away little portions of her that he could retrieve in the future, when his longing for her became unbearable.

Agitated, he shifted his weight and bumped against one of the redwood planters lining the balcony rail. He looked down, and the row of neatly pruned rose bushes brought a sudden, sweet memory of summer fragrance filling the apartment and the sight of Tori's roses, yellow with orange edges, spilling out of vases and pitchers in every room. They looked forlorn now, their bounty of summer growth brutally amputated by winter's cold and Tori's shears. "It's for their own good, Ryan," she'd told him, as she executed one merciless excision after another. "The new growth will be stronger and healthier." He had frowned in doubt. "Trust me, Ryan." Her smile was irresistible. He'd pulled her up into his arms, and then he'd kissed her.

Ryan glared at the row of deformed little figures and noted with bitterness their swelling buds already anticipating the spring. "Don't bother," he said. "She won't be here to look after you." He added, "And Vicki doesn't know how."

He didn't hear her slide the door open and step out behind him. Her arms circled his waist, and the faint scent of ginger spice shot twin arrows of joy and pain through his body. Wordlessly, he turned and brought his mouth down on hers. Enveloped in the soft twilight hush, they shared a kiss that was deep and long and achingly sweet. When they pulled reluctantly apart, Ryan let his eyes linger over her, already naming the vision being etched in his memory. *This is how my love looked in twilight.*

She was wearing her white robe, and her blond hair curled softly, just brushing her shoulders. *It's gotten longer,* Ryan thought. He suddenly wanted her to cut it again, as if keeping her hair short would somehow help her to keep her claim on this body—on this life—and prevent Vicki from coming back.

Tori moved to the rail and stared out over the city deepening into dusk. "It's started, Ryan," she said quietly.

He moved to stand beside her. "What's started?"

She turned and leaned an elbow on the rail, holding him with a steady gaze. "What we've dreaded. I dreamed about the bridge." She lifted a shoulder. "It's only a week away. I should have expected it." She drew in a breath that trembled. "She was already there, standing on the bridge. Waiting for me."

At his look, she put out her hand and covered his. "Don't hate her, Ryan. She didn't ask for this to happen any more than I did." She smiled faintly. "I would have, though, if I'd known you would be here. I wouldn't have missed this time with you for anything. No matter what happens, I'll carry you in my heart until the day I die."

Ryan couldn't speak. He couldn't move, couldn't breathe. He could do nothing but stare at her in mute despair.

She turned her back on the glittering city and leaned both elbows on the rail, staring through the glass doors into their living room. The soft light of the table lamps was growing imperceptibly brighter as the dusk surrendered to night.

"Do you ever wonder, Ryan, what Victoria will be like when she comes back?"

"She's not coming back." His voice cracked.

"She's had a whole year, Ryan, just like me. A lot can happen in a year. She may surprise you."

"She won't get the chance." His jaw tightened. "I'm not letting you go, Tori. I can't. Vicki doesn't belong here anymore. This is your home, with Christina and me." He covered the crack in his voice with harshness. "How can you stand there and calmly talk about Vicki coming back while you just up and vanish from our lives? Like it's already decided, like it's so *easy* for you —"

"Easy!" She drew herself up, and her eyes flashed. "You think it's *easy* to hold that precious little girl in there — *our* baby, Ryan, not yours and Vicki's — and tell myself that soon, oh, so soon, I'll have to give her up?" She swallowed. "And I can't think at all about how it will feel to give you up, Ryan. To imagine waking up in a world that doesn't have you in it. To know that I'll never be able to touch you or kiss you or make love with you, never hear the sound of your voice whispering tenderness to me in the dark." Angry tears brimmed her eyes. "To know that I'll never again see you looking at me the way you're looking at me right now." Her voice broke. "To know…even though I'll never be able to find you…it won't stop me from searching for you…every day…for the rest of my life."

Despite her angry stance, her mouth trembled, and Ryan longed to pull her against him and still that trembling with his lips. But he didn't dare. The mere touch of her skin against his might very well ignite flames that would consume them both.

So he stood where he was, his arms dangling uselessly at his sides, and instead filled himself with the glorious sight of her. And with a sudden burst of intensity, his love for her expanded into a new plane. He knew he would travel there in the long nights when he was alone and could no longer reach out for her, and he would spend his life roaming its mountains and its hidden valleys and never find its boundaries.

She saw the shift in his eyes, and the flame in hers softened. She took his hands in hers and folded them carefully against her heart. The two of them stood motionless, gazing silently into each other's eyes, and for a brief time they traveled that new, boundless terrain together.

* * *

Ryan fumed as he sat in his idling Jaguar, trying to see through the long, writhing lines of vehicles trapped by an accident on the Bay Bridge. *This is crazy,* he thought, glancing at the dashboard clock for the fortieth time in as many minutes. When he and Tori moved to the East Bay, he would have to consider taking the BART train into the city.

His stomach clenched in excitement and dread as he imagined how it would be when he walked through the door of his apartment and confronted his wife. *It's done, Tori. I put down the deposit today. The property is ours.*

He knew what she would say, what he'd steadfastly refused to hear since he'd first told her about the property. "It won't stop it from happening, Ryan. Nothing can stop it. All we can do is accept."

Well, if she thought for one minute he could ever let her go without putting up the biggest fight of his life...

He winced, remembering the bargain he'd made.

He didn't know with whom he'd made that bargain, maybe just with himself. Anyway, it didn't matter. He couldn't keep it. He could not, *would* not lose her.

Ryan glanced at his plans lying on the seat next to him and recalled his dream of a house with many rooms and wide windows overlooking gardens and the slopes of a mountain. Miraculously, he'd found the very spot— an older house on five acres of land bumping up against the boundaries of Mount Diablo State Park. With some renovation and expansion, his bedroom terrace would hold an unobstructed view of the lower slopes. The three bedrooms would multiply into six, with a room for Stephanie, a room for Christina, a room for another sister or brother.

Finding that property wasn't coincidence. It had to mean that his hopes for the future wouldn't be shattered with the coming of tonight, that his dream hadn't been just wishful thinking but a prophecy of what was to come.

He would find a way to convince Tori of that and then hold her right through the dark, moonless hours until the dawn confirmed that he was right, that the future was indeed theirs together. Forever.

Impatiently, he tried her cell phone again. After four rings her husky voice thanked him for calling and asked him to leave a message.

Where in blazes *was* she?

He waited for the beep and said crisply, "It's me.

Where are you? I'm stuck in traffic, but I'm on my way home. I'll see you soon. I love you." The words repeated in his mind: *I'll see you soon...I love you...I'll see you soon...*

He gripped the wheel with clammy palms, his excitement over acquiring the East Bay property suddenly eclipsed by a rising wall of fear.

* * *

"Tori?"

He meant it to be a shout, but it came out a scared whisper. No matter. The silence echoed back to him what he already knew, what he'd known before he'd parked his car and run up the stairs, two at a time, because he couldn't stand to wait for the elevator.

She was already gone.

Fear, like a shapeless monster, shadowed him as he ran down the hall, whispered to him as he passed Stephanie's empty room and Christina's empty crib, taunted him as he burst into their empty bedroom. Ryan's gaze slid over the gold satin bedspread and caught on the cream envelope propped against the pillow. His name, written in her bold, sloping hand, mocked him as he picked up the envelope and stared at it.

Rain just beginning to patter against the bedroom window competed with a sudden, dizzy throbbing in his head. He sat down heavily on the smooth satin and stared at the envelope, hating the way his hands shook, hating the sound of his own heart hammering in his ears.

The flap was unsealed. Ryan slipped out the single sheet and unfolded it.

My love:

Please don't despise me for my cowardice. I told myself I was saving you the grief of a painful good-bye, but that was a lie. The truth is, I couldn't wait any longer. If what is to be is to be, then I want it over now. I'm afraid that if I look into your eyes one more time or feel the loving circle of your arms around me, my mind will shatter, and I will go mad from wanting to stay with you.

Christina and Stephanie are with my mother. I borrowed her car. Please, my darling, don't follow me. There is nothing you can do. There is nothing either of us can do. We are in God's hands.

You are my heart and my life, now and forever.

It was unsigned.

Ryan stared at the slanting words drifting up the page at an odd angle, telling of her distress when she wrote it. Then they blurred and ran together, and he realized he couldn't breathe. The monster had crept inside him and was closing around his heart, trapping the air in his lungs. His quaking hand dropped the sheet, but he didn't notice. For a measureless moment, the world stopped. Time, life, death, love—nothing existed, nothing was real. Nothing mattered. Not his pain or his loneliness or his bright future abruptly dashed to pieces. The horror had happened. She was gone.

Rain tapped insistently at the window and eventually roused him. He turned his head mechanically and stared at the glass, at the drops of water clinging and slipping down the pane. And he realized that the horror, indeed, had not happened yet. The rain that fell against the window was also falling on *her*, somewhere in *this* world, in *this* life. He still had time to get to her. But he would have to hurry.

He jumped to his feet, wobbling a little before his legs were steady enough to support him. He stepped away from the bed, and his shoe crushed the letter from his wife.

He scooped it up and jammed it angrily into his jacket pocket.

"It's not over, Tori," he said. New resolve quickened his blood and drove the monster from his head. "I know exactly where you've gone. And I swear I'll go to hell and back again to bring you home."

* * *

The storm made the moonless night even darker. Ryan fought to keep both his temper and control of the car as he peered through the rapid sweep of his wipers and dodged between wet, snaking lines of traffic heading north on Highway 101.

A horn blared, and Ryan swerved to avoid hitting a black Mercedes he could swear hadn't been in that spot a moment before. He jerked the Jaguar back into his lane and slammed on his brakes, fuming behind the staring red taillights of a GMC truck. Heavy sheets of rain were making drivers cautious, but time prodded Ryan with a white-hot spear, pushing him beyond mortal concerns of safety and caution.

It seemed like hours, but was actually less than one, before Ryan cleared enough of the traffic to speed ahead into the dark night. Grateful for his many recent trips to the Golden Springs Ridge building site, he skimmed the familiar road with absent attention, leaving his mind free to imagine what would happen when he caught up with his wife at the bridge over Two Trees Creek. For, of course, that's where she was headed, to give herself up to the whims of fate. His only clear thought was to physically get to her and pin his arms around her, like steel bands. If supernatural forces came for her, then, by God, they would have to take him, too.

Ryan looked around in pleased surprise, recognizing the dim landforms that told him he was close to the Springstown Highway turnoff. He was making good time. It couldn't be more than forty minutes from here.

Once he was on the Springstown Highway, Ryan picked up speed. *Tori,* his mind called to her, *wait for me. Hold back until I can get to you, darling. Wait for me!*

He didn't see the jackknifed truck until he was almost on top of it. Even if he weren't speeding, it would have been difficult to stop, coming around a blind curve into the looming broad side of the trailer. As it was, there was nothing he could do. Quick reflex saved him from crashing headlong into the great steel wall by jerking the wheel and slamming on the brakes. The Jaguar spun in a crazy circle before it bounced off the unforgiving steel and flipped, sliding easily on its top across the slick road to stop precariously near the edge of the rise overlooking Cougar Canyon.

When Ryan groped his way back to consciousness, his first sensation was searing pain in his head and his legs. His second sensation was the cold realization that he had to free his body from whatever held him trapped.

He struggled to open his eyes, but blood ran into them, and he couldn't get his arm up to wipe his face. He stopped struggling a moment to listen, but all he heard was the relentless patter and hiss of rain splashing on the Jaguar's hot steel belly. *There's no one to help me,* he thought, fighting a strong pull to slide back into comforting oblivion. *I have to get myself out of the car before it blows up.* Then, with a stab of panic, *I have to get to Tori!*

He arched his torso and cried out as hot pain tore through his legs and threatened his fragile thread of consciousness. Gritting his teeth, he mentally prepared himself for another pull. *Come on, Ashton. Time to make all that upper body work pay off.*

Deprived of vision, Ryan sensed a gap of cold air on his left, and he instinctively pulled himself toward it. It took him precious minutes to realize his seat belt was still pinning him, and he groped for its release button. Like a worm slithering out of an apple, Ryan inched and twisted his torso out of the car. But when he tried to move his legs, the pain of jagged steel slicing into them made him scream in agony and pushed him dangerously near that dark brink of nothingness again. His head lolled back into the mud, face up, and the gentle rain began to wash him clean. It diluted the blood still seeping from his forehead and cleared his eyes enough so he could blink them open.

The night was black without moon or stars and utterly deserted. He wondered vaguely if the driver of the truck was dead. If he himself soon would be. "I'm sorry, Tori," he whispered, trying to reach out to her with his last shreds of consciousness. The rain pounded harder, and his head sank deeper into the mud. "God keep you safe, my love. Wherever you are."

The water rose, and the dark was sucking him under, taking away the patter of the rain and the smell of his own blood. With a sigh that shuddered through his body like a sob, Ryan surrendered to the dark.

Victoria

Chapter Twenty-One

Tender flames from a dozen candles tangled smoky fingers in the still air above Isabel's head. They wreathed her face in soft light and defended her against the indifferent December daylight peering in at the high square windows of her chapel.

Dora's great pudding bulk hunched on the floor beside her mistress. Her head was bowed, whether in prayer or exhausted stupor, I couldn't tell. I crept up behind her and touched her shoulder. When she didn't respond, I gripped both shoulders and shook her gently.

"Dora. Dora, wake up."

Her grizzled head raised slowly and wobbled. I knelt beside her and put my arms around her.

"You go back up to the house for a while and rest. I'll keep watch here."

She blinked at me and glanced at the high windows to read the hour. Wordlessly, she nodded and began to rise. But her legs, bloodless from hours of kneeling, would not support her. She stumbled and almost pitched us both to the floor before she recovered herself. I helped her take the first few steps and then, like a mother with a toddler, watched worriedly as she stumbled away from me. When I started after her and took her arm, she shook her head.

"It's best you stay here. Don't leave her alone." She met my eyes briefly, her own still leaking weary tears, her expression desolate. She patted my arm and turned away.

By her own request, Isabel had been laid out in the chapel for the long vigil before her burial. She wore her wedding gown, her satin-sleeved arms laid close to her body, her dark hair spilling loose over an elaborately embroidered pillow. I stepped up to the table and stood over her, touching her hair lightly but unwilling to touch the porcelain skin now pasty and tinged with gray. Death could not rob Isabel of her fine features, but it destroyed the illusions her vitality had created. Without the haunting blue-violet gaze, without the proud carriage of her head and the stubborn tilt of her chin, her human form was appallingly ordinary. She looked thinner to me, and older. Her dark hair was unmistakably threaded with silver; the lines and imperfections of her face stood out cruelly. I had never before noticed the V-shaped scar below her left ear, nor the slight asymmetry of her cheekbones gently tipping the line of her still mouth.

I lit another candle and knelt beside her body, folding my hands dutifully. But prayers wouldn't come. I had dreaded this moment, this final, private vigil when I would say good-bye to the woman I had come to love as my mother. I let my gaze roam her beloved features, and in my mind's eye, they came alive for me. I saw her eyebrow arch in humor, her chin lift in stubborn pride, her lovely mouth curve in an unexpected smile. I recalled how every head turned when Isabel walked into a room, how grace and dignity were hers to command, even up to her last moments.

My reflections shaped themselves into a prayer, after all. I gave thanks for the mother's love I would never have known but for Isabel. And I prayed for a way to memorialize this remarkable woman as no cold gravestone or brass plaque on the door of her chapel ever could.

* * *

I held Robbie's mittened hand in my own and stared at Isabel's coffin lying at the bottom of the hole. Father Philippe stood beside me, next to Leon and Ana. A brisk December wind blew brittle leaves around our feet as old Father Gabriel, who had christened Isabel as a baby and secretly married her to Alexander, drew a final cross in the gusting air over her grave. His gaze fell on me, and he nodded.

I stooped mechanically and released a pitifully small handful of dirt into the hole. It trickled dully onto the coffin's wooden lid. Father Gabriel next looked at Robbie, who shrank against me and buried his face against my arm. "You don't have to, Robbie," I whispered, and shook my head at the old priest. Leon stepped up and took a handful of soil, followed by Ana and Dora. Others lined up and followed their example, paying their last respects to a dignified but remote woman who had lived a good deal of her life apart from them, asking for neither their respect nor their approval but stubbornly following her own heart.

As we turned away from the graveside and started

toward the house, a tall, heavily veiled woman approached me and laid a gloved hand on my arm.

"*Señora?*" Her voice was old but with a hint of lilt that caught my attention and turned me to look at her. She lifted her veil, revealing startling blue-violet eyes in a delicate face. She extended her hand once more. "I am doña Elena Cuerello. Isabel was my daughter."

I stiffened. Robbie, still clutching my hand, stared at the stranger, his eyes widening as he realized that this woman was his grandmother.

Mine, too, I thought, and I stared at her with frank curiosity. She was both tall and slender, like Isabel, her hair and finely arched brows turned a beautiful silver-gray. Her mouth, too, was like her daughter's, although its frown lines seemed permanently etched, and there was a coldness in those extraordinary eyes that kept my spine stiff.

The woman suddenly dropped her hand, and I realized I had made no move to accept it. Her eyes glittered.

"I suppose I cannot blame you for refusing me welcome." Her voice was sharp and more heavily accented than her daughter's. She gave Robbie a long look before she dropped the veil over her face and turned away.

"No, wait. Please." I touched her arm and felt it stiffen as she glanced back at me. "Forgive me, *señora*. I was overcome by surprise." I tried to peer through the veil hiding her face. "Of course you are welcome here. I'm Katherine, Isabel's daughter." I put my arm around Robbie's shoulders. "This is my brother Robert."

Robbie offered a stiff little bow. "How do you do?"

Isabel's mother nodded, her veil whispering as it settled over her features. It puffed softly with her breath as she said, "I am pleased to meet you both." Then, to Robbie, "You have the look of your mother about you."

We stood in awkward silence until, surprisingly, Robbie took charge. He offered an arm to his grandmother and said politely, "Permit me to escort you into the house, *señora*."

Elena hesitated. Then she laid her gloved hand lightly on Robbie's coat sleeve. The three of us turned together and followed the others up the front steps of Rosswood House.

* * *

Doña Elena ensconced herself in a corner of the parlor sofa and remained there throughout the afternoon. When laid in her great-grandmother's arms, Elise was quiet and seemed content, as if she knew by instinct that this woman was kin. Robbie was enthralled with his grandmother. As the afternoon wore on, he eagerly produced treasures from his room to show her—everything from sketches in his drawing pad to his brand-new, store-bought pants to the ragged stuffed elephant no one was supposed to know he still slept with. He nestled against her, seeming not to mind her stiffness, and jumped up to get her more tea or a sandwich from the buffet set up in the dining room.

After some failed attempts to draw her out, I contented myself with observing her from a distance. I watched her hold Elise with an expression of wary interest, watched Father Gabriel bend over her with the familiarity of one who had known her for years, watched Leon make stiff, courteous attempts at conversation with her. Ana steered clear of her, always finding some task or other to divert her attention. To be fair, Ana had taken much of the funeral supper responsibilities upon herself, giving me the freedom to move among the guests or slip off by myself when I needed to. She and Leon had come immediately in response to my telegram. Although it was foolish, I kept watching the door, hoping for the sight of one more person.

But no one else arrived.

It was late afternoon when our guests began to drift away. In the foyer they took my hands and murmured final words of condolence as they slipped into their coats and hats. I turned from Laura Crawford's parting hug to find Elena pulling on her cloak behind me.

"Surely you're not leaving already?" I couldn't hide my dismay, and she glanced at me as she pulled on her bonnet. Her hands, I noticed, were bent with arthritis, making the task of tying the bonnet strings difficult.

"I must leave," she said, and in her tone I recognized the implacable will she had passed on to her daughter. "I have already stayed too long."

"But we will see you again soon?"

She shook her head. "I see no need. I have defied the don, your grandfather, by coming here at all. He expressly forbade it."

"But—" I was puzzled. "You told us he was dead."

"Yes." She crossed herself dutifully. "Nevertheless, I respect his wishes, *señora*." She had discarded the afternoon's habit of calling me by my name and retreated into the safety of formal titles.

Her aloofness stung.

I thought of Robbie, of the hungry, eager plea in his eyes as he'd snuggled next to her on the sofa, and my anger rose. "Are you just going to walk into our lives, after all these years, and walk right back out again?"

She replied stiffly, "You don't understand."

"What is there to understand?"

She drew back at my vehemence. "It is out of my hands," she insisted. "It is the don's wish."

"He's *dead*. What can you possibly owe him?" Guests were staring. I lowered my voice. "Think what you owe to *us*, to Isabel's children. To Elise, your great-granddaughter. Do we mean so little to you?"

She regarded me coldly. "Good-bye, *señora*." She extended a gloved hand to me in formal courtesy. I fisted my hands at my sides and kept them there. I saw her eyes narrow before she pulled the black veil over her face.

Without so much as a backward glance, doña Elena Cuerello brushed past me and walked out of her daughter's house.

* * *

The Stovolsky clock stood silent, its pendulum motionless and draped in black out of respect for Isabel. I tiptoed down the great staircase, and the eerie absence of the clock's measured sweeps made the sleeping house seem even quieter. I'd glanced at the small clock on my writing desk before leaving my bedroom and was shocked to see its hands approaching eleven-thirty. How was it possible, I wondered, that I could still be so wide awake after all that had happened today?

I clutched Katherine's journal against my chest as I made my way past the dining room, long since cleared of the funeral supper, and headed toward the library. I thought perhaps a brandy would give me courage enough to at least open the book.

Once the journal was back in my possession, I found a hundred excuses not to read it. I was too tired; I was too depressed. I couldn't think of Katherine and her problems now; I could only think about Isabel. Once the funeral was over, I promised myself, once I was rested, then I would find time to read Katherine's last entry.

Well, the funeral was over, and I was wide awake. The weak excuses fell away, exposing me to the real problem—I didn't want to read the journal. The truth was, Katherine's personality and life had become so interwoven with mine that I could no longer draw clear boundaries between them. Reading the details of how Katherine had murdered her husband would somehow tie me to the crime. It would be like reading about my own past. As curious as I had been at first to discover what was written on those mysterious missing pages, the prospect of reading them now filled me with dread.

I opened the library door to the bright light of a lamp and a cheerful fire. Father Philippe sat in one of the high-backed chairs, his feet propped on a stool, absorbed in a book.

Dressed as I was in a nightgown and bathrobe, my hair loose over my shoulders, I considered withdrawing quietly and fleeing back up the stairs. But in that moment he saw me. Hiding his astonishment, he smiled and rose to greet me.

"Mrs. Kamarov! How delightful. Please, come and share the fire." He gestured, quite genuinely, I thought, to the other armchair. As we sat down, he held up his book sheepishly. "I'm afraid you've caught me in a little indulgence, Mrs. Kamarov. My late-night habit of reading novels." He smiled ruefully. "I read them for pleasure and also to study human nature. Every emotion and behavior known to man appears in these tangled stories of people who love and struggle and make their mistakes. I confess, I find them quite captivating."

He pointed to the journal on my lap. "You are a late-night reader yourself, I see."

I glanced down. "This isn't exactly a novel, Father, although it reads like one. This"—I laid my hand over the cover—"is Katherine's journal, the one I told you was missing. I've only just recovered it."

I watched his face for a response. He drew back a little, his expression deepening from friendly to serious. But not, I was relieved to note, skeptical. He nodded. "I was hoping for a chance to speak with you about your...intriguing situation. Tell me, how are you faring...*Victoria*, is it not?"

"Yes. Although I hardly feel like Victoria anymore. So much has changed."

Father Philippe nodded and settled back in his chair. He rested his gaze on me and propped his chin on his thumb, rubbing a finger over his lower lip as he prepared to listen.

Perhaps because of the funeral, I started in the middle of my story, with the shift in my relationship with

Isabel. The pain of losing her sharpened as I recounted my childhood struggles with my own mother, and then finding my unexpected capacity to love and receive the love of Katherine's mother. "It changed me, Father. Even the way I feel about myself. I know it sounds strange, but sometimes I look in the mirror, and I don't know who I am. Of course, I'm not Katherine. But I'm not Victoria anymore, either. I do things Victoria would never do."

I told him about the rape and slicing Raymond's throat and my passionate but defeated attempts to see him prosecuted. I described confronting the town gossips and compelling them to accept Elise despite her questionable parentage. I told him of Emily's plight and offering her sanctuary, of taking responsibility for Robbie's welfare, of running the ranch when Isabel could no longer manage things herself. Of finding courage when I had always despised myself as a coward.

"So, you see." I spread my hands. "I've changed so much, I don't know what to call myself anymore. And March is looming only a few short months away. I know I can't go back to that life, to being that shy, cowardly woman. I won't be Ryan's compliant wife again nor that beautiful, empty-headed icon for my grandmother's stores. Victoria is gone, and she'll never come back. I've banished her, and someone very different — someone I hardly recognize — has stepped into her place."

Father Philippe shifted in his chair and brought his fingertips together. His dark eyes penetrated mine.

"Are you certain you must go back?" he said.

I shook my head. "Nothing is certain. That's the horror of it all. I could make such a lovely life here. I could be happy. But it's not my choice."

"Are you certain of that?"

I stared at him. "Well, no. But it wasn't my choice to come here in the first place, was it? I hardly knew anything about Katherine or her family. Then, suddenly, here I was, smack in the middle of her chaotic life."

The priest steepled his fingers and pressed his palms together. "And now you've smoothed the tangles and rooted yourself in relationships you are reluctant to leave."

"Yes."

"And this task you were sent here to perform. You mentioned it when we spoke before." I nodded. "Have you given more thought to what that could be?"

I hesitated before answering. "Isabel often told me she believed I was sent from God to teach Robbie, and to teach her, about love. Dora said something similar." I lifted a shoulder. "I've been assuming that I was sent here to help bring Robbie out of himself a little, to be a protector for Elise, maybe to restore Summerwood Cottage. These are all things Katherine would never have done."

Father Philippe laced his fingers together and dropped them to his lap. "Did it never occur to you that the good God intended to work through you was actually *for you*, my dear, for *your* benefit?" He smiled at my startled look. "I can see it has not. In my experience, people who minister to others become themselves transformed by the very love they give away. Put simply, one who blesses others is blessed himself. Love is strong, and its power to transform human life is unbounded."

He gave me a moment, studying me with his dark eyes.

"I don't believe you've banished Victoria at all," he said. "In fact, you've saved her. You redeemed her and gave her a new life—her own. I've listened to you describe some amazing challenges and how you've met them. Give Victoria her due credit. Remember, she arrived here last March with little more than her own good character and innate resilience, but they were sufficient to bring you to where you are today. Don't despise her, my dear. Love her. She has shown herself to be a remarkable woman. Your truest ally."

He leaned forward for emphasis.

"No matter what happens next March, you won't lose the person you have become. Perhaps that is God's greatest gift to you through this whole strange experience—the gift of discovering who you really are, independent of place or time or the expectations of others. You've found yourself, my dear, for now and for always."

Chapter Twenty-Two

My startling conversation with Father Philippe decided me against the brandy. The priest retired just after one o'clock, and I waited until I heard his footsteps on the stairs before I opened Katherine's journal. The pages were whiter, fresher than when I had last seen them, and Katherine's bold script seemed as familiar to me as my own. I resisted the urge to lose myself in a rereading of her earlier life and resolutely flipped toward the end of the journal. Almost through the written section, I was surprised to find a sudden change in handwriting.

I turned back a page, to Katherine's familiar script, and recognized her words about Anton as the last I had previously read: *He thinks he has won, but he has always underestimated me. Tonight, in the darkness of the new spring moon, I shall beat him at his own game.*

I flipped over the page to the new handwriting and realized with a shock that Isabel, not Katherine, had written this last entry. It was dated four weeks before her death.

My Dearest Katrina:
Dora, my true and faithful guardian, has promised not to return your journal to you until I

have departed this world. Forgive me, *hija mía*, for showing you my heart only through these scratches of ink across an impersonal page. But my confession brings me grief and shame, and I could not bring myself to present it to you in any form but this. Indeed, if I could not resort to such cowardly means, I would carry my secrets to the grave with me and leave you ignorant of the role I have played in certain events. Or perhaps I take the cowardly route by confessing to you and unburdening my soul at your expense. Forgive me, *querida*, for the pain these words may cause you. But you must know the truth and then decide how best to proceed.

I came across your journal quite by chance on the night you tried to harm yourself. I read it over and over in the following days while you lay delirious on your bed and muttered strange names and raved about a burning bridge. I spent hours on my knees, lighting candles and praying that God would spare your life. The possibility that you might take your own life had never occurred to me. The very irony that such an act would rise up and defeat my own seemed like God mocking me. It would be His third punishment.

The words of your journal confirmed what I never wanted to admit but I always knew. May God forgive me for not protecting you from your father, Katrina, for not taking you away from here. My pride has been my bane; I could not go back to my father's house and admit he had been right about Alexander. No, it was worse than that. I could not admit to myself that my love for Alexander not only made a prisoner of me but of you as well. And so we remained, I the willing captive and you the innocent one.

I did not know you blamed yourself for your brother's death. It was I, not you, *querida*, who was responsible. God's first punishment to me for choosing a life with Alexander was to take away my beloved Nicholas. His second punishment was to give me another son, a son I did not want. I was never certain if Alexander knew that Roberto was not his child. But I think not. I cannot imagine he would have allowed me to live if he knew I was carrying Anton's bastard.

I blamed Alexander for giving Anton so much freedom on the ranch. I blamed God for deserting me. I blamed Ana for bringing her despicable brother into our midst.

I can still hear the rain tapping on the roof of the chapel and see the way the altar candles flickered as I knelt at my prayers. They almost gusted out when the door opened suddenly and shut against the harsh January wind. Without turning, I knew with the clarity of the hunted scenting the hunter that Anton stood at the back of the chapel. I cursed myself for allowing him to catch me alone. Ever since he had taken to following me with his arrogant eyes and making opportunities to corner me alone, I had tried to keep in the company of others. Dora usually accompanied me to the chapel. But that day she was in bed with an illness, so rare for her, so unfortunate for me. But, no, it had nothing to do with fortune. I turned and saw Anton's eyes, so like Ana's, fixed on me, and I knew he had only waited and watched and seized the opportunity when I laid it in his lap.

I tried to run, but he caught me and threw me down on the stone floor, where he shamed and brutalized me before the very eyes of God. If I wasn't before, I was convinced then that God hated me, and I hated Him right back. When I discovered I was pregnant, I prayed for God to take away my unborn child. God heard my prayers. But He took my beautiful Nicholas instead and left a dark changeling in his place.

I was so filled with grief and hate, I thought I might die from it. I cared for no one and nothing. My life seemed only a painful nightmare from which I could not awaken. I am ashamed to think how I abandoned you, Katrina. I was so afraid Alexander would find out my terrible secret that I blinded myself to the fact that you needed protection from him even more than I. Dora had cared for me as a child, and I trusted her to care for you as well. I never learned how to be a mother to you, *niña mía*. I wanted to believe you didn't really need me. It would have hurt me to believe otherwise. I was so selfish.

Please believe me when I tell you I never expected that others would blame you for Anton's death. I planned it so carefully, to make it look like a sudden, mysterious illness. It was soon after I discovered I was dying of the consumption that I made my plans. I needed no doctor to confirm what I suspected — I had watched my grandmother die of it when I was a child, so I knew the symptoms. I also knew I did not want to seek help. I was prepared to die; indeed, I felt half-dead already. It is astonishing how the knowledge of impending death takes away one's fear. I had neither the heart nor the courage to lift a hand against my husband. But I could rid the world of Anton Kamarov as easily as swatting a fly. And then let the world do to me whatever it wished. You, my Katrina, would be saved from a future of pain and humiliations, the kind of life I knew only too well.

When I guessed you were pregnant, I realized I would have to act soon. Anton was counting on inheriting the ranch if the child you carried was a boy. If it was not, the ranch would remain under my control, and I knew Anton would not hesitate to make public his claim to Roberto as his son if he thought it would force me to share the ranch with him. I told myself I was getting rid of Anton to save you and Roberto, but I'm not that noble. I hated Anton, and I added to that my hatred for Alexander. In my mind the two men had become like one — a devil I could not allow to live.

Buying what I needed from the old Chinese woman was tricky. I knew you were friendly with the eldest son, and I was afraid he would tell you my secret. So I made a bargain with the old woman — I would give them money to leave town quietly and never return. Before they went, they were to burn down their shop and their house to make it look as though someone hating Chinese had driven them out. I knew the old woman would keep our bargain, for I threatened to accuse her family of murder if they came back. She knew no one would believe a Chinese against a Rostnova.

It was simple, really. A little bit in Anton's food for a few days, then the final dose of poison. When you took sick that same night, and I realized you had given yourself mistletoe, I cursed myself for not taking you into my confidence. Dora later assured me you intended only a miscarriage, waiting for new moon to enhance the safe passage of your child's soul into the arms of God. It was a miracle that you not only pulled through but that your child was also saved. I took it as a sign that God intended a new life for you both. I did not feel regret over Anton's death, *querida*, only that you suffered needlessly. I was furious with you for putting yourself and your child in such danger. But later I understood it was fury at myself and terror when I considered what had almost happened to you.

I cannot understand how, in the aftermath of such wicked deeds, God granted me in the last months of my life a joy and peace beyond what I have ever experienced. When you, my daughter, should despise and revile me, you came to me with love and forgiveness in your heart. When I could only see Roberto as the curse of God, you showed me he is a lonely child who was not responsible for the accident of his birth. Because of you, Katrina, the heavy cloud of grief and hate that darkened my life has thinned to admit new light. Even my prayers have changed because of you. The unexpected gift of your love has pierced me like an arrow and lodged in my heart. I never realized that love is stronger than hate, or that truth is stronger than evil. I don't know if I can still make my peace with God. Because of you, I want the chance for that peace. After so many months of wanting to die, I wish now I could stay with you, *querida*, and learn more about this miracle of love you have brought into my life.

I am so tired. I have written this account so that you might know the truth and decide what is best to do. I trust you to know what to tell Roberto, whether or not he should know that he is Anton's son and that it was his mother, not his sister, who was responsible for his father's death.

May God be always with you, Katrina *mía*.

And there, pressed on the page like a signature, was a small, perfect violet.

* * *

I slept very late the next morning. When I finally dressed and went downstairs, Marta informed me that Leon and Father Philippe were waiting for me in the library as soon as I could manage to join them.

The two men were sharing a bottle of port. Leon rose when he saw me and smiled broadly. A little too broadly, I thought.

"Katherine, my dear! Come join us. You remember

Father Philippe, of course?"

Father Philippe rose and took my hand. "Good day, Mrs. Kamarov." He looked amazingly fresh and rested. I smiled and nodded politely, appreciating his tact.

"Good morning, Father."

"Morning? Heavens, girl, it's past noon." Leon's booming voice resonated unpleasantly in my head. "Sit here, Katherine." He held out a chair beside the priest's. "I hope you don't mind my asking the padre to join us. I wanted the benefit of his expertise before you and I discuss this."

"Discuss what?" I shot Father Philippe a questioning glance.

Leon coughed a little and cleared his throat. "Well, it's like this, my dear." He coughed again. "We've been reading over my brother's will. He made it, you know, before your marriage." He thrust a finger into his collar and tugged vigorously. "I'll come directly to the point, shall I? The truth is, Alexander has left everything to me. The land, the house, the livestock, the money. I'm sorry, my dear. The padre here confirms that the assets would have gone to you in trust for the son of your marriage. But, as your child turned out to be a girl—well, you see." He spread his hands. "Upon Isabel's passing, your father specified that it should all come to me." He tugged at his collar again.

I blinked at him. "You mean," I said slowly, "Robbie and Elise and I must look for another place to live?"

Leon looked shocked. "Good God, no! Oh, sorry that, Padre." He glanced an apology at the priest. "My dear, you are welcome to stay here for as long as you like. As *long* as you like." His beetle brows drew together like a thick black brush above his eyes. "No doubt this comes as a shock to you, Katherine, on the heels of losing your dear mother." He lowered his voice. "I'm sorry."

I glanced at Father Philippe, who was watching me silently. "Alexander left us nothing?"

The priest's dark eyes were soft with sympathy. "Nothing. Your uncle inherits completely, my dear."

Leon spoke gently. "I'm certain your father never intended to disinherit you or Robert, Katherine. Despite his shortcomings, my brother was a fair man. He must have meant that I would look out for you, which, of course, I fully intend to do. Have no fear on that account."

I stared at Leon and wondered why Alexander would have willed his estate to his brother over the head of his own son.

But, of course, the answer was obvious. Alexander had known, after all, Isabel's terrible secret. I glanced from Leon to Father Philippe and wondered who else knew about Robbie. Isabel may have confided in her old priest, Father Gabriel. Did Dora know? Of course, she must. Dora knew everything about Isabel.

I reassembled my thoughts. "Will you live here now, Uncle?"

"Well, my dear, we have a comfortable residence in San Francisco, as you know." He cleared his throat uneasily and glanced at Father Philippe. "I must say, though, I've been thinking about what you said. That an earthquake may be coming." He held up his hand. "Not that I'm superstitious, mind you. But it might be prudent to move some of our belongings up here. You know, not to have all our eggs in one basket, so to speak. What would you say to that? Mind if we take up a little space for some objets d'art?"

I smiled. "That sounds very sensible, Uncle, and not in the least superstitious." I caught Father Philippe's grin before he hid it behind his hand. "And now that Isabel is gone, I hope you will feel free to discuss with me any plans you have for the ranch, such as buying and selling land or where to invest your resources."

Leon's black eyes brightened. "I was quite hoping to enlist your help, my dear girl. After our…discussion over Russ Paxton's offer to buy up the north valley, I spoke to several acquaintances in the city. It seems that grape growing is becoming quite a lucrative enterprise. I've got my lawyer looking up the ownership rights to those grape varieties the old man was cooking up. You were wise to keep Isabel from selling." His grin softened. "I won't underestimate your business acuity again. In fact, I would welcome your counsel at any time. This is, after all, a family business. And you'll always be a Rostnova, even if you marry again."

I nodded and leaned back. "Robbie, too. I wish you would set up something for him, Uncle, now that all this belongs to you. Even if Alexander intended no harm, his son should not be left without an inheritance."

Leon pulled thoughtfully on his mustache. "I'm ashamed I didn't think of that myself. I will, of course, set up something for him right away." He picked up his glass of port and took a swallow. "And what about you, Katherine? What can I do for you?"

I didn't even pause to think about it. "Give me the cottage, Uncle, and enough money to finish the repairs and keep up the maintenance." I clasped my hands. "We're only halfway through repairing the damage from the fire. Then I'll need money to replant the rose garden, and I'd like to hire a regular gardener to maintain the property."

Leon smiled tenderly. "You have the old man's heart, Katya, well and truly. No one has cared about that place except you since the day he died. Of course it's yours. I'll have the papers drawn up." He added, "Anything else?"

"Yes, there is one more thing." I took a breath and looked him in the eye. "I want clear title to the north valley and the timberland slopes around it. And," I continued, ignoring his sudden scowl, "once the vineyard gets going, I want thirty percent of the profits."

Leon's black eyes flashed. "What in blazes—"

It was my turn to hold up my hand. "Thirty percent isn't so much, Uncle. You just admitted you wouldn't have a wine-growing business at all if you'd sold the land to Russ Paxton."

There was a sharp silence, broken by Father Philippe's soft chuckle. "She drives a hard bargain, Leon, but she's got a point." His handsome face beamed like a mischievous boy's. "I'd want to stay on her good side from now on, if I were you."

Leon reddened. "Devious wench," he muttered. But his eyes twinkled under the fierce draw of his brows. "All right, young woman. You've got your cottage and your land." I arched an eyebrow. "*And* thirty percent of the vineyard profits, blast it all! *Which*," he added, wagging his finger at me, "is hardly more than wishful thinking at this point."

"But it won't be for long." I matched his slow grin with one of my own. "And we both know it." I rose from my chair and held out my hand. "May I say it's a pleasure doing business with you, Uncle."

Chapter Twenty-Three

Christmas was less than a week away. Feeling anything but festive since Isabel's death, I had done nothing to decorate the house or prepare for any kind of Christmas supper. I didn't even know what sort of tradition the Rostnova household was accustomed to observing. I would have to find out.

I was climbing the stairs, considering when I could get into town to make some secret purchases, when I spied Dora and Ana huddled together in the doorway of Ana's bedroom. There was an unmistakable air of conspiracy about their bent heads and soft voices. I froze on the second step from the top and watched them, puzzled and curious. Then I saw Dora pass something into Ana's hands, and my heart leaped in my chest. I recognized the box from my writing desk—smooth and round, made of bamboo. I remembered the Chinese letters drawn on the hinged lid. And the deadly white powder hidden inside.

Ana watched Dora's face, concentrating on her words, which I could not hear. She glanced at the bamboo container in her hands and then furtively over her shoulder again. She whispered something back to Dora. Then she nodded and slipped into her bedroom, shutting the door very softly. I stayed where I was until

Dora retreated down the hall.

I went straight to my desk and pulled open the drawer with the hidden compartment, just to confirm it was empty. I stood there, staring at the light dusting of white powder showing a faint impression of something round, and I wondered. Had Isabel hidden the telltale box in Katherine's drawer after she poisoned Anton? Or had Dora herself hidden it there, possibly to keep her mistress from taking her own life once the deed was done?

That was crazy. Isabel would never kill herself. But why hide the evidence here? Why not just get rid of it? And why give it to Ana?

As if in response to my thoughts, Dora appeared suddenly in the doorway. She stood there, watching me as I closed the desk drawer and turned.

"Come in, Dora. And please shut the door." She did as I asked and then stood by the door, her arms folded, her face expressionless. I pointed to the desk without taking my eyes off her. "Did you take the moonseed out of this drawer?"

She shrugged. "Why ask me? You see me give it to your aunt."

I stared at her. "Come sit down." I walked to the window seat and sat. Dora crossed the room but stood before me, her arms still folded, her mouth a tight, defensive line. "What did you tell Ana, Dora?" When she didn't reply, I persisted. "You told her about Isabel, didn't you?"

She looked puzzled, and I hesitated. Didn't Dora know, after all? I searched her face, but her stubborn expression told me nothing.

"Do you know what Isabel wrote in the journal, Dora?" She shrugged again, which could have meant anything. Losing my patience, I got to my feet and began to pace. "That powder should have been disposed of long ago. There was no point in keeping it. I forgot it was in my desk until just now, when I saw you give the box to Ana." I stopped pacing and stood before her. "What did you tell Ana?"

Dora shrugged again. "I tell her how to use the root powder."

I stared at her, incredulous. "Why would Ana need poison?"

Dora peered at me as if I were very stupid. "For the misery in her hands and her feet." She seemed annoyed.

"To treat her arthritis? That poison treats arthritis?"

Dora reached out and patted my shoulder. "I make the mistake and forget that you are not Katherine. She always makes warm possets for her mama when cold winter winds make the pain worse. When it starts again in November, I come here and take to make the possets. I know you don't know how. Then Ana asks me, and I give it to her. I explain how to make, how much to use so she doesn't get sick." She squinted at me. "Too much medicine makes poison."

"But," I sputtered, "you were so secretive. I thought—"

"Your uncle doesn't like Chinese medicine. He doesn't like Indian medicine, either." Her sudden grin flashed like bright sun through a gap in a craggy cliff. "He is a very modern man. Very little patience, very little sense." She chuckled at her own joke.

I sat down hard on the window seat and stared at her. "Then you didn't tell her about Isabel?"

Her grin faded, and her eyes were once more expressionless.

I took a breath. "Dora, I know that Isabel must have told you." I glanced at the closed bedroom door and lowered my voice. "You must know that she used the poison to kill Katherine's husband."

Dora stared at me for a moment. Then she folded her arms and shook her head. "No."

"Yes, I'm afraid it's true, Dora. Isabel poisoned Anton Kamarov."

"Oh, yes. Poison, yes. But not this." She unfolded her arms and gestured at the writing desk. "Not root powder. This is only for her pains. She uses rattlesnake venom to kill that bastard. After she uses the bamboo, then she kills him. Kills him good." She grinned. "He suffers, that devil, before he dies."

My mouth went dry. Dora gave me a shrewd look and then lowered herself onto a chair with a heavy sigh.

"That Chinese gives her the idea," she said. "Little slivers of bamboo in his food for a few days. Sharp like razors, cut inside his stomach, makes bleeding. Then, on the last day, she gives snake poison in drink. It gets into that man's blood through the cuts in his stomach and makes him suffer before he dies." She looked at my expression, and her voice rose. "Makes him pay for what he does to her. For what he does to *you*." Her little eyes narrowed into glimmering slits. "You dare judge her? You think she's wicked to save you, to save your child?"

I jumped to my feet and started pacing again. "I'm not judging her, Dora. But, yes, I think it was wrong. Murder is wrong. And such a painful, awful—" I shook my head. "I can't believe Isabel could do something that cruel. Even if she hated him. There's no excuse—"

"*Ha!*" Her short bark brought me to a halt. "You stand here alive because of what she does." It was one of the few times I'd ever seen Dora angry. Her big nostrils flared; her little eyes scorched me with accusation. "Is it better let that monster live and you and your baby die? You think he lets you live if he knows about Chinese boy, your baby's father?" She snorted. "You think you are better than Isabel? You almost kill that Delacroix man. Almost slice his throat good to save you, to save your daughter. How does that make you better than her?" She saw my face change, and she nodded with a *humph* of satisfaction. "Better to spill his blood than yours or Elise's. Better to kill that Anton before he hurts anybody again. Nobody is sorry to see him die, not even his sister. Everybody is glad."

Nobody blames you, Kat. Michael's words came back to me. *He was a scoundrel. I'm glad he's dead...*

"But—" I gestured weakly. "What I did to Raymond Delacroix was self-defense, an instinctive reflex. What Isabel did was so calculated, so cold-blooded—"

"Hot blood, cold blood." Dora shrugged and tapped a finger to her head. "Your mother is clever. Very careful when she sets the trap to catch the bear. She knows that sooner or later he comes charging again from the forest looking for blood. She doesn't wait this time until he attacks. She kills him while he sleeps. If she waits—"

Dora shrugged again. "She is only a weak woman fighting against the devil. How can she win? Only if she is very clever. And you see." She spread her hands before her. "Nobody catches her. Nobody can say he dies of anything but stomach sickness. Clever. My clever *niña*."

Her proud eyes gleamed. "She is always strong, always full of spirit. When she's only a child, she defies the don, her father, and he beats her to set example for her sisters to obey. But he doesn't break her. When she marries her love, she loses her family. But she doesn't complain. She knows her own heart, and she follows it. Always."

In a rare moment of affection, Dora reached out and took my hand. "You are not the daughter of her body but surely of her heart. You love with spirit and courage. You, like no one else, can understand her. Isabel sins, yes. Isabel lives her own way and chooses wrong path sometimes, yes. But Isabel is *good*. She loves her family, even when they curse her name and drive her away. She loves that devil she marries and is faithful to him always. She loves her old nurse." Her eyes filled. "And she loves you. She begs God to forgive her." Tears trailed over the rough terrain of Dora's cheeks. Her voice turned gruff. "You remember Isabel's goodness and her spirit, and you tell your daughter these good things. When Elise is old and tells her stories, she brings honor to her grandmother's name. Yes?"

My eyes widened, and Dora nodded sagely. "Elise becomes a storyteller. And you. You find your own way to remember Isabel." She smiled through her tears. "Yes?"

* * *

In my dream I am a lioness crouching on the dark, wet grass, straining my ears toward the line of trees. Waiting. My cub presses against my side, trembling with cold and fear. My heart reaches out to her like loving hands, and I take her inside my body, where I know she will be safe. Now, as one being, we stare with crescent eyes at the dark line of trees.

There is no warning this time. The trees part, and the bear rushes toward me. For the first time I see my enemy — powerful jaws and sharp teeth, fire in its eyes as it charges into the clearing.

There is no time to think. With a mighty roar, I rear up on my powerful hind legs. I bare my teeth and lash the air with my claws. The bear also rears up, and I notice a golden seam running down its underside.

The seam widens, and a golden woman steps out from the belly of the bear. Astonished, I realize that the bear is only a coat of skins, which the woman casts aside in a lifeless heap.

She opens her mouth, and a sweet song fills the night air. It curls around me like a fragrance I've known before. The woman reaches into her breast and pulls out a golden key. Laying it flat across her palm, she offers it to me.

When I reach for the key, I notice my hand is human. Looking down, I see my lioness body had taken the form of a woman. With human eyes I read words inscribed on the key: "Love opens doors."

I look up, a question on my lips. But the woman has vanished. The clearing is empty except for me, my golden key, and the tender light of the moon.

Chapter Twenty-Four

In the four months of his absence, I had begun to doubt that I would ever see Michael again. Despite the vague promise that he was coming for Christmas, one day followed another, and Ana had no word from him. So it came as something of a shock when he suddenly arrived the day before Christmas Eve.

I had been out for my morning walk, taking longer than usual because rain had kept me indoors for nearly a week. An hour of tramping through mud and redwood needles and inhaling a forest scent almost too rich to bear took me the long way around to the family graveyard. Wind had driven dead leaves to mix with the bright flower offerings on Isabel's grave, and the hard rains had flattened them together like a thick, protective coverlet. I straightened the simple wooden cross marking her head until a proper gravestone could be carved. I'd given the order myself for the inscription: "Beloved mother and grandmother, taken from us too soon." I knew it wasn't enough. As Dora had hinted, I would find another way to memorialize Isabel. In fact, I already knew the form it would take.

A few drops on my head scarcely got my attention before the skies broke in a torrential downpour. Although I wasn't far from the house, I was soaked through by the time I reached the back door, cursing myself for not wearing a protective rain cloak. Through the screen door, I heard voices in the kitchen, and I recognized Emily's laugh. *Good,* I thought. That probably meant she had hot tea waiting.

With water running into my eyes, I blindly lunged into the kitchen, letting the screen door bang shut behind me.

"Jiminy Christmas!" I exclaimed, grabbing a towel from the hook by the door and burying my sopping head in it. I rubbed the towel over my face and pulled it down my braid as I glanced up. "That'll teach me to go running off without my—"

The words died in my throat.

Emily was sitting at the kitchen table. She turned bright eyes to me, her cheeks flushing prettily. "Katherine, look who's—" She stopped as she saw me. "Lord, Katherine, you're soaked clean through!"

No kidding. I was painfully aware of water running rivulets down my face and neck, pouring off my braid and dripping into puddles around the hem of my skirt. My disarray made even more striking the contrast between me and the elegant young man who leaned gracefully against the sideboard, his long legs crossed casually at the ankle.

"Hello, Kat," Michael said quietly.

I stared at him with wide eyes. The only sound I made was the annoying drip of water running off me and spoiling Carmen's immaculate floor.

Michael gave a sudden laugh.

"*Jiminy Christmas* is right! You look worse than a cat

who fell down a well."

He made no move to help me, just stood there with a smug grin on his face.

From the corner of my eye, I saw Emily glance between us. "I think I'll get some towels." She rose quickly and disappeared through the kitchen door.

My mind couldn't take it in. It was more than the suddenness of seeing him. The truth was, he was so changed, I had the fleeting sensation that he wasn't Michael at all. As I gaped at him, the word that came to my mind was a term I would never have used to describe Michael Carey: *gorgeous*.

He seemed older, that awkward hint of youth matured into an easy confidence. His long, graceful body was still lean but had filled out a little, as if he had grown into himself. His hair, always so wild, was cut short and shaped by an expert, his sideburns tapered slightly longer, his upper lip sporting a fashionable little mustache. He had new glasses with gold frames more square than round, giving him the look of a businessman rather than a scholar. The vested suit he wore looked expensive and was tailored to fit him exquisitely. My gaze trailed down his long legs to his boots, square-toed and shiny black.

"Finished?" he asked politely.

I scowled at him. "It's just that you're so changed, Michael. I hardly recognized you."

His gaze resting on me was thoughtful. "I haven't made up my mind if you've changed or not." A smile played with his mouth.

My cheeks flushed hot under the trails of water still

trickling from my plastered hair.

The door opened, and Ana swept into the kitchen.

"Michael! My dear boy!" She wrapped him in a fierce hug and drew back for a thorough appraisal. "Well, just look at you. The young New Yorker. I must say, I'm impressed!" She cocked her head. "I'm not sure about that mustache, though. It might take some getting used to."

I snorted, and Michael threw me a look. "It goes with the suit," he said lightly, but his finger stroked the absurd little brush self-consciously. I smiled to myself.

Ana saw me, and her brow furrowed. "Heavens, child! What on earth have you been doing?" She pulled away from her nephew and crossed the kitchen, taking the towel from me and pushing me into a chair. She sponged vigorously at my hair just as Emily reappeared with more towels.

"Thank you, Emily." Ana's voice was brisk with disapproval. "It won't do, Katherine, if you come down with a chill." She applied a fresh towel with renewed vigor. "Michael! Come here and help your cousin get these filthy boots off."

Michael approached without a word and squatted before me. He bent his head to unlace my boot, suddenly so close that his familiar, clean scent knocked a wave of pure longing through me. My hands reached for him, but I pushed him away instead.

"Don't bother, Michael," I said hoarsely. "I can manage it."

He raised his head and looked directly into my eyes. His were the gray-green I remembered—no amount of fancy living in New York could change that. It pierced my heart, however, to find no tenderness in them now. "Suit yourself," he said indifferently. He rose and turned away to wash his hands in the sink.

I finished the job Michael had begun while Ana fisted her hands on her hips and scowled at me.

"Tell Dora to fix you a hot bath, Katya. Then you'd better have a rest. I'll send Marta up with a tray later."

She was showing off for her nephew. The thought made me bristle.

"You needn't give me orders, Aunt," I said. "I'm a grown woman, quite capable of looking after myself, thank you."

Ana's retort was swift. "A grown woman doesn't go traipsing around in the pouring rain, soaking herself to the bone and risking pneumonia. Not when she has a baby to look after." She gentled her tone. "Go on upstairs, Katya, and stop spitting at me like an angry cat." She gave my shoulder a conciliatory pat. "Off with you, now. I'll see the boots are cleaned."

Emily's arm slipped quietly around me. I glanced up at her and then uneasily at Michael. He was still at the sink, wiping his hands on a towel and staring out the window. He didn't turn as we left the kitchen.

* * *

It annoyed me that Ana was right about my needing a nap. After a long, hot bath, I decided I would lie down for just a little while. I didn't open my eyes for nearly two hours, and the clock on my writing desk told me I was too late to go down for dinner. So I took my time dressing, wishing my dark green gown were clean—I liked the way it brought out the brown of my eyes. Tired of mourning attire, I rejected my black merino wool and selected a navy silk with cream lace at the collar and sleeves. I frowned, wondering if it were too dressy. I wouldn't want Michael to think I was preening for him. Maybe I should wear the calico…

I ended up in the black merino, perversely pleased with its unrelieved severity. I no longer needed Dora to arrange my hair, and it wasn't long before the black, silky curtain was firmly secured in a soft twist, and ebony bobs swung from my ears. I artfully applied makeup, perhaps overemphasizing my eyes, which I considered my best feature. I couldn't completely hide the dark shadows of grieving from my face, but a little pink in the cheeks and on the lips helped distract from them. Deciding it was the best I could do, I put away my makeup pots and chided myself a little as I spritzed on the jasmine scent I knew Michael liked.

Elise slept in the nursery now. I pushed her door open softly to see if she was awake and found her crib empty. Either Ana or Emily must have taken her downstairs already to meet Michael. Feeling cheated, I pressed my lips together and stalked out of the nursery.

Peals of laughter drifted from the open parlor door. I crossed the foyer and stood in the doorway for a moment, unobserved. Despite my pique, my frown melted into a smile.

Elise was propped on Michael's lap and staring at Robbie, who was capering on the carpet in front of them. Every so often she turned her head and stared up at Michael, and her look was at once so solemn and so comical that it broke new waves of laughter from everyone in the room.

Ana was the first to see me.

"Katya, dear. Come and see how your daughter is charming her cousin!"

Michael grinned as I approached. "Katherine, I am completely besotted by your daughter." As if on cue, Elise opened her mouth in a wide toothless smile and banged her fists together. "You see? She's irresistible." His slender hands circled her waist and gently lifted her into the air above his head. Elise beamed down at him and cooed.

"Looks like the charming is mutual." My words were gruff because I had to push them over a lump in my throat at the sight of Michael and Elise together. I had imagined this scene a thousand times. Michael gave me a swift look as he settled Elise back on his lap.

"Katya! Look what Michael brought me all the way from New York!" Robbie tugged on my hand, and I let him lead me to a corner of the room. A cardboard theater as high as the sofa back was set up, with real cloth curtains that rose and fell with the pull of a cord and screens of different background scenes. The actors were cardboard cutouts with wedged bases to make them freestanding and paper costumes that could be changed like paper-doll clothes. "Michael went to see real plays, and he's going to teach me how to do one using these cardboard people." He held up a muscular specimen. "You want to play with us?"

I glanced at Michael, who looked at Robbie. "No parts for girls in this play, Robbie. Only ferocious pirates.

Then again," he added, with a sidelong look at me, "your sister might be just right for Gertrude, the loudmouthed parrot." I dropped open my mouth to protest, and Michael winked at Robbie. "See what I mean?"

I snapped my mouth shut, and Robbie shrieked with laughter, startling Elise, who scrunched up her face and prepared for a good wail. But Michael lifted her to his shoulder and patted her back, rocking her and crooning gently. I watched her little body relax and nestle into his neck. My own body went soft.

I sank to the sofa beside Emily.

"I gave Elise some applesauce when she woke up, and I brought her down," Emily said, with a trace of unease. "I hope you don't mind, Katherine."

I forced a smile. "Of course. That's exactly the dress I would have chosen for her." It was my favorite—petal pink with little embroidered ducks and flowers around the hem. It brought out the creamy translucence of her skin and softened the intense dark of her eyes.

Ana spoke up. "Michael was just telling us about some of the exciting people he met in New York. Imagine, sitting to dinner with the Vice President of the United States and the Prime Minister of England!" She shook her head. "I'm afraid you'll find our San Francisco society quite dull, Michael, after the glamour of living with the Stratfords."

Michael lifted a shoulder, careful not to disturb Elise, who was beginning to drowse against him. "I'm a San Franciscan, Aunt. New York is an exciting city, certainly, but it isn't home. Do you know, even the fog smells different here on the west coast? And the color of the

Pacific is a perfect blue I've never seen anywhere else."

His voice was soft, but I smiled at the subtle passion in it. It was always there when he talked about the things that mattered to him—finishing his novel, promoting social causes, dreaming of a career in writing. Marrying me.

I suddenly saw through the polished veneer, and he was Michael again, or very nearly. He'd changed from his fine traveling clothes into casual slacks and a thick cable-knit sweater that made him look achingly familiar. But the new elegance was still there, that almost imperceptible shift in manner, in the way he held his head, in the way he smiled and spoke. There was a hint of distance about him, as if he had moved just beyond my reach.

But, of course, how could I expect otherwise? He was a successful novelist now, rubbing elbows with the elite of the publishing world, being groomed to marry the daughter of one of the wealthiest men in San Francisco. I shuddered inwardly. Vivian Stratford. He hadn't mentioned her name yet, but I suspected it wouldn't be long.

Elise had fallen asleep. I rose and approached Michael, holding out my arms. "I'll take her upstairs now," I whispered.

But Michael rose instantly from his chair. "Let me," he whispered back. "She might wake up if I give her to you."

I nodded, and Michael followed me from the parlor, carrying the sleeping child in his arms. When we reached the nursery, he laid her gently in her crib, and I settled the quilt over her. Without opening her eyes, she heaved a big sigh and then resumed her quiet, regular breathing. Michael and I stood in silence, our hands resting side by side on the crib rail, and watched my daughter sleep.

In the magic of the moment, I could believe that Michael was my husband and Elise was our child.

Michael, can you feel it?

"She's beautiful, Kat." Michael's voice was soft beside me. He raised his head and looked at me in the dim light. "Ana told me about your ordeal when Elise was born. She told me you delivered her all by yourself in that god-awful attic at the cottage. And Dora found you unconscious the next morning." He leaned an elbow on the rail and stared at me. "What made you go wandering off by yourself like that? You both could have died." There was an edge in his voice. "It's a miracle you didn't."

I bristled. "We came through it all right, Michael." I added, "No thanks to you."

It was an unfair blow. I don't know what made me say it. Michael stared at me, and I looked away. Curling my hands around the crib rail, I fixed my gaze on my daughter's peaceful face. After a moment Michael reached down and lightly brushed Elise's cheek with his knuckle.

He left the room without another word.

* * *

Leon was thrilled to see his nephew again. Several times he leaned across the supper table toward Michael, beaming and booming, "So good to see you again, son!" Our places at the table had changed somewhat. Emily sat across from me, beside Michael. Robbie now sat with us, in Ana's old place beside me. Leon sat at one head of the table and Ana at the other, in Isabel's chair. I inwardly bridled at her presumption and had to remind myself that Ana had a perfect right to sit wherever she liked. The servants still treated me with deference, but it was clear that Ana was now mistress of the Russian House.

Despite my resentment, I was relieved to discover that Ana always took charge of the Christmas festivities, even when Isabel was alive. Robbie informed me that, according to Russian custom, the Christmas tree was brought in and decorated on Christmas Eve after the children were tucked into bed. And if we had been very good all year, Father Christmas would leave gifts under it on Christmas morning.

As if reading my thoughts, Ana spoke up. "Michael, I've managed to find some plump cranberries for your favorite Christmas dish." Her eyes twinkled as her nephew's face lighted in a grin.

"*Kissel*?" Seeing Emily's puzzled expression, Michael went on to explain. "*Kissel* is a special cranberry pudding they make in Russia. In fact, Emily, you're in for a true Russian Christmas. Everything from the food to the decorations is the way my aunt's family used to do things at home."

"Except for the snow." Ana sighed. "I miss a snowy Christmas. You can't go sledding down these California hills like you could in Russia."

Leon snorted. "Romantic nonsense. Your father lost nearly a third of his livestock one year because of the cold. I'm grateful for California weather." He stabbed a small red potato with his fork and pointed it at her. "You think that pain in your hands would be better back in the snow? California is a paradise compared to the old country."

Ana bristled. "That's because you weren't born there, Leon. You don't have the strong ties that I do. My sister and I loved the Christmas sledding and going for rides in our father's *troika* and making a snow maiden in our front yard—"

"Snow maiden?" Emily looked from Ana to Leon. "You mean, instead of a snowman?"

Robbie piped up. "She means like the real Snow Maiden, right, Auntie Ana?" He sat up importantly. "Russian children know the story of the Snow Maiden, the *sniggle*—" He stopped and looked at his aunt for help.

"*Snegurochka*," Ana said. "A little girl made from snow. There is a legend, Emily, of an elderly Russian couple"—Leon groaned, and Ana glared at him—"who were so desperate to have a child of their own that they decided to make one from snow. They fashioned a little girl from their own heart's desire, with delicate little hands and feet and a smile sweeter than a thrush's song. Then, by miracle, the snow girl came alive and lived with them for the whole of winter. She was kind and good, and they loved her very much. The mother made her a coat and cap of the softest, whitest fur. The father taught her to play the *balalaika*, and together they sang songs of old Russia. But, sadly, as the winter drew to an end, the little girl grew weaker, and finally she told her beloved parents that she had to go back to the land of snow and ice, which was her birthplace. The couple were so upset, they vowed they would not let her go. The father bolted the door, and the mother held her daughter tightly all through the last night of winter. In the morning, when the mother opened her eyes, all that was left of her beautiful daughter was the white fur cap and coat she had made for her and a puddle of pure, clear water on the floor."

There was a moment of appreciative silence around the table.

"That's a *horrible* story!" I blurted out. Ana looked at me in surprise.

"Why, Katya! You've heard that story every year since you were born."

Robbie touched my arm. "But the Snow Maiden came back the next winter," he said. "Didn't she, Auntie Ana?"

Ana shrugged. "Some say that. Some say she never came back, and the old couple still watch for her every winter. Others say she visits a different couple every year. The way I heard it, the important lesson of the Snow Maiden is to accept a blessing when God sends it your way. And then be willing to send the blessing on. Maybe if the mother and father hadn't tried so hard to hold onto her, she could have left when it was her time instead of melting. Then she might have come back to them the next winter—"

Ana saw my face and stopped. "My dear child, what is it?"

My head felt light, as if all the blood had left it. "I *hate* that story!" I said. I shoved back my chair and tried to stand.

Both Leon and Michael rose, but I waved them back.

"No. Please." My throat closed, making my words inaudible. "Forgive me." I stumbled from the table, nearly knocking over my chair in my rush to escape.

I ran blindly toward the stairs. By the time Michael caught up with me, I was huddled halfway up the staircase, clutching the banister with both hands and sobbing uncontrollably.

He dropped to his knees beside me. I felt him grip my shoulders, trying to turn me away from the banister.

"Katherine, what is it? What's the matter?" His voice was no longer cool and distant. It was frightened.

I jammed my forehead into the banister, needing the pain of it to keep me from dissolving into my grief. "I don't want to go back, Michael," I sobbed. "Please don't let me go back. *Don't let me go back!*"

He tried again to turn me, but I clung harder, shaking and sobbing. Then I heard Ana's voice above me.

"It's delayed shock, poor child. She's been so brave since her mother died. I didn't realize she was still so vulnerable, but I should have expected it. All that nonsense about the Snow Maiden. It was thoughtless of me."

I felt her hand on my head, smoothing my hair. "Katya, dear, you can't stay here. Michael and I will help you to your room now. That's it, child, up you come."

I allowed Ana to pull me away from the banister and help me stand. Michael took my other elbow, but I lifted it away from him, afraid to let myself lean on him. He dropped his hands but stayed by my side as Ana led me down the hall. He spoke over my head.

"I'm sorry I wasn't here for Isabel's funeral. I didn't get your telegram until a week too late. We were staying with friends of the Stratfords on Long Island, and then Vivian wanted to visit a cousin in Connecticut before we headed back to New York. Your message was waiting for me."

"There was nothing you could have done, Michael." We arrived at my bedroom door, and Ana stopped. "You go on downstairs and finish your supper. I'll get her settled."

I didn't look at him as he touched my shoulder. "Get some rest, Katherine," was all he said.

Ana helped me to my bed and slipped off my shoes.

"There you are, dear." She pulled a comforter over me and sat down on the bed beside me. She stroked the hair off my forehead, and the motherly gesture reminded me so much of Isabel that I brimmed over with a fresh gush of tears. In silence she let me sob, stroking my head and my arms until the shudders quieted and the tears began to ease.

"Sometimes what we all need is a good cry," she said in her practical way. She pressed a handkerchief into my hand. Then she rose and tucked the comforter around me. "Rest now, Katya dear." She dimmed the lamp beside my bed and slipped quietly to the door. "I'll look in on you before I go to bed. Try and sleep."

I heard the door shut softly behind her. I quickly reduced her handkerchief to a useless, soggy rag, but I was too tired to get up and find another. I lay for a long time, cocooned in the warmth of the comforter, while tears continued to roll from my eyes and soak the pillow under my cheek.

My pain drifted aimlessly between thoughts of Isabel and Michael and the Snow Maiden, and as the first mists of sleep crept closer to claim me, I began to understand something about grief. I saw that one loss blends indistinguishably into the next, and you can't partition them off, like drawers in a chest. No matter what triggers it, no matter how bravely you have faced it, grief has a way of snatching you back into that dark, familiar place where all losses are kindred and all tears flow from the same deep well.

Chapter Twenty-Five

Christmas Eve arrived, and for once Robbie accepted an early bedtime without protest. Once he was tucked away, but certainly not asleep, Leon and Michael brought in the fir tree and set it up in a corner of the parlor. Then Ana shooed everyone but her husband upstairs, declaring that Father Christmas could not come until we were all snoring in our beds. Michael stopped in the library for a book, and Emily and I went to my room for a cozy talk before going to bed.

I looked forward to these companionable chats with Emily. In the months since her arrival, she had become both a friend and the sister I'd always wanted. We talked a lot about babies but never about the father of her child. We talked about how sweet Robbie was with Elise but never about how much Emily missed her own family. There had been no invitation to her to come home for Christmas and no effort to reach out and accept her and her child. Missing Isabel as much as I did, I wondered how Lillian could sever so completely relations with her daughter and prospective grandchild. And I wondered how Theresa, raised with the same abuse and fear as Emily, could hold back her sympathy and support.

Emily sat in my armchair with her hands laced over her rounded abdomen. She smiled as she felt her baby move.

"I think he's going to be a musician," she chuckled. "The kicks always come in threes, like he's counting out a rhythm."

I smiled and laid my head back against the chaise, glad that Elise was already asleep so I could just relax and enjoy the fire. Rain drummed at the window, but its persistence only made me feel more snug and content.

"You know what's funny, Katherine?" Emily's voice lapped gently against my drowsing senses. "I've known Michael Carey since we were all children. I even saw him last spring, but I guess I was too occupied with—" She caught herself and glanced at me as I rolled my head to look at her. "Anyway, I just never noticed before how attractive Michael is. I mean, the man is downright handsome. Have you noticed?"

I rolled my head back and stared at the ceiling.

"Yes," she murmured. "Perhaps you have."

I gave her an impatient look. "I think his new mustache looks infantile."

"Infantile?" Emily chuckled. "I wouldn't say that. In fact, I'd say Michael is every inch a man, and then some."

I frowned and stared hard at the fire. It hadn't occurred to me to look at Michael through Emily's eyes. I realized with a jolt that Emily was closer in age to Michael than I was. He was sensitive and a sympathetic listener. I'd seen them talking together several times since his arrival, but I hadn't considered—

"Do you think he's really going to marry that rich Miss Stratford? Ana seems to think so."

"You asked Ana?"

"Yes. I was just curious." Emily's voice was dreamy. "He seems pretty available to me. I've never really thought about it before, but I think Michael would make a good husband. He's smart; he's gentle. And he's wonderful with Elise. He must like children, don't you think?"

"I suppose." Jealousy bolted through me like an electric current, leaving an odd metallic taste in my mouth. I sat up straighter on the chaise and stared stonily at the fire.

"I wonder if he could be happy settled in a place like Springstown," Emily persisted. "I mean, after growing up in a big city like San Francisco and then hobnobbing in New York. I wonder if he'd content himself with a quiet country life."

"I suppose his wife could live with him wherever he wanted to go. San Francisco, New York." My tone was dry. "Borneo."

"Yes, but what about a wife who already has a child? She would want to stay close to home, to raise her child near her family and friends."

I turned my head to look at her. "At this point, Emily, I wouldn't think leaving your family for the man you love would present much of an obstacle for you."

Her eyes were gentle. "I wasn't thinking of myself, Katherine."

I stared at her and felt my cheeks flame. "Am I that obvious?"

She gave me a sympathetic grin. "You might as well have 'I'm crazy about you, Michael' printed on your forehead." She tilted her head as I sighed and dropped my chin onto my chest. "Is it so impossible, Katherine?"

I nodded. "It is."

"Why? Do you know how he feels about you?"

I raised my head to stare at the fire again. "He's going to marry Vivian Stratford. That's what's best for him. You said it yourself. How could he be happy buried here in this tiny little corner of Sonoma County?"

"I don't know. Maybe you should ask him."

I shook my head and stared at the snapping flames.

Emily's voice rose a little. "If I loved a man like Michael, I'd tell him. I'm *hanged* if I wouldn't!"

I shrugged. "It's complicated. Ana doesn't approve. And Michael's just beginning his new career. He needs people like Julian Stratford. I...don't know exactly what I can offer him. I don't know what my future is holding for me."

"Well, for heaven's sake, who does?" Emily clacked her tongue impatiently. "Michael doesn't strike me as the type to marry some heiress just because her father's got money and influence. He has more integrity than that. He always did, even when we were children." Her voice softened. "If there ever was a man who would marry for love, I think that man is our Michael." When I didn't respond, she sighed and pushed herself up from her chair, stretching her arms over her head. She gave a long, lazy yawn. Then she leaned over me and put her hands on my shoulders.

"Tell Michael how you feel, Katherine. Give him a chance to answer for himself." She quickly kissed the top of my head. "Anyway, it's something to sleep on tonight."

* * *

Christmas morning dawned with a dazzling sun made brighter by the crisp, rain-rinsed air. According to house rules, no one was allowed to open the parlor doors and see what Father Christmas had brought until everyone—adults and children alike—was assembled together. Robbie took charge of rounding us up, policing stragglers, and leading us, yawning and bleary-eyed, down the great staircase. He raced across the foyer and had the doors to the parlor open before the first adult reached the bottom step.

"Wizard!" he shrieked, and lunged into the room. His crows of delight pealed into the foyer as I followed Emily's blond braid into the parlor.

The Christmas tree was magnificent. Robbie exercised masterful patience until we were assembled well enough to begin opening presents. He opened mine first and was thrilled with his fire wagon. About three feet long, it came with a real clanging bell and yellow extension ladders hooked to the sides. When Henry and the only kitten we had kept came snooping around the tree, the clang of the bell and Robbie's shrieks sent them leaping from the room in terror and bounding back up the stairs. Ana was pleased with the silk shawl I had selected for her, and Leon thanked me for his favorite brand of pipe tobacco. Emily got teary-eyed when I pulled a wooden cradle from behind the sofa. I had painted it with sprays of wildflowers I thought wouldn't be too pretty if her baby turned out to be a boy. Inside the cradle I'd tucked a soft yellow receiving blanket and a woolly stuffed lamb I couldn't resist. Elise got a doll much too big for her but one she could dress and carry around with her when she started walking. For Michael I'd chosen a soft woolen vest of sea green, exactly the color of his eyes.

My gift from Michael was a smart little hat made of mink and black felt. I held his bit of extravagance carefully in my hands and smiled at him.

"It's lovely, Michael," I said.

We were sitting on the floor in our robes and slippers, Robbie busily driving his fire wagon between us, two of his cardboard actors propped in the front seat.

"I wanted something dark to set off your eyes," Michael said. "Vivian helped me pick it out. We went to five different stores before I found what I wanted."

He couldn't have known how his words stung me. I turned the hat in my hands and imagined Vivian Stratford tucking it over her chestnut waves and tilting her head, waiting for Michael's approval. *Yes, Vivian, it's just what I'm looking for. Of course, any hat in the store would look lovely on you. Any hat in the world —*

"Katya, let me look." Ana took the hat from me. "Michael," she said, shaking her head, "this is charming but so extravagant. Where on earth would a woman like Katherine wear such a hat?"

With a *humph*, Michael walked on his knees across the carpet and snatched the hat out of his aunt's hands. "She can wear it to Christmas breakfast." He plunked the hat onto my head and gave my cheek a friendly kiss. "Happy Christmas, Cousin." He cocked his head and grinned. "I knew it would go with your blue robe the minute I saw it."

I touched my cheek where Michael had kissed it, caught Emily's grin, and flushed. Michael was watching me, and I felt my cheeks flush hotter as I slipped off the hat and carefully settled it back in its tissue paper nest.

"Open my gift, Katya!" Robbie was hopping on one leg, a cardboard actor in each hand. Gratefully, I turned away from Michael and picked up a wrapped gift roughly the size of a shoe box.

"Let me guess." I held it to my ear and shook it gently. "A new chair for my bedroom?"

"No!" Robbie laughed and plopped down on the rug beside me.

I started pulling at the red satin ribbon. "A new garden rake?"

The shocked look on Robbie's face made me pause. "No, but that's pretty close." Curious now, I pulled off the paper. "It's garden tools!" he shouted, unable to wait until I could lift the lid and see for myself.

Lying in the box were a small trowel and a sturdy weeder.

"See?" Robbie took the trowel from the box and ran his finger over the pointed tip. "It's really sharp, so you won't have to hurt your hands anymore. Now you can plant more roses in our garden and make it look the way our grandfather planned it."

He smiled gleefully as I took out each tool and admired it. I grabbed him into a tight hug. "Robbie, I couldn't love anything more. Thank you." I gave him a noisy kiss, and although he squirmed, he didn't pull away. "Between you and me, we'll have Grandfather's rose garden looking as beautiful as it ever was."

* * *

The Christmas sunshine was so inviting that I couldn't resist taking Elise to sit with me on the porch swing. Ana had outdone herself with the dinner. I was so stuffed with borscht, roasted chicken, pickled mushrooms, and delicious little meat dumplings call *pelmeni* that I thought I would burst. When Michael warned me to save room for the *kissel*, I groaned that it was already too late—I might never eat again.

Like an angel, Elise slept right through dinner. We voted five-to-one to postpone the *kissel* until later in the afternoon, and I left Michael pouting at the table while I went upstairs to check on my daughter. She was just stirring as I bent over her crib, and I picked her up and held her warm against me as she lapsed into a final little doze against my shoulder. I sat in the rocker by the window, nursing her and singing snatches of "O Little Town of Bethlehem" and "The First Noel." It was a strange Christmas for me, both satisfying and curiously empty. I smiled into Elise's dark eyes as she watched me over the mound of my breast, and I felt love for her as strong and steady as a heartbeat. And yet I missed Eleanor's Christmas Eve dinner parties, the ice rink set up in Union Square, and the giant, glorious tree that had stood in the rotunda of the five-story emporium every Christmas that I could remember. I closed my eyes and recalled my visit with Michael to the emporium, then called the City of Paris, and the beautiful rose locket Michael had chosen for me but was too expensive to buy. I wondered if there was a tree there now, and if Samuel M. Prescott decorated his haberdashery shop for the holiday.

Elise was singing her "I'm finished now, Mom" song, which consisted of coos and gurgles and excited little shrieks. I held her to my shoulder until she burped her air. Then I changed her diaper and dressed her in the new red dress and cap Ana and Leon had given her for Christmas. I wrapped a blanket around her and settled us on the front porch for a long, slow swing.

Crystal raindrops clinging to the tree branches made the stretch of forest across the drive sparkle in the sunshine like Christmas trees with millions of tiny electric lights. The cloudless sky was the deep, brilliant blue of winter, and the air stirred with a gentle breeze that occasionally nipped. Henry came meowing to join us, accompanied by Petey, the sleek white kitten who reminded me of a gangly teenager these days. Henry jumped onto the porch railing and settled herself for a wash while Petey joined us on the swing after asking only once. He stretched his slender body across the cushion with a sigh and promptly closed his green eyes.

"Is there room for one more on that swing?"

I shaded my eyes and looked up. "I'm afraid you'll have to ask Petey."

"How about if I *tell* Petey?" Michael scooped up the limp white body and sat down beside me. He settled the cat on his lap and stroked it, and I watched Petey stretch out his paws and sigh again. Green glimmered momentarily through slanted slits and then disappeared.

"Did you stop badgering poor Ana about the *kissel*?" I asked.

Michael squinted at Henry, who was settled on the

rail. "Heck, no. Christmas isn't a day for patience. I still don't understand how you could all agree to postpone the best part of the meal." He stopped stroking Petey and lifted a hand. "But I'm a reasonable man, known at times to bow to the majority opinion."

"You got Carmen to sneak you some, didn't you?"

His grin was wicked. "You won't tell on me, will you, Kat?"

I shook my head and laughed. "You're worse than Robbie."

"Yes, but I also have my good points."

"Like what?"

"Like I won't tell Ana that you didn't eat your string beans." I opened my mouth, and his eyes gleamed. "You always did hate string beans."

I stared at him because Victoria had always hated them, too. "I didn't realize anyone noticed," I said. I looked down at Elise, who was drowsing against my chest.

"Let me take her." Michael urged the cat off his lap, and Petey dropped to the porch. He stalked a short distance away and sat with his back to us, twitching his fur, while Henry looked on with mild interest.

Michael cradled Elise's head with his hand while I spread her blanket on his lap. He laid her down carefully and folded the blanket over her.

"You look like you've been around babies before," I said.

"Vivian's cousin has a baby just about this age." His smile was a little bashful. "It's not hard, once you get the hang of it."

He leaned back and pushed a little on the swing.

"I'm sorry about your mother, Kat." He fingered the rim of Elise's red knit cap. "I'm sorry I wasn't here." He looked up at me, and his eyes were gentle. "It must have been terrible for you. I know how much you loved her."

I nodded and looked away, willing my tears away before they could surface. "She was very frail at the last. But her spirit was strong. I decided I'm going to paint her, Michael. I'm going to paint her exactly as I finally saw her—strong and beautiful and very human." I saw in my mind the black silk dress with the froth of delicate lace and the brooch of violets Alexander had given her. And the startling blue-violet of her unfathomable eyes.

"No one could do it better, Kat. It will be nice for Elise when she's older. She won't remember her grandmother."

"But she'll know the stories." I caught myself and smiled. "I can see into the future. Did you know?"

A ghost of a smile touched his lips. "I heard that." He looked at my left hand. "No ring, I see."

I followed his gaze. "No ring."

"What happened with Delacroix? Ana wrote only that you'd broken off with him." When I didn't answer, Michael looked away, across the drive, to the glittering stand of redwoods. "I asked Emily, and she told me to ask you. She seemed rather mysterious about the whole thing."

"Raymond Delacroix," I said, "happens to be a vicious animal masquerading as a human. If he values his life, he won't darken my doorway again."

"Our silver-tongued pretty boy is 'a vicious animal

masquerading as a human'?" Michael sounded amused. Then he looked at me sharply. "Wait. What are you saying? Did he—"

"Don't worry about it." I met his gaze steadily. "I've given him some shrewd advice that's certain to make him a pauper. And I'm selling his ring to buy new furniture for the parlor he destroyed."

Michael sucked in a breath. "He set that fire?" I nodded, and he jerked his head around so I couldn't see his expression. "And nobody's put him in jail yet?"

"He's a silver-tongued pretty boy," I reminded him, "from a rich Philadelphia family. The long arm of the law doesn't reach that far." I touched his sleeve, lightly, so he wouldn't feel it, and drew my hand back. "It doesn't matter anymore, Michael."

His gaze whipped back to me, his eyes smoldering. "*Doesn't matter?*" He stared at me with such frank horror that I flushed uncomfortably and rose from the swing. I moved to the railing and rested my hands on it. Annoyed at having to share her space, Henry jumped down and ambled over to Petey, swishing her tail irritably.

I steadied myself before I turned to face Michael.

"I haven't congratulated you on your book, Michael. You really did it. You said you'd get it published, and now you have. You must be so happy."

Michael shifted Elise on his lap and said nothing.

I ventured further. "I'll bet you're glad you went to New York with the Stratfords, after all. You've got your dream now, Michael." I tried to sound enthusiastic. "You're on your way. Doesn't it make you proud?"

He looked up at me, his eyes solemn. "Yes. It is what

I wanted. What I dreamed of. And Julian has been wonderful. He took a chance on me, set me up with people of influence. I'm deeply indebted to him."

I forced a smile. "I understand you and Vivian Stratford are to be married." Michael gazed at me, his mouth still. I babbled on. "She's lovely Michael. Quite beautiful, in fact."

"Yes. She is."

"And you must be great friends by now. Her name comes up all the time when you talk about your trip."

"Vivian and I spent a lot of time together."

I licked my lips and made my voice bright. "Well, I know Ana is very pleased about it. I guess you've got everything you always wanted now."

After a silent moment he said quietly, "That's a strange thing for you to say, Katherine."

We stared at each other. Perhaps sensing tension, Elise began to stir.

"I only meant to say that I hope you'll be very happy, Michael. Truly."

"I hope so, too. Truly." His expression was utterly flat.

I felt my cheeks flame. Elise rubbed her eyes and gave a few squawks, winding up for a wail. "I was only trying to be nice, Michael," I said. "But if you're going to be rude, I take it all back."

"You can't take it back," he said calmly. "You can't take anything back, even when you've made a mess of things."

Elise began to wail in earnest. I scooped her up from Michael's lap and raised her to my shoulder. Patting her back, I walked to the door and stopped.

"Are you coming in, Michael?"

"No." He gave the swing a lazy push and looked out at the redwoods. I couldn't see his eyes behind the afternoon glare on his glasses—his new, sophisticated, Vivian Stratford-approved glasses.

"Suit yourself," I muttered.

I let the door bang shut behind me.

Chapter Twenty-Six

My head ached for the rest of the afternoon. Perversely, Michael was relaxed and even jovial. He was in rare form, clowning with Robbie and teasing Ana until she vowed she would either hug him to death or choke him to death. He entertained us with stories of New York publicity parties, acting out the parts of a nervous waiter and a haughty magazine editor and her pampered Pekingese until even I was laughing.

Robbie's incessant pleas to play theater eventually wore him down, and Michael helped him set up the little stage for a pirate story. When they invited me to play the part of Gertrude, I crisply refused. Robbie was disappointed, but Michael suggested they keep the parrot in the hold, where she couldn't distract the crew from their dangerous work. He further suggested they occasionally feed the parrot with fingers and toes from the pirates' unfortunate victims, which cheered Robbie immensely and led to grisly improvisations as the story progressed. Eventually the parrot was eating entire carcasses, including the entrails, and she wore the dead men's gold earrings on her beak, which Michael said was often bent out of shape. The play ended when Captain Robbie, Peg-leg Michael, and Loudmouthed Gertrude discovered an island with a big treasure chest sitting right on the beach, filled to the brim with gold doubloons, jewels, dead snakes, and big jars of peppermint sweets.

"Speaking of sweets—" Michael pushed himself off the floor and stretched his body like a cat. "I think I spy Marta with our Christmas pudding. *Finally.*" He made a face at Ana and turned to Robbie. "Anybody interested besides me?"

"I am!" Robbie shouted, and he raced to be the first one at the table. "*Kissel* is the best part of Christmas dinner!" He beamed at Michael.

Michael sat down and took Robbie onto his lap, warning him not to eat the pudding with his fingers, or Ana would make him wash all the dishes. I smiled as I sat down across the table from them. Their heads were close together, their eyes in identical, exaggerated stares as they anticipated the pudding. I was struck again by the remarkable resemblance between them, and I suddenly realized that the resemblance wasn't just my imagination. If Anton were Robbie's father, then Robbie and Michael were first cousins. When Isabel had observed the two of them in the coach that day, she'd looked as if she'd seen a ghost because she truly had.

The *kissel* was delicious, but I was too agitated to eat. I noticed, however, that there was nothing wrong with Michael's appetite. He downed his portion of the rich pudding and offered to finish mine if I wasn't going to eat it.

"I don't know where you put it, Michael," I said crossly, threatening him with my spoon as he tried to steal my dish. "I'm still full from dinner."

"That's because you ate too much and didn't leave room." Michael snatched his hand back but kept his eye on my pudding. "Self-control is the key. And we pirates are paragons of self-control. Right, matie?" He winked at Robbie.

"Right, Peg-leg." Robbie valiantly took up another mouthful of pudding, but he'd clearly had his fill.

"Pirates also share, so no one goes hungry." Michael dipped his spoon into Robbie's dish and lifted it to his mouth. Robbie shot a questioning look at Ana, who was watching them fondly. Isabel would be scolding Robbie, I thought suddenly. My heart gave a painful little twist.

I watched the boy relax under Ana's indulgent smile, and he chuckled when Michael scooped up the last of the pudding and then feigned shock and dismay to discover it all gone. *Michael is so good for Robbie*, I thought. *Like a father. Robbie needs a father.*

After the *kissel*, we settled in the parlor. My headache had eased, leaving me in a soft, sleepy sort of melancholy. I sat on the floor with Elise, pointing out the candles on the Christmas tree and dangling a shiny ornament so she could see it and touch it. Then I scooted back and leaned against the sofa, close to Ana's knee, and watched Michael and Robbie on their stomachs over a chessboard. Emily had already gone up to bed, and Leon was nodding beside Ana, occasionally snorting himself awake and dropping his head again over her shoulder.

I drowsed myself and didn't realize I was dreaming until I felt a hand on my head. "Mother?" I said sleepily. I blinked my eyes open, and the first thing I saw was Michael watching me, his eyes soft with compassion.

Then Robbie turned and looked at me, and I realized I had spoken my dream aloud.

"I'm sorry." I lifted away from Ana's knee, where my head had fallen, and glanced at Elise. She was curled in a ball on my lap, sound asleep.

"Nonsense, child." Ana's voice was thick, and she cleared her throat. "You're exhausted, and no wonder. It's high time we were all in bed. You too, Robert."

"No!" Robbie's protest was automatic, even as he yawned and rubbed his eyes. Michael reached out and tousled his hair.

"Time for bed, old man. We'll leave the game and finish up tomorrow after breakfast." He shook a finger at him and winked. "And no coming down in the middle of the night to move the pieces around. I'm winning, you know."

"You are not! *I'm* winning!" Robbie had captured five of Michael's men, and Michael only three. Michael looked disconcerted.

"Oh. Well, in that case, maybe *I'll* come down in the middle of the night and move them around."

Robbie opened his mouth and then caught Michael's grin. He grinned back. "I know where every piece is, so you'd better not," he said loftily.

Michael chuckled and pushed himself up from the floor. I thought he was going to help Robbie up. Instead, he crossed over to me and lifted the sleeping baby from my lap. "Let me help you up, Katherine," he said gently. He offered me his hand.

I took it, looking up into his eyes as he helped me stand. The soft look was still there, so deep and full that I simply left my hand in his for a moment and felt his gaze tugging on my heart. With an effort I dropped my gaze to Elise, who lay peacefully in the crook of his arm.

"Thank you, Michael. I'll take her now." He laid her carefully in my arms and gently brushed his knuckle over her rosy cheek. To my surprise, he did the same with mine.

"Good night, Cousin," he said. I thought I heard tenderness in his voice. "Sleep well."

* * *

I lit the lamp in Elise's nursery and spotted a package lying on the table next to the rocker. Elise was beginning to fuss, but I sat down and took the package into my lap. "Storyteller" was written across the plain wrapping. I untied the ribbon, folded back the paper, and pulled out a beautiful blanket woven in soft yellows and greens and blues. It was one of Dora's own, and I suddenly understood.

The symbols woven into it must represent storytelling. It was Dora's legacy of good fortune to Elise. I remembered Dora had done the same for young Katherine on her birthday, just as Dora's own mother had once done for her. I thought back over the days since Isabel's funeral and realized that this gift for Elise had been Dora's task as she sat at her loom, alone in the sitting room, day after day. She'd been more silent than usual, more withdrawn. When she wasn't at her loom, she either kept to her bedroom or visited the chapel for prayers. When Ana had invited her to share Christmas dinner with us, she had quietly refused.

I changed Elise into her nightclothes and sat down in

the rocker to nurse her back to sleep. I spread her new blanket over my lap and ran my free hand over it, thinking about Dora. I wondered if she had made a blanket with a special symbol on it for Isabel when she was a child.

Elise was hungrier than I had thought, and she nursed vigorously while I leaned my head against the back of the rocker and looked out the window at the Christmas night. The hills and forest were dusted with silver, and words I'd known since childhood tiptoed into my mind. *Silent night, holy night, all is calm, all is bright.*

Tears slipped down my cheeks. I let them come. These weren't the stinging shards that had spilled from my shattered heart every day since Isabel's death. In some mysterious way, the merciless beating of those harsh tears had softened a place where my soul now rested, finally at peace, and the tears that came now were like a gentle rain soothing a heart that was preparing to heal and let go. They were tears of love and gratitude and surrender. They were tears of acceptance.

Elise fell asleep, but I kept rocking us gently. I watched the Rostnova hills shimmer under the Christmas moon and let my mind drift and settle with light wings on thoughts that comforted me: the shine in Robbie's eyes as Michael drew him into a special bond of male camaraderie, the tender way Michael held Elise and brushed her cheek with his finger, the quiet compassion in Michael's eyes when I'd called out for my mother in my sleep. The brush of his hand against mine when he laid Elise in my arms, the clean male scent of him that made my knees go weak. *Michael.*

* * *

It was nearly midnight when I finally tucked Elise into her crib and retired to my bedroom. Numb with fatigue, I mechanically undressed and pulled on my warm flannel nightgown and robe. I sat at my mirror and pulled the earrings from my ears, the pins from my hair, and watched the heavy tresses tumble over my shoulders before I began to brush them.

The moon had risen higher, sending a silver patch across my bed. As I turned my head to begin braiding my hair for the night, something winked on my pillow, catching my eye and bringing my busy fingers to a sudden stop.

I sat for a moment, staring stupidly and wondering if it was a trick of light. My hair fell loose as I rose and crossed the floor to the bed. Then I clamped my hands to my mouth, muffling a squeak of surprise.

I recognized it at once—the beautiful locket with a delicate yellow rose unfolding across its enamel center. Tucked under the fine gold chain was a note: "This is your real present. Happy Christmas, Katherine. Love, Michael."

I walked to the mirror and watched myself fasten the chain around my neck. The locket settled on my breast, exquisite against the plain blue flannel of my robe. I traced it gently with my fingertip and stared at my reflection.

I hardly recognized myself. My eyes were enormous, my cheeks flushed as if with fever. My heart began to flutter like a wild bird as I came to a sudden decision. Not daring to stop and think for fear I would lose my nerve, I left the mirror and quietly opened my door. Slipping into the dark hallway, I followed the banister around until I was standing at the door next to Emily's, my hand raised to knock softly. But Michael's door was ajar.

I swallowed hard and gingerly pushed the door open on blessedly silent hinges. I slipped soundlessly into his room.

Michael wasn't there. Moonlight outside his window was bright enough to show clearly that his bed had not been slept in. Disappointed, puzzled, I returned to the hallway and made my way down the staircase. As I reached the foyer, I saw shadows flickering on the parlor walls.

The candles on the Christmas tree were snuffed out and the lamps were turned down, so the fire was the only source of light in the room. I tiptoed across the carpet and stood still, looking tenderly down at Michael. He was sleeping in an armchair, his cheek propped on a fist, his glasses lying on the table beside him. An arm and a leg were flung carelessly over the side of the chair, and his lips were slightly parted. As I knelt on the carpet before him, I heard his deep, regular breathing.

I felt torn between wanting to touch his face and wanting to stay still so I could have the pleasure of watching him sleep. He looked young, his neat hair finally rumpled, his long lashes faintly shadowing his cheeks. His vest and tie were discarded, and his shirt was open at the neck, revealing little curls of golden hair. My body trembled and not just with indecision.

To both my relief and disappointment, Michael

settled the matter himself by suddenly coming awake. He blinked at me and then rubbed his fists into his eyes and yawned, exactly like Robbie. I smiled at the thought.

"I didn't think you were coming." His voice was gruff with sleep, and he yawned again, pulling his leg back from the arm of the chair. "I guess I fell asleep before I could get myself up to bed."

I touched the locket. "I only just saw your gift, Michael. It's so beautiful. I had to come and thank you." I closed my hand over it and looked up at him.

He fixed his gaze on my face. "Did you open it?"

"Open it? No. Was I supposed to?"

He slipped to his knees on the rug beside me, so close I could feel the heat of his body. "Careful," he cautioned, as I fumbled with the tiny clasp and eased the locket open. Tucked inside was a folded wedge of white silk. And inside the silk was a ring.

"Oh!" A small round diamond winked at me from a simple gold mount. "Michael, it's beautiful."

"I should light a lamp," he said, beginning to rise from his knees. But I put a quick hand on his arm.

"No, the firelight is so nice. Let's just move closer to it." Together we crawled to the edge of the rug and knelt close to the hearth.

"I admit, it's not much." His voice was soft and shy. "But I bought it with the advance against royalties from my book, which was only fitting. Without you, there wouldn't even be a book."

I looked up at him, loving the way his mouth was lifting in that crooked, wistful smile. It was exactly the way I had drawn him that night in the attic at

Summerwood, the night Elise was born. "Michael." I raised my hand to his cheek. "I don't know what to say."

He pulled my hand down and took the ring from me. "Say yes." He slipped the ring onto my finger, and we both stared at it. "Say yes, Katherine."

My mind froze, but my heart responded without hesitation. "Yes!" I whispered. "Yes, Michael, yes!" I threw my arms around him and buried my face in his neck. "Yes, yes, yes!" His arms swooped around me and pulled me against his. Through the layers of our clothing, I felt our hearts pounding against each other like two wild horses on a crazy midnight gallop.

With a happy little laugh, he pushed me away so he could see my face. "Katherine." His voice was misty, like his eyes. He smoothed back my hair and cradled my face, carefully, as if he couldn't quite believe I was real. "Katherine." Something flared in his eyes, through the mist and the wonder. I closed my eyes and arched my body to meet his kiss.

I wasn't prepared, however, for the shock of our coming together. All the pain of being apart, all the love and the longing sharpened our kiss into a fine point that pierced my body like an arrow and lodged with a painful jolt in my loins. I gasped and broke away from him, shaking with surprise and need. Michael seemed as stunned as I was. We stared at each other without speaking, without touching, almost without breathing.

Michael smiled and lifted his hand to my face. With fingertips light as butterfly wings, he traced my eyebrow, the contour of my cheek, the tender interior of my parted lips. I closed my eyes as his sensitive fingers rounded my chin and began a trail down my throat. He pushed the robe off my shoulders and brought both hands to trace my collarbones out to my shoulders and then down the sides of my chest, curving beneath my breasts to meet at center, just above my heart. I shuddered a little and opened my eyes in time to see the heat in his eyes before he slipped his hands behind me and brought me up against him.

We slipped down to lie on the rug before the fire, our bodies twined together like a silken cord. Unlike the first kiss, our second started slow, a bare brush of lips that triggered sparks of delicious anticipation. Moving off to explore cheeks and noses, our mouths returned to each other and tasted slowly, carefully. Michael gripped the sides of my head with his hands and held it firm as he deepened his kiss, locking my mouth with a new, urgent hunger. His long legs moved against mine, parting them, and I yielded with a little moan of pleasure.

Michael suddenly wrenched his mouth away and sat up. "God forgive me!" he said. He raked his fingers through his short hair. Then he looked at me, still lying disheveled and trembling with need on the rug beside him. He leaned on his elbow and gently stroked my face. "I'm sorry, Katherine." His voice shook. "I didn't think...I didn't mean to..." He brought his fist under my chin and rubbed his thumb over my lower lip. "I never want to hurt you, love. I want to take away all the bad things in your life that have hurt you. I want to lift you up and cherish you and make you safe."

He pulled his hand away and raked it through his

hair again. "What you must think of me," he said. "Especially after Delacroix—" He jerked himself upright.

I sat up, too, and I clamped my arms around him. "Don't even mention that man and yourself in the same breath, Michael. I do feel cherished and safe with you. And I love you with all my heart." I turned his face toward me. "In case you didn't notice, Mr. Carey, I was a willing volunteer." It was my turn to rub a thumb over his lower lip. "I seem to have no will power when it comes to you."

He grinned and snatched my hand, kissing my fingertips. "When the proper time comes, I'm going to remind you of that, Kat."

"I'll make you a deal," I said suddenly. "I promise not to compromise your virtue until we are well and truly married if you'll do me one particular favor."

He winced. "What is it?"

"Lose the mustache."

He looked startled and then burst out laughing. "Well, if I must. But only for you, love." He kissed my fingertips again.

After eyeing my locket, or rather the two flanneled mounds cradling it, Michael suggested that I put my robe back on. He built up the fire before disappearing into the kitchen to fix us some tea. He returned shortly with not only tea but also chicken sandwiches and raspberry scones Carmen had already prepared for our breakfast.

We picnicked on the rug in front of the fire, talking and laughing quietly and loving each other with our eyes. At times we were silent, each of us staring into the flames and hugging our own secret thoughts, reveling in the miracle of our love reborn. It was the happiest night of my life.

Into one of those comfortable lulls, Michael spoke quite casually, through a mouthful of raspberry scone, "Who's Ryan?"

Chapter Twenty-Seven

My happy, quiet heart gave a painful stab of alarm. Michael was lying on his side, propped on an elbow, calmly licking crumbs from his fingers.

"Who's Ryan?" he repeated. "You said he's someone you used to know."

"Yes." I studied him, trying to measure the openness in his eyes, remembering how much I loved him. And, somehow, the words came easily. "Ryan was my husband."

He stared at me without moving. Then he eased himself up and rested his back against the sofa, stretching out his legs on the rug. "Go on," he said.

The words continued to come easily. I identified the woman in the drawing he had seen in the attic at Summerwood and gave a brief account of Victoria's history—her childhood in a rich and famous family, her marriage to a man she didn't love, the desperate life she longed to escape. I told him the story of meeting Katherine at the bridge and seeing the dream come to life on Elise Delacroix's canvas—"*Our* Elise?" he interjected—and everything from the exchange of lives to this moment, sitting before the fire, wearing the ring of the only man I had ever truly loved. He listened patiently, sometimes exclaiming or dropping his mouth open or swearing under his breath. But he never challenged my story, and he let me tell it in my own way.

By the time I'd finished, both the fire and I were exhausted. Michael didn't speak. I watched the dying flames send up their last valiant strokes before sinking into smoldering mounds of ash.

"I know it's a fantastic story," I said. "Sometimes I almost can't believe it myself. But I do have Joanne Greenly's letters in a box upstairs. You might want to look at them."

"There's no need, Kat." Michael's voice was gentle. "I believe you."

I looked toward him through the darkness of the fireless room, wishing I could see his expression. "You believe me? Just like that? Without proof?"

"You're the proof, love," he said. "I knew you were different, even that first night when you didn't want to mount Gretchen, remember? And you wouldn't lean against me in the saddle but kept scooting up in that prim little way of yours, nearly slipping off a couple of times." He chuckled. "And then after dinner, when you came out to the stables to apologize. It was the oddest thing, but I wanted so badly to pull you into my arms. I couldn't understand it; I'd never felt that way about you in my life. By the time summer rolled around, I was a goner."

The darkness made his voice curiously intimate and almost painful in its honesty. "Michael," I said softly. "Thank you...for believing me. I wanted to tell you so many times. I was afraid you'd think I was crazy."

He laughed lightly. "No. You weren't the only one

raised at Dora's knee, believing all those Indian ghost tales. Say, do you remember that time I dared you to stay overnight in the haunted caves—" He broke off. "But that wasn't you, was it? That was her, the other Katherine." He sounded amused. "Well, anyway, there were these old caves that Dora told us were haunted by the spirits of the dead. I dared Katherine to stay in them all night with me. We were doing okay until she started making weird noises and pretending she could see things in the shadows. She got me so scared, I was climbing out of my skin. I finally rode back here and got my uncle, and we practically had to drag her away by the hair. I've never been back to those caves." The grin faded from his voice. "I always admired Katherine's spunk. But she was wild, reckless with people's feelings. She could be cruel, and I didn't admire that." His voice gentled. "You have courage, like her, but you could never be cruel. It isn't in your nature."

I started crying softly. Michael knelt beside me and folded me into his arms. "You're shivering, Kat. Come sit on the sofa with me."

We sat close together, and Michael wrapped us in a quilt. The long day caught up to me, making my head heavy against his chest. He kept a firm arm around me and used his free hand to stroke my cheek and play with my hair.

"Before you nod off, Kat, there's one more thing I need to know." He nudged me. "Are you listening?"

"Hmm?"

"Wake up. This is important."

With an effort, I lifted my head and lolled it back on

his shoulder. "What?"

"Remember the other night when you were so upset? You were hanging onto the banister for dear life, and you said something very strange. You said, 'Michael, don't let me go back.' You said the same thing outside that little bakery on Powell Street, the one with that witchy old woman."

I raised my head and squinted through the dark, trying to see his face. "I didn't think you heard me."

"Well, I did. And I need you to tell me what it means." His voice was tight, and I knew he'd already guessed what I was going to say.

I sighed. "The witchy old woman was Victoria's great-great-grandmother. Being with her in that shop was like being back with Eleanor again." I shuddered. "I had a sudden taste of what it would be like to go back to Victoria's life, and it scared me, Michael. Then, there was the other night—that story Ana told about the Snow Maiden disappearing with the coming of spring, losing the new family she loved." I shuddered again, and Michael tightened his arms around me. I buried my face in his neck, and this time the words wouldn't come.

Michael spoke them for me. "You have to go back." His voice was hollow, like an echo of his real voice.

I burrowed further into his neck. "I don't know. Father Philippe seems to think I'll have a choice. But I don't know."

"Who is Father Philippe?"

"A priest from the mission in San Rafael. I told him my story, and he thinks maybe I'll have a choice about going back. But I won't know until March."

"At new moon, you mean." He said it thoughtfully, rubbing his cheek against my hair. I looped my arms around his neck like a child, and he kissed me gently. "Okay, no more questions. Sleep now, love. And I'll hold you."

That's how Robbie found us a few hours later when he raced downstairs to check on the positions of the chessmen. Michael and I were both sound asleep, wrapped tightly together under the quilt, with Michael's locket gleaming on my chest and his ring winking on the third finger of my left hand.

* * *

We were married on the third Sunday of the New Year. Ana, when she'd gotten over the shock of our engagement, wanted to give us a lavish wedding and reception in San Francisco. But Michael firmly refused. Neither of us wanted to wait for the long preparations such an event would require. Instead, we decorated Isabel's chapel and asked Father Philippe to perform the ceremony. I asked Emily to be my bridesmaid, and Robbie stood with Michael in front of the altar, beneath the crucifix Leon had carved for Isabel. Together they watched me walk down the aisle on Leon's arm. My dress was a simple gown of butter yellow, with long sleeves and a short train, bought on a day trip Emily and I made to Santa Rosa in the protective company of Alfred. Michael had returned to San Francisco to clear up business at the paper and arrange for another leave of absence. And to buy me a wedding band.

Clever with her hands, Emily made my bridal bouquet, which consisted of white lilies, violets, and yellow roses. The heavy fragrance of the lilies brought back memories of being a child in my mother's bedroom, where she kept her favorite flowers on her dresser. In the process of mourning Isabel, of understanding her weaknesses and complexities, I realized that I had also begun to forgive Christine. At last able to set aside old resentments, I carried lilies and violets on my wedding day to acknowledge, and to release, the two most important women in my life. And I carried roses for my new hope with Michael.

I held Leon's arm and followed Emily into the chapel. The small benches were filled with people, and many stood along the walls. I recognized Laura and Betty and other families from town who had become friendly with Robbie and me. Many guests I did not recognize, friends of Leon or Michael from San Francisco. I was glad to see Bruce and Theresa standing with June, although Lillian and John were conspicuously absent. As we neared the front, I saw Dora standing with Ana, who held Elise, and beside her a distinguished couple I suddenly recognized as Julian and Irene Stratford. Vivian stood behind her mother. Our eyes met briefly, and she nodded very slightly.

Then Emily reached the front and stepped aside, and I saw Michael, looking impossibly handsome, grinning and so full of love that I caught my breath. And I saw nothing but Michael until he kissed me soundly at the end of the service, and we turned, hand in hand, to face the world together.

The day was cold but gloriously sunny. The gardeners outdid themselves in dressing up the formal garden with winter annuals and setting up little tables and chairs for the wedding guests. My hand was hardly ever out of Michael's as we mingled with friends, introducing each other to guests, smiling and accepting congratulations, catching each other's eyes to exchange wordless messages of love and happiness. Elise wore a yellow dress, thick white stockings to keep her legs warm, and a ruffled bonnet to keep the sun out of her eyes. Michael carried her on his arm and introduced her as his daughter, and my heart, already melted with love for him, melted again. Late in the afternoon, I stole some time to take Elise to her room and nurse her quietly. I rocked her and sang to her, and I showed her the new gold band nestled against my diamond on my left hand.

"Michael is your new daddy, darling." She yawned, and her eyelids fluttered closed. "No matter what happens to me, Michael will take care of you. You can depend on him."

I looked up as Emily tiptoed into the room. "Asleep?" she whispered, and I nodded. I rose and laid my daughter carefully in her crib. Her thumb immediately found her mouth, and she gave it a few tugs before she relaxed and was still.

Emily touched my arm and motioned me over to the window. Then she showed me her left hand, and I gasped. A small diamond glittered on her third finger.

"Emily! It's got to be Alfred, right?"

"Who else?" Emily's smile was radiant. "I guess this love business is contagious. You and Michael are so happy together, it made all my little excuses seem foolish. Alfred proposed again, and this time I said yes.

We're getting married next month." She hugged me, and I felt joy shiver through her body. "Did you see Theresa and June?" I nodded, and she nodded back. "Theresa asked June to come and live with her and Bruce. Rescued her, actually. With June the only girl left at home—" Her face clouded. "But now June is safe, and I have my sisters back again. Who knows? If we stick together, my child might get to know his grandparents, after all."

I squeezed her hands. "Alfred is a wonderful man, and he worships you. You'll be so happy!"

"I know." She bit her lip. "Thanks for talking sense to me, Katherine. I didn't want to hear it, but you were right. About everything."

There was a light tap on the door. Ana stuck her head in. "Katya, dear, some of the guests are leaving. And your husband is looking for you."

"Coming, Aunt." I turned to Emily with a soft smile. "'My husband.' I like the sound of that."

* * *

The winter sun had already set behind the hills when the last guest drove away. I stood on the steps beside Michael, waving good-bye, and then turned with a sigh to go back into the house. But Michael stopped me.

"Not that way, Mrs. Carey." He caught my arm and pointed to a sleek carriage that was curving up the drive. "This way."

"Michael, what on earth—" I let him lead me down the steps, and the carriage drew to a halt before us. Michael opened its door and bowed to me with a flourish. "After you, my dear."

"But Elise—"

"Is in Emily's competent care for the night." He grinned and gave me an impatient nudge. "Up you go."

I stepped up into the carriage and spotted a bouquet of yellow roses lying on the seat. With a little cry, I swept them into my arms and buried my face in them. Michael climbed in behind me and shut the door.

"Michael, where are we—" My words were smothered against his sudden kiss on my mouth. The roses crushed between us as our arms wrapped around each other, and their sweet scent pressed itself into a memory I will always have of that magical drive to Summerwood. When the carriage stopped, the driver opened the door for us and coughed discreetly. Reluctantly, we let each other go, and Michael helped me down. In a happy haze, I looked up at the cottage and gasped with delighted surprise.

Satin bows and streamers propped on tall stakes lined the pathway leading to the front steps. Inside the cottage dozens of candles lined the unfinished hallway that led to the master bedroom. Marta emerged from the bedroom and dropped a low curtsey.

"There is a cold supper in the hamper, *señor* Michael, and wine in the ice bucket. I'll bring your breakfast tomorrow morning."

"Not too early, Marta."

She dimpled. "No, *señor*. Not too early." She curtsied to me and dimpled again before disappearing through the front door. A moment later we heard the carriage pull away.

"Welcome home, Mrs. Carey." Michael scooped me up in his arms and carried me into the bedroom.

I caught my breath, dazzled by a hundred pinpoints of candlelight. Michael set me down gently on the rug, and I just stood and stared around me at candles and flowers spilling from every surface and corner of the room, enclosing us in a magic circle of light and color and scent. I saw the hamper Marta had promised sitting under the window beside the ice bucket chilling two sleek bottles of wine. The bed was made up with a new coverlet and plump pillows with embroidered satin cases. I recognized my suitcase sitting on the floor beside it, and I guessed that Emily had packed it with the new gown and slippers and robe we had purchased in Santa Rosa for my wedding night. A cheerful fire in the corner fireplace spilled flickering light and solid warmth into the room.

"Michael." I turned to him, knowing all this was his wedding gift to me, and my heart melted for the third time that day.

Light as a whisper, his hands circled my waist as he brought his mouth down on mine. It was the sweetest, gentlest kiss I had ever known. The beautiful room spun dizzily for a moment, and I might have floated away on a cloud of pure happiness if Michael's hands weren't anchored on my waist. When he lifted his mouth away, I slowly blinked and stared at him, unable to speak. He brushed my cheek with his knuckle, and his smile was tender.

"I expect you'll be wanting your privacy now." He cleared his throat, and his ears turned pink. "I'll take a turn outside, to make sure everything is buttoned down tight." He kissed me lightly on the nose. "When you're ready for company, just leave the door ajar." He paused with his hand on the doorknob. "And *don't* touch the wine till I get back." He grinned and disappeared through the door.

Emily, bless her, had remembered everything. I took off my wedding clothes and pulled on the silky nightgown. Then I spritzed myself with jasmine scent. I took down my hair and brushed it until it shone like black satin in the soft candlelight. My eyes looking back at me in the mirror were dark and deep, my cheeks flushed with high color. I slipped on the matching robe and thrust my feet into my dainty new slippers. Before I opened the door, I turned down the coverlet and fluffed the pillows.

At my signal Michael pushed open the door, carrying two fluted glasses and some china plates. "I was just checking out the upstairs." He set down the glasses and plates and uncorked the first bottle of wine. "I think I could turn one of those rooms into a study, the one looking out on the oak tree. I can set up my typewriter and write my next novel in the comfort of our country house."

"You'd actually live here, Michael?" I held out the glasses, and he filled them with rose-colored wine. "I mean, wouldn't you miss living in the big city?"

He shoved the half-empty bottle back into the ice and took a glass from me. "Are you kidding? Writers need lots of peace and quiet so they can think profound thoughts and compose impossibly complex sentences." He touched his glass to mine. "Here's to living a long, happy life together, to filling those rooms upstairs with our children, to growing old together and creating beautiful memories every day, for the rest of our lives."

Our eyes held as we drank our toast together. And in that moment and for the rest of that enchanted night, I believed it would all come true just as Michael had said.

* * *

Some lunatic rooster with no sense of respect kept up a grating chorus of crowing and chortling until my eyes forced themselves open. It was not yet sunup. Lying on his stomach beside me, Michael groaned, pulled a pillow over his head, and lay still.

My hands, already learning the lines and hollows of his body, instinctively reached for him, but I drew them back and made them still. Instead I lay on my side and let my thoughts wander back over the long hours of our first night together. I pulled up one tender moment after another, savoring them like pictures in a memory book.

After our wedding toast, we took grapes from the hamper and settled with our wineglasses on the rug before the fire. We fed each other grapes, kissing fingertips and lacing our fingers briefly, teasing ourselves with the hours of love that lay ahead. Finally the grapes were eaten, the glasses were empty, and I was beginning to feel the warmth of the wine curling through my blood and bringing a dewy flush to my skin. Michael stood first. He reached down and pulled me up, and our eyes locked for a brief, trembling moment.

We fell into the kiss like divers into a silky lake. My senses swam in the softness of Michael's mouth against mine and the way our bodies fit and melted together. We broke apart, gasping and both a little dizzy. Michael laughed softly as he scooped me up and carried me to the bed. He lay down beside me and propped himself up on his elbow, his fingers fiddling with my hair while his gaze roamed hungrily over my face. He untied my robe and opened it, and his eyes glided over the gossamer fabric of my gown. He caught his breath, and his eyes shot back up to mine.

"I love you, Katherine," he whispered hoarsely. "How I've waited for you!" He pulled me against him and kissed me, murmuring my name against my lips. Then, somehow, the silky folds of my robe and gown were lying in a heap on the rug. Michael's strong, lean hands skimmed over my body, exploring, possessing.

His clothes quickly followed mine, adding to the heap on the rug. When he turned to face me again, I caught my breath and took him by the shoulders to hold him still. "Please," I said. "Just let me look at you for a moment."

He looked like a young god out of Greek mythology, descended straight from Mount Olympus. The hair tousled on his head and curling along the pale skin of his body shone like burnished gold in the candlelight. His limbs were lean but well-muscled, and he held himself with an easy strength that was graceful yet thoroughly male. His eyes were full and dark, like glimpses of the ocean, surging with passion pulled up from a hot, deep place. I sat up and ran a reverent hand over his chest, down his hip to rest on his thigh. "Michael," I said breathlessly. "You're beautiful."

He grinned his boyish, lopsided grin. "No—"

But I laid a finger on his lips to silence him.

"Yes, you are." When he saw that I meant it, his grin softened. "Beautiful," I whispered again, and I leaned over and kissed his mouth.

What followed was a rapturous blur of sensation and emotion and blind, urgent need. Michael's lean, powerful body became one with mine—skin against skin, wild heartbeat against wild heartbeat. We were once again that silken cord, inseparably twined—one flesh, one mind, one desire.

Much later, when the candles had burned low and we lay in each other's arms, exhausted and drowsing in sweet satisfaction, I came to a startling realization. Never once in our long hours of lovemaking had I sought that secret refuge with the cornflowers I had always needed with Ryan. I had loved Michael with all my heart and body, without fear, and received his love with open trust. I pressed my lips to his chest—warm and pale and lightly furred with gold—and felt his arms tighten around me as he sighed in his sleep. Then I, too, fell asleep, lulled by the steady life-beat of his heart under my ear.

Chapter Twenty-Eight

Michael moved into my bedroom at Rosswood House until renovations could be completed at Summerwood. January and February were unusually rainy, holding up the work until I thought I would scream from frustration. Good as his word, Leon transferred legal title of the cottage and property to me and assigned me funds to make every improvement I could want. Under my strict supervision, gardeners transplanted dormant rose bushes from the formal garden to the patch at Summerwood, and I ordered brass nameplates to label the row for each variety.

Robbie was thrilled with my marriage to Michael but also apprehensive about my moving into the cottage. We reassured him that Summerwood was only a short walk away and that we would keep a room ready for the nights he would stay over with us. Ana and Leon settled into Isabel's house with an air of permanence. Ana ordered a thorough redecorating of Isabel's bedroom and sitting room, which she shared with Leon, and I couldn't help feeling resentful. Ana understood, however, and she was kind and patient with my frowns or sudden tears as I saw little traces of Isabel steadily disappearing from the house. On the day that Isabel's headstone was delivered, Ana accompanied me to the gravesite to watch the workers lower the heavy white stone into place.

Michael and Leon were in San Francisco, and my loneliness for Michael seemed to sharpen my grief for Isabel. When the stone was finally in place and the workers had gone, Ana put her arm around my shoulders and drew me close to her.

"Katherine, I've something to say to you." She cleared her throat. "I'm afraid I misjudged you rather badly, my dear. I'm sorry. It's no secret that I was against your relationship with Michael. I didn't believe he could be happy with you. But I was wrong. And I ask your forgiveness." She squeezed my shoulder. "I've never seen two people more devoted to one another than you and Michael. He told me repeatedly that you were the only woman in the world for him. Now I believe him. When I see him with you and Elise, I know he's chosen a good life for himself."

Her eyes were the same somber gray as the winter clouds above us. "I realize I can't take your mother's place, Katya. I won't even try. But Michael is like a son to me, and now you are my daughter." She leaned close, and I felt affection in her kiss on my forehead. "We are your family, dear. I hope Elise will come to think of me as her grandmother and let me love her as I would any child of yours and Michael's." She searched my face earnestly.

I answered her with a warm embrace. After a long moment, Ana pushed herself away and patted my cheek. "I'll leave you alone now, Katya." Her tone was brisk. "Hot soup will be waiting when you get back to the house."

She turned away quickly, and I watched her go. Then I knelt beside Isabel's grave and laid my bunch of purple pansies against the new stone, just below the words "Taken from us too soon."

"Rest easy, Mother," I said. I raised my hand and traced the letters of her name with my fingertips. "I love you, and I miss you. But I love Michael, too, and I'm so happy with him. Elise and Robbie and I have a family to care for us. You don't have to worry."

A gust of wind came up suddenly and snatched up my words. I watched leaves swirl in a dance above my head, and I fancied that wherever Isabel was, she had heard me, and my words had made her smile.

* * *

Emily and Alfred were married in town on a bright mid-February day that hinted strongly of the coming spring. I was shocked and angry that so few people turned out for the ceremony, owing to Emily's state of unwed pregnancy as well as her "unsuitable match." Lillian and John refused to attend, as did Lillian's nephew. Rumor had it that Raymond was courting Russ Paxton's eldest daughter and had talked Russ into investing money in the Golden Springs Valley land deal.

Despite their parents' boycott, both of Emily's sisters attended her as bridesmaids. Emily walked down the aisle on Leon's arm with a smile so radiant that I put my anger and indignation aside and felt only happiness for her.

Alfred looked ten years younger and unexpectedly elegant in a pressed black suit and a spanking new haircut. The look of adoration in his eyes as he watched his bride approach made me turn to Michael and press my hand over his heart. He smiled and pulled me against him, and my happiness for Emily was brighter because of my joy in my own love.

As it happened, both Emily and I moved out of Rosswood House the same weekend. Emily and Alfred rented a house in town close to Theresa, and Michael and I moved the last of our possessions into Summerwood and took up residence there.

We settled into a quiet routine. Marta came to work in our new kitchen while I tended Elise and spent most of my afternoons in the attic, working on my portrait of Isabel. Michael worked in his "study" down the hall from me, writing feature pieces for Julian Stratford's paper and beginning his second novel. I learned to judge his mood from the rhythm of the keys tapping on his Remington, or from the length of the silences in between, occasionally broken by a sharp explosion of expletives. Michael could be moody and at times obstinate. But he was also gentle and loving and sensitive. His smile was like sunshine and his kisses like a magic potion that could soothe and comfort me or else flame me with desire so intense that it shocked and delighted me.

Robbie was lonesome for us, so we invited him for many afternoons after school to play with Elise and read to me from his new primer. Michael took time to sit with him on the porch, and they talked about everything from trains to why God made termites to Priscilla, a third-grader to whom Robbie had lost his heart. Sometimes when I saw them sitting with their heads together, their ankles pulled up on their knees in identical poses, the family resemblance was so strong that they seemed like father and son.

One day I confided to Michael that Robbie was Anton's son. He didn't seem surprised.

"Isabel told you?" I said, shocked.

Michael shrugged. "Isabel wasn't the only one who knew." At my look, he nodded. "Among his many faults, Anton was also a braggart. At least to me. He didn't dare tell anyone else because he was afraid of your father—I mean, Alexander. Anton was always obsessed with Isabel." He shook his head. "He was an evil man, Kat. I'm glad you never knew him."

Before we went to bed that night, I brought Katherine's journal down to the parlor, where Michael was reading in one of the comfortable armchairs that Raymond's ring had purchased for us. He looked up as I tore Isabel's pages from the book and threw them into the fire.

"I don't want Robbie to ever know the truth about his father," I said. I watched the pages curl briefly over Isabel's handwriting before they browned and shrank into ash. "He'll remain Alexander's son. He'll keep the Rostnova name. And Leon will always be his uncle." I stood before Michael, clutching the journal against my chest. "You and Dora and I are the only ones who know, Michael. Please promise me you won't ever tell him."

Michael set aside his book and took me onto his lap. "I promise, Kat. No one deserves a legacy like that, least of all our Robbie."

I put my arms around his neck and rested my cheek against his forehead. We stared in silence at the fire until

Michael lifted his mouth and caught mine in a slow, lingering kiss. "Is Elise asleep?" he murmured, against my lips.

"Um-hmm."

His hand moved from my waist to stroke my thigh. I caught my breath at the delicious sensation of my bones beginning to melt in anticipation.

He raised us both, still locked in a kiss, and began leading me to the bedroom. But Katherine's journal weighed heavily in my hand. Reluctantly, I pulled away.

"I'll join you in a minute, Michael." My voice was husky, and I had trouble focusing on his face through the haze of my longing for him. It still amazed me how quickly and completely that longing could overtake me. "There's something I have to do upstairs first."

"Well, don't take forever." He twisted a stray lock of my hair around his finger and tugged gently. "If you're not down here in five minutes, I'm coming up after you."

The oilskin cloth was already in the attic. I opened Katherine's journal one last time and flipped through the pages, through the sloping black letters that chronicled her life and finally to the blank pages relieved only by a delicate flower already flat and dried to near transparency. I wrapped the oilskin around the red satin covers and slipped the package into its secret chamber beside the ink bottle. Then, with the reverence of sealing a burial tomb, I lowered the wooden plank and covered it with the rug, hiding it away for the future.

* * *

My terror began on the night of Ana and Leon's thirtieth wedding anniversary. We ate an elegant supper at the house, and I presented them with my portrait of Michael as a gift. Now that I daily held the real Michael in my arms, I didn't need the drawing to give me comfort. As I'd hoped, Ana was thrilled.

"It's so clever, Katya! So like our Michael."

Leon nodded and boomed, "Amazing likeness, Katherine! Well done." He beamed at Robbie. "There's the Rostnova talent, young man. Can't get away from it. Comes from a long line of artists, starting with the first cousin of Catherine the Second. That's why we have the crown in our family crest, boy, for royalty. You come from a proud line, Robert. Don't ever forget that."

"No, Uncle Leon." Robbie smiled up at me. I smiled back, a little fiercely.

"Robbie isn't only a budding, artist, Uncle," I said, steering us away from the subject of pedigree. "He's becoming quite a reader as well. Robbie, let's hear that poem you read for me the other day. The one about the dog and the crooked bridge."

We spent a comfortable evening listening to Robbie read and Leon telling stories I'd never heard about his boyhood in California and his education in Moscow. Michael and Robbie spent an hour pouring over the chessboard, which they left permanently standing on a table by the piano. They took such pains over each move that I wondered if it wasn't the same game they'd begun on Christmas Day. Robbie was yawning uncontrollably, and Elise had been sleeping in the nursery for over an hour when we decided it was time to go home.

Walking with Ana across the foyer toward the stairs, I suddenly noticed the Stovolsky clock was missing. I pointed to the tall curio standing in its place, and Ana turned to look.

"Oh, I had the clock moved upstairs. There was no other place to display my Lomonosov porcelain. Anyway, we needed a clock upstairs." As we climbed to the second floor, I didn't need for Ana to tell me where the clock had been placed. We passed it just outside the nursery, where it would measure out time for the next century. I started to enter the nursery, but Ana stopped me with a hand on my arm. "Katya, I didn't want to tell you this downstairs. Dora has left us, dear. She decided to go back and live out the rest of her days with her people." At my look, she patted my arm. "She couldn't bring herself to tell you good-bye, so she asked me to do it for her."

I stared at her. "But how could she go? *We're* her family!"

Ana shook her head. "She was devoted to Isabel, but Dora was always apart from us. You know that. Now Isabel is gone. Michael and Elise are your family, and Robert has Leon and me to look after him. There was no reason for her to stay." She squeezed my arm. "She left something for you, Katya. I'll go and get it."

She moved down the hall toward her bedroom while I went into the nursery and gathered Elise into my arms. I was rigid with shock and an acute sense of betrayal. Ana returned and held out a blanket.

"I think it's quite beautiful. Dora said her mother made it for her. She said you would understand."

Ana shook out the blanket, and I saw the design Dora's mother had woven for her in rich colors of blue and green and shining silver. I didn't understand all the symbols. But I knew the blue water represented peace. A round moon hung in a dark sky, reflecting twin bands across the water, and it seemed somehow benevolent.

* * *

It had to be close to two o'clock in the morning, the night cold and windless. Michael and I were nestled under thick covers, sleeping in each other's arms when I suddenly jerked upright and started screaming. Michael sprang up beside me and grabbed my shoulders, shaking me.

"Kat! Kat, wake up!" When I burst into sobs, he pulled me against him and rocked me. "It's all right, love. You're safe. You're safe with me." My sobs quickly turned into shivers, and he pulled me down with him under the covers, wrapping me tightly against his body. Only when the shivers began to ease did he loosen his arms and pull away enough to look into my face.

"What was it?" he asked, smoothing a damp tangle of hair from my cheek.

In the pale light of the waning crescent moon, I could just make out the sleepy rumple of Michael's hair and the dark worry in his eyes. When I tried to speak, a wave of love became a stab of pain and despair, and I cried out. Shutting my eyes, I rolled into him and buried my face in his neck.

"It's begun, Michael," I said, my words muffled against his throat. "I was at the bridge, and I saw her. I turned around, and she was standing on the bank, looking down at me."

Michael's body jerked. "It doesn't mean anything,"

he said quickly. I recognized the familiar, stubborn edge.

I pulled my head back and looked him in the eye. "We both know better than that, Michael. It's only a week away. We may only have one more week together—"

"Don't say that!" He gripped my shoulders and shouted at me. "I won't let you talk like that!" His mouth trembled, and he suddenly crushed me against him, burying his face in my hair. "I'm sorry, love. I'm sorry." I felt a tremor ripple through his body. "The dream wasn't real, Kat," he whispered. "This is real. You and me together. This is all the reality we need."

Then he kissed me, a deep, desperate kiss, and I surrendered to it. Without speaking, we sat up and pulled off each other's nightclothes, our gazes locked together. This time there was no playfulness, no laughing or teasing or stretching out the moment to savor and anticipate. We moved our hands impatiently over each other's bodies, frustrated that no matter how tightly we pressed together, we couldn't erase the physical boundaries that kept us from merging into one solid being. Michael's mouth groped hungrily at mine, and I answered with a need that was just as fierce, just as demanding.

Our passion peaked and then abruptly stilled. In the dim light of the weakening moon, I saw Michael's eyes staring down at me, dark and full of pain. We didn't speak, and we didn't put our clothes back on. Michael pulled the covers over us, and we lay quietly, pressing flesh against flesh—curve for curve and limb for limb—until there was no space between us. Neither of us slept. The molten fire inside me cooled and could no longer protect me from the cold horror of what lay ahead. I began to shiver, and Michael moved, tucking the blanket closer, bracing his arms around me as if he could keep the chill from my heart by the sheer force of his love.

Eventually I drifted to sleep, wondering vaguely if my cold fear would turn me into ice and then melt me before morning, leaving Michael to awaken shivering and alone in our bed.

Chapter Twenty-Nine

In the following days, the chill around my heart expanded, systematically closing me off from the world around me. Instead of cherishing each remaining moment in the life I had grown to love, I found them slipping through my fingers like sand, leaving me cold and untouched. I would pick up Elise and hold her close, but I couldn't feel her. When Michael surprised me with roses, I couldn't smell them. When we made love at night, I watched us from a distance, watched my body respond to his touch, and I felt nothing. The days passed, and I shrank further into a small corner of myself. The blue cornflowers had once again given me shelter, but this time I didn't know how to get back. And so my final week slipped away from me, and it was as if I could only watch helplessly from inside my little space in Victoria's wallpaper.

I don't remember leaving the cottage. I don't remember the walk along Two Trees Creek or climbing onto the bridge. In fact, I didn't know I was poised at its very center, looking past my dangling toes at the tumbling creek water far below, until I heard Michael shout, "Kat! Don't move! Stay right where you are until I can get to you!"

As if in a dream, I watched Michael run along the

path on the high bank of the creek. He lunged onto the bridge and snatched me back from the edge, gripping my arms so hard that the pain of it penetrated my stupor.

"You're hurting me," I said.

He didn't respond, just clutched me against him and shuddered.

I became aware that my feet hurt and looked down, surprised to see them bare and covered with dirt and blood. Not only that, I was wearing my flannel nightgown.

"Michael," I said. "I don't...what on earth?" I looked up at him, bewildered.

Michael peered into my face. Then he turned me within the firm circle of his arms. "Look." He pointed to the spot where I had been standing.

The middle section of railing was completely gone. I had stood with nothing but air to keep me from falling into the creek. I gasped and shrank against Michael and then cried out from the pain in my feet. He picked me up in his arms and carried me off the bridge. On the shady bank he sat me down and bent to examine my feet.

In grim silence he began to pick thorns and debris from my bleeding flesh while I bit my lip and whimpered in pain. Grasping a foot, he looked up at me, his mouth a thin, unpleasant line. His eyes were smoldering. "Mind telling me what in blazes you were doing up there?"

His anger surprised me. "I was following the moon," I said. "I didn't feel the cuts in my feet."

Michael's grip on my foot made me wince. "There *is* no moon, Kat. It's *daytime*." His voice was tight, like a cord stretched almost to breaking. He released my foot and knelt forward, gripping me by the shoulders. "What's happening to you, Kat?" I looked at him curiously. "You've disappeared somewhere. Don't you know you have to fight this thing? That you can't just give up?"

I stared vaguely at him, and he shook me. "Your child was crying, Katherine. Do you hear me? You went off and left her. Marta came to me and told me she couldn't find you anywhere." He released my shoulders, and he stood up, scowling down at me. "I looked everywhere. I was on my way to the house when I suddenly guessed where you'd gone."

He turned his back and walked a few steps away, staring down at the creek water. "What were you going to do, Kat? Throw yourself over?" His voice shook. "Are you so eager to leave us that you're not even going to wait until new moon tonight?"

I watched him with limp eyes.

He strode back and stood over me, tall and strong like one of the redwoods. "I don't understand how you can just give up, Kat. Isn't our life together worth fighting for? I'd walk through the bloody fires of hell to stay with you. I thought you'd feel the same way."

"I don't have a choice, Michael," I said crossly. "You talk as though it's all up to me."

"Father Philippe thinks it is."

"Father Philippe is guessing. He doesn't know anything."

"Well, neither do you!" Michael shouted. "Up until now you've had more courage and spirit and love than anyone I've ever known. Don't give up now. Don't give *us* up. Don't let them take you away from me!"

I pulled my feet under my nightgown and sat up straighter. "This isn't one of your novels, Michael," I said. "I can't just make everything turn out the way I want."

"But maybe you *can*." He dropped to his knees and gripped my shoulders again, forcing me to see the agony in his eyes. "Listen to me. I can't go with you tonight. This is something you have to do on your own for us. For *us*, Kat — for you and me and Elise and Robbie and everyone who loves you. We're all depending on you." He found my hands and clutched them against his chest, where I could feel his heart hammering. His eyes were desperate, his voice urgent. "I believe in you, Katherine Carey. I believe in our love. And I believe that, when the time comes, you *will* have a choice, and, somehow, you'll find your way back to me. *You'll find your way back to me!*"

Roughly, he pulled me into his arms, and he kissed me. His lips were warm and familiar, and suddenly I was back in my bedroom at Ana's in San Francisco, standing in my nightgown, kissing this man and hearing him tell me for the first time that he loved me. He was the first and only man who had ever loved me. The only man I would ever love.

The thaw began in the middle of my chest, spreading slowly like rings in a pond from a center of love. And when the ice was gone, I wasn't melted at all but solid and gloriously alive in Michael's arms. He felt the change and lifted his mouth away to look at me. The stark relief in his eyes brought tears to mine.

"You're wrong about one thing, Michael," I said

gravely. "I won't be alone tonight. I carry you inside me, always. Your love is the anchor that keeps me centered, the beacon that always points the way home." I laid my hand along his cheek. "Be my lifeline tonight, Michael. And for God's sake, whatever you do, don't let go."

* * *

The night was unexpectedly quiet. I had anticipated a lightening storm, like the previous year's, but the skies were clear and bright with a thousand stars. Even the wind was still, as if the world were holding its breath.

Elise was asleep, and Michael and I sat together in the parlor, watching the fire. We didn't speak but held each other tightly. Indeed, we'd hardly been out of each other's arms all afternoon. Occasionally, we turned to one another, and our eyes would meet and hold, sharing the same thoughts, the same fears, the same desperate hope.

My arms were around his waist, and his were around my shoulders. I leaned my face into his neck, breathing in the clean, familiar smell of him, and rubbed my cheek against the rough cotton of his shirt. Little curls of hair peeked from the open neck of his collar, and I brushed them with my fingertip. He stirred and looked down at me, and I raised my face to look at him. Without his glasses, his eyes had that soft, vulnerable look. I remembered lying on the blanket with him in Golden Gate Park and thinking how incredibly beautiful his eyes were. They had been gentle and tender and smiled love at me, just as they did now. Even then, Michael had loved me.

He kissed me gently, on my forehead and my nose

and then on my mouth when I offered it. I sighed and rested my head on his shoulder. "Michael," I whispered. "I'm afraid."

"I know." He laid his cheek on my forehead. "I am, too. But fear can make you brave, Kat. And you're so loved. You have everything you need to make it through this." His arms tightened. "I believe in you."

The mantel clock ticked a slow, monotonous rhythm that was making me sleepy. I yawned several times and noticed that the fire was going out. Or, rather, there was a curling, black emptiness at its center that was spreading into the room. I watched it, fascinated, and suddenly realized that I could no longer feel Michael's arms around me. I tried to sit up, but my body was paralyzed.

I was suddenly looking down on the top of Michael's head, at his tousled hair glowing like burnished gold in the firelight. His arms still held my body. I called to him in a voice I knew he could only hear in his dreams.

Without warning, the current snatched me from behind. It tore me away from the sight of Michael and the warm, comforting room and hurled me into the bowels of the long, dark tunnel I knew.

New Moon

Ryan fought to keep from drowning. Murky water covered his face and sucked at his body. He could see nothing. Weeds curled around his legs like slimy dead fingers, somehow familiar to him.

He knew he was trying to escape, but from what he couldn't remember. Moreover, he was trying to get somewhere, to accomplish something important. But he couldn't remember what that was, either.

With each new thrust of his face above the water, Ryan noticed that the darkness was thinning. There was light in the distance, and a current was carrying him toward it. Kicking free of the tugging weeds, he managed to keep his head clear of the water. He swept past familiar landmarks and realized that he was being carried *upstream*, to what end only the current seemed to know.

* * *

Snatched from the comfort of Michael's arms, I am hurled through miles of dark tunnel and dropped abruptly before a towering wall of white mist. There is no sound, nothing else around me. I call out, "Katherine! Are you here?" but my shouts die in the mist.

Then…someone unseen brushes past me. A sweet, familiar scent holds me briefly, tenderly, and lets me go. Michael's words return to me: You are so loved, Kat. You have everything you need to make it through this.

I swallow down fear, stretch out my arms to feel my way, and resolutely step into the wall of mist.

Like a stage curtain, it parts before me, enough to reveal four steps. At the top of the steps is another wall with a door almost twice my height and made of gold.

I mount the steps and try the door. It's locked.

* * *

The current swept Ryan steadily toward the light. He saw a pale moon hanging low in the sky and then a bridge, outlined in silver, directly ahead of him.

The current slowed, and two women appeared, one of them fair and one of them dark, approaching the bridge from opposite banks. A thick white mist curled down from the moon and enveloped the bridge, hiding its center. The blond woman stretched out her arms and started forward into the mist. The other woman did the same.

In a burst of clarity, Ryan remembered his mission.

"Tori!" he shouted. The dark-haired woman paused and seemed to look toward him. "Tori, stay back!" Ryan struggled toward the bank, but the current was too strong. The harder he struggled, the weaker he became. "Tori!" he cried again. But it was no use. Even his voice had weakened. She could no longer hear him.

Horrified, Ryan watched one woman and then the other disappear into the mist. The white cloud seemed to expand, brightening until it was a painful, blinding light. Then everything went dark. The bridge, the moon, and the mist were gone.

Water sloshed over Ryan's head. He screamed and thrashed as the dead fingers gripped his arms and legs again, and he knew he was going down for the last time.

* * *

The golden door bars my way. In a flash of insight, I remember my gift from the golden woman. From my pocket I retrieve the key she gave me. I read the inscription: "Love opens doors."

My key fits the lock and turns easily. But still the door will not open. I hammer on it with my fists, twist the knob, but to no effect. It won't budge.

I realize the door must be locked from the other side.

"Katherine!" I shout. "Are you there? Katherine, do you have a key? Open the door!"

The mist bursts with sudden brilliance, like a sheet of lightning, and begins to swirl around me. Momentum builds, whipping my hair over my face and sucking greedily at my limbs. Fighting the growing vortex, I cling to the knob with one hand and pummel the door with my fist.

Everything suddenly blackens. Wind roaring like a tempest tries to pry my fingers from the knob. I grab hold with both hands and scream, "Katherine! Do you hear me? Open the door!" My fingers begin to slip. "The key, Katherine. Use your key!"

* * *

Water filled Ryan's mouth and nostrils, making him gasp and cough. The dead fingers became living hands that felt gently over his body.

"He's coming around." A gruff voice floated in the dark above him. "Easy, fella. Don't try to move." Then, "Somebody hold an umbrella over his face, or this rain's gonna drown him."

The rush of water abruptly stopped. Ryan squinted his eyes open. At first all he saw was a red light intermittently flashing in the darkness, then dim forms bending over him. Hands raised him, and he cried out as hot pain seared his legs.

"Careful, guys." The same voice spoke again. "His legs are torn up pretty bad. Watch that gash on his head. Okay, let's get him into the ambulance."

Pressure tightened across Ryan's chest and thighs.

"Weirdest thing I ever saw." A different voice came through the dark. "I thought for sure the guy was gone."

"Makes two of us," the gruff voice agreed. "Knock on the head like that should have killed him. Metal sliced his legs to the bone but missed the femoral by a hairbreadth." A soft chuckle. "My opinion? That guy's got Somebody Important looking out for him."

Ryan was lifted into a place suddenly dry and warm and quiet. He felt a prick in his arm and opened his eyes. A young woman was bending over him.

"Ryan?" Her voice was clear and sweet. "We're taking you to the hospital. You're going to be okay."

"Tori?" The effort of speaking brought new pain stabbing through his head. Ryan shut his eyes and worked his throat. "Did she...my wife...?"

There was a long pause. He heard the woman's voice, muffled, and far away. " —passenger in the car?"

Then the gruff voice, "No...maybe out the other side...tell CHP...have another look."

"Tori." Her name was only a movement of his lips as the ambulance took off with a low wail of siren.

* * *

The dark tempest lifts and twists me, prying my fingers loose. Screaming, sobbing, I feel them slip when suddenly a key grates in the lock, and the door swings open. The howling dark pitches me forward. In the same instant Katherine and I are thrown together — two leaves whirling in the wind. I feel her pass through me like a spirit breath. Then we are wrenched apart, and Katherine is gone. I am alone in the dark, drifting in a thick and profound silence.

Through the darkness a pinpoint of light catches my attention. "Michael!" I cry. Hope surges, and the far-off beacon brightens, tugging faithfully at my heart. Within moments I can feel the warm fire again, and Michael's arms wrapped tightly around me. I hear his voice pleading, whispering my name over and over, like a prayer.

Summoning all my strength, I lift an unsteady hand to the orange-blond head pressing against my cheek. "Michael," I whisper, barely audible, but the bright head snaps up.

"Kat?" His voice is hoarse and shaky. "Kat! Kat!" Then Michael is kissing me. I taste salt from his tears and see love shining for me in his sea-green eyes, and I know I'm home.

Epilogue

"It's the painting we saw at Rosswood House last year, remember?" Lisa Knight pointed to her housewarming gift leaning against the newly painted living room wall. "I read in the paper that Elise Delacroix died, and they were selling her paintings. So Chris and I went up there and got this one for your sumptuous new country home." She raised her glass of iced tea in a toast. "May you live a long and happy life here on the sunny side of the Bay!"

Sitting beside his wife on the sofa, Chris tapped her glass with his beer bottle and took a swig. "Nice work, Ashton." He nodded at the new expanse of windows overlooking green lawns and colorful flower beds. "I hear they want to feature your place in *Homeowners* magazine. You know, the before-and-after thing. Quite a coup." He grinned wickedly.

"Yeah, the competition was pretty stiff." Ryan grinned back. He was leaning against the mantel, testing himself to see how long he could stand erect. He'd been walking without the canes for two weeks, but his legs still got tired, and sometimes the pain came unexpectedly. The doctor said that was normal and not to get impatient.

Well, patience was something he was learning about.

And being grateful for every single day. Ryan looked over at his wife, who was sitting in a pool of summer sunshine by the window, her hair gleaming like spun gold. She caught his gaze and smiled at him, her emerald eyes reaching across the room to hold him in that intimate caress that always made his heart skip.

Love you, Tori, his eyes told her.

Hers whispered back, *Love you.*

Stephanie emerged from the hallway, balancing Christina on her hip. She stopped in front of the painting to study it. "Cool. Hey, that lady looks just like Tori." She glanced around for other opinions.

"Amazing, isn't it?" Lisa pulled a brochure from her purse. "Here's some interesting history about that little storyteller artist." She unfolded the brochure. "It says she was born Elise Kamarov to a widow who soon after married Michael Carey, a novelist remarkable for the uncanny accuracy of his futuristic stories. Elise lived her entire life in Sonoma County. She made her reputation as an artist, and she was the great-niece of Leon Rostnova, a Bay Area artist who was educated in Russia and lived with his wife at Rosswood House after they lost their San Francisco home to the 1906 earthquake and subsequent fire. In 1923, Elise married Douglas Delacroix, a local rancher who inherited from his grandfather, Russ Paxton. Douglas grew up on the ranch with his mother after his father, Raymond Delacroix, lost all his money in a failed land venture and deserted his family. It is uncertain whether Raymond was murdered over a gambling debt or committed suicide when he was caught in a swindle over a silver-mine deal. The eldest of five children, Elise was the last surviving child of Katherine and Michael Carey and grandchild of Alexander and Isabel Rostnova. Katherine's younger brother, Robert, married but remained childless, so the proud Rostnova name died with him. Sonoma County will miss Elise's artistic talent as a colorful storyteller as well as a gifted painter of local life."

Lisa sat back and glanced at her husband. "I'll tell you something else," she said with a slow grin. "The picture framer told me that under the torn paper on the back of the painting, there was a handwritten title, *Bridge Over Two Trees Creek*. And under the title was a signature and a date: *Katherine Carey, 1902*. So it had to be Elise's *mother*, not Elise, who actually painted the picture. How about *that*!" She looked from her host to her hostess, and her grin faltered. "What? Did I say something wrong?"

Ryan glanced at his wife and thought his own face probably looked just as stunned. He cleared his throat. "No, that's just...quite a story." He shoved away from the mantel. "Thanks for the painting, you two. We'll give it a place of honor." He jerked his head. "Come on outside, Knight. You haven't seen the finished terrace."

"Yeah, this I gotta see." Chris drained his beer bottle and stood up. "It's not everyone who has a *mountain* in his backyard!"

Stephanie handed Christina over to her mother and hurried to catch up with Lisa. "Tori's showing me how to grow vegetables. I have my own patch with tomatoes and cucumbers and summer squash. But no string beans," she added, with a grin. "Tori *hates* string beans!"

Ryan glanced at Tori as he followed their guests to

the door. "We'll be out in a minute," he called after them. He crossed the room and joined her where she stood studying the painting.

"So she married my cousin Michael," he heard her say, "and they had four children together. I never would have guessed it." She looked at him. "When Lisa started talking about those people, they were strangers, Ryan. Like characters from a book I read and then forgot about." She shook her head slowly. "It's strange to think of them long dead and buried. And now the baby Elise, too. All of them gone."

Ryan slipped his arm around her. "But you know better than that, Tori. They're alive right now, right this very moment, in that different space. And they're creating their lives one day at a time, just like us."

Stephanie was back at the door. "Are you guys coming or what? Chris and Lisa want to walk down to the creek."

"Be right there, Stephanannie." Ryan cradled his wife's face and gave her a searching look. "I love you, Tori Ashton." He kissed her solemnly, tenderly. Then he took his baby daughter on one arm and slipped the other around his wife's shoulders.

Together they followed Stephanie out the door into the July heat shimmering off the rising slopes of Mount Diablo.

About the Author

Judith Ingram weaves together her love of romance and mystery as well as her training as a counselor to create stories and characters for her novels. She is also the author of a Christian guide to forgiving and posts weekly devotionals on the role of forgiveness in healing relationships.

She lives with her husband in the San Francisco East Bay and makes frequent trips to beautiful Sonoma County, where many of her fiction characters reside. She confesses a love for chocolate, cheesecake, romantic suspense novels, movies that require three hankies, and all things feline.

Judith would love to hear from you! You can e-mail her at judith@judithingram.com or visit her Website at judithingram.com.

Judith Ingram

Author Acknowledgements

My thanks to family and friends for your support and encouragement in bringing this story to life: my husband, Frank, and my daughter, Melanie; Joy McGuire, my first author friend and literary auntie to my characters, Victoria and Katherine; and Angela Bartels, who read early drafts and gave me sound feedback.

My thanks also to Vinspire Publishing for believing in this story and working to make it the best it could be, especially editor-in-chief, Dawn Carrington; cover artist, Elaina Lee; and editor extraordinaire, Rory Olsen.

Among the many resources I used for historical research, most helpful to me were the following books: *My Life at Fort Ross: 1877–1907* by Laura Call Carr (1987; Fort Ross Interpretive Association, Inc.: Jenner, CA); *Sonoma County: The River of Time* by Simone Wilson (1990; Windsor Publications, Inc.: Chatsworth, CA); *Christmas in Russia* by World Book Publishing (1992; World Book, Inc.: Chicago); and *Bed & Breakfast Guide: California* by Courtia Worth, Terry Berger, Naomi Black, and Lucy Poshek (1991; Prentice Hall Travel: New York).

Judith Ingram

Questions for Discussion

1. Do you think the copper coin had magical powers? Why or why not?

2. What did Victoria need from Ryan that he seemed unable to give her? Did she find what she needed in Michael?

3. What did Katherine mean when she told Christine, "You are the mother I've always wanted"? How was Christine a better fit than Isabel to give Katherine the mothering she needed?

4. Discuss the dream images of the lioness and the deer. What does it say about the characters that Katherine saw herself as a lioness who became a deer, and Victoria as a deer who became a lioness? What images have been especially meaningful in your dreams?

5. What is the significance of the bear that haunted Victoria's dreams?

6. How do you think Katherine acquired the key to open her side of the door in the final new moon exchange?

7. How did Stephanie help to tell Katherine's story?

8. Do you think Ana's love for her nephew justified her attempts to discourage his infatuation with his cousin Katherine, who had a reputation for cruelty? What would you have done in her place?

9. Why was Ryan so angry with Katherine after he read her journal? What was the deep fear that compelled him to distance himself from her?

10. Eleanor claimed to have loved her husband, Matthew, and her son, Luke. Do you believe she was capable of love? Did she love her granddaughter, Victoria?

11. How did Eleanor's treatment of her daughter show up in Christine's adult behaviors and self-image? Does Christine deserve to be forgiven for her own failures as a mother?

12. Why was Christine so afraid to love Dan? What convinced her to take a chance and commit to a relationship with him?

13. Isabel wrote in Katherine's journal that she could not admit to herself that her husband was abusing their daughter. Given the legal and economic limitations of women in the late 1800s, what could Isabel have done differently?

14. Compare and contrast the death scenes for Isabel and Eleanor. How were the scenes alike and how were they different? What insights do you have into these two women?

15. Why was Summerwood Cottage so important to Victoria? Why did the fire's devastation make her feel as if she "had been raped a second time"? Discuss the spiritual significance of her efforts to rebuild the cottage.

16. What originally caused the Elizabeth personality to emerge? What do you think facilitated the ultimate integration of Katherine and Elizabeth into one whole personality who called herself Tori?

17. Why did Emily seek out help from Victoria? Has there been a hardship in your life that equipped you to help others?

Judith Ingram

Dear Reader,

If you enjoyed reading Into the Mist, I would appreciate it if you would help others enjoy this book, too. Here are some of the ways you can help spread the word:

Lend it. This book is lending enabled so please share it with a friend.

Recommend it. Help other readers find this book by recommending it to friends, readers' groups, book clubs, and discussion forums.

Share it. Let other readers know you've read the book by positing a note to your social media account and/or your Goodreads account.

Review it. Please tell others why you liked this book by reviewing it on your favorite ebook site like Amazon or Barnes and Noble and/or Goodreads.

Everything you do to help others learn about my book is greatly appreciated!

Judith Ingram

Judith Ingram

Plan Your Next Escape!
What's Your Reading Pleasure?

Whether it's captivating historical romance, intriguing mysteries, young adult romance, illustrated children's books, or uplifting love stories, Vinspire Publishing has the adventure for you!

For a complete listing of books available, visit our website at www.vinspirepublishing.com.

Like us on Facebook at
www.facebook.com/VinspirePublishing

Follow us on Twitter at
www.twitter.com/vinspire2004

and join our newsletter for details of our upcoming releases, giveaways, and more!
http://t.co/46UoTbVaWr

We are your travel guide to your next adventure!